Ruby Spencer's
Whisky Year

Ruby Spencer's
Whisky Year

Rochelle Bilow

BERKLEY ROMANCE • NEW YORK

BERKLEY ROMANCE
Published by Berkley
An imprint of Penguin Random House LLC
penguinrandomhouse.com

Library of Congress Cataloging-in-Publication Data

Names: Bilow, Rochelle, author.
Title: Ruby Spencer's whisky year / Rochelle Bilow.
Description: First edition. | New York: Berkley Romance, 2023.
Identifiers: LCCN 2022025644 (print) | LCCN 2022025645 (ebook) |
ISBN 9780593547885 (trade paperback) | ISBN 9780593547892 (ebook)
Subjects: LCGFT: Romance fiction. | Novels.
Classification: LCC PS3602.I476 R83 2023 (print) |
LCC PS3602.I476 (ebook) | DDC 813/.6—dc23/eng/20220708
LC record available at https://lccn.loc.gov/2022025644
LC ebook record available at https://lccn.loc.gov/2022025645

First Edition: February 2023

Printed in the United States of America
1st Printing

Book design by Elke Sigal

For Rachel S.

Ruby Spencer's Whisky Year

Chapter One

Ruby Spencer was absolutely, positively sure about three things.

1. Quitting her job and moving to a random town in the Scottish Highlands for a year to write a cookbook was the craziest thing she had ever done.
1.5. (Would ever do.)
1.75. ((The crazy thing was the Scotland part, not the cookbook part.))
2. In all her thirty-five years, she had never lived anywhere as beautiful as this tiny stone cottage, overgrown with ivy and moss, with its sweet mint-green door.
2.5. Even if it didn't have a kitchen.
2.75. Hahahahaha.
3. After two delayed flights, a canceled one, an overnight snooze on a bench in Heathrow Airport, and one missing piece of luggage later . . . her armpits absolutely, positively stunk.

Ruby set her canvas duffel on the cool floor, closed her eyes, and inhaled deeply. *God, I smell awful.* On her next breath, she focused her attention on the cottage around her. She wiggled her toes inside her Keds and shimmied her shoulders on the exhale. The air inside the cottage smelled sweet and heady, like cinnamon and smoke, black tea leaves and vanilla. Which was nice. Which was much better than her armpits, which smelled like curry and garlic.

She kept her eyes shut as she listened for the tiny sounds that tend to hide in old stone Scottish cottages. To her right and slightly above: the wind whistling through the chimney and into the hearth. In front of her and through the window: gentle clucking from a flock of hens scratching at the ground. Behind her, the creak of the heavy wooden door she'd left open, swinging on its hinges. To her left: nothing. But wait—Ruby pressed her fingers into her palms and bit the inside of her cheek. A frenetic scamper, followed by a squeak. A mouse! Ruby's eyes flew open and she laughed. The mouse had gone, but, she surmised, not for long.

"Of course," she said, running her palm down her messy fishtail braid. "I would be disappointed if there *weren't* mice."

Next, Ruby held her arms out by her sides and felt the air on her skin. It was mid-April, and the Highlands were still chilly, but, as mentioned, she was a bit ripe. She had stripped down from her three-season traveling jacket and sweater to jeans and a cotton camisole, and the breeze was a treat. The air inside the one-room home she had agreed to rent—Sight unseen! After a few short phone calls with the owner! For a whole year!—hung cold from years of vacancy. But it was thick with potential. Ruby could tell that much was true.

She sniffed a little and caught heather on the breeze. *Classic Scotland, right there. It's just like I imagined*, she thought. Ruby wondered what other Scottish stereotypes would prove to be true. She hoped the one about strapping bearded men who guzzled whisky and whispered sweet nothings was. But maybe she had just been watching too much *Outlander*. Her mind trotted past the image of a sexy Scot kissing her against a pile of oak barrels to Benjamin. She immediately cringed. No. Mustn't think about Benjamin here. The man had occupied far too much of her brain space for far too long.

The breeze picked up again and Ruby was pulled into the present. She reached for the sweater she'd tied around the duffel straps and slipped it over her head. It was cream colored and cable-knit, long in the sleeves, and reached halfway down her thighs, but it was soft and comfortable, perfect in the way that favorite sweaters always are.

She looked around and drank in the scene. There was a massive stone hearth, almost large enough to hold the height of her five-foot, two-inch frame. The fireplace dwarfed the rest of the cottage. Or perhaps anchored it? Hard to say. It was big. Directly across from the door Ruby saw a dusty window held together by thin timber muntins; one of the glass panes was missing and was nailed over with a wood board. This was the sort of thing that would have driven her mad in Manhattan, an injustice that would've had her hollering at her landlord for a replacement and reduction in rent. But she was in Scotland! So now it was charming, and she didn't have to be angry about it.

3

In front of the window sat a bed to rival the hearth. It was made from wood, like every other piece of furniture in the cottage, with an enormous head- and footboard, and thick posts for legs. It looked like it weighed a ton. Two tons? Numbers were not Ruby's strong point. The mattress was covered in a white sheet and a worn velveteen green quilt that looked about a trillion years old. Again: super charming. Because, Scotland. Spread across the quilt, at the foot of the bed was a real sheep's pelt. Ruby touched it with her fingertips and brought them up to her nose; she could smell the lanolin. There were plenty of pillows, both functional and furry, piled against the headboard, giving the whole bed a look that was at once soft and wild. Ruby kicked off her shoes and flopped onto the mattress. It was surprisingly comfortable, although she would've dealt with it no matter what. Having sold all her earthly possessions and moved across an ocean, she didn't have much room to be picky about details like beds and mattresses. On the other side of the cottage, pushed up against the stonework, was a small writing desk and minuscule chair. A tapestry throw was artfully draped over the desk. On top of that, a tapered candle in a brass holder and a delicate vase holding a few yellow cowslips.

Ruby reached off the bed and rummaged in her duffel bag for her dictionary, which—okay, *yes*, she had brought a dictionary in her carry-on luggage. And, *yes*, she realized ten minutes into her wait at the security check that it had been a monumental (and monumentally heavy) mistake. The thing of it was, Ruby really wanted to make a fresh start here: not just to write a cookbook but to become the sort of person she wished she was. The sort of person she never got around to becoming in New York. The sort of person who, when reading novels and encountering a word she didn't know, looked it up in an actual dictionary, rather than grabbing her phone and googling "meaning of alacrity" or whatever. To be clear, *not* the sort of person who immediately exited the dictionary.com app and spent the next forty-five minutes blacking out on Instagram's explore tab. Not naming any names, but . . . ugh. Ruby's life had become very stale and very uninspiring over the course of the last few years. The dictionary felt like—what? A reminder of that intention? Sure. Let's go with that. Anyway, she placed the dictionary—Oxford, not Merriam-Webster, because, Scotland—on the writing desk. There. Transformation complete. She was now a calm and stable human who could do hard and good things, like move to the UK in her midthirties and learn new words.

The cottage couldn't have been more than eight by eight feet; if Ruby wanted to, she could cross the whole thing in one big step (and a half). But how did they measure things in Scotland? Centimeters? Ruby wasn't positive. She had a moment of panic. *How could I have moved to a country without knowing their units of measurement?* Ruby grabbed her phone to google it. Wait. No Wi-Fi in the cottage. Right. She'd look it up later. It probably didn't matter that much, honestly. What did she need to measure? She was only writing a cookbook.

Sigh.

She stretched her arms over her head, then brought her hands down underneath her sweater. She scratched her rib cage and yawned, bone-tired from the international flight, the train ride from Glasgow Airport to Inverness, the taxi ride from the station, and the polite touch-base conversation with the cottage's proprietor, Grace Wood. "It's perfect," she murmured to herself now, curling up into a small ball in the center of the bed. The door caught a lively gust and slammed shut with a thud. Somewhere along the baseboard, the mouse exclaimed in surprise. Ruby pressed her palms together and tucked her hands underneath her cheek. She imagined the rodent wearing a miniature kilt and drinking from a thimble of whisky. *Scotland is going to be great. Everything will work out. This was definitely not a mistake. Nope. Not at all. No mistakes here. Not a single one.*

Ha ha.

And then, even though her brain very much wanted to keep thinking about the cottage, about her future cookbook, about awful Benjamin, about how she'd earn enough money to live here for a year, about why the hell she'd thought a cottage with no internet would be *charming*, and about every single embarrassing thing she'd ever done in her whole life, exhaustion overtook her body. Her fringe of black lashes fluttered once, and she was asleep.

When Ruby woke, it was dark. How long had she been sleeping? The cab had dropped her off at the pub shortly after noon; it couldn't have been much past one when she drifted off. She rose and fumbled around the walls for a light switch. The fixture on the ceiling crackled and sparked a few times before it settled into a dim glow. Two weeks ago, a rustic cottage in the small town of Thistlecross was all she could think about. And she was finally here. She was about to spend an entire year exploring Scotland

and drinking whisky. So why did it suddenly seem . . . less awesome? Harder? Ruby needed better ambiance; that would help, for sure. She found a box of matches in the desk drawer, struck one, and lit the candle. Light threw itself against the stone walls and made dancing shadows.

"Oh, that's nice," she said, and rifled through her bag for a toothbrush and some clean jeans. Ms. Wood had set a pitcher of water on the windowsill, along with a ceramic mug. Ruby filled the mug and drank it down, then brushed her teeth. There was a small bathroom tucked in the southern corner of the cottage. She'd shower later. Eventually. She wasn't in a rush; there didn't seem to be anyone to impress in Thistlecross. She slid into her shoes again and walked outside, around to the back and surveyed her domain in the dark, stretching her legs and doing a couple of yoga poses to move her spine. *Buck up, girl. You wanted this.*

Why had she wanted this, exactly? Ruby had figured that the minimalist setup and a "closer to nature" existence would help her write her cookbook: reduce distractions and keep her focused on the task at hand. Plus, it seemed romantic and poetic. Very Walden Pond. Very literary. But had Thoreau had a small pub nearby? Ruby seemed to recall some sort of story about him doing laundry at his mom's. *Ugh. Just like a man.*

She looked around for the hens; it appeared they had retired for the night in the coop near the rowan tree. Ruby ducked back inside and shrieked. One of the hens had decided to roost in the cottage instead of its perfectly decent home, and was perched on a bedpost. (Mental note to close the cottage door in the future.) She approached the hen, who careened around the cottage. What was she going to do . . . catch it? No. That was absurd. She could not. She would not. Maybe she could just guide it out of the cottage. Ruby smacked her hands together to startle it into action, which resulted in her clapping after a hen and shouting "Go home! Go home!" for no less than seven spins around the interior of the cottage. The bird finally skittered out the door and ricocheted toward the coop. Of course, this was all *very charming*, because it was *Scotland*. This was fine. Everything was great! Scotland was great!

Not a mistake!

Mentally, she was spent. She wished she could burrow under the quilt and sleep until morning, but she had promised Ms. Wood she would return to the pub for supper. Besides, her stomach was howling, and she'd foolishly packed the granola bars, nuts, and bags of dried fruit in the rest of her luggage, which was . . . well, where, exactly? Delayed. Hopefully not lost. Somewhere between New York, London, Glasgow, and Thistlecross.

She gingerly blew out the candle, turned out the light, and walked the path to the pub, aptly named the Cosy Hearth. A combination of the building's warm glow and the near-full moon lit her way. Ruby noted the places where the walkway had gone from unruly to overgrown. It was laid with stones, smoothed from weather and almost entirely covered under a carpet of bindweed and grass. The pub itself was a compact stone structure, similar in style to her cottage but two stories tall. There were two chimneys; one was puffing out a steady stream of woodsmoke. The roof had been reshingled semirecently, and the doorway was painted the color of a ripe melon, but other than that, it looked much as it might have two hundred years ago. With one hand on the doorknob and the other stuffed into her back pocket, she took her millionth deep breath of the day. And then she entered the Cosy Hearth.

Chapter Two

Ruby, my dear!" called Ms. Wood from behind the bar. She held her hand up to pause a chattering man sitting on one of the oak stools. The man was weathered, either in his mideighties or one hundred and eighty-five, in a dapper vest that was large enough to appear as though it was wearing him. He looked very *Scotland*, Ruby thought.

"Are you coming in, or would you rather stand in the doorway all night?" he said. Ruby ducked into the room; the frame was almost shorter than she was. Charming, just charming.

"Ms. Wood. Hi," said Ruby. And, to the man at the bar: "Good evening." She did a little curtsy which she hoped came across as sweet and fun, not weird. She was always getting them mixed up.

Ms. Wood wiped her hands on a linen apron tied around the wide girth of her waist and shook her head. "From now on, it's Grace." Then, sensing Ruby's hesitancy: "Please. Otherwise, you'll make me feel ancient." She brushed back a strand of white hair that had come loose from her bun. Grace was not ancient, but she was old. Oldish. Older than Ruby, who was not old, but not young, either. Ruby was middle-ish.

"Grace," Ruby said, rolling the word around in her mouth and trying to repeat the intonation. When Grace had said her own name, it sounded like an exclamation: *Grrrace!* There was a vague *d* sound in there, too; right after the *r*. Or was it before? Ruby wasn't used to the Scottish tongue, and when she tried to say Grace's name out loud, it just sounded dumb.

Grace motioned for Ruby to take a seat. "This is Neil Mackintosh," she said, and Ruby smiled. "He's lived in Thistlecross for forever and a day."

"That name I can manage. Neil. Hello."

The man took off a tweed cap and held it over his chest, then extended his other hand to Ruby. "It is with great pleasure and vast intrigue I welcome the first permanent tenant of Thistlecross's famed flophouse." Ruby took the glass of amber brown liquor Grace set on the bar and raised her right eyebrow.

"Oh, Christ's cross, Neil," Grace said, blowing another wisp of wiry white hair out of her face. Her thin bun was tied with a red satin ribbon, but the small hairs around her face kept escaping it. "Don't scare the poor woman away. She's only just arrived."

Neil placed his hat back over his mop of gray hair and raised his glass to meet Ruby's. He winked, then sniffed around the air a bit like a bloodhound. "Ah, the scent of whisky in the springtime," he cheerily commented. Ruby self-consciously craned her nose down toward her armpit. Whisky in the springtime, indeed. She took a sip and felt the day's tensions melt and puddle around the edges. She held the alcohol on her tongue for a few moments, then enjoyed the sensation as it warmed her throat. "I can tell who the town troublemaker is," she volleyed back. "Hi. I'm Ruby. Roo. Everyone calls me that."

"A pleasure, Ruby-Roo," said Neil as he motioned toward the ceiling. "Welcome to the club." Ruby looked up and saw that dozens of mugs and beer steins hung from an iron rack. They all looked different, some with names painted on, surrounded by a couple of cobwebs.

"Ah, a nickname. You did not tell me earlier," scolded Grace, retreating to the kitchen behind her. When she returned, she was carrying two plates heaped high with food. Ruby caught the scent of pork fat and felt her knees weaken. It was a good thing she was perched on the stool. She turned around to see who had ordered the supper, but there were no other patrons, not even at the worn brown leather chair that sat in front of the crackling hearth. Ruby made another mental note: she had a feeling she would be spending a lot of her evenings curled up in the chair with a book. And her dictionary.

"I figured, we have a year to get acquainted," Ruby said, suddenly shy. A whole year. She really hoped that she'd become friends with these people. Otherwise, she was in for a long, lonely haul.

"Aye, you are pure done in, I reckon," Grace said and set the plates down in front of her and Neil.

Ruby moved her braid behind her shoulder and leaned in close to the plate. "This smells amazing. What is it?"

"Dinna ask," Neil said, sawing into his plate with a fork and knife, "dinna tell."

Grace reached over the bar and smacked Neil. Ruby grinned. Grace winked. "It's nothing special, and for that I apologize. Bacon and beans, I'm afraid, for tonight." Ruby used her fork to smash a few beans onto a heel of bread and took a bite. Salt, smoke, and fat hit her like a tidal wave. She closed her eyes and sighed. Heaven. "This is perfect."

"You don't have to be kind," said Grace. "I had hoped to have something more traditional . . . or at least exciting for a New York City food writer."

Ruby swallowed and looked down at the bar. "Please. First of all, I don't live in New York City anymore. I live here. And second, you forgot the word *ex*–food writer. I'm your employee now." She winked and Grace clucked. Neil kept shoveling in food. "Anyway"—Ruby brightened—"I love this. It's my favorite kind of meal. Comforting and hearty. And this whisky is unreal." It was. Thick and sweet on the tongue, with curls of clove and honey, perhaps a small slice of coconut cake.

"I'm glad you like it. It's one of the many secrets kept here at the Cosy Hearth," said Grace.

Ruby's eyebrow went up again. She speared a piece of bacon. "So many secrets. I suppose I have a few, too. So what's this about a flophouse? I thought I was staying in your *cottage*."

"Pay old Neil not one shard of attention," Grace said. "He likes to exaggerate."

"Aye, I do. But there's no embellishment on the history of the stone cottage." He turned on his stool to face Ruby. "Many years ago—some will say as far back as the sixteenth century"—Grace snorted and threw down her bar rag, crossing her arms across her chest to hear the rest—"there was a whisky pub in this very place."

Ruby looked around again, taking in the dark wood-beamed ceiling and antique-looking paned windows, not unlike the one in her cottage. There was a damp and cool smell to the room. Fat, dripping candles, she suddenly realized, were everywhere and yet the place still felt dim. In a cozy sort of way. *Sorry, cosy.*

A shaded electric light fixture was affixed to the ceiling in the center of the room, but if it was on, it was only just so. There were more cowslips, and violets, too, in vases at the end of the bar and on the dining tables arranged near the fire. The whole thing felt very authentic—the kind of place a movie set designer would use to demonstrate what an old bar in Scotland was meant to look like. Ruby shrugged. "I believe it."

Neil continued, "Now, we all know that the Thistlecross folk can drink just about better than any Scot—Highlanders *or* Lowlanders"—here, Grace nodded—"although there was one special whisky that could set even the sturdiest Scot's kilt off-kilter." Ruby smiled. Neil was clearly putting on a show for her benefit, but he was also having fun. And she wasn't about to let a good story go untold.

"Some do say"—Neil's eyes darted around the bar—"that there are a few bottles of this very whisky still in existence. Old though they may now be." He coughed and nodded in the direction of Ruby's glass. She brought it to her lips and took a whiff, deciding to play along. She crossed her eyes and stuck out her tongue. Neil slapped his knee.

"Thatta lass. Now, on the rare night that the barkeep declared worthy of such sinful, golden pleasure, the drinking folk of Thistlecross would place a wager. The most strapping, solid lads in the town were chosen to drink of this whisky until they could not hold another drink." Ruby loved the way Neil said the word *drink*. The *d* sounded like a trill, and the *k* settled with a satisfying ting. "Afterward, if the winning lad could walk from the end of this very bar to the end of the stone path that leads to the cottage, he would be rewarded richly." Neil leaned in, whispering in a fake aside. "Translation: he got to take home all the wagers placed against him." By now, Neil's eyes were shining. He took another sip from his glass. "Sure, the distance was short. But the whisky was strong! If the lad so much as stumbled on the path, he had to settle the cost of the whole town's drams that night."

"And then what would happen?" asked Ruby, swiping her bread across the plate to mop up some sauce.

"Well, either way, the laddie wasn't about to walk all the way home!" Neil chortled. "By that point, he was properly pissed. So down he would flop in the old stone cottage."

"He's mostly right," said Grace. "Although I don't remember it being centuries ago, nor should you, Neil, considering you passed many a night there in your youth and vigor." She turned to Ruby and rolled her eyes. *Men*, the look said. *Am I right?* "But this place has been in existence for a long time. Since the mid-1800s. The whole town of Thistlecross was built around a very grand estate run by Lord and Lady Tweedkins."

Lord and Lady Tweedkins. Charming. Beyond charming.
Delightful.
Scotland!

"This is all extraordinary," said Ruby. "I love it. I love that *I'm* staying in the flophouse now. I promise to use it well." She drained her glass to prove the point. "But what about the special house-made whisky? Did that really exist? I wasn't aware there had ever been a distillery in Thistlecross."

A dark cloud passed over Neil's face, and Grace's shoulders slumped. "Oh, dear," she said. "I'm afraid that part of the story has just become a piece of folklore. Thistlecross had a handful of grain mills, so it bears to reason there were more than a few rogue distillers. And of course, this was all before branded single malts became popular. People just made whisky, and they drank it." Grace shrugged.

"In large quantities!" Neil added, motioning for more.

Ruby could tell something had soured, and she was holding on to so many more questions than she had before dinner. But she didn't want to press. Not on her first night in a very small town. "So. No more drinking games? When was the last time someone won? Who was the lucky *laddie* to stay in my cottage? You, Neil?"

Neil finished his glass, too. "No, Ruby-Roo," he said, setting it firmly on the counter. "I reckon that would have been Brochan. Brochan is"—he cleared his throat with an exaggerated cough— "very tall, dark, and handsome. Scotland's most eligible bachelor. And—"

"Neil. Please, let's pace ourselves." Grace was about to switch him with a towel. She looked equally cross and amused.

"Mea culpa. You'll meet him soon enough," Neil said, but when Grace turned her back, Neil waved his hands in front of his face like he was overheating, to demonstrate to Ruby that Brochan was dreamy.

The three sat in reflective silence for a few moments before Grace explained to Neil that Ruby had come to Thistlecross in search of a change of pace from her previous career as a food journalist in New York. On paper, Ruby would be helping bake and cook at the Cosy Hearth—it was the most efficient way to a temporary work visa, and both women had agreed to blur the lines around the truth a touch. But actually? "A lass after my own heart," Grace said, "Ruby is writing a cookbook." Ruby nodded, and Grace noted with pride that Ruby would be using the kitchen at the Cosy Hearth to work on her recipes.

"Well, of course," Neil said. "Where else would she do it? There's no kitchen in the cottage."

Ruby had a feeling that Neil had known all this for hours, but she didn't mind her story being shared. "That's right," she said. "I, along with every other thirtysomething journalist in the big city, have burned out and come in search of the elusive fairy tale: the mythical Highlands life." She knew how ridiculous her story sounded. *Why leave everything I knew for a place I've never met and a half-baked dream?* But how could she answer a question she hardly understood?

Neil was kind. "I know the allure of the Highlands. I tried to leave it once in my twenties but soon found myself longing for home. Although I didn't make it as far as you. Just Glasgow." He paused and thought for a moment. "I know, also, that the allure here can be hard to explain." He paused once more and this time, he frowned. "Then there was that Sassenach lady television show. Ever since that came on the scene, Americans have been pouring into Inverness like there's something to see there. But tell me: Why *Thistlecross*?"

Ruby laughed and turned her eyes to Grace and the bottle on the shelf. She didn't admit to Neil that although she had no actual delusions of an eighteenth-century Scot sweeping off her feet, she had been influenced by the "Sassenach lady television show." Neil's question was a fair one. Thistlecross held none of the sexy intrigue of other, more popular Highlands destinations. It was best known for a towering waterfall and for being the birthplace of the first-bred golden retriever. Ruby liked waterfalls and she liked dogs. (She was not a psychopath, after all.) But did she like them enough to cross the Atlantic? It was a little early for a midlife crisis. Ruby decided to take the easy route and give a quippy answer instead of a real one.

"Why Thistlecross? Well, *that*"—she sipped her second whisky—"is very easy to explain." The puddles of melting tension turned into deep pools. This was very, very delicious. Top-notch stuff.

And there, in the oldest, smallest, stoniest pub in Thistlecross, Ruby Spencer told the two oldest, kindest, loveliest people in town about the night she pinned a map of Scotland to the door of her Manhattan apartment, blindfolded herself, spun around three times, and threw a dart for the very first time.

Chapter Three

The next morning, Ruby woke early, courtesy of a rooster near the door. She rolled over and crammed her head under a pillow. "How could I have missed *you* yesterday?" she said, and reached for her cell, which she'd set on the windowsill behind the bed. Just shy of six o'clock. She blinked and looked around the room. Her room. *Eek.* Her room!

Although she'd hung her hat in Manhattan for more than a decade, the city had never felt like home. So why did she miss it all of a sudden? It wasn't Benjamin. Or Lucas, or Jason, or Aaron. Or Seth. Or . . . *Damn it, Ruby! Must. Not. Think. About. Idiot. Men.*

She missed Manhattan because it was familiar. That was the only plausible explanation. She had no real love for New York, with the exception of its superior bagel industry. (*Note to self: Find out about Scotland bagels in general and Thistlecross bagels in specific.*) New York had been just a place to throw herself into work and forget about her daily existential crises of job dissatisfaction and life goals. She hoped that the grittiness of her stone cottage would force her to actually show up to her life with some sort of intentionality, and not just use her home as a physical place to store her body while she existed inside her head.

But it wasn't like the city had any strong pull on her. She drifted there after school because early-twenties Ruby had thought living in New York would be cooler than living upstate. Then she got a cool job to match her cool city, and settled into the grind. And, damn, it was a grind. Ruby felt like New York had lied; it wasn't the glossy, sexy playground she'd imagined. It was hard, and most of the time, living there sucked. She'd shared that with her parents a few years back, hoping for sympathy—or at the very least, a fifty-dollar bill. But Deirdre, her mother, had gently asked Ruby if the city hadn't been honest all along; if she had just placed an unfair expectation on it.

Ruby thought about her parents as she burrowed deeper under the quilt. They were gentle and supportive. Good people with an awesome marriage. They had gotten together young, straight out of high school, and created a life in Ithaca. They'd had Ruby not long after they wed, and declared her to be so perfect they'd never top her. So it had been just the three of them, for Ruby's whole life. Being an only kid wasn't so bad when your parents adored you, and, really, she'd had a pretty privileged childhood.

When she was in primary school, she wanted for nothing and did all the things girls her age liked to do: horseback riding lessons, ballet lessons, T-ball (that lasted all of three games until she was hit on the head while stringing together a crown made of dandelions), and crafting dozens of shitty boondoggle key chains. Deirdre still kept her house keys on one, actually. There had been posters of boy bands plastered to her walls with tacky putty, press-on nails during sleepovers with stuffed-crust pizza, and marathon telephone sessions with her best friend, Lee Demarco. Ruby was loved and accepted, and had all the Limited Too glitter lip gloss her heart desired. Eventually she traded the boondoggle for boyfriends and turned into a moody teen who wrote dramatic poetry with gel pens in a journal. And painted her fingernails alternating shades of sparkly purple and black. And listened to Dashboard Confessional every damn second of the day. But those were all very normal things for a teen of that time, and there was no *real reason* to experience a sense of ennui and longing. As far as these things go, Ruby didn't feel that she had any major trauma in her life. Unless you counted the increasingly common gray hair sprouting up from her part. Which she did not (most days).

And yet.

The bugger of it was that Ruby had always felt there was something broken inside her. Which made her feel guilty, because she'd had it a lot easier than many other girls. But even so, deep down, Ruby suspected that no one would really ever *get* her.

But doesn't everyone feel that way?

It's hard to tell, not knowing everyone else.

Is it possible that it's the yearning for identity that threads us all together, rather than separating us?

Am I overthinking this?

Probably?

As she truly woke, Ruby reminded herself that she was in Thistlecross. Scotland. She propped herself up and pulled the elastic from her topknot. He hair tumbled down past her shoulders in curls the color of good milk chocolate. She twisted a corkscrew around her finger—the damp, heavy air in the Highlands was good for her locks. In New York most days, Ruby's hair hung flat and limp on top, wavy on the bottom. It was the sort of hair that stylists hated to cut, because it never looked good. But it looked nice here. Ruby reached for a slim leather-bound notebook she had placed on one of the pillows last night and jotted down a few things.

1. *Call Mama*
2. *Coordinate kitchen schedule with Grace*
3. *Find luggage (??? ugh)*
4. *EARPLUGS*

For as long as she could remember, Ruby had lived and breathed through her notebooks. Her mind moved so quickly that she'd think of something and forget it seconds later. So she wrote down everything: dinner ideas, to-do list tasks, people's names and places, juicy quotes from an interview, and even some of her heart's darkest secrets. Lee, Ruby's bestest, joked that Ruby ought to permanently stitch the notebook to her left hand, so she'd never be without it.

She studied the list. She wasn't going to accomplish any of it without breakfast, so she stretched one last time and rolled out of the big bed. She almost pulled the quilt back up and arranged the pillows neatly, but decided that it looked nice like that, all rumpled and imperfect. For the typically organized Ruby, it was an out-of-character decision. But then, so was booking a one-way plane ticket to Scotland. Well, technically a three-way ticket. She had plans to go back home for a week, to visit her folks in August. But still. Scotland! For a year! This was a whole new chapter.

After a tepid shower, Ruby yanked on tan leggings she'd packed in the duffel, along with a pair of thin wool socks. She had fallen asleep in her sweater, and put it back on now: a permanent uniform. She laced up her shoes and walked the path to the Cosy Hearth with a bit more precision than she had the night prior. That scotch was really something. Something strong.

Grace, who lived upstairs, was already rummaging around in the kitchen just off the bar area; Ruby could hear the clanking of pans against stove top, utensils against pans. Ruby drew in her breath sharply when she entered the building. *Lovely, just lovely.* The sun had sneaked in through the windows and was presenting itself on the stone floor in wide slices. It was unlike any sunlight Ruby had ever seen: rich and warm, not so much golden as it was sweet cream butter. And speaking of butter—Ruby could smell something baking. "Grace!" she called, once again attempting the Scottish flair and once again butchering it. "Good morning!" She glanced down at the bar; on it was a teacup with a faint smear of coral-colored lipstick and a paperback novel with a well-worn spine. Ruby read the title and blushed a little; it was the first book in a romance series that had been popular about a decade ago.

Grace appeared with flour dotting her cherry-tomato cheeks and strong forearms. Her hair was wrapped in a bun, this time secured with a royal blue ribbon. "Mornin'," she said, noticing Ruby's gaze at the book. "I come down here from my flat upstairs to read sometimes, when I can't sleep." She looked at Ruby as if to say,

Any further questions can be directed up your arse. "I'm making scones, and I'll be needing you to put the coffee on." Ruby grinned. She kind of liked being bossed around. It was good, how comfortable things felt already with Grace.

After Ruby's one-woman game of darts in New York had selected Thistlecross as her new home, she began researching the area. Through some journalistic sleuthing (that bachelor's degree wasn't a total waste, after all), she found an ad Grace had placed with Thistlecross's regional newspaper, looking for a tenant to occupy the stone cottage. Ruby first reached out with a bold email followed by a shy phone call. When she explained she was hoping to spend the year testing recipes and writing a cookbook, Grace had enthusiastically offered her the spot. The rent payment was even reduced, so long as Ruby lent a hand in the kitchen when Grace needed it. And best of all, she was willing to vouch for her as an "essential" employee.

The Cosy Hearth's kitchen was as charming and quirky as its bar. A very old cast-iron oven with a gas-powered stove stood against one of the stone walls, which were lined with a few sporadic rough wooden beams for shelving. There was an old but sturdy refrigerator and a small walk-in pantry. The sink must have been a new addition. It was a deep, wide, farmhouse-style behemoth in which a few mixing bowls were already stacked. There was little in the way of countertops, but a large butcher block table with stools on two sides sat in the middle. Grace was standing at the table's head, using a pastry cutter to mix butter into flour. Just a linen curtain separated the kitchen from the bar, which Ruby realized was a genius stroke of advertising: All the intoxicating smells from the kitchen would quickly reach the patrons. Well, if there were any patrons. Ruby had yet to see another soul at the Cosy Hearth, beyond herself, Grace, and Neil. Grace wiped her hands on her apron and pulled a tray of scones from the oven. They were just lightly golden at the edges and dotted with currants. Ruby eyed the pastries as she reached for a tin can of coffee on one of the shelves and filled the kettle on the stove with water.

"What time does the Cosy Hearth open for customers?" Ruby measured out coffee into the French press. "Surely these scones aren't all for us?"

Grace chuckled. "No, you're right about that. The Cosy Hearth opens—well, as soon as I wake up, though it doesn't much matter because aside from a few loyal friends like Neil, we don't have much in the way of customers."

The kettle made its presence known and Ruby poured water over the grounds.

"Speaking freely, if I may," Grace said, and Ruby nodded in encouragement, "the town owns this building, and I'm lucky that they recently reduced my rent payments. The Traveler Hotel has gobbled my business whole."

Ruby was aware of the Traveler Hotel from her internetting. It had been constructed a few years ago, in 2016. And it sat just a couple of streets away from the Cosy Hearth. Although it catered to out-of-towners who dared venture away from the tourist centers of Inverness and Loch Ness, Ruby wondered if the glossy espresso bar and bistro on the ground floor were attracting locals who had previously been Grace's patrons. Ruby stirred the coffee with a butter knife and plunged the French press.

"I'm lucky also," Grace said, "that they order scones from me three days a week. The payment isn't much, but it's *something*."

Ruby smiled sympathetically and handed a mug of steaming coffee across the table. "If the scones are a fraction as good as last night's dinner, the hotel is the lucky one. May I?" Grace nodded and Ruby reached for a pastry. She wiped the coffee grounds from the knife and split open the scone. Steam escaped to reveal a dense crumb. Ruby dipped her knife into the crock of butter and slathered some onto half. She took a bite and started laughing. "Oh, wow. Grace. You are a gift."

Grace beamed and turned the contents of the mixing bowl onto the counter as she set about shaping another batch of scones.

Ruby chewed thoughtfully. "I'm sorry about the great migration to the hotel. Honestly, anyone who gives up on a real-deal place like this is a fool."

The same rain cloud that had crossed Neil's face the night before appeared over Grace's now. With a cluck of her tongue, Grace shifted the conversation. "Well, it'll free up the space for you and your cookbook research," she said. "Don't be shy; we can always work around each other if we need it at the same time."

"Or *with* each other," Ruby said, licking her thumb and picking up a few crumbs from the plate.

"Or with each other," Grace agreed.

The two women were quiet for a few minutes. Ruby sat on a stool. She let the mug of coffee warm her hands and she watched Grace work. After swiftly portioning the dough into eight pieces, she brushed each one with cream and added a sprinkle of sugar on top. Once she'd put them in the oven, she turned around and placed her hands on the table. "So. I've shared my heart's sorrow with you. I'll be needing you to tell me yours."

Ruby cradled her coffee on her knees. She'd spent so long as a writer telling other people's stories, she was out of practice telling hers.

"I don't know where to start."

Grace clucked. "With the first thought that comes to your mind, naturally."

Ruby took a sip.

"Well . . . both my parents love to cook. When I was young, we'd spend our whole weekends driving around Ithaca on grocery store adventures. Then we'd come home and they'd cook these elaborate meals. Coq au vin, beef bourguignon, that kind of stuff. It was pretty glamorous, now that I think about it." Ruby's heart melted a little as she recalled one of her first memories: helping her mom stir a pot of risotto with chanterelles and hen-of-the-woods mushrooms. She had even let Ruby pour a splash of white wine in the pot, assuring her that all the alcohol would cook off by the time the food was ready. Risotto was still Ruby's favorite comfort food, although these days she followed the "splash for the pan, splash for my glass" rule of cooking with wine.

Grace had settled in across the table. "Go on."

"As I got older, it just seemed obvious that I'd start cooking, too. At first it was routine, but I realized I actually loved doing it. And"—Ruby's voice got quiet and shy—"I realized I was pretty good at it."

"What's that, dear?"

Ruby repeated herself at the same volume.

Grace nodded. She'd heard the first time. "And how is it, when you cook?"

"Oh, gosh. It's so intuitive. Once I learned the basics, I stopped using recipes. I just toss stuff in a pot and adjust as I go. A little bit of this, a touch more of that—you know? You know." Ruby grew more confident as she continued. "The food I make—it's wholesome. Hearty but not heavy. I'm obsessed with vegetables, but I hate when they taste like rabbit food. There's always rivers of olive oil and butter. But fresh herbs and citrus. It's not indulgent or guilty. It's just . . . nourishing."

"I learned how to cook from my da," Grace said. "And I'm with you on the rivers of butter. I could stand to eat a few more vegetables, though." She tilted her head. "But you didn't end up a chef. You became a writer."

"Yeah, I'll be honest, line cooking was not for me. I tried, but it was awful. Being surrounded by a half dozen coked-out dudes simmering in a vat of their own testosterone?" Grace snorted. "Gross. I got a job at a food website, and it turned out I loved that so much more. I rose through the ranks, I guess. Eventually I became the features editor, and that was just . . . a dream."

Ruby had soared through the job for almost an entire decade. But as her ten-year workaversary crept up, she realized that she was burned-out. The thrill of scoring a major story or getting tweeted at by a *Times* staffer had lost its luster. She was tired all the time. New York was grating on her nerves. And, worst of all, turning her passion into her career had had one unfortunate consequence: she had kind of, sort of, just a little bit stopped caring about food.

So she had quit. Just like that—walked into the editor in chief's office and handed her a letter of resignation. Then she cried. In her editor's office. Which was weird. Then she went to a bar and sat alone and drank a very expensive glass of white burgundy. Which she could not afford. But made her feel happy. So it was worth it. Then she had to go back to work for another two weeks. Which was awkward, after the crying thing. And then she left for good. And she called her mom and said, *Help me I don't know what I'm doing with my life.* And her mom smiled through the phone and said, *Remember how much you used to love feeding people? Why don't you finally write that cookbook everyone's been asking you for?* Even though no one was asking Ruby for a cookbook. Except her parents. But they counted. So Ruby googled "How to write a cookbook proposal" and then she wrote one. And sent it to a literary agent. And the agent said, *I like where this is going but you need a more cohesive theme; you need a hook. Take another crack and send it back to me.* And Ruby tried, but she had forgotten how hard it was to write recipes, and she kept getting distracted by Manhattan (sirens, trash everywhere, rats dragging around slices of pizza, etc.). So she sold all her furniture and broke her lease and found a very adorable stone cottage for rent in a small town in the Scottish Highlands. And she moved there. To find a cohesive theme.

"It seemed like a logical next step in my career, but now I'm not so sure. What on earth would I title a cookbook?" she explained to Grace as she poured them both a second cup of coffee. "*A Bunch of Random Things a Random Woman Likes to Eat*?"

Grace reached over the table and touched Ruby's cheek with her knuckle, leaving a trace of flour.

"I like that title," she said. "But I think you can do better."

Ruby gave a small shrug and stayed quiet.

"There's more, isn't there?" Grace asked. "And I won't press if you don't want to share. But I notice I opened my cottage to a single renter, not two."

Ruby groaned. "It's been eighty-four years since I was a twosome."

Chapter Four

That wasn't quite the truth. And Ruby wasn't always so jaded. Like any thirtysomething woman living and working in Manhattan, Ruby dated. But she had been burned, and badly, in her twenties, and the experience left her both cautious and unenthusiastic about men. And the deeper she got into her thirties, the less worthwhile the whole dating thing even seemed. The first date or two was enjoyable (it was nice to have someone else offer to pay for her white burgundy), but once things progressed, Ruby found it hard to show up in the way you're supposed to when starting a relationship. Vulnerability, which felt so easy on the page, seemed impossible to access when cooking dinner with a man. Let alone sleeping with him.

For a while, Ruby had half-heartedly swiped around on dating apps, being sure to note that she was not looking for a relationship. "Why bother?" she had written in her bio. That commentary caused an avalanche of replies from men interested in one-night stands, which would have been fine, except . . . Well, the thing of it was, most of them didn't know how to spell. Or formulate a complete sentence. Or couldn't be bothered to. Ruby wasn't looking for a life partner, but she wasn't about to divulge her orgasm face to a man who thought "'Sup???" with three hand-wave emojis was a quality opening line.

Honestly. Men. Be better.

In fact, the last time Ruby had had sex was . . . *Um, hold on.*

There was Aaron, the finance guy. And that had been two whole years ago. Ruby kept running into him during her morning commute. At the time, Ruby had thought it was romantic, like there had to be a *reason* they kept brushing elbows on the subway. As it turned out, the reason was that their apartments were close to each other and they started work at the same time. They struck up a flirtation and eventually she asked him to dinner, which led to her going back to his place for a nightcap. Which led to perfectly acceptable, perfectly boring sex in the missionary position. Ruby hadn't even gotten off, but after five minutes of that weird jackrabbit thrusty thing he apparently liked so much, she didn't feel the need to try for another round. She went home with the intention of studying alternate subway lines that passed by her office, because obviously she never wanted to see him again. But then he texted her the heart-eyes emoji and said he couldn't stop thinking about her, and that felt nice. Ruby knew he wasn't *the one*, and he wasn't great in bed, but she somehow found herself in a three-month situationship with him. Those three months were as expected: dull sex, lots of ignoring each other at the dinner table, and generally feeling like she had made a mistake. Like she had settled for less than she deserved and desired. When she finally called it off and texted Lee the update, her friend sent the eye-rolling emoji. **obviously, roo . . . it's not like ur going to fall in love with a finance bro who plays golf and wears polo shirts?**

Lee was right. Ruby was not that kind of woman. And that meant she got lonely sometimes. But it also meant she didn't have to deal with the disappointment of yet another man turning out to be a chemistryless dud. Nothing an extra-long bubble bath with candles and her vibrator couldn't fix.

Okay, Ruby was lying. Just a little bit.

She had definitely had sex since two-years-ago Aaron.

It just wasn't the sort of sex that fit into her personal ideal of who she was, so she kept conveniently forgetting about it.

But since we're being *honest* here, there was Jason, who happened immediately after Aaron. Jason was a tattoo artist who'd inked a tiny gemstone (it wasn't a sapphire or diamond . . .) onto the soft flesh of her inner wrist. Afterward, he told her he dug the way she bit at her lip when the pain got too intense, and one thing led to another, and that's the story of how Ruby had sex with a stranger in a janitorial closet of a tattoo shop in Williamsburg, Brooklyn.

Oh, and of course there was Lucas, from hot yoga. He showed up at her studio one Saturday morning a few months back, and she was so distracted by his blond ponytail and cheese-grater abs that she fell over, like, actually tumbled onto the ground, during dancer pose and got a nasty bruise on her thigh. They chatted after class, and he revealed he was in town for a week, visiting his San Francisco firm's NYC office. They spent an incredibly sexy few days together, eating at trendy restaurants and screwing in his mind-bendingly beautiful SoHo hotel, but then he went back to

33

the West Coast and Ruby went back to standing on her head without ogling hot men. Every once in a while, she Liked his stuff on social media and he Liked hers back.

Ruby cringed as she remembered Seth, the *actual* last guy she was with. Seth had been all potential, no delivery. He was a political reporter for an intellectual news magazine; they had actually worked for the same media conglomerate before Ruby quit her job, and had occasionally bumped into each other at the work cafeteria. Ruby dug his writing (the man had a way with subjunctive mood), so when he said yes to her offer for happy hour drinks after work on her last day at the office, she was genuinely excited. But then he spent the whole time telling stories about celebrities he'd interviewed and talking about his Pulitzer nomination. Ruby wasn't impressed—it's not like he had won. But she had kind of, sort of been hoping for a one-night stand before her yearlong adventure in Scotland—where she was pretty sure she'd be having zero sex. So they wound up back at his place, and things were getting heated until he revealed he struggled with ED. Technically, they hadn't even had sex. Technically, it had been an epic fail. Afterward, Ruby berated herself for getting her hopes up for a man who seemed so good on paper. She'd been around the block; she knew better.

But before all that—before the parade of unexceptional men—there had been Benjamin.

Benjamin, the biggest disappointment of them all.

Benjamin, who was irritatingly taking up so much of Ruby's brain space, even after all these years.

Ruby had fallen for Benjamin (not Ben, *never* Ben; Benjamin believed that nicknames were stupid and beneath the dignity of grown adults) straight out of college, during an internship at a digital magazine. He was whip-smart and ten years older than she, with all the money, style, publishing accolades, and gravitas that came with a decade of experience in New York media. He also happened to have been the editor in chief of the website at which Ruby found herself. These days, Ruby would never accept a workplace superior's advances. But early-twenties Ruby was dazzled by him and too confident for her own good. *What's the worst that could happen?* she had thought as his interest in her grew from her job performance to her thoughts on the latest Salman Rushdie novel, or her take on the new dumpling place that had just opened on Canal near Mott Street. Before Ruby understood what was happening, she was fully committed, deeply in love, and in an intensely adult, monogamous relationship with Benjamin.

It was breathtakingly romantic for two whole years—and with none of the intern-boss drama her coworkers predicted. Six months after starting the internship, she was offered another opportunity elsewhere and took the gig. She and Benjamin had agreed it was for the best. He'd even given her a professional reference before her interview. In retrospect, Ruby saw the problematic nature of his recommendation, but at the time it just confirmed her feeling that Benjamin considered her his true equal. She wasn't Ruby, the naive intern; she was Ruby, his *partner*. (*Boyfriend* sounded so unworldly. So college!)

As they continued deeper down the path of coupledom, Ruby introduced Benjamin to her parents, who adored him. She spent

Thanksgiving with his whole family, and shone with pride when he introduced her as "the smartest, most exceptional woman I've ever known." She moved into his Carroll Gardens apartment at breakneck speed, and immediately settled into a blissy domestic routine. They cooked dinner together every Friday, feeding each other from the spoon as they stirred sauce. They thumbed through *The New York Times* together in bed every Sunday, reading aloud passages from the front page. Ruby secretly loved gorging on the Styles section, but she waited until Monday, on her commute to the office. Benjamin thought the Styles articles weren't "real journalism," a stance to which Ruby had agreed on their first date—even though she felt otherwise. And every weekday morning, after Benjamin left for the office, Ruby woke to find a handwritten note for her, next to the toothpaste in the bathroom. Every weekday morning. Even when they were grumpy with each other, or he was in a rush.

So Ruby never saw it coming when, one Saturday afternoon as she tackled the toilet bowl with bleach and a scrub brush, Benjamin sat on the sink and quietly, calmly announced he'd reconnected with his ex over drinks and wanted to be with her. Like, as soon as possible. Like, yesterday. He told Ruby that she remained a unique and special person, and even went so far as to tell her that she'd always have a "quiet place" in his heart. But his ex? She was the one. Surely, he said, Ruby would understand that.

Ruby had thrown the toilet scrubbie, hitting him square in the forehead. She hadn't meant to—it was instinctual—but now, years later, she still couldn't clean her bathroom without feeling a rush of nausea.

She'd moved out within a week, subletting a dingy studio in Yorkville until she saved up for a nicer place. It was a bleak time in Ruby's life, marked by an upsetting amount of takeout dumplings and Facebook-stalking her ex's ex turned lover. Benjamin never contacted her again; never even accidentally butt-dialed her. It was like those two years had never happened to him. It was like she'd never existed.

But Ruby had been changed by the experience, deeply shook. Eventually, the fresh wounds in her heart scabbed over, but instead of healing, they started to calcify. By the time Ruby found herself sipping vodka with *Womp-womp* Seth, she had become an impenetrable fortress. She was untouchable, but she was also safe.

Even though Ruby always insisted on condoms and got tested regularly, she couldn't help but feel her behavior was a little . . . reckless? Wild? Stupid? A cacoëthes? (Pause for dictionary.) *Pointless?* That one; that last word fit the bill. Because she never felt *satisfied* after these types of encounters. Even if the sex was good, she was sick of investing emotional and mental energy in entertaining men her age who couldn't be bothered to make a dinner reservation, let alone ask her a question or two about herself. It all ultimately felt like a distraction from herself. She didn't love having sex with random men, but she also didn't love not having sex at all. She didn't want to be in a relationship with someone who didn't light her up, but she also grew restless on her own.

Ruby did not really know what she wanted.

———

Back at the Cosy Hearth, she tried to explain this all to Grace. Well, without mentioning Tinder or screwing Aaron in his obnoxiously minimalist FiDi loft and getting herself off in her bathtub. Or Tattoo Artist Jason, Hot Yoga Lucas, or *Womp-womp* Seth. Or Benjamin.

"I guess I'm just not meant to be in a relationship. And that's fine. My only fear is that I'm becoming a bit odd and eccentric in my 'old age.'" Ruby rolled her eyes to demonstrate that she was joking—um, sort of—and Grace nodded.

"I understand. I know someone just like that. However, as I have always told him: He just hasn't found his person." And, before Ruby could ask: "You'll meet him soon enough."

Chapter Five

Ruby spent the next day walking everywhere and drinking in the landscape. She wanted to see all of Scotland, but it seemed more important to orient herself here first. The Cosy Hearth and the stone cottage were on the eastern side of the tiny town; and as she strolled toward its center, she noted the small houses, the rolling hills in the distance, and the silver birch trees that bordered the farmland and fields. She more than noted the surprisingly robust collection of food shops: a greengrocer, a butcher, a cheese shop, and a bread bakery. There was plenty to see here, but the landscape wasn't dramatic or jaw-dropping, the way it was on the coasts or islands. There were no cliffs or sweeping valleys, but it felt quiet and homey. Thistlecross wasn't a place to have an epic adventure; it was a place to make a life.

As she wandered past houses in town, she noted that many had gardens in window boxes and cold frames. She hadn't come to Scotland to grow vegetables, but decided right then and there that she would plant a garden. It would be a fun distraction, and maybe even help her pull the cookbook together . . . in some mysterious, yet-to-be-determined way.

Although Ruby had never farmed, she had friends who did. She loved working in the fields and barns, and every year, she spent long weekends upstate, helping with planting and harvests. In exchange for the manual labor, she was fed well and welcome to whatever gardening knowledge she could absorb—and she'd discovered a green thumb for vegetable growing. She consulted with Grace that evening, who chuckled and gave her the green light, although she also warned that the Highlands did not enjoy the fertile ground or more hospitable weather of the Lowlands. Grace suggested that Ruby focus on hardy crops; things like potatoes, kale, cauliflower, and root vegetables. Or easy stuff, like herbs.

The next day, Ruby visited the general and hardware store on High Street. It was thankfully more than a collection of batteries with a few toiletries and packaged loaves of bread thrown in for good measure. The shop was manned by a distinguished-looking man in his midsixties with a trim little pencil mustache. "Carson Chapman," he said by way of introduction. "A transplant, like you."

"Thrilled!" said Ruby, extending her hand. "Where from?"

Carson neatly folded the newspaper he'd been reading and set it on the counter. "Spent some of my prime working years in Manchester." He firmed the crease with his thumb. "Before that, I was a boy in Leek."

Ruby didn't offer up her details. She had a sneaking suspicion Carson knew everything about her except her social security number. The cheesemonger had. The postal worker had. Whether it was Grace, Neil, or a little Scottish mouse, someone was spreading the news about her arrival. So instead, she shifted the conversation to the task at hand. "That's exactly what I'm here for. Leeks."

Carson gave her an odd look. "Well, seeds, really," Ruby clarified and Carson's look said *Ah*. "Leek seeds. And carrots, and kale, if you've got them." Carson proffered a variety of seed packets. They looked quite old and dusty, and Ruby hoped they'd germinate. She selected a handful's worth of the most robust-looking varieties, but noted there were no tender salad greens or herbs. While Carson rang up the tally, she jotted a note in her journal: *Buy parsley, etc. seeds online.*

In addition to a weirdly large cache of knowledge about sheep castration, Ruby's farm stints had taught her that the delicate stuff grew best in a hoop house—a simple freestanding greenhouse made with polyethylene stretched taut over PVC piping. It was a great setup, and she would have loved to build one here. But she didn't have enough hands to construct it behind her cottage; it was decidedly not a one-woman job. She also didn't want to place too large a bet on her growing abilities before getting started.

She explained the issue to Carson. Luckily for Ruby, Carson had dabbled in amateur garden and landscape design as a way to blow off steam on the weekends during his time as an estate lawyer in Manchester. He sketched out plans for a simple wood raised bed with a hinged top covered in poly plastic. The top would keep her veggies warm during the chilly spring nights and could be lifted up to weed, water, and pick her crops. A baby greenhouse. How cute. How Scotland!

As the amount on the till crept up, Ruby watched the pile of tools and equipment grow into a small hill. "How do you like the flophouse so far?" Carson asked, documenting each purchase in a ledger with a ballpoint pen.

"You're the second person to call it that," said Ruby. "As far as flophouses go, this one is superior. Neil told me all about the she-nanigans that used to happen there. Well—I guess, the shenanigans that led to people staying there." Carson chuckled. "Did you ever?" she asked, seeking the type of confession best told to a near stranger.

"Heavens, no," he said, looking offended. He put the seeds in a small paper bag that he slid across the counter. "Although I was at the pub the last time the fellows did battle with a few bottles of whisky. Neil started it 'for old times' sake,' which will likely not surprise you, having met him yourself."

"Did he win?"

"Well, it depends on how you quantify a win, doesn't it? The rules are clear as mud, and the point of the whole exercise is even murkier." Carson rolled his eyes but left a grin on his mouth to signify that although he thought it was a silly game, he still liked that it was tradition in Thistlecross. "But no—a young man named Brochan took home the honors. It was down to him and Neil at the bitter end. Neil claimed he was drinking to remember; Brochan said he was trying to forget. What weighty troubles a nineteen-year-old has to forget, I'll never know. Neil fell asleep by the fire eventually. Heaven help the old man who challenges a youthful one to any match that isn't won through wisdom."

Brochan. There was that name again. Her curiosity was bub-bling over. "How long ago was this?" Ruby asked, trying to sound like she couldn't care less about the answer.

Carson thought about it. "Oh, now. Years ago. Fifteen? Twenty?"

Ruby did some quick calculations. That would put the mys-terious Brochan right around her age.

"Well, if they ever try it again, I'll be pulling for you."

"If I find myself at the bottom of a whisky bottle, you'll be pulling my head out of the loo," said Carson with a laugh disguised as a dignified sniff.

Ruby tittered and nodded goodbye to him as she headed toward the door, her arms full. She was midway through jostling paper bags into the crook of her elbow when the door swung open from the outside. "Savior! Thank you," she said, adjusting her purchases to a more comfortable position.

"No bother." The voice attached to the door-holding hand was deep and low, and Ruby lifted her eyes to meet it. Wow. The voice was *hot*. The voice was bearded and tall and made her belly do flip-flops. She stood there for a few moments, holding her seed packets and gaping at the handsome Scot in front of her.

"Brochan!" Carson's voice jolted Ruby back to reality and she blinked awake. "Thanks," she repeated, only this time her voice came out like a whisper. Brochan tilted his head in her direction and stepped aside. Realizing that she was about thirty seconds past her cue, Ruby hopped past him and out onto the street.

The door sealed shut as Brochan returned Carson's greeting. Ruby opened and closed her mouth a few times, recalling Grace and Neil's teasing hints. So this was Brochan. A man so gorgeous, he rendered her practically speechless.

As Ruby walked home, her heart hopeful and her bank account considerably less robust, she twitched her nose nervously and wondered for the umpteenth time that week if she'd bitten off more than she could chew.

Chapter Six

The next day, Carson delivered the rest of Ruby's haul in his truck. Thankful for any excuse to procrastinate writing her cookbook proposal, Ruby opened her notebook to the page where Carson had drawn the plan and written instructions.

It's not that Ruby didn't know her way around a hammer. She had lived alone for years, after all, and pictures don't hang themselves. It was just that building a raised garden bed with a hinged top was way more complicated than it had seemed yesterday, standing at the counter with Carson. But it was either that or stare at the judgmentally blinking cursor on her laptop. She tied her curls back into a quick braid and got to work.

After clearing away a four- by six-foot patch of weeds and long grass near the path that connected the Cosy Hearth and her cottage, Ruby lugged the untreated wood—thankfully, already cut to size—to the site, and set the pieces on their sides in the shape of a rectangle. She reviewed Carson's notes: *Use screws to secure the framing.*

Ruby grabbed the first screw and set its tip against the piece of wood where it met its neighbor. "Eek!" she squealed a little, both in fear and the thrill of doing something hard and good. She aligned an electric drill over the screw and pulled the trigger. The screw made it halfway in before the wood started splitting apart at various points. The plank looked like it was in danger of completely splintering. "Eek," she said again, more quietly this time.

"You didn't ask advice but—if I were you, I'd mark the places you mean to screw before doing it. And predrill the hole."

Ruby turned around, still in a squatting position, the drill still in her hand. Leaning against the cottage was a well-built Scot with a truly heroic beard. Brochan. His facial hair was trimmed neatly around his mustache and well maintained at the edges, coming to an unruly rounded point about an inch lower than his chin. It was a *great* beard (not that she was a connoisseur or anything). The man attached to the beard was at least a foot taller than Ruby, wearing a white linen shirt rolled up at the elbows, the hem grazing the waistband of his gray canvas work pants. His facial bone structure was strong; but the presence of round, ruddy radishes for cheeks made his features seem kind, rather than severe. Clearly he'd spent much of his life outdoors; the time was showing on his skin, with deep creases around the outside edges of his eyes. Which were almost black. His hair was thick and the color of good dark chocolate, just long enough to tuck behind his ears. Which it was. Tucked behind his ears. And that beard. Ruby couldn't tear her eyes from it. It managed to somehow look full and bushy without being wild, and there were hints of red around the edges.

Eek, squealed Ruby internally. How long had she been staring? Long enough to drink in all those details. Long enough to become creepy? Definitely.

"I did not . . . ask for advice," said Ruby, "but I'm also not about to turn it away when it shows up at my door. I mean, in my garden." She blushed and her neck felt hot. The man stood there, in no apparent hurry to make the situation less uncomfortable. He crossed his arms and waited for her to speak again. Ruby caught a glimpse of the roped muscles that snaked along his forearms. They were strong, but not grotesquely big—his muscles—and looked like they'd been formed with years of manual labor. They were not the kind of muscles built on barbells and rowing machines. *Wait.* Had she just done a flirt? No. Impossible. She was merely caught off guard. *Slow it down, girl*, she thought. *Introduce yourself. Before this gets any creepier.*

"What I meant was, thank you. That's probably very wise. Is it obvious I've never done this before? Ha. I wanted to grow some vegetables over the summer, but judging from the weather lately, they'll need all the help they can get." Ruby shivered as a breeze picked up, and wished she had dressed in more than a thin tank with her trusty leggings. "Oh! I'm Ruby. I'm renting the stone cottage from Grace. You can call me Roo, though. Everybody does." *Awkward, just stunningly awkward.*

The man laughed and kept his post against the cottage. "Brochan."

Ruby set down the drill and stood. Brochan kept leaning and smiled. Ruby waited. Brochan waited longer.

"Brochan." Ruby took the word in her mouth, attempting to gently roll the *r* in the way he had.

"Brochan," he repeated it, correctly this time.

"Brochan," Ruby tried again.

"Call me Broo," he said.

Ruby giggled. Was *he* flirting? Um, how old was she? Twelve, apparently. She extended her hand. "I'll work on it." He took her palm and squeezed, rather than shook. She let her gaze travel briefly along the length of his arm to his chest and collarbones, which were carpeted with thick dark hair. *Brochan.* That name. This man. The last *lad* to spend a night at the stone cottage before her arrival. A man who could hold his scotch. A man who, by nineteen, had already felt tortured by memory. Probably a super great person for her to get involved with!

Both Neil and Carson had made it seem like there was something mysterious, or secretive, about Brochan; but as Ruby studied his face, she couldn't notice anything weird or unnerving. He didn't seem like a serial killer or town drunk (the town drunk was probably Neil, all things considered).

"Are you from here? I mean—Thistlecross. Not the cottage," Ruby asked and attempted to cram her hands into her pockets before realizing she was in leggings and had no pockets.

"Yes," said Brochan, squatting down and looking first in the direction of town, then back at the cottage. He picked up the drill and gave it a quick whirr. "I'm from here." Motioning for Ruby to join him, he flashed a smirky grin, and the corner of his mouth turned up at the same time his eyes brightened. "Now. Let's make a home for those lettuces of yours."

Chapter Seven

Brochan and Ruby worked together all morning. When they spoke it was about the project at hand, but mostly they were quiet. Which was weird for Ruby. Every bone in her journalist's body wanted to pummel him with questions, starting with *Who the hell are you?* and ending with *Are you single?* Which was also weird. Because she wasn't supposed to care about meeting men. Because she had decided that she wanted to be single. Because she was here to write a cookbook (and grow vegetables). Ugh! But, Ruby thought as she watched Brochan attach metal brackets to the wood, his face an uncomplicated canvas of pure concentration, maybe it wouldn't hurt to add a little adventure.

It was well past noon when they pulled the plastic tightly over the frame. Ruby was hungry, but glad they had powered through lunch. The garden bed looked good. And she had created it. Well, with the help of a sexy Scottish man. But nobody said she had to do everything on her own.

"How can I repay you?" Ruby asked, opening and closing the cover a few times with a smile on her face. She could hardly wait to fill the bed with topsoil and seeds. Before Brochan could answer, she tugged at her braid and nodded in the direction of the Cosy Hearth. "Can I make you lunch?"

Brochan fitted the drill bit into the grooves of the carrying case and latched it shut with a satisfying snap. He stood and rubbed his hands together a few times, his palms making a scratchy sound. He extended an arm toward the path, indicating that Ruby lead the way. And then he said, "Yes."

There was no one inside the Cosy Hearth—per usual, Ruby thought with a sigh. *Poor Grace.* "Hello?" she called out, before spotting a note on the bar, held in place under a vase filled with bluebells: *Closed for the day on account of errands.*

"Poor Grace," Ruby repeated out loud. "I have a feeling we're the only ones who will see this note." Brochan frowned and for the first time that day, Ruby saw an entire thunderstorm gather in his eyes. So curious. So many questions. She held on to them all. "Well, we'll have the kitchen to ourselves," she said. "And I know where Grace keeps the good butter."

While Ruby cooked, Brochan gathered plates and flatware for them, then helped himself to the taps behind the bar, where he poured two glasses of ale. He delivered one to Ruby, who had just cracked a couple of eggs with bright orange yolks into the cut-out centers of bread frying in bacon grease. "Mm, thank you," Ruby said, taking a sip. It was heavily malted and almost chewy. Nothing like the death-by-hops beer her dad enjoyed or the pale lagers Lee chugged like water in the summer. It was different, and a little weird. She liked it.

"Thank *you*. For the bacon," Brochan said as he peeked into the pan. He set his glass on the butcher block table, crossing his arms across his chest like Grace so frequently did. Ruby again noted toned biceps with another flash of heat rising from her neck. "I guess they do teach you some valuable things in the States, after all," Brochan observed.

"Excuse you!" said Ruby, transferring the eggs and toast onto two plates. She pinched her fingers into Grace's salt well and made it rain over the toast. "I loved bacon *way* before it was cool. In fact, I once wrote an article about how the bacon trend has become so overdone that it died and came back to life. I interviewed chefs and pig farmers and everything. I *know* bacon." Ruby was bragging, and she realized that she wanted to impress Brochan; prove to him that she had talents even if they didn't lie in the construction realm.

"I loved bacon before you could walk," he said, taking another sip and raising his thick eyebrows toward his hairline.

Was that a question about her age? Or another flirtation? Both?

"Maybe that's true," said Ruby, using a knife to cut a big bite of her lunch. "Maybe not. How old are you?" She brought an egg-drenched piece of toast up to her mouth, aiming to look cute and coy as she ate it, but a trail of yolk ran down her chin. She reached for a napkin and tried to seem unruffled.

"Thirty-eight."

"Thirty-five. But I'm not sure when I learned to walk. Or first tried bacon."

"So I could be right."

"Fine, I don't want to fight about it!"

Unlike every other recent romantic encounter she'd had, their flirty banter was imbued with a sense of curiosity. They were teasing and learning about each other, not just racing toward the bedroom. It felt foreign, but certainly not bad. Ruby savored the crusty bread turning tender in her mouth. Was her knee-jerk animalistic attraction to him made more exciting by the conversation they were sharing? *Definitely.* It seemed like Brochan considered her to be an equal, which was a sensation Ruby hadn't felt since he-who-must-not-be-named.

They ate in silence, then, standing across from each other at the butcher block table. Ruby's left hip stuck out as she rested her right heel at her left ankle. Brochan took hearty bites, finishing his meal in under two minutes. He watched her chew for a moment, then placed a hand on the wood, following a line in the grain with his middle finger. "Grace used to make this for me when I was little."

Ruby looked up through her lashes. *That* was an interesting piece of information.

Brochan finished his ale. "She called it egg-in-the-hole."

Ruby swallowed her last bite. Brochan collected both their plates and brought them to the sink, where he washed them and the frying pan. "My mom always called them duck eggs," she said. "Which is not really a thing. I don't think anyone else would know what I meant if I said that. But she stamped out the middle of the toast with a duck-shaped cookie cutter. I loved it."

Brochan turned off the tap and wiped his hands on his thighs. He smiled at Ruby.

Ruby sipped her beer. God, it was so hard not to ask him all the questions. She settled on an easy one. "So, Broo," she said, and saw a small spark of laughter shimmer in his throat. "I'm sure you've heard all about me. New Yorker turned wannabe Scot, writing a cookbook, offensively bad with power tools. What do you do for a living?"

"What makes you think I know all about you?"

"Because everyone else in Thistlecross does!"

He chuckled. "You're a spitfire. I don't know your birthday. But I know who you are."

"February nineteenth. But seriously: What do you do?"

"What we did this morning, mostly. Carpentry and adjacent things. Fixing broken windows. Installing new washers and dryers. Minor renovations. Leaky sink repair." Brochan shrugged. "I do whatever people need done in order to live *their* lives."

"The town handyman, it would seem," said Ruby. "Arguably the most important position."

"Don't be telling that to Mayor Dunbar," Brochan said, asking with his eyes if Ruby wanted another ale. She held her thumb and forefinger together to indicate just a little bit more. A *wee* bit.

"I haven't met him yet. Thanks."

"Her."

"Ooh, nice, I love a woman in political power."

Brochan gave a flat, forced smile and handed over the beer.

Ruby took the half-glass and toasted him. "Slainte." Coming from her, the word sounded like a sneeze that had been held in for too long.

"Your pronunciation leaves a lot to be desired, but the effort is noted. And appreciated," Brochan said. "Slainte." When he said it, it sounded impossibly alluring. "Mayor Dunbar is . . ." He paused and combed his fingers through his hair. Ruby inspected her split ends. "Complicated. We grew up together, went to the same primary school." He smiled. "Kind of hard to avoid becoming mates with everyone in your age bracket, bustling metropolis that Thistlecross is. We used to cause all sorts of trouble." Brochan let his smile transform into a conspiratorial grin. "Once, we got read the riot act for writing dirty words on the bathroom stall. I told our teacher the fairies had done it." Brochan met Ruby's eyes. "I don't think she believed me."

"What words did you write?"

"Shite. Knockers. The like."

"Nice."

"After highers, she worked in the town hall as the secretary, which was great. We were proper adventure hooligans. Supposing she was my best mate. But Thistlecross was apparently too small for her, and she left for New York City. We had a huge row—she called me a 'small mind attached to a big—'" Brochan's cheeks turned red and he brushed a few crumbs onto the floor. "Well, never mind. We didn't speak for the whole time she was gone. I stayed here, mucked around. Plowed driveways. Fixed doors. Built wee greenhouses." Ruby smiled. "When she came back four years ago, I could see we had nothing in common. She'd changed, had become entirely focused on *growth* and *unmet potential* in Thistlecross. Like she thought the rest of us were backward eejits. At first she tried to create advertising campaigns for the local business, but the local businesses are all just—I don't know—people who make soap as a side job. Nobody had the means to pay for advertising. And everyone already knows that Sofie makes soap—they know every scent it comes in. Anyhow. She—Mayor Dunbar—

kept blethering on about getting on the tourism bandwagon. She thinks Thistlecross is stuck in the past. I think we're doing just fine. Finally went and got herself elected mayor a few years ago. It was quite the upset. A lot of folks still have their knickers in a twist over a woman in the position."

Ruby frowned. This was hard. She could see what a sore spot this was for Brochan. She couldn't imagine having gone through a falling-out with Lee. But also, hell yeah, for feminism and strong-ass women. But also, the tricky bit about change versus tradition in the Highlands. How do you move forward as a place steeped in—and known for—its history? She wanted to tell him that she understood how he was feeling, but that seemed silly. Because she didn't. She'd never felt connected to a place the way Brochan seemed to feel about Thistlecross.

He leaned across the butcher block table like he was about to share a secret. He was very close to Ruby. Close enough to kiss her. *Oh my god* was he going to kiss her? He wet his lips with his tongue and raised his left eyebrow. She leaned in a little closer. She was so close that he could count her gray hairs if he wanted to. She hoped he didn't want to. She was certain there was black pepper in her teeth.

She held her breath and tried not to move.

Finally, Brochan spoke. "Anyway. She's become quite the patronizing arsehole."

Ruby let the silence hang heavy between the two of them. She was still trying to figure out what to say when they heard the door creak open. "Ruby, is that you? Either that or Neil's helped himself to the larder. I smell bacon grease!" Before either Brochan or Ruby could move, the curtain to the kitchen parted, and Grace entered. Ruby jumped backward. Grace only paused for a half of a second before chattering introductions. Ruby had a feeling that she witnessed their whole morning in the singular moment she observed. She was a sly one, that Grace.

"Brochan, I see you've met Ruby. Ruby's staying at—"

"The flophouse. Yes, I know."

"The cottage," Grace corrected and playfully knocked his cheek with her knuckle.

Brochan checked the frayed leather watch on his wrist. "Time for me to go. Mrs. Finley will be waiting for her call-a-plumber. Thanks for lunch, Ruby," he said and turned toward the bar.

"Roo. It's Roo. And thank you for this morning. I still don't know how I'll repay your kindness."

"You don't have to," said Brochan with another million-pound smirk. "I know where you keep your vegetables."

He seems great," Ruby observed to Grace after he'd left.

"Oh." Grace smiled, and let her eyes wander to the two empty beer glasses on the table. She crossed her arms over her chest and looked pleased with herself. "He is."

Chapter Eight

The next morning, Ruby woke at a reasonable hour, thanks to some ear plugs she'd thrown on top of the pile of seed packets at Carson's shop. Take that, rooster. Her luggage had finally arrived, too. She was immensely happy to be reunited with her full collection of leggings and her old denim overalls. She massaged her scalp a bit with her fingernails and looked in the small mirror hanging at eye level on the wall. Her hair was a mess—honestly, since when did she have curls like this?

She almost jumped out of bed to start the day before remembering that there were no rules anymore, and that although she was technically supposed to be writing a cookbook proposal, there were no deadlines, and she could work at her own pace. So instead, she gave herself another handful of minutes to luxuriate in bed and scribble in her journal. After a few doodles and observations about the cottage, she found herself trying to nail down the top ten most influential dishes of her cooking and writing career. Which was difficult. Because she had eaten countless tasty and important things. And because the exercise felt a little pointless.

Like, you don't create a cookbook out of ten random dishes. But it was a starting point. So far, Ruby had written:

1. *Mushroom risotto*
2. *Duck eggs, a.k.a. egg-in-the-hole*
3. *Chocolate*
4. *I am an idiot.*

That last one didn't count.

Last two?

Not really, anyway.

She hadn't gotten very far.

Writing a cookbook was hard work.

She sat cross-legged on top of the quilt and stretched her back. Well, maybe Grace would have some ideas.

Almost on cue, there was a knock at the door and Ruby called, "Grace? Come in," expecting the tray of coffee and scones her new friend/best landlord ever had insisted on delivering the last couple of mornings.

It was not Grace.

"Oh! Ack! Shit! Hi!" She cried, tossing the journal two feet in the air.

It was Brochan.

Ruby was wearing her cable-knit sweater over a pair of old cotton underpants patterned with palm trees. Brochan was wearing more than that. His cheeks turned red and he stumbled backward, knocking into the desk and sending the candleholder tumbling to the floor. As he retreated, he mumbled something that sounded like, "Sorry! I'm an arse!" Ruby yanked a pair of leggings from the storage trunk and pulled them on, then ran out the door after him. He'd made it almost all the way back to the Cosy Hearth by the time she caught up.

"Augh!" She waved her arms over her head, hoping to inject a little levity to the situation.

"I'm so sorry," he said. He refused to look at her.

"I'm so sorry!" she echoed. Her face was melting off. "You must think I'm some kind of lecherous predator, inviting you in like that . . . with me wearing . . . not wearing . . . stuff. . . ."

He shook his head. "You must think I'm some kind of brute for barging in."

"I don't. You knocked. I was in my own little world. Writing. Trying to make sense of something that doesn't seem to want to work."

"Best not to force it, then." Brochan gave a weird laugh—ha *ha*!—and shook the shameful expression from his face. "Maybe try caffeinating and give it another go?"

She nodded because she wasn't sure what you were supposed to say next in this sort of situation. But Brochan was: "There are some renovation projects the cottage sorely needs," he said. "And I have the morning available." Ruby started to argue but Brochan wouldn't hear it. "Don't tell me you like rooming with a mouse, because I won't believe it. Also, that light fixture is an electrical fire waiting to happen. I was surprised to hear that Grace had leased the cottage to you in its condition."

"It's fine, really. It's got character. How did you know about the mouse?"

"You forget. The cottage was first a flophouse. And no matter how knackered you are at the end of the night, the sensation of wee feet scampering across your chest is not something you soon forget."

Ruby gasped. "No!"

"Yes. But first: You need coffee. And shoes."

Brochan sent Ruby back to the cottage and met her there a few minutes later with a steaming mug of coffee and a warm scone from Grace's kitchen. Ruby invited him to sit and share it with her, but he declined and got straight to business. He worked all morning. All afternoon, too. Ruby didn't ask if he had anywhere else to be, and he didn't leave. While Ruby bounced back and forth between the kitchen at the Cosy Hearth and the writing desk (her list had grown to six influential dishes), Brochan found the mouse's secret entryway and sealed it. He worked some magic with the electrical wiring, and the light no longer crackled. He added caulking around the windows, and cleared away all the overgrown weeds and wildness that threatened to envelop the building. Ruby was happy he'd left just enough moss and ivy to keep the cottage looking quaint and homely. And to accentuate the beautiful door with its heavy iron hinges.

Although Brochan didn't come back the next morning, he did return the day after that. For the next few days, he stole time from himself and his other projects to better the cottage.

At first, Ruby used his presence there as an excuse to admire the way sweat dampened the collar of his shirt and trickled down onto his pecs. And the way his adorable Scottish *arse* looked in his canvas pants. But soon, she found herself looking forward to their talks as he worked and she avoided her cookbook proposal. They chattered almost constantly, covering cooking and carpentry and whisky and wine and Ruby's life back in New York. As Ruby handed him tools and performed small tasks to help, like sweeping up sawdust, she began to understand what made Brochan so genuinely enjoyable to talk to: they were having conversations. Every man she'd been with in the last, oh, forever since Benjamin, was like an interview subject. They all answered Ruby's questions (*What are your hobbies? Tell me about your family. What charitable causes are important to you?*), but they would never ask her about herself or keep the volley going. If Ruby wasn't peppering them with queries or stories, they'd just lapse into silence and reach for their cell phones. Not Brochan. He was often the one to initiate conversation, asking her thoughtful questions about what she liked and where she was from—he understood the natural swell and flow of listening and speaking. It was pure heaven for Ruby. Better than a five-course meal that involved mushroom risotto and chocolate ice cream. Better than a double orgasm.

Ruby kept attempting to press bills into his palm, but he wouldn't take them, promising that he'd owed Grace the favor for a long time. Plus, he liked the work, he said. He liked the conversation. He liked (here, he inserted a wink) the company.

Since he wouldn't take her money, Ruby started to feed him. And the more she cooked for Brochan, the more excited she got about her cookbook. She may not have cracked the code on her "co-hesive theme," but she was creating food that made her heart dance.

She baked hard-crusted boules made with Grace's sourdough starter; those she would slip into Brochan's knapsack when he wasn't looking. She picked the pinkest stalks of rhubarb from Grace's patch behind the cottage, and simmered them with honey and cinnamon to make a sauce. She ladled that into a jar and left it next to Brochan's toolbox. She gathered eggs from the henhouse and hard-boiled and shelled them, finally sprinkling them with salt and snipped tiny chives. Those, she delivered on a plate with the toasted heel of a baguette and a smear of homemade mayon-naise. She went foraging for morels and sautéed the bounty with butter and thyme, then tossed it all with rustic sheets of hand-rolled pasta. When it was ready, she artfully arranged it in a bowl and carried it out to Brochan, who was performing some delicate kind of surgery on the broken windowpane. He took the plate and fork and offered her the first bite. She hesitated, feeling silly and self-aware. No one had ever fed *her* before. She opened her mouth and held her hand under her chin to catch the sauce as he gently deposited a forkful onto her tongue. She closed her lips around the tines as he slowly pulled it out. She made a soft sound. It really was delicious.

"I like watching you eat," he said, his dark eyes glinting.

She swallowed her pasta and laughed. "I am not a graceful eater!"

"I never said you were. That's not what I like about it."

"Oh, well—then." She blushed and scuffed at the dirt with her toe like one of the hens.

"It's the way your pleasure heightens everyone else's. You make me want to slow down and actually enjoy things." He said it like it was no big deal, not the keenest observation and nicest compliment anyone had ever given her. He tasted the pasta. His eyes rolled back in his head.

"Ruby, this is too much," he said.

"It's not too much," Ruby said. She suddenly noticed what he'd been doing while she cooked lunch. "It's not nearly enough."

The five other panes were still the same forever-dusty glass as they'd always been, but the bottom left one—the broken one—had been replaced with a pattern created from pieces of beveled glass, held together by thin strips of metal. The pieces worked together to create a picture. From far away, Ruby hadn't been able to observe the details, but now she saw that the glass depicted a patch of heather grass blowing in the wind on a small hillock. The work was so intricate that Ruby could easily discern the scene, even though there was no color and each piece of glass was clear. It was beautiful. Ruby had never seen anything like it, let alone owned anything like it. "Did you—?"

"Install it? Yes," Brochan said with a mouth full of pasta. "Regrettably, I did not make it. I'm so glad you found where the morels hide, by the way. This is absurdly good."

Ruby beamed. "Thanks. My mom really loves mushrooms. I guess I do, too." She turned her attention back to the window. "This is stained glass?"

"Leaded glass, actually. Stained glass is a type of leaded glass. Like all squares are rectangles but not all rectangles are squares. So if color's used in leaded glass, you'd call it stained.

Sorry . . ." He trailed off. "This is very boring and uncool, and you do not care in the slightest."

"Actually, I care in the mostest," Ruby said and touched the bars on the window.

He briefly placed his hand over hers, pressing the pads of his fingers into her nails and then picking up his fork again. Ruby forgot to breathe for a few moments.

"I had some leaded panes kicking around from . . ." He paused and considered his words. "An old building in town. I used a few of them at my place in the barn." Ruby tried to interject— *the barn?*—but Brochan grinned and shook his head. "This pane was waiting for a special home. So I should be thanking you for giving me a reason to finally get off my arse and showcase it the way it was meant to be."

Ruby ran her hand all the way around the curves and arcs of the grass. She had seen heather in the fields around town, but had never noticed how beautiful it was. Or how much she apparently loved glass window work.

"I'm glad you're here and that I met you, Brochan," she said. Nothing veiled about it; that was how she felt.

"I'm glad for you, too, Ruby."

"Roo! It's Roo."

He laughed. "I'm trying. I like a good nickname. And yours is a great one. It just feels like something I have to earn first."

Ruby had never thought about it that way, but Brochan was right. Even though she always introduced herself as Roo, only the people she really loved called her that. There was an intimacy to it. Maybe she should guard it a little more closely.

Brochan packed his tools and gave her a wave as he drove away. Damn that man. Why did he have to be so sexy? And sensual. And kind. It was very distracting. And annoying. She knew little about him, but she was beginning to learn the things that really mattered. Like what he valued (working hard without complaint, taking good care of your belongings, speaking your mind). She knew what he liked to eat and she knew what he didn't. (There wasn't a drop of sauce left on the pasta plate, but her rhubarb jam had been returned earlier that week with an apologetic grin. "I didn't want it to go to waste," he'd said.) Ruby knew the way his cheeks betrayed his laughter before it sounded. She knew the way he'd make a small huff of annoyance every time hair escaped from behind his ear. She still caught herself daydreaming about twisting her fingers all up in his beard, but increasingly she let her thoughts stray to cooking dinner together on Friday evenings, and taking him home to meet her parents. But she'd gone down this road before, with Benjamin, and she knew it was a dead end, not a cute cul-de-sac with a white picket fence and hydrangeas blooming by the doorway.

Ruby Spencer hadn't come to Scotland to fall in love. Absolutely, positively not.

Chapter Nine

Bolstered by her crush, Ruby strengthened her resolve to focus on the cookbook proposal. She hated to admit it, but she was working this steadfastly so she'd have something to brag about to Brochan. So she didn't admit it, and just committed to a little bit of work on her proposal every morning. *Hey, maybe even Thoreau caught feels during his stint in nature. Whatever gets the job done, right?* Once she'd banged out a few recipes, she rewarded herself with time spent in the garden. Every afternoon, when the light was bright and strong, she'd hinge open the top of her small greenhouse and pull weeds, leaving their roots to shrivel in the sun. After a couple of weeks spent filling a watering can directly from the spigot outside the cottage and trekking over to her greenhouse, she relented and paid Carson another visit for a length of hose to make the job more efficient. Carson gave her a knowing smile—"I wondered when you'd be back for this." The hoses were in a back storage room, yet to be unboxed for the season, but he promised to deliver hers to the cottage later that afternoon.

Ruby thanked him and stepped back out onto the street.

It was a beautiful day; clear as the old-fashioned bell that chimed above the door as she exited. The air was surprisingly light, and the sun warmed her shoulders. Across the street, a few guests exited the Traveler Hotel clutching plastic cups of iced coffee.

Ruby's mouth watered. Buying and savoring her first iced latte of the spring had been one of her favorite traditions in New York, and although she appreciated Grace's French press coffee at the Cosy Hearth, she found herself now aching with want for an espresso drink. She crossed the street and stood in front of the hotel, debating. The automatic doors opened and closed, opened and closed, as she took in the building with curious eyes. It looked as glossy and sleek as any modern hotel anywhere in the world, which made it stand out against the quaint, old stone buildings that surrounded it. Its name was printed above the doors in neon green lettering, in lowercase: the traveler hotel. The *travel* part of the name was hot pink. The windows were all clean lines and sharp angles, and the building's exterior was a smooth charcoal color.

She peered into the lobby and saw a clerk at the desk looking annoyed as the doors continued to slide open and shut. Ruby took a step back, feeling guilty for being there, in light of how Grace clearly felt about it and its role in disturbing business at the Cosy Hearth. But no one had forbidden her to visit it, and even if they had, that would be ridiculous. She just wanted an iced coffee. The next time the doors whirred open, she stepped into the lobby. Low-slung purple couches and mid-century modern coffee tables dotted the space; there were a great many potted palms. Ruby shrugged. It did not look evil. It looked nice; a dead ringer for any chain hotel she'd stayed in over the course of the last decade. The clerk pointed her in the direction of the espresso bar, an adjoining room near a wall of packaged granola bars and veggie chips.

Ruby blinked and shook her head when she entered. The bar was bustling with people, all drinking coffee and chatting. A few were eating scones, which Ruby recognized from the batch she and Grace had baked earlier that morning. She got in line and studied the chalkboard behind the barista. It looked pretty standard, with espresso drinks and drip coffee, a selection of herbal teas, and a few specialty lattes. There was also a short food menu, offering a Moroccan chickpea salad and curried chicken sandwich.

"The usual, Mayor Dunbar?" the cheery teenage barista asked. Ruby's ears perked and she surreptitiously checked out the woman in front of her. She was tall, miles taller than Ruby, with thick, glossy red hair that reached the middle of her back. She wore an emerald-green pencil skirt with an impeccably fitted matching blazer, nipped in at the waist. Ruby peeked at her shoes; nude pumps, a three-inch heel. Damn. Mayor Dunbar was a fox.

She paid for her double espresso, then twisted a lemon peel over it and drank it in two sips at the counter.

As she turned around, her eyes gave Ruby a quick once-over. "Hallo!" she said, extending her hand. "We don't know each other. You have excellent hair."

Ruby took her hand and shook. "I'm Ruby Spencer. Yours is better."

"Thanks. Anne Dunbar. Proud to be mayor of Thistlecross."

"*Lady* mayor," coughed a voice at the back of the line. Anne's eyes flashed in anger. The barista looked at Ruby expectantly, and she mumbled an order for an iced oat milk latte.

"Kindly bugger off, Sean," Anne said, tossing a cold stare at the fortysomething guy in a grubby flannel.

"Real nice words for a mayor," he complained.

Anne turned back to Ruby and reached into her handbag for her credit card. Before Ruby could argue, Anne had paid for her latte and added a scone to the order. "Please ignore idiot men I went to school with," she said with an apologetic smile. "I'm so chuffed you're staying at the Traveler. Here, try a scone." She indicated to the barista for a pastry. "We get them from the sweetest old woman in town."

Ruby clutched at her latte with a death grip. "Grace. I know."

Anne looked confused.

"So, I'm not staying at the hotel. I'm renting her cottage."

Anne gave Ruby another up and down, this time slower and more purposed. It took just a second, but Ruby felt supremely scoured. Anne gathered herself into a welcoming smile. "So it's you. The American. You'll love it there. It's dear, a proper Thistle-cross institution. How long are you staying?"

"A year is the plan."

"A year! Well, you'll have to check out Moss Glen Falls. Have you done that yet? And the golden retriever museum." The two women stepped away from the counter after Sean coughed again. Anne leaned in closer, and Ruby could smell a delicate floral perfume. Anne put a hand up to her mouth, as if she were about to share a classified secret. "We're the birthplace of the first golden retriever."

"I've heard. But there's a museum?"

"It's in the post office. More of a wee display."

"I like dogs. I'll pay it a visit soon."

"Hurrah," said Anne, glancing at a clock on the wall. "Shite, I'm late." She pumped Ruby's hand again, and Ruby noted her nails, pristine and lacquered beige, to match her high heels.

As Anne walked toward the lobby, Ruby called out, "Thank you! For coffee!"

"Anytime. Seeing as you're my new best mate, I'll be looking forward to having a blether with you soon." She laughed and shot finger guns at Ruby, and then she was at the door, greeting a tall man with an old-school brimmed hat and briefcase, and then they were walking out of the hotel, and then they were gone.

Ruby's jaw dropped.

Mayor Dunbar was . . . awesome?

Also, what was a blether?

She took a sip of her creamy latte and sighed in pleasure. She knew that she couldn't, in good conscience, frequent the Traveler Hotel, but *wowee*, did this hit the spot. She started for the lobby and the doors slid open when she got within ten feet. Maybe she could talk to Grace about investing in an espresso machine. A small one.

Ruby started back to the cottage with a new vigor and caffeine running through her veins. She had forgotten how helpful a change of scenery can be when stuck on a writing project. Maybe she'd bring her laptop out to the garden and work for a while near her plants. She watched a young couple coo over a leashed golden retriever puppy on the opposite side of the road. She was pondering whether more people owned golden retrievers here than elsewhere, or if it just seemed that way because they were more jazzed about it, when she walked into Brochan.

"Oh!" she said, stepping on his toes, her latte sloshing up against the plastic lid.

"Oh yourself." He was carrying a brand-new green garden hose over his shoulder.

"Hi."

"Hallo yourself." He trailed his eyes from her coffee to the direction she'd come from, and raised a dark eyebrow.

"Don't hate me?"

Brochan looked at her amusedly. "Because you drink expensive lattes? I already knew you were from New York City."

Ruby leaned in close. *"Because I went to the bad place."*

Brochan adjusted the hoses, hoisting them higher up on his shoulder, and took the cup out of Ruby's hand. He drank from the straw and made a *not terrible* face. "What makes you think that I'd hate you for buying a coffee there?"

Ruby took back the latte and pulled a *gee, I don't know* face. "Because it's stealing all Grace's business?"

Brochan shook his head. "Appreciate the loyalty, but you're a free woman, Ruby. You can do whatever you want; eat whatever and wherever you like. I won't be rescinding my friendship over a coffee milkshake." He shrugged. "Besides. I like their chicken sandwich. I'm not saying that I make it a habit to frequent there. And I'm not saying I'd admit it to Grace. But it's not so black-and-white. The hotel employs a lot of people in Thistlecross. Some of them are my mates."

Ruby's body relaxed. "I hear you. Hey, is that hose for me?"

"Aye. I stopped by Carson's to pick up some grout—exciting times, I know—and he asked if I could deliver your hose if I was going to the cottage later."

Ruby's face flushed. "How did Carson know you come around?"

Brochan tilted his head in that direction, and they started walking again, their strides matching. "Because I've been doing work on it and buying a feck-ton of tools and materials from him for the job?"

"Oh."

Brochan looked sideways at Ruby. "And because everyone knows everyone's business in Thistlecross."

They looked at each other for a moment.

"I met Mayor Dunbar, just now."

Brochan didn't flinch, but Ruby could feel the energy between them change.

"She paid for my coffee. She seems chill. Definitely not like a patronizing asshole. Or even a patronizing arsehole."

Brochan gave her two thumbs up, but he rolled his eyes.

"Okay, fine. She's an ogre and I hate her already?"

"Like I said. You're a free woman. Be mates with whoever you want. But just . . . watch out for her."

"Um, okay?"

They walked the rest of the way to the cottage in silence. Ruby finished her coffee, which had gotten watery and lukewarm. Brochan heaved off the hose and pushed his sleeves farther up his arms.

"I don't mind doing it," Ruby said.

"I got it," he said and quickly joined the hoses to the spigot on the side of the cottage. He attached a spray nozzle and tested the water pressure.

"Hey, thanks," Ruby said, grappling for the easy banter they had shared minutes earlier. "Can I make you lunch?"

"Dinna fash yersel," he said without checking his watch. "See you around."

Chapter Ten

The next morning Ruby took a soak in Grace's bathtub. Her small shower in the cottage was nothing like this claw-footed monstrosity. She was pushing the tap with her toe to warm the water when she heard voices downstairs. It was early still, not yet eight, and she wondered if Grace was finally entertaining a customer. But as she craned her ear toward the doorway to listen in (hooray for thin old Scottish walls), she caught Brochan's steady cadence. She sunk in lower, letting the water lap at her chin while the conversation carried up the stairs.

"Come on, Grace. Don't be naive. You know who this is from."

"But it might not be him! It says *Wanker* on the delivery address."

"As appropriate as that name is, this package was meant for Winkler."

There was a tremendous pause. Finally, Grace spoke. "But why would a delivery come for him *here*?"

Brochan's frustrated sigh sounded loudly. "That's what I'm saying. There's no good reason for this. It's from American Uniforms Unlimited. What does that bloody mean?" There was an agonizing pause. "I'm going to open it."

Grace's indignant gasp was just as resonant. "We will *not* be opening it!"

Ruby didn't want to miss the rest of this drama, so she pulled the plug in the tub and toweled off, then put on a pair of olive green leggings and her sweater (or, as Grace had recently corrected her, *jumper*).

As she walked through the kitchen, she grabbed the half-full French press and an empty mug. She bit back a laugh and took in the scene at the bar.

Brochan was holding a piece of purple plaid fabric in front of his chest; a drapey sort of thing, part dress, part apron, and part bustier. It was tiny and wouldn't even cover his thigh had he tried to shimmy into it. The effect could have been comical if he wasn't wearing a look of rage.

Grace nodded a hello at Ruby before directing her attention back at Brochan. Brochan balled up the garment and tossed it back in the box. "It's clearly Winkler."

The air in the room felt suffocatingly thick. Ruby poured the coffee into the cup and held it out to Brochan. Maybe it would help? He shook his head vigorously and pounded once on the bar with his fist, then stalked out of the pub, the cantaloupe-colored door slamming behind him.

Ruby brought the mug to her lips and sipped. The coffee had gone cold. She set it down and looked into the box. There were a few different versions of the garment inside. One was dark green; another was red plaid and made of two separate pieces, a bikini top and a miniskirt. She wrinkled her nose and looked at Grace hesitantly. "What's going on?"

Grace crossed her arms, then uncrossed them. "Ruby, I'm not quite sure."

"I don't want to push . . ." said Ruby, even though that was a lie and she did.

Grace let out a low whistle. "There's so much to this story, and I don't know how much is mine to tell."

"I'll listen to however much you feel comfortable sharing."

Grace looked toward the door, and, confident that Brochan was out of earshot, started talking.

"The Cosy Hearth used to be a more traditional pub. Busy all hours of the night. It did a swift business in ale and crisps."

"No scones?"

"No scones. But plenty of whisky, and good fare, and bright conversation. It was the heart of Thistlecross." She looked out one of the windows for a few moments before continuing. "A businessman stole away the owner to manage a chain of Scottish-themed restaurants in the States. Losing him meant losing the pub, in a way. It—and he—left a void in a lot of people's lives." She paused and checked to make sure her hair ribbon was tied tightly. "Even though I have tried my best to keep things running."

"How does Brochan factor in here? He seemed, um, upset."

"It was hard on him. The pub has been an important part of who he is."

"In what way?"

Grace shook her head. "That's his story."

Ruby picked up the faux-tartan bikini top. It was made of

polyester and the plaid patterning had been printed on; it was wiggly in places. "So . . . this box of ugly uniforms? This package is somehow connected to the restaurateur?"

"He came to town decades ago, to make the offer. I thought we'd never see or hear from him again. He got what he wanted; a real Scot to run his dog and pony show. I just can't work out this showing up, here, now. But I'd never forget his name."

Ruby tucked the fabric back in the box. She didn't have anything helpful to offer, so she just crossed her arms and said, "A pox on *Wanker*!"

Grace laughed even though her eyes betrayed worry, and invited Ruby back into the kitchen for a fresh batch of coffee.

As they waited for the water to boil, Ruby scrunched her nose and worked up the courage to press Grace a little further. "Has business been slow here ever since he came? Winkler? Since the pub manager left?"

"Oh, no," said Grace. "Well. It didn't become slow; it had been that way for a while. But the place has felt a wee hollow since he left. It's just in recent times that I've become a proper relic. The Traveler Hotel is so busy and the Cosy Hearth is so . . . not."

"You really did not need my help in the kitchen, did you?"

Grace smiled softly. "No."

"And you really do need a full rent payment on that cottage."

Grace kept the smile on her mouth, but her eyes squinted. "Well . . ."

"Grace! If this is a matter of your livelihood, why did you agree to reduce the payments and vouch for my visa?"

The oldish woman clucked her tongue. "Lass! How could I

not? You didn't even know you needed a visa, dear thing." Ruby blushed. That was true. International travel was more complicated than the movies made it seem.

"Besides. And more important, I just had a good feeling about you. My intuition."

"Do you still? Have a good feeling?"

Grace's eyes relaxed again. "The very best."

Chapter Eleven

The weeks tumbled forward, measured in the height of Ruby's parsley plants. Warmer weather became not just a promise but the present. And although in New York she had fantasized about Scotland's windswept moors and abandoned castles, the reality of it was that Ruby was quite happy staying here in this tiny town. Yes, the coastal cliffs were calling. But their song just wasn't quite as inviting as the quiet, warm comfort of the Cosy Hearth.

Nothing more had come of Wank—Winkler, or his tawdry uniforms. Grace shoved the box under the bar and neither woman spoke another word about it. Ruby couldn't help but feel that they hadn't seen the last of those uniforms, but she knew well enough to let sleeping golden retrievers lie.

Meanwhile, she found herself spending almost all her time in the kitchen; Grace was easy to be around. She was also Ruby's only friend in Thistlecross. Well, unless you counted Anne Dunbar. But that connection seemed like a live wire.

Brochan had gone distant and cold since their last encounter. She saw him occasionally, finishing a plate of food at the Cosy Hearth, or driving past with an old appliance bursting out the back of his truck, but since the package arrived, he hadn't come to the cottage or spoken directly to Ruby.

Ruby was mad at herself for getting her hopes up after promising herself she wouldn't. She was also mad at Brochan. Because, *What the hell, dude?* The man had spent weeks flirting and making her eat pasta from his fork, then ghosted her. Everyone had made him seem desirable and exciting, but from where Ruby sat, this was just depressingly predictable.

What had he said, that day with the garden hoses? Dinna fash yourself. Well he can go fash *HIMSELF.* Ruby had more important things to worry about.

Together, Grace and Ruby brainstormed and tested cookbook recipes. Although the process remained difficult, it had become enjoyable with Grace signing on as Ruby's unofficial partner in the project. She helped rein in Ruby's wild creativity. (*Yes, dear, a three-day process for salt-cured fried fish does sound wonderful . . . but how realistic is it for the folks at home?*) Ruby appreciated having Grace's company and insight, and began to wonder if it was fate, rather than a clumsy dart toss, that had brought her to Thistlecross.

And Ruby was helping Grace, too, in her own way. Where Grace was content with breaking even on her scones, Ruby convinced her to make the case to the Traveler Hotel for a price increase. When Grace reached for the jar of currants on the third day in a row, Ruby subtly pushed a pile of shelled hazelnuts and a skillet of browned butter her way.

Ruby figured that time spent cooking was time well spent, even if you can't see how in the moment. At least, that's what her mother had always told her as the two of them whisked together salad dressing and roasted chicken legs for their Sunday suppers. Ruby kind of missed those dinners now, even though she hadn't been a part of them regularly for years. But Grace was a good stand-in for Ruby's mom, if Ruby's mom was a cheery Scottish woman who walked around with poufs of flour on her nose.

In addition to the morning scones for the Traveler Hotel, Grace had been hired to cater a few events and dinners for their constantly rotating, but always full, guest list. This week it was a "Traditional Scottish Feast" for a birding tourism group who had their binoculars set on the red kite. The hotel had requested haggis, neeps, and tatties: as stereotypical as Scottish dinners come.

"Explain to me again why they're called 'neeps,'" Ruby said as she peeled the tough skin from a vegetable she was pretty sure was actually a rutabaga. Grace laughed, setting a large pot on the stove and bringing it to boil.

"The vegetable you're holding there is called a swede. No, not a person from Sweden; I know what you're about to ask. It's akin to a rutabaga." Ruby grinned triumphantly and transferred the peels to a large compost bucket. "But somewhere along the way, the dish got bastardized and turnips were used. Neeps . . . turnips . . . I reckon it's all the same." Ruby dropped the chopped swedes in the boiling water, and Grace added a shower of salt. "Some Scots swear by parsnips, but that's just wrong."

"Hmm," said Ruby, arranging parboiled potatoes—tatties— on a baking sheet. "What do you use for seasoning?" In her small Manhattan apartment, Ruby always roasted root vegetables and potatoes with rosemary, thyme, oregano, and plenty of black pepper.

"Salt. Pepper. And a healthy amount of this." Grace passed over a crock of rendered pork fat. *But of course.* "Some people use oil, but since we're going traditional . . ." She paused. "Authentic would more likely be suet. But I don't want to send any of the tourists running for their mother."

Ruby understood. Suet, or beef fat, was used in cooking across many cultures. She had once eaten a savory pie crust made with it. But these days, the tourists were more likely to have experienced suet as the glue that held their birdseed cakes together for winter birds. She dipped a spoon into the lard and dolloped it all over the potatoes, then added salt and pepper. She pushed up her sleeves with her opposite elbows, and used her hands to work the fat into every millimeter of every potato. Into the oven they went at two hundred degrees Celsius, or, as Ruby calculated later, just shy of four hundred Fahrenheit. Once the neeps had boiled, they'd get dried out and roasted, too. Grace said they'd rewarm all the veg and gently mash them with butter. (*How much butter?* So much butter. All the butter.) So now, onto the haggis.

Ruby was no shrinking violet when it came to food. She had prepared tongue in culinary school, and she enjoyed blood sausage. But even she had to admit that there was something a little scintillating about a recipe that started with "lamb's pluck," a.k.a. the heart, lungs, and liver. She wondered if the hotel guests actually knew what went into the "must-try" Scottish dish. Grace had already cooked the pluck by steam-roasting it for a couple of hours. She had also prepared a lamb's stomach by cleaning it and soaking it in a brine bath overnight. Where had Grace gotten a lamb's stomach? Mysteries of the universe. Now, she handed Ruby a mixing bowl full of the organs and spare beef trimmings. "Chop them up finely," she instructed, and set about readying a needle and thread.

Ruby was grateful to have her favorite chef's knife from her once-lost, now-found luggage. It felt good and powerful in her hands as she ran it over the meat. "Does it bother you?" she asked Grace.

Grace looked over the rims of the small wire-framed glasses she wore for intricate tasks. Ruby suspected it was mere pride that kept her from donning them all the time. "What? Cooking haggis? Lord, no. I grew up eating this. My da would make it for my brother and me. It was his specialty."

"No," Ruby clarified. "Making haggis for *the hotel*. They're taking all your business, and you have to spend your time working for them just to make ends meet. Does it ever just grate on you? Especially after everything that happened with the pub."

Grace pulled the thread through the needle's eye. "True as that may be, I'm grateful to have my health and my home."

Ruby kept chopping away at the meat; it was starting to re-semble finely ground beef. "But don't you see? They're making you put on a show. Parading your culture and heritage for their entertainment."

A thoughtful smile spread across Grace's lips. "Oh, and you believe the tourism industry to be bad, then?"

"Isn't it?"

"Is anything entirely bad?"

"I . . . That feels like a trick question."

"Let me ask you a more direct one, Roo." Ruby set down her knife and bit her cheek.

"What brought you to Scotland?"

Ruby's cheeks flushed. Guilty as charged. She had no connection to the land or its culture. Sure, she had always felt inexplicably *drawn* to it, but wasn't that the same sort of exoticism that she rallied against when her friends did an African safari, or visited the ancient ruins at Machu Picchu? Point taken.

"Ugh. I am a jerk." Ruby scraped the meat back into the mixing bowl and poured in chopped onions and rolled oats. More salt, more pepper. Ground nutmeg and mace.

"It wasn't my intention to make you feel that way," Grace said, taking the bowl from Ruby. "This looks good. The consistency is right." She scooped it into the sheep's stomach, then began to sew the package closed. With an actual needle. Ruby was rapt with attention. "What I'm trying to help you see is that it's a complicated issue. Tourism has done a lot to upend real Highland culture. But it's also been a boon in other ways. Our country's whisky exports are up, and the majority of restaurant owners and innkeepers have more business than they know what to do with." Ruby nodded. "It's also a privilege to be able to share our traditions—the things we love—with other people. Like I'm doing now. With you."

Ruby felt properly schooled and let Grace's lecture wash over her. Finally, she stood up. "Tea? I could use some." Grace agreed and continued speaking.

"My business has changed, but it has not died. There's room

for interpretation here. Some people believe that change always indicates progress. Others think that with change comes death."

Ruby's brain lit up like a pinball machine. *Mayor Dunbar. Versus Brochan.*

"I think that the truth lies somewhere in the middle." Grace touched her hair ribbon and sighed. "I suppose it makes me feel a trifle sad to know that my wee, sleepy town will never be the same as it was when I was young. But then, what is? I'm sure the old ladies in Thistlecross were cranking on about similar things when I was a girl."

The kettle screeched and Ruby spooned black tea leaves into the pot, then poured the water over them.

"I suppose what I'm trying to say is that if you want to have coffee at the Traveler once in a while, it won't bother me any." Grace let the words hang between them.

"Oh. You knew?"

"Thistlecross may keep secrets from you, but you can't keep secrets from Thistlecross."

"I thought I was being sneaky!"

Grace winked. "You're going to have to try a lot harder to sneak around me, lass."

"I think that you are a wise and incredible woman."

"I think that I am an old one. Now, we'll set the lamb's stomach in a pan of boiling water and let it roast for hours."

Ruby refilled the kettle and put it back on the stove. "An *incredible* one."

Chapter Twelve

Later that week, Ruby sat against the cottage doorframe with a bottle of farmhouse-style saison. It was early evening, and although *hot* was an exaggeration, the weather had felt genuinely, consistently warm for the first time since her arrival in Thistlecross. Fresh air breathed new life into the cottage, blessing her sheets and pillowcases with the scents of the Highlands. The beer was refreshing, like citrus and herbs. She had just finished working in her miniature garden, after putting the finishing touches on her cookbook proposal and drafting an email to her agent. Crossing her fingers and feeling hopeful. Brochan's greenhouse cover was functioning well, trapping every bit of sun and throwing it back onto the seedlings. The radishes were already looking promising, and she could swear the chervil was getting taller by the second. Although—she chuckled into the neck of the beer bottle, her breath making a small *ooooooo* sound—it is difficult to observe growth progress if you're constantly checking.

"Care for some company?" Ruby looked up from the spotted beetle she had been watching trek across one of the stones in front of the doorway.

Brochan stood in front of her with his knapsack slung over a shoulder. He was lit by the fading sun, the rays accentuating the red in his beard and a shy spray of freckles across his cheekbones and the bridge of his nose. How had Ruby never noticed the freckles before?

She considered serving him a little sass, maybe making a sharp joke about his disappearance, but decided against it. What point would it serve? Bolster her wounded pride over his three-week snub? Meh.

"Please, anything to distract me from the prison of my own mind," Ruby said and immediately blushed. "Beer? It's a little warm; I brought over a couple from the kitchen, but that was a while ago."

Brochan accepted the bottle and produced a metal opener attached to his key chain. He flicked off the cap, then caught it in his hand before pocketing it. He did the smirky grin thing he had apparently mastered. "I like your tattoo," he said, motioning to her inner wrist. "Been meaning to tell you that."

"Oh. Thanks. It's a ruby."

"I'd hope so."

He sat across from Ruby, his back against the doorframe. Her knees were tucked up into her chest. His legs were splayed out into the doorway and path. He looked effortlessly comfortable, like he was the benevolent king of Thistlecross. Or at least this small patch of it.

"So. What do you want to talk about?" asked Ruby.

"Who said I wanted to do any talking?"

Hmm. That sounded like a flirt *and* a snub.

He noticed her scowl and softened his words. "All I really want to do is watch you drink that beer and notice the wee smile you make after each sip. But that'd be mildly odd, no?"

Ruby's heart tripped over itself. "Oh, I don't know. Mildly odd doesn't sound so bad." Brochan touched the neck of his bottle to hers. *Clink.* "Missed you at the cottage lately . . ." she said, lilting the end of the sentence up into a question, an invitation to explain himself.

"I miss being here. Alas, Grace has finally deemed it worthy of occupancy, so it appears I'm no longer needed." He waited a beat. "You'll have to tell me if anything goes wonky. Or if the mouse returns."

Ruby tried to maintain normalcy in her features, but she could feel her shoulders slumping. *Brochan had only come around so often because Grace hired him to? Of course. How silly of me.* His daily appearances and their long conversations took on new meaning with the knowledge that fixing up the cottage had just been a job. And to think she had tried to pay him! Not to mention, all the food she'd shared.

"Which isn't to say I didn't enjoy the work," Brochan said steadily. "I rarely have such braw chats with my customers."

Ruby gave him a half smile and decided to switch gears. She still had questions about the mysterious package delivery. "Weird about the uniforms, huh? Grace told me a little bit about what happened with the pub."

Brochan raised an eyebrow so high it almost disappeared into his hairline. "How *much* did she tell you?"

"A normal amount? I don't know. How much is there to tell?"

"A great deal. *What* did she tell you?"

Ruby gave him a curious look. "That the Cosy Hearth used to be a whisky pub owned by someone else. That the owner left to work for a weird chain restaurant from my old stomping grounds—the States." She shrugged. "That's about the long and short of it."

Brochan nodded as he weighed this. "Aye. That's a good summary of things."

"And this is somehow connected to the uniforms, yes?"

"I do think."

"Was it a weird accident, or something else?"

Brochan set his beer on the ground and ran all ten fingers through his hair, shaking it out at the ends. "I'll hope for weird accident. 'Something else' would be bad for Thistlecross. And that would mean a square go. A fight," he clarified, noticing Ruby's perplexed look.

Ruby understood advocating for her career. In fact, for the last ten years, she had fought tooth and nail to make it happen. But she'd never felt the call to stand up for a *place*. "Tell me more about that. Tell me about you and Thistlecross."

"That's too big a question."

"Then tell me about your childhood here. If you've left and moved back or if Thistlecross has always been home."

He edged a little closer and knocked his knee into hers. "That's better. I was born here. Raised here. I've never lived anywhere else. I'm not a simpleton . . . though I'm sure there is a lass or two in town who'd be happy to provide evidence of the contrary." Ruby chuckled a little, even though the idea of Brochan with another woman sent an irrationally sharp bolt of jealousy down her spine. "I've traveled. Been to London, the Hebrides. Those are the islands off the western coast."

"I know what the Hebrides are!" Ruby assured him quickly, not wanting to seem uneducated. "There's Jura and Orkney and Mull and—"

Brochan's laugh was gentle and kind. "Okay, lass. You know your Scottish geography. The isles are special to a lot of Scots. This Scot, included. When I was a boy, my dream was to move to St. Kilda, the—"

"Outermost island in the Hebrides," Ruby finished for him, then clapped her hand over her mouth. "Sorry. I should let you actually answer the question I asked you."

He knocked her knee again, twice. One, two. "I've always been drawn to them. The isles. The more desolate and untamed, the better. A disappointment to learn St. Kilda was evacuated in the 1930s. I'll admit to daydreaming about spending a month or two there, camping. But I know that life would be hard in the Hebrides. It's nice to be able to drive to the shop and buy epoxy if I need it. Not have to take a ferry to see my family."

"And where is your family?"

"Not worth blethering about. It was small to start, and has gotten smaller."

Ruby let his nonanswer slide. "So it's not the stunning views. And it's not your parents. What *is* it about this place that lights a fire in you?"

"I just . . . You are relentless, woman!"

Ruby smiled in a *sorry-not-sorry* way.

"I've never felt the pull of anywhere else as strongly as I do here. Well"—he tossed a wry smile to Ruby—"that, and the price of beer is madness in the cities."

Brochan squeezed his right trap muscle and drank his saison. Ruby pulled her shoulders toward each other and created a small hollow between the cottage and her lower back. The stretch felt delicious.

"You like your work, then?" she asked.

"It's not about that. Yes, I have good work; steady work. It's challenging, sometimes even rewarding. But I don't love it. It's . . . it's the people here, then. They've been more of a family to me than my own. Neil, and Carson. Sofie and Mac from the other side of town—you'll meet them soon, I'm sure." Brochan frowned, concentrating. "It sounds so provincial in words like that, but my neighbors raised me into a man. Takes a village, I s'pose. I feel obligated to Thistlecross.

"At some point I decided to stop skulking around town like a cretin and dreaming of becoming an outdoorsman on a North Atlantic island." He rolled his eyes at himself. "It's my home, for better or for worse." He finished his beer. "I'm no savior. But I do my best to keep the worst from happening."

The sun was setting now; it lit up Ruby's hair like a crown. "Good god, are you a beautiful woman," Brochan said, as he moved his hand down to rub the soreness away from his bicep. Ruby choked on the mouthful of beer she was swallowing.

"Oh, you're drunk," she said, cautiously reaching up to touch her flyaways and wispy bits. No man had praised her like that since Benjamin. It was always *sexy* and *cute* and *so fucking hot*.

"My turn to ask you a question. Why is it so difficult for you to accept a compliment?"

"Ew. That's a sticky one."

"I answered yours. . . ."

"No, you're right. Fair is fair. I guess I'm not used to receiving them. Not like that, not in a genuine or honest way." Brochan started to protest but she continued, pointing at him. "If I'm relentless, you're very disarming! I don't know—it's hard for me to believe unsolicited compliments. Or nice gestures. From men, anyway. I did believe, once upon a time." Ruby scrunched her nose and furrowed her brow at the same time. "So that's my flavor of relationship trauma. What about yours?"

"Strawberry."

Ruby groaned.

Neither one said anything for a few minutes. Ruby tried not to peek at him and she tried not to be the first one to speak, but it was hard because she wanted to do both things. She fiddled with the bottom of her braid. He tucked his hair behind his ears.

"You're quiet," Brochan observed.

Ruby exploded into laughter. "I'm not! Not really. *You're* quiet."

He tossed a smile her way. "Comparatively, it would seem."

Brochan was quiet for an eternity more.

Ruby couldn't take it. "Tell me: What did you do today?"

"When the handyman business is slow, I spend time on my own project. I've been fixing up an old barn—to turn it into a home—for years. Finally got it to the point of habitable last fall."

"I have so many questions! Where is it? How big is it? What has the experience been like? Do you love it? What does it look like?"

Brochan laughed. "Striking previous comment about you being quiet from the record, Ms. Journalist." She made an *ugh, I am insufferable* face, and he shook his head. "It's nice to have someone intelligent and curious to have a blether with." He made sure to answer all her questions in order by counting them on his left hand. "It's a five-minute walk from here, near the pine forest. It's small. Ish. Was once a horse barn, so we're not talking about a massive hay loft sort of situation here. The experience has been maddening, and I do love it." Brochan brought his eyes up to meet Ruby's. "It's hard to describe what it looks like. Red? Barny? I guess you'll just have to see it."

Ruby's heart roared and she felt a warm rush flow from her belly to her thighs. *Easy, Roo.* "I'd like that," she said quietly, feeling anxious. Brochan's disappearance from the cottage may have been all business, but were his feelings for her personal? Seemed that way. She pushed the questions from her mind and continued to steer them in the direction of surface-level niceties. "I hope that working on the cottage wasn't keeping you from your own stuff."

"No one held a pistol to my head," Brochan reminded her. "But, as I said, that cottage has been special to me for a long time. And Grace is a good customer, of course. It was my pleasure." Brochan frowned and his brows knitted themselves together. "There's still plenty more to do, though. It needs better insulation before the cold weather sets in."

"Which should be in—what—a couple of days now?" Ruby laughed. It was late May. She was used to harsh winters followed by sweltering city summers. Today was warm, but what would tomorrow bring? Rain, probably. The persistent, constant chill of the Highlands still felt foreign to her. Foreign, but not bad. Like someplace she could grow into.

Ruby reached across the doorway and gave his shoulder a small squeeze, like she had watched him do for himself, minutes earlier. It was the first time she had touched him. It was the first time she had touched a man since *Womp-womp* Seth. And Seth had sucked. He did not count. The sensation was thrilling and nostalgic at the same time, and even better than when he'd touched her fingertips over the glass window. Because she was initiating it, reaching for what she wanted. She could feel the thick sinew of his muscles, and she worked her fingers into the knots that revealed themselves to her touch. He groaned a little bit, and a meteor of excitement landed in Ruby's center, then rippled outward. She could feel the heat of his skin radiating through his thin V-neck. She left her hand there for a moment. Too shy to meet his eyes, she focused on the small holes along the neckline of his shirt, holes that betrayed the thick black hairs on his chest.

"The pub." Brochan was weighing something in his mind. He placed his hand on top of hers and squeezed back. It felt so good, so intimate, that it shocked her and she slid her hand away, busying it with the label on her beer bottle. "It was more than just a place to get hammered."

"Tell that to Neil."

"Ha! Clever lass."

Ruby beamed. It felt good to make him laugh.

"How can I explain this? In Scotland, bars aren't just an opportunity to drink. Not like America." Ruby started to protest but realized his evaluation was pretty much spot-on. Evidenced by literally every Manhattan bar she'd gotten drunk at. And every Brooklyn one, too. She let him continue. "A pub is the soul of a town. Even if there isn't a municipal building, there will be a pub. Frankly, I think that's better. When the pub in Thistlecross first began, it was the only place in town." He gave a wisp of smile. "Now it's the only place no one goes to. That said, pubs are also excellent places to get smashed."

"So what was special about *that* pub?" Ruby asked. "Besides the fact that it was here, in lovely little Thistlecross, of course."

"The owner always distilled and aged whisky for the patrons. Always, for as long as the pub was in existence. Knowledge was passed down through generations, and all that. Hell if I know where the first aging barrels came from, but after a while, they were bought from Dewar's. Under the table of course." Ruby nodded; she was familiar with Dewar's. Her father always had a bottle of it in the liquor cabinet. He drank it over ice cubes, sometimes with ginger ale mixed in.

Brochan continued. "Not that you'd be able to find a bottle of Thistlecross whisky on the shelf in any off-license—that means liquor store, bottle shop," he added, taking note of Ruby's perplexed expression.

"Why not? Wasn't it good enough? Neil seemed to think so."

"Oh, sure. It's the best whisky I've had in my life. It's sad that the tradition died, but Grace doesn't do it, and it just . . . faded out."

"You've tasted it?" Ruby wondered if it was Thistlecross-made whisky they drank during their flophouse competitions.

"Aye. You probably have, too. I think Grace said she gave you some on your first night here. But it was never an official operation. Nobody used to care about that sort of thing. Now everyone's up in arms about legality and other such shite." Brochan coughed, and the cough sounded suspiciously like the words *Mayor Dunbar*. "So far as I know, nobody ever lost a life from a dram of it, though if they did it was their own damn fault." Brochan paused, as if he was weighing something in his mind. "The whisky still was kept in an old barn in town."

Ruby hugged her thighs in close. There was a new crispness in the evening air, and she wished she hadn't left her sweater in the kitchen. "Oh? And would this barn happen to be red?"

Brochan's grin could have moved mountains. "Legend says."

A gorgeous bearded man who lived in a barn with an old whisky still. Could you get any more Scotland than that? She decided to poke at the bear a bit. "Do you know anything about the pub's previous owner? It seems like he was a special man."

Her words were a slap that knocked the smile from Brochan's lips. He looked pained. Ruby could feel an impenetrable wall erect itself in seconds. She rested her chin on her kneecaps and waited to see what would happen.

Brochan gazed in the direction of the Cosy Hearth and picked up a pebble close to the path. He turned it over in his hand, rubbing it with his thumb. "No. I don't know anything about him," he said, and tossed the pebble into the hen yard.

Chapter Thirteen

The next night, Ruby set up her laptop on the bar at the Cosy Hearth. It had been surprisingly busy, all things considered. Neil had stopped by for a meal and some gossip. Carson, who typically kept a strict schedule and dined alone in his flat above the general store, breezed through after he closed up shop to have a drink and check on Ruby's garden. That was nice, she thought; it made her feel like she was becoming a part of the neighborhood. She had also met a couple Grace identified as Sofie and Mac, sharing a platter of cheese and oatcakes, giggling by the hearth. Ruby remembered their names from her conversation with Brochan and introduced herself. Through their chat, she learned that they worked at the Traveler Hotel; he was a clerk and she cleaned rooms. She also made soap from Highland cattle tallow and garden herbs, another detail Ruby recalled. Sofie seemed particularly thrilled to learn that Ruby was growing her own herbs, and offered to bring over some mint cuttings soon.

Sofie and Mac had been coming to the Cosy Hearth since it was whatever mysterious pub it had been before it was the Cosy Hearth. So in a way, they existed in the gray area between tradition and progress. "We had our first date here," Sofie told Ruby as Mac grabbed his wife and planted a huge kiss on her cheek. They were sweet. Everyone in Scotland was sweet. Everything was going according to plan.

Now, the bar was empty and Grace had gone upstairs. When she'd said good night to Ruby, she had given her hand two quick squeezes and said she thought their busy night was a sign of better days. Ruby's heart broke a little and she kicked the box of uniforms further into the dark shadows under the bar. Four customers did not a profit make, but the hope and pride they brought to Grace's eyes was worth all the money in the world. The fire was slowing to embers, and the candles were still glowing; Ruby reminded herself to snuff them when she left. She looked around the room and sighed contentedly. The flames danced gracefully on the stone floor and the walls. Moonlight poured in through the small windows. Grace's collection of old cast-iron skillets hung over the hearth, and the bar smelled like honey and warm milk, which Ruby had just frothed on the stove top. It really was the happiest little place, she thought.

She turned to her computer. Ten o'clock. It was time for video calls. Because the Wi-Fi signal didn't reach her cottage, Grace told her that she was welcome to conduct her catch-ups here.

First, she called her parents. Her joy swelled when their faces appeared on the screen. They were holding the cell phone sideways, and Ruby laughed as she tilted her head to see them properly. Even after years of FaceTime and Zoom, her parents had never quite gotten the hang of it. Ruby updated them about her kitchen adventures with Grace and her small-but-mighty greenhouse. She fudged the numbers a bit when explaining how far along she'd gotten on the cookbook. Tackling the proposal, thanks in large part to Grace's encouragement, was a big accomplishment, but until she had an advance check from a publisher, she wanted to shield them from worry. Which she *knew* they would. Worry, that is.

Before Ruby left New York, her father had given her a lecture on fiscal responsibility and the dangers of "intentional free-falling." At the time, Ruby had rolled her eyes and assured him she was fine. *Ugh, whatever, Dad.* But with her savings account dwindling, she was starting to wonder if she had underestimated how challenging it really is to start over at thirty-five. And if it had been absolutely, positively necessary to do so in Scotland. But these were the sorts of questions she saved for two a.m., when she was alone and amped-up on anxiety. They were not the sorts of questions to lob to your parents on a pixelated video call while they got tipsy off white wine. She gave them a quick walking tour of the Cosy Hearth, then blew a kiss and said goodbye. Deirdre and Mark were about to cook dinner; apparently it was tofu stir-fry night.

Next, Ruby dialed Lee. She felt a little nervous. The two women hadn't shared a city in years, but they had also never gone weeks without talking. Somewhere between the haggis and the handsome town handyman, Ruby had let their phone calls slide. Her friend worked as a politics reporter at the Ithaca newspaper, and promised she'd take a break from chasing leads to finally catch up. Ruby desperately needed Lee's straight talk and crash-through-life sort of blind optimism. She was freaking out about Brochan. (*Seriously, why hadn't he made a move on her? What did the man actually want?*) If this was all too good to be true, Lee would tell her.

"Ruby Shoes!" Lee shouted when Ruby's video materialized. She raised a martini glass to the screen. *Three olives, extra dirty*, Ruby thought, if she knew anything about her best friend. Ruby toasted back with her glass of milk. "Shouldn't that be brown liquor?" Lee teased.

"Oh, trust me. I am getting my fill of that. Hey, before we start: I'm sorry for dropping the ball and going a little incommunicado."

Lee waved away the concern with a flick of her wrist. "You only moved halfway across the world; it's fine."

"I'm technically just an ocean away."

"Technically fucking Greenland is separating us."

"Not true! The latitude of Greenland's tip is one degree higher than Scotland!"

"And she's a maps expert now, in addition to a Scot." Lee took a sip and rolled her eyes. She leaned in close to the camera, and Ruby could see smudges of mascara under her lashes after a long day spent hounding sources for answers and typing up stories in the newsroom. Lee may have sometimes presented herself as a lighthearted, happy-go-lucky blonde bombshell, but she was extremely smart and she worked hard. She could be both things, and she was proud of them equally. Ruby loved that about her. "How the hell are you?" Lee asked.

"I'm . . ." Ruby paused. Sometimes, she thought she would like to move here permanently. Such as when she had slow, thoughtful conversations with people on the street. Or when she cooked with Grace. Spending time with the people in Thistlecross made her feel like everything was okay, even when it wasn't. Plus, there was Brochan. Whom Ruby thought was just okay. Kidding; she was mildly obsessed with him. So: Thistlecross had given her community, a slower pace, people who felt like family. . . . Those were all arguments in the pros column. But other times she thought, *This is absurd; I cannot move to Scotland for real. Obviously I am just running away from hard things. Obviously all my doubts and fears about what I should be doing and where I belong would shout at me just as loud from Thistlecross.* In other words, Ruby didn't have a clue what she was doing with her life. Like most thirty-somethings. She wasn't special; she was just in Scotland.

"Good," she settled on a mild word for Lee. "I'm good. Scotland is good. It's beautiful. The people here are sweet. My cottage is adorable. The kitchen I'm using for my recipes is awesome. Everything is retro, but unironically. You'd be jealous of the sink. Oh! I'm growing a garden! There are chickens! It's good! I'm good."

Lee narrowed her eyes, waiting for Ruby to drop the act and say something real.

Ruby set her glass on the counter and picked at a cuticle. Her hands had always been rough, but they'd gotten downright rugged over the course of the spring. "I am good," she said. "But things are heavy, too. Truth told? The whole 'I'm going to move to Scotland and write a bestselling cookbook' thing is a lot harder than I thought it would be. Mostly because I am having a minor crisis of identity. Why the heck did I think I needed to come here in the first place?"

"Because you are brave and badass and because you do hard things that will make sense someday," answered Lee. "Even if they feel like shit now." She was not the type to let anyone wallow, especially her best friend. She was also not the type to believe her best friend when she had declared that she was giving up on love. So now she took a conspiratorial sip of her cocktail and coquettishly perched her chin on her knuckle. "Next question: Any new men in your life? And I swear to God, if you tell me about another idiot stockbroker, I am going to fly to Scotland myself and find you a weird kilted man who will do gross things to you on a moss bed. They have moss beds there, right? I'm not making that up? I feel like Scotland has moss beds."

Ruby was laughing so hard that her stomach hurt. "Scotland has moss beds."

Lee nodded righteously and sipped her martini.

Once her laughter slowed to a few spontaneous giggles, Ruby looked around to make double sure she was alone and then leaned in. "Funny you should mention the whole 'Scottish man' thing, though. There is this guy. No—he's a man, for real. His name is Brochan."

"DOES HE DO GROSS THINGS ON MOSS BEDS?!" Lee shouted, and Ruby aggressively tapped the lower-volume button on the keyboard.

"I don't know!" Ruby got in extra close to the screen and whispered, even though she didn't need to. "We haven't even kissed!"

Lee looked shocked and gasped. "YOU? Haven't kissed him?"

Ruby felt hurt and ran her ring finger around the rim of the glass. "Whoa, wait. What's that face about? What are you implying?"

"Oh, babe. Don't take offense. It's just that you haven't been . . . slow to jump into bed as of late. Aaron? Jason? Lucas? Seth?"

Leave it to a best friend to give it to you straight.

"Yeah, but they didn't mean anything. Bad sex is a bummer, but it's nothing compared to the crushing realization that men always fall short in the relationship department. Everyone since Benjamin is just, *blah*. You know that better than anyone! You've seen me go through it. You've gone through it, too."

"Totally valid. And, Roo, you know I'm not trying to throw shade at you for having casual sex. I'm just trying to point out that historically, even when you *say* that's what you're doing, you still show up with a suitcase of miserable expectations about men, which they inevitably fulfill. So be casual if you want! Put your heart out there if you want! But if you do make it an actual *thing*, maybe try and trust him a little bit? I don't know, give him a chance to actually be a good guy?"

"You know I'm trying to have more chill when it comes to men. I guess that's why I'm confused-slash-terrified. Because this time actually feels different. But I can't quantify how. I'm trying to figure that out. If I can trust my instincts. If I can trust him." Ruby looked into the camera. "Lee, he asks me questions."

"Praise be; unicorns do exist." Lee finished her martini and grabbed the laptop, depositing Ruby on her kitchen counter while she mixed another drink. "You're right. I'm sorry if I sounded a smidge judgy. I mean, who am I to question your choice in men? You're talking to a woman who spent half the afternoon sexting with the new videographer at work."

"So . . . Truce?" Ruby extended her hand.

Lee pretended to shake it through the screen. "Truce. We're wild women who can have as much or as little sex as we want, and we'll always have each other's backs."

"Isn't that what our first friendship necklace said?" mused Ruby.

"Nerd. Now tell me about this Broken guy."

"Brochan!"

"That's what I said."

"It was not."

"Details, shmetails." Lee settled back into her loveseat and wrapped a blanket around her shoulders like a cape. "Okay, lady. Start from the beginning and don't leave anything out."

Chapter Fourteen

As it tends to do, spring turned into summer. By July, Ruby had come no closer to figuring out Brochan—or kissing him—but she had accomplished three things. True to form, she marked them in her journal so that years later, she could look back and fondly remember that weird year she spent drinking whisky in Scotland.

1. She had finally submitted the cookbook proposal. The "cohesive theme" was seasonal cooking: salads and grilled veggies in the summer; neeps and tatties and beef stews in the winter. That sort of thing. Her fingers were crossed; and every time the email alert dinged on her phone, her heart stopped for a few seconds. But she hadn't heard anything from her agent yet.
2. In lieu of having a *real* job, she had basically become a part-time miniature vegetable patch farmer.
3. In light of the vegetable farmer thing being kind of dumb, she and Grace had begun a weekly pop-up Sunday supper for the locals.

3.25. They named the event the Family Table, and charged a small fee for the suppers to cover the cost of food and make a bit of a profit.

3.5. Although Grace helped her crank out the food, Ruby was really in charge of the theme and the flavors. She let her creativity run wild, marrying traditional Scottish dishes with her modern-fresh spin. For example: clootie dumpling, an old-school steamed pudding, was made with goat's milk and served with a cardamom-mint cream; pot pie was stuffed with cannellini beans and lemony kale.

3.6. People loved it.

3.7. And Ruby loved doing it.

3.8. Maybe even more than she had loved being a food writer.

The first dinner started out after a happenstance gathering. Grace had wrapped up a day of marathon cooking for the Traveler, one of her traditional Scottish feasts, when Ruby wandered into the kitchen after going for a walk around the trails in the pine forest. She took out her earbuds and noted the extra pieces of dough that littered the butcher block table, as well as a frying pan of leftover ground lamb. She asked Grace if she could "do something" with them. *Have a go*, Grace had said, and before Ruby knew what she was getting into, she was rerolling the dough and cutting it into rectangles, then seasoning the lamb with fragrant curry powder, then mixing it with finely chopped scallions and sultana raisins, then piling all that on the dough, then closing it into a neat little pocket, and . . . well, you can probably see where this was all going, even if Ruby didn't at the time. She was cooking purely on instinct.

By the time she pulled the lamb hand pies, crackling and golden, from the oven, the crew at the bar had turned into a small crowd. A small crowd that was clamoring for a taste, so Ruby happily served Neil and Carson, Sofie and Mac, Aileen the postal worker and dog museum curator, and Brochan, as well as a few tourists who had wandered in off the street, lured by the aroma of curried lamb and buttery pastry. Folks were gathered at the bar, some perched on stools and others standing around. Ruby and Grace held court behind the counter, pouring more whisky.

"Ruby," said Mac, his mouth full of lamb, "this is so good, I would pay for it."

"You will be paying for it." Grace frowned.

"Thanks," Ruby said, and her cheeks burned with pride.

"Wait a minute," said Brochan.

"Yes, even you will be paying. This isn't a poorhouse!" Grace smacked Brochan with a tea towel, and Ruby wondered again at their familiarity. *Had Brochan worked at the Cosy Hearth as a teenager or something?*

"Of course I will be, and tipping, too," he said. Grace nodded, satisfied with that. "But here's what I was going to say: I think I speak for everyone in the room when I say that I'd happily pay whatever you charged for a meal like this." Everyone in the room agreed. "Ruby and Grace—together, you're some sort of dream team. Grace, your food has always been the soul of Thistlecross." A few people clapped. "And, Ruby? You bring that certain . . . I don't know what."

"Je ne sais quoi," said Ruby.

"What?" said Brochan

"Never mind," said Ruby.

Grace looked from Brochan to Ruby and hummed to herself in a wise sort of way.

Brochan continued. "Right, then. It's just nice to share a meal with you again." Everyone murmured in agreement, even the tourists who were feeling very pleased they'd stumbled upon this pub and were now having a Genuine Scottish Experience.™

Carson grew a little misty-eyed and mentioned that when he first moved to Thistlecross with his wife—God rest her soul—the regular dinners they ate at the pub were what helped them integrate into the community. Mac pinched his wife's bottom and reminded everyone (again) that their first date was at the pub. Neil grumpily noted that he had never stopped eating there, unlike some people, but would be happy to have company once again.

Brochan nodded. He was getting excited. "Aye. We used to always eat here together. Even if we weren't *together*. It was like a family dinner. What if we did that again? A Family Table; that's what we ought to call it."

"What are you getting at, lad?" asked Neil. "Don't be so obtuse."

"I'm saying that Ruby and Grace ought to host a special weekly supper and that we ought to pay them to do it."

Ruby let his words sink in as the rest of the patrons looked toward her and Grace.

"Don't look at me," said Grace.

"Don't look at me!" squeaked Ruby.

"We're looking at you, Ruby," said Brochan.

He was. Very intensely.

Damn it, Brochan.

Ruby thought about it. Of course she wanted to do this. Cooking at the Cosy Hearth with Grace made her happier than almost anything. The only warmer memory she held was cooking Sunday suppers with her parents. But Ruby couldn't shake the feeling that she remained an interloper; a temporary curiosity that could never move around Thistlecross like she truly belonged there. A community dinner curated by her was such a very big thing. She stammered a few times, trying to find a way to explain all that. "I—I'd love to do this. But it seems like I'd be imposing. I'm not a part of the family."

"You are not imposing," assured Grace.

"That lamb pie was the most delicious thing I have eaten in years," said Sofie.

"When you're here, you're family," said Neil.

"Like the Olive Garden?" said Ruby.

"What?" said Neil.

"Never mind," said Ruby. She cocked her head and observed everyone's faces, shining and hopeful. How could she say no? "My answer is *yes*."

She waited a beat, for dramatic purposes, then said, "Next Sunday. Seven o'clock. And be ready to drink lots of whisky and wine, too."

Chapter Fifteen

Later that night, rubbing cocoa butter into her knees and watching a candle slowly melt down into a blob of wax, Ruby thought, *Maybe everything is going to work out.* She thought, *Maybe coming to Scotland was the craziest AND best thing I have ever done.* She thought, *Maybe I was just overthinking this, and life is going to be extra super easy from now on.*

Unfortunately, the next day something bad happened.

Ruby was in the process of marinating prunes in some bottom-shelf whisky for the first Family Table dinner when her phone pinged with an email alert. She almost didn't check it right then and there, but she wasn't the kind of woman who had that kind of restraint. She wiped her hands on the back pockets of her jeans and swiped up to see who had written.

It was Ruby's literary agent. *(That was good.)*

The subject line was **Regarding your cookbook proposal.** *(That was neutral.)*

The body of the email was surprisingly long and professionally thoughtful. It essentially said, "Listen, Ruby, I think you're a great writer; you always have been. But this concept just isn't unique enough to make a splash on the current market. There is no shortage of seasonal cookbooks these days. Besides; no one really knows who you are, unlike the assorted rappers, singers, models, and actors who have published cookbooks this year. I love your style, but I don't feel confident I can sell this cookbook to a publisher." The email went on to encourage Ruby to shop her proposal around to other agents. *(That was the bad part.)*

Ruby's heart stopped for a moment.

She bit down on her cheek so hard that she tasted the metallic tinge of blood, and her mind began to race. Her thoughts hadn't crystallized into emotions yet. For some people, emotions come first. For Ruby, it was the thoughts. And often, she got so busy writing and researching and cooking and doing dumb things like moving to foreign countries on a whim that the thoughts just swam around in her head forever as baby feelings. And everyone knows that babies are exhausting.

Rejected. Her cookbook was dead in the water. It never even stood a chance. She had quit her job, moved across an ocean—completely ravaging her savings account in the process—and all for this stupid, stupid pipe dream. Which had apparently drowned somewhere off the southern tip of Greenland. Fucking Greenland!

Ruby set her phone next to the prunes and wrapped her hand around the neck of the whisky bottle. She gripped tightly as the thoughts crashed over her.

I want a drink.

Everything seemed so wonderful yesterday and now it is awful.

Coming to Scotland was the craziest and WORST thing I have ever done.

I walked away from the only thing I've ever been good at and now I have no clue who I am.

Is it too late to beg for my old job back?

But the matter still stands that I would rather become a desolate fisherperson on the northern coast of Greenland than jump back on the hamster wheel in New York City.

What did I expect? No one buys cookbooks anymore. I don't even buy cookbooks.

Oh my God, am I a thirty-five-year-old fuckup or what?

(Indecipherable mumblings about fear, shame, regret, and loneliness.)

Then the feelings began.

Ruby took her hand off the whisky just in time to catch the first tears with her knuckle. She sank down onto the floor of the kitchen of the Cosy Hearth and she cried. Her sobs were big and loud. She didn't know where Grace was, but she was glad to be alone. It had been a long time since Ruby had cried, and honestly, she wasn't sure if she had *ever* cried like that before, with such unselfconscious abandon. All of a sudden, she was feeling so many things. Which was curious. Because Ruby generally went about life completing to-do lists and having adventures, *not* indulging in weepy emotions.

It was only a dumb cookbook. Why did she care so much?

As the tears fell into her mouth, salting her lips, she admitted that she wasn't crying about the cookbook. It was just . . . *everything.* Moving so far from home while simultaneously trying to figure out where home was; taking a career leap of faith and hoping for the best while not knowing how to create her future; wanting Brochan but not understanding how, or in what ways . . . grappling with how to be alone without getting lonely. So many moving parts, and none of them seeming to have answers.

Finally her sobs dried, slowing to sniffles. Ruby felt exhausted. She pulled her thighs close to her chest and jammed her eye sockets into her knees. There, that was better. Everything was dark and she was alone.

Except—well, she wasn't.

Ruby jumped when she felt the hand on her back, but she kept her face hidden. She knew who it was, and she did not need him to see her swollen, red eyes.

How dare Brochan show up here when all she wanted to do was be miserable and feel sorry for herself?

Brochan didn't say a word, but Ruby felt him shift his weight so that he was sitting on the floor, too. His hand moved gently, slowly over her back, and his calluses caught on the fabric of her tank top. It was a very curious experience to be curled on the kitchen floor of an old pub, getting stroked like a cat by a sexy Scottish man as she sucked snot back into her nasal cavity.

Eventually, Ruby peeled her face away from her denim and turned her cheek so that she was kind of, sort of looking at Brochan. *Oh, Brochan.* The man was undeniably masculine with his big hands and big arms and excellent beard, but now he also seemed deeply gentle, with those soft eyes and full lips that no mustache could ever really hide. No matter how hard the mustache tried.

"Hi," said Ruby.

"Hi," responded Brochan, using his knuckle to mop up her last few leaky tears.

"Sorry you caught me during my weekly breakdown," Ruby joked, twiddling the laces of her Keds and sniffing once more.

"You're allowed to have emotions."

Ruby smiled a little; and although she looked like a mess, she did feel calmer. Brochan reached up for the bottle of whisky. Instead, his hand found the mason jar of prunes, which he brought down. He unscrewed the top and ate one ("Odd. But tasty."), then offered the jar to Ruby. She ate two, and heard Lee's voice ricocheting around her skull. *Give him a chance to actually be a good guy.*

"Wanna talk about it?" asked Brochan.

And Ruby, surprisingly, did.

"That cookbook I came here to write? It's apparently not going to happen."

"What do you mean?"

"My agent rejected the project. In other words: no one is interested in what Ruby Spencer, ex–food writer, has to say about dinner."

"I think you've got a crew of mates here who would disagree with that." He let her process this. "Will you be wanting sympathy or advice, or both?"

Ruby blinked twice. No one had ever asked her a question like that. She'd never even considered she could have a choice.

She laced her fingers around her shins and leaned back. "Advice, please."

Brochan thought for a minute or two, then started with a disclaimer that he knew next to nothing about cookbooks. Ruby smiled and assured him nothing he said was legally binding. He smiled back.

"Is writing a recipe book the only thing you see yourself doing next? Or could there be other options?"

Ruby pulled in her cheeks between her top and bottom rows of teeth and gave him a tortured look. She wasn't sure.

"You don't have to tell me," Brochan said. "That's just for you: the question and your answer. Listen. I know my observation matters little here, but if you want to do something else, it seems to me there's plenty you could. You're brilliant with people. You light up a room just like Grace. You're a gardener. . . . There's more. You're good at a lot of things."

He licked his thumb and wiped away a salt trail from underneath her eye, then pressed the pad of his finger into the center of her bottom lip. Her mouth opened slightly.

"I think you could be anything you want to be, Roo."

The feeling of his thumb on her mouth had whipped her sadness into a potion that simmered low and steady between her thighs. Magic, the man was magic. She wanted to kiss him. She would kiss him. Here, on the floor of the Cosy Hearth kitchen. With prune breath. He just had to be the one to initiate. It had to be him. So then she would know it was real. And right. She closed her eyes. She leaned in. She was ready. Ruby was so ready to kiss him.

Brochan's pants started beeping madly with texts.

He let his thumb slide down to her chin, which he cupped

briefly before reluctantly reaching into his pocket. Ruby pretended to look away as he checked the screen, but on it she saw a stream of incoming notifications from **Margaret**. There was an apple emoji next to the name. Brochan held the phone in his hand just long enough for Ruby to catch the last message: **No strings. Think about it.** He quickly shoved the phone back into his pants and tousled Ruby's hair, like a big brother would do.

She looked at him curiously but pushed his bicep, like a little sister might. And that was that; he left, off to work on a leaky bathroom sink faucet. Ruby puttered around in the kitchen, every so often licking her bottom lip and pretending she could still taste the grassy, smoky imprint of Brochan's thumb. Wondering if he was thinking about apples or about prunes.

Chapter Sixteen

So that was Monday.

Ugh.

On Tuesday, Ruby composed a very professionally thoughtful email back to her agent. It essentially said, "I completely understand and obviously respect your opinion. I'm just so grateful for the chance to have my proposal even be considered and it's amazing that you took the time to read it. If you ever change your mind, I'm totally here, like, for anything. I'll literally write any cookbook in the world, even if it's something dumb like, 'Microwave Dinners for Sad Single Women.' Heh heh. *Kidding obviously*. But also serious."

On Wednesday, Ruby unpacked a set of watercolor paints and drawing paper that had been buried in the bottom of her suitcase since her arrival. She'd started painting a few years ago, and was absolute shit at it, but that didn't matter because she enjoyed the process. Now she laid it all out on the floor of the cottage and brought over a little glass bowl of water and some old rags. She painted a few signs advertising the Sunday supper. In addition to a rustic floral border snaking its way around each page, she used a thin brush to paint on the details and a few teaser menu items. She also asked folks to please RSVP with a sign-up sheet at the bar. Old-fashioned. Low-tech. Authentic. The whole thing was a bit over-the-top for a casual dinner party, but then wasn't moving to Scotland itself a bit extra?

Once the paint was dry, Ruby delivered a sign to Carson's general store, tacked one up to the bulletin board at the town hall, and pasted a third onto the base of a golden retriever statue on High Street. In any other town it would have been weird to have a golden retriever statue, but this was Thistlecross, birthplace of the first golden retriever. So it wasn't weird at all.

Ruby then walked to the Traveler Hotel. It was a gray area of acceptability to advertise there, but if people like Sofie and Mac could hang at both places, so could she, she reasoned, posting a sign on the community bulletin board in the espresso bar. Plus, the errand provided an excuse for a latte fix. She had just taken her first sip when she noticed an evil-looking briefcase on one of the tables. Not that briefcases are inherently evil, but this one was giving off bad vibes.

In truth, the briefcase was quite average looking, brown and leather, but it did seem familiar. Again, the vibes. Hadn't Mayor Dunbar met someone with a briefcase last time she was here? Yes! It must have been the same one. Who carried a briefcase these days? It wasn't the sort of accessory you saw often.

Deciding to put on her detective hat, Ruby perched on a purple chair nearby and busied herself with a day-old newspaper. A few minutes later, sure enough, the same man returned from the loo and picked up a frothy, whipped cream–smothered drink from the bar. It was exceedingly funny to her that this sixtysomething guy was a coffee slushy fan. He was tall: sharp angles held together by knobby joints. All elbows and chin. His eyes were darting around the room as he removed his hat and drank his training-wheels coffee. Ruby thought he looked like a Disney villain.

He clicked open the briefcase and shuffled a few papers. Not long after, Mayor Dunbar entered the room with a chic large tote bag and walked straight past Ruby toward the man. Ruby sank lower in the chair behind the newspaper. She pretended to be absorbed in an article about the local quilting club as she listened in to their conversation.

"Trust your trip was decent?" Anne said, motioning for an espresso from the barista. She looked unreal, in a black power suit unbuttoned just enough to hint at a cream-colored camisole. Her pumps were sky-high and two-tone, color-blocked in seafoam and teal. *I mean, come the fuck on.*

"Oh, sure," he said. "Had a naughty little stay in Glasgow last night."

Ew, thought Ruby, w*hatever that means.*

"Och, Louis," Anne said, her glossy lips pulling down into a frown. "Could we not? Not talk about brothels during this business meeting?" The man looked chastised and started to apologize, but Anne raised her hand to shush him. He sputtered. She sighed. "Let's move on."

"Sorry, really," he said before taking a gulp of his drink. A whipped cream mustache adorned his upper lip and Ruby crinkled the newspaper to mask the giggle that escaped her.

Anne folded her hands, cappuccino-colored nails resting on top of opposite knuckles. "It's fine. So I've had a lawyer draw up a contract for the sale. It was a massive pain, to be honest with you. Our usual man Carson refused to do it."

The man shrugged. "Well, you found someone."

"I'm just trying to impress upon you the paroxysm of anger that is about to be unleashed here."

Paroxysm. Ruby mouthed the word and reached into the depths of her brain, coming up short. One for the dictionary. Or not. Because, context clues.

"I understand."

"No you don't." Anne's voice lowered and Ruby instinctively leaned in. Just a touch. "You dinna know at all. Selling the Cosy Hearth is a big deal." Her cadence had become a little more musical and a lot more Scottish. She sounded fiercely protective of her town.

Ruby's heart raced.

Anne pulled a pen from her tote and clicked it a couple of times. "Folks here have fond feelings for the pub, even if they don't always show it. Your restaurant may not be happily received by locals at first. Or . . . ever." She looked upset for a heartbeat, then rearranged her features into a steady, cool downward gaze as she removed a folder and passed it to him.

The man shuffled through the papers briefly before placing them neatly in his case. "Money makes everyone happy," he said. "This town is about to be overjoyed."

Anne stood, indicating the meeting was over. "I'll have my secretary send it in an e-file as well."

"Thanks for that. I'll look over everything this evening. I'm sure there'll be no problems—we'll connect tomorrow."

They shook hands, and he put his hat back on his head, then started for the door. Ruby set the newspaper on the table. Once he was gone, Anne sank back into her chair and looked glumly into her empty espresso cup.

The briefcase really had been evil. Damn.

Ruby looked up from the knot she had braided her fingers into and met Anne's gaze; they had both happened to raise their heads at just the same, incredibly awkward moment. She worked her hands loose and gave a meek wave, whispering the word, *Hi*.

Anne's eyes flashed in panic, then recognition, then panic again, then finally, she laughed. "So," she said, leaning toward Ruby. "Time for a dram?"

Chapter Seventeen

Five minutes later, Anne Dunbar and Ruby Spencer were perched on stools at the hotel bar. Ruby was drinking a glass of Sancerre; Anne was sipping a whisky with sparkling water. ("It's like a spritzer for boss hens," she'd said.) They had ordered a little plate of almonds and olives to share.

Once Anne had handed over her bank card, she turned to Ruby and said, "Orighty. On a scale of one to I'm screwed, how much of that did you hear?

"Thanks for this," Ruby said, swirling the wine and sticking her nose in the glass. She inhaled and let the grassy scent pummel her. *Holy yum.* "And, um, I'd say . . . call me an electric drill?"

Anne tossed her head back and cackled. "Wow, I'm in love with you."

Ruby sparkled and took a sip. "*I'm* in love with this wine list. It's low-key one of the best I've ever seen at a hotel bar."

It was Anne's turn to beam. "*Thank you.* No one here appreciates it. But tourists do! And I do, obviously. I got properly into wine when I studied abroad. In New York. I helped get this place off the ground; no one here knows shite about marketing or design or good taste. Sorry, I'm blethering. Where are you from, by the way?"

"New York! Well, raised upstate. But I moved here from the city."

"Stunner! I wonder if we overlapped. We must have."

"Must have. So—I actually knew you lived in New York for a while . . ." Ruby let the sentence fizzle out.

Anne leaned forward, intrigued.

"Brochan told me, when I first met him. And that you two were friends when you were kids."

Anne's terrible poker face revealed a look of intense surprise before she settled into a fond smile. "Right. Well, he's a doll. Even though he properly hates me. Seeing as I represent all things evil and have a forked tongue. Allegedly." Something registered in her consciousness, and she lifted an eyebrow. "Are you knocking around with him?"

"No!" Ruby nearly shouted. "I mean . . . maybe? I want to?"

Anne took a slow sip of her spritzer on steroids. "I bless this union. Just keep your wits about ye." She took another, slower sip. "He can be tricky—a cantankerous old man, which is why I'm so bothered over this whole deal with the Cosy Hearth."

"I understand bits and pieces of this whole . . . situation. But can you tell me what's actually happening?"

"Not fully my story to tell," Anne said, igniting a spark of annoyance in Ruby. She'd heard that before. Who *would* explain what was happening here? "How much do you know?"

"Next to nothing."

"So—obviously the Cosy Hearth is special. It's a glorified

hobbit home with beer taps. But I don't know how Grace has held on so long. She's deep in it. I coordinated the scone deliveries and catered dinners with the Traveler; it was breaking my heart to walk by and watch her reading by the fire every day. A miserable scene; no one in the pub. Except for Neil. You've met Neil?"

"Oh, I've met Neil."

"Brilliant. Love that bastard. Och—anyway." Anne pressed the pads of her fingers into her temples. "Ruby, I don't expect you to understand this but Thistlecross is struggling. Tatties over the side."

"Sorry, say again?"

"Tatties. Potatoes. Over the side. Of the boat, I suppose. Just meaning . . . we're fucked. We haven't got a distillery or cliffs or the sea or castles. There's nothing to draw tourists beyond Moss Glen Falls. And that's not a lot. As we discovered after building a new hotel. So not only are visitors spending time at other places in the Highlands, our people are leaving. To work at those places."

"I think it's nice here," said Ruby, feeling odd for defending her adopted town against its mayor's harsh words.

"Oh, me, too. It's the best place in the world. And I lived in New York for years. But Thistlecross hasn't exactly got sex appeal. And we shoveled *a lot* into this hotel. Probably a heap more than we should—" Anne stopped herself and shook her head, as if waking up from a dream. "Why am I telling you all this? Please don't repeat it. Please."

"I won't."

"You have to promise me," Anne begged, holding out her smallest finger.

"You have pinkie swears in Scotland?"

"Do it, eh?"

Ruby hooked her finger around the mayor's and they squeezed. The two women locked eyes. "Your secret is safe with me. I promise."

"Thanks, Ruby. Is it obvious that life is a little lonely up here for the first 'hen mayor' of Thistlecross? Sorry for throwing myself at you. I'm not normally this desperate. Or maybe I am? Shite."

Ruby gave her a reassuring smile. "You don't have to apologize. I'm here for it. At the very least, I owe you for the coffee and the wine. So . . ."

Anne dove back into the story. "Right, so we need to make some cash. Fast, and for the long term. Sorry to be so blatant about it, but I'm scraping the bottom of the barrel when it comes to the simplest things. Road maintenance, that sort. Not sexy, that stuff. But important!

"Winkler—that's the man you saw me with—wants to open an American chain restaurant here. It's Scottish . . . adjacent. They serve whisky; everything is covered in fake tartan. He wants to open it in the Cosy Hearth building." She made air quotes with her fingers. "Authentic ambiance."

Ruby nodded, taking care not to betray her familiarity with Winkler's name.

"It's the right choice for tourism. For Thistlecross, full stop. It's not just quick money from the sale. . . , It's everything. New jobs, a beacon to tourists looking for something comfortable. If we can't offer the landscapes and clan culture that people want, we'll draw them in with scran and whisky. Winkler's business model works. Everyone in the States loves his restaurants."

"Do you love them?"

"They're all right. A bit embarrassing, to be sure. But they're familiar to Americans. And they deliver the concept of the Highlands in a reliable package." She shrugged and studied her glass. "It would help Thistlecross become the Scotland that people expect. The Scotland that people flock to."

"So Brochan is mad because . . . Grace is his mom?"

"No, who told you that?"

"No one. They seem close. So why does he care so much?"

"He has a lot of history with the Cosy Hearth. Ask him about it sometime. Get him steaming first, though."

"Okay. I will. Just one question. *Steaming* means . . . ?"

"Pished, plastered, goosed, minced, oot yer tree, wrecked—essentially."

"So . . . drunk?"

"Yes. Get him drunk. He won't go in fer the blether unless he's in the Balvenie."

Ruby raised an eyebrow. That didn't sound right; the Brochan she knew happily shared conversation without knocking back shots. But then, how well did she actually know him?

"He already suspects something's up. That guy—Winkler?—sent a box of uniforms to the pub. Kind of an aggressive move, no?"

"*That's* where they went? Oh, I want to laugh, but I think I'll gouge my brain out with this wee fork instead." Anne picked up the olive fork and twirled it once between her fingers.

"He seemed creeped out that day, but I think he's forgotten about it by now. Or at least, written it off as some weird mistake."

"I understand I can't keep this from him and Grace. But I'm not ready to tell them. Not until everything's proper. I need to have some kind of damage control plan at the ready."

"But you will tell them? Before it all goes public?"

"I will tell them." Anne used the fork to impale an olive and Ruby took an almond. "But this is dull. Tell me what brought you to Thistlecross. You're not, er, related to Grace, are you?"

Ruby shook her head. "I just needed a change of pace from the city. I quit my job at a magazine and decided to write a cookbook."

"Hurrah!"

"Well, the cookbook got rejected."

"Boo."

"But Grace and I are starting a Sunday supper club at the pub."

"Hurrah again!"

"The first one is this week. You don't . . . you don't want to come, do you?"

"Blah. I do want to come. But it doesn't feel right to get too close to Grace right now. Professional distance, all that."

"Understood. Well, maybe you can help me choose a few wines to pair with the meal? I'd love someone else's insight."

Anne tied her heavy curtain of hair back with a beige elastic and motioned for the menu. "Better yet, I'll get Lachlan, the bar manager, to slip us a few bottles. You can be mysterious about your source."

The two women leaned in to the bottle list.

"Now tell me," Anne said, "what's your first course?"

Chapter Eighteen

Ruby went back to the cottage that night with some good red wine and a couple of bottles of bubbly. As her Sancerre buzz wore off, she tried to untangle the events of the afternoon. It seemed wrong to keep this secret from Brochan. But more or less wrong than breaking the trust of a friend? Because that's what Anne was, right? A friend? Ruby felt for her—mayoral life seemed hard, and harder still as a woman in a stubborn old town. It would be pretty great if she and Brochan could reconcile their differences, Ruby thought, because sneaking around kind of put a damper on this awesome new girl gang. But maybe everything would work itself out on its own. Maybe nothing bad would happen further, and everything would magically fix itself.

I mean, stranger things have happened.

On Thursday, Ruby checked her email a dozen times to see if her agent had said anything about the microwave cookbook. She had not.

All morning, she tried to focus on pulling weeds, finding it impossible not to think about her conversation with Anne, the contract that sat in Winkler's briefcase, or the impending dinner party. As she ripped out dandelions, she wondered again what Brochan's actual deal was. She was angry that he hadn't shared whatever full story everyone else kept hinting at in mysterious half-truths. Then she wondered if she actually had a right to know.

But how can I ask him to tell me all that . . . without sharing the secret I'm keeping, too?

In the afternoon, Ruby and Grace sketched out the plan for their meal and shopped for ingredients. Grace drove them to the local shops as well as a few in nearby towns. They visited Sam, the butcher, for ground beef. They stopped at the cheese shop, where Eliana gave them samples of a dozen different cheeses; they finally settled on a few. Rory, the greengrocer, let them have their pick of vegetables. Of course, they couldn't conclude their errands without a visit to Donnie, the chocolate and candy maker, who boxed up intricately painted gin-filled truffles.

Once back at the Cosy Hearth, the two women cleaned and readied the vegetables, created seasoning blends and sauces. Every time Grace looked at Ruby from across the butcher block table and smiled, Ruby's cheeks flushed. She had to physically bite her lip at times to keep the rush of words from spilling out: *Could you pass the pepper oh-and-also-Anne-is-one-hundred-percent-selling-your-pub-but-please-don't-hate-her-because-she's-trying-her-best?*

By Saturday, consumed with nerves, Ruby sat with a mug of tea, sunning herself near the garden patch and admiring her hard work. It felt good to pick away at something with quantifiable results. There had been weeds earlier this week; now there were none. She was skimming the list of to-dos in her journal when she heard Brochan's laughter. She looked up and shielded her eyes from the sun. He was riding a rugged-looking bike with a man about his age. Both were wearing stretchy clothing covered in mud splatters. Brochan was a mountain biker? Brochan had friends? Ruby wasn't sure which surprised her more. She felt a bit shy and grabbed the garden hose, pretending to become very interested in the saturation level of her soil.

They hadn't spoken since her sob fest in the kitchen, when she'd unleashed a barrelful of tears and weepy fears. When he'd touched her lips and almost kissed her. Then gotten a sketchy text message from Margaret. They hadn't spoken since she'd overheard his childhood best friend tease at the secrets Brochan was keeping, and the one Ruby was now guarding. Despite the fire hose of complicated thoughts, when Ruby looked at him, all she felt was unfettered desire. Desire that pounded in her chest and throbbed beneath her navel. Suddenly, she realized she had no idea what to say to Brochan.

She hoped he'd ride by without seeing her.

He didn't ride by without seeing her.

Brochan broke off from his partner and crested into the yard. Ruby watered the thyme and pretended not to notice. Lalalalala. *What was it about this man that made her feel so damn awkward?*

"He's just *too* sexy; that's what it is," Ruby said to herself, playing with the folds of her faded tartan sundress. She'd gotten it from Grace the week prior, as the two women explored an old trunk that held treasures from the proprietress's past.

"I wore this for every party and dance for years," Grace had murmured, rubbing her thumb over the muted red and piney green pattern. She held it out toward Ruby. "It looks to be about your size." And so it was; the bodice fit perfectly around Ruby's small waist, with a simple scoop neck and zippered back. The skirt flared, hitting just above her knees; it made a pleasant swishing motion every time Ruby turned around.

"Who's too sexy, then?" Brochan asked, taking off his helmet and shaking out his gorgeously textured mane.

Ruby gestured toward the herbs. "Mr. Cilantro."

Brochan gave her a questioning look, then reached for the hose. "Can I? I ran out of water on the trails." He motioned toward the plastic bottle clipped into his frame. Ruby handed the hose to him, and he adjusted the pressure from a shower to a stream, then brought it up to his mouth. He drank, the water catching in his beard and dripping onto his Lycra shirt, unzipped halfway down his chest.

Ruby stared wantonly at the hair that spread across his pecs, then shook her head, to transport herself back to reality. *He. Is. Such. A. Man.*

"I had no idea there was good biking in Thistlecross," she said.

There was good biking all over the Highlands, Brochan corrected as he unwrapped a protein bar. He took a big bite, then offered it to Ruby. She shook her head, but thought it was sweet he had offered. "Kyle—fellow village ruffian—and I have a standing weekly ride. It keeps my head from becoming mince."

Ruby understood. Until she left New York, she hadn't missed her thrice-weekly hot yoga class. The sweaty flows made her head feel un . . . mincey. She told him that, and made a mental note to do a few sun salutations at some point.

"I've always been curious about yoga," Brochan said thoughtfully, finishing his bar and pocketing the wrapper. "Maybe you could teach me a few moves. Oh, hey. How are you feeling, since— earlier this week? All that?"

Ruby couldn't help it; she laughed loudly. "You're just so perfect!" she said. "If this were a romance novel, I would be about to find out that you lost your wife and children in a tragic cider-making accident and were finally ready to open your heart to someone new." She was surprised at how bold she was acting, but after the week's weird start coupled with the brazenness of his touch in the kitchen, all her little inhibitions no longer felt like they held power over her. She shook her fist in the air in mock indignation at his goodness to drive home the point. As she did, the spaghetti strap of her dress slipped from her shoulder and settled on her upper arm.

Brochan came a little closer and guided the strap to its proper place.

"No wife. No kids. But . . . cider? I'm not sure I get your meaning."

She gulped.

"I saw your phone the other day. In the kitchen. Someone texted you, there was an apple. Oh my god, I'm psychotic. Sorry. It was wrong of me to look." Her words turned into a mumble by the end of the sentence, and her cheeks betrayed her embarrassment.

Brochan lifted his head in a slow nod. If he was angry she'd peeked, he didn't say it. "Old flame. Meant nothing, means nothing. And who cares about apples when I've got rhubarb preserves right here?"

Ruby opened her mouth, then closed it. Hard to argue with that logic.

Brochan ran his finger across her clavicle. "And what's so wrong about a wee romance novel, anyway?"

"Nothing's wrong with a romance novel, except that— Brochan, come on. No guy is ever as unrelentingly *good* as the leading men are made out to be. They're always screwing up, then doing something completely over-the-top and ridiculous to atone, like showing up under the heroine's window in the rain with a boom box blasting 'Signed, Sealed, Delivered.'"

Brochan laughed, big and jolly. "What do you have against Stevie Wonder?"

"I take issue with people using his musical genius in such grotesque context!"

"Genuine shows of affection are grotesque?"

Ruby rolled her eyes. "You know what I mean. Oh, and the authors are always describing the clothes the leading women wear in ridiculous detail, like it somehow matters to the plot. Nobody cares about my clothes!"

"I care about your clothes." Brochan gathered the skirt of Ruby's dress in his fist and pulled her a little closer, then released her. "For example, I like this dress and I like you in it. And, aye— I think it's nice, having something to aspire to. An ideal. And if nothing else, they make you feel good. Hopeful."

"You do *not* read romance novels."

"I do read romance novels!"

Ruby glared at him. He was so full of shit.

Brochan held his hands up in an *okay, okay* gesture.

"So I have read—past tense—one or two. There were always a bunch kicking around when I was a lad. I thought they were scandalous, basically proper pornography."

Ruby put her hands on her hips and shook her head. "No doubt, you triple underlined every time the word *knockers* appeared."

"Ha! I fully assign all guilt in such capers to Anne." Brochan's softhearted memory turned crispy around the edges, and he swatted at the air, trying to be casual.

His reference to his old friend and Ruby's new one made her flush, but she pushed it out of her mind.

"Anyhow," he said, "you write a romance novel that includes the word *knockers*, and I will read it."

They shook hands. *It's a deal.*

Brochan took a step back, then, and raised the garden hose, pointing it inches from Ruby's nose. "If this was a romance novel," he said, his voice wicked and delicious, "you'd be soaking wet."

Chapter Nineteen

On Sunday, Grace and Ruby pushed together every table in front of the fireplace at the Cosy Hearth to form a long table. A family table. They had a very respectable amount of guests signed up, including the crew from last week (well, minus the tourists) and one of Grace's friends from her monthly knitting circle. Grace laid two extra places, one for her and for Ruby, but Ruby shook her head. *No way.* She was going to be far too busy cooking, plating, and making sure each dish looked picture-perfect. Also, she was massively nervous and needed to be doing something with her hands, not watching everyone eat the food she'd prepared.

For the first course, Ruby had laid an extravagant cheese board on the bar and set a small stack of mismatched plates beside it. If she'd learned anything from her time attending fancy publishing events in New York, it was that these things tended to go more smoothly if you allowed guests to roam around a bit before forcing them into a seat. Ruby had unearthed a large wooden cutting board from the depths of Grace's cabinets. Now, it was crammed full of cheeses—an aged goat milk cheddar, a soft, creamy Brie-style cheese made from sheep's milk, and a stinky blue that would surely separate the food warriors from the dabblers. In between the cheeses were bunches of grapes, dried apricots, tiny bowls of the whisky-soaked prunes, walnuts Ruby had caramelized in honey and chili peppers, and rustic crackers made with fresh rosemary from the garden. There were also, courtesy of the Traveler's Lachlan, two chilled bottles of Lambrusco, a sparkling red wine that was meant to be served cold. As Ruby prepared the main course, she could hear the lull and hum of conversation grow louder with each passing moment. She smiled to herself, happy that everyone was having a good time and that she had a part in creating the experience. This was not what she had come to Scotland for, but suddenly she couldn't imagine her life without the Cosy Hearth or the people in it.

God, she hoped the contract with Winkler fell through.

Grace poked her head between the curtains and smiled so big, her cheeks became rounder, fuller cocktail tomatoes. Ruby was smashing down beef patties with a spatula as they crisped in a large cast-iron pan. She was covered in fat splatters, and the bandanna she had tied around her head was all askew. She also happened to look happier than she had in a long time. Something good was happening in Ruby's heart. "Almost ready?" Grace asked.

Ruby grinned back. "Almost ready. Round 'em up."

Five minutes later, Ruby emerged balancing three plates between her two hands. She had planned on trekking back and forth from the kitchen until everyone was served, but Brochan jumped up to help, his linen napkin tumbling from his lap to the floor. Grace caught Neil's eye and the old man didn't try to conceal his wink. Were they really that obvious? At that moment, Ruby didn't care. She was grateful for the help and also a little bit grateful for how excellent Brochan's torso looked in his worn-out, pale gray button-down. It complemented his dark eyes.

Not that she had noticed.

Once everyone was served, Ruby stood at the head of the makeshift table and thanked them all for coming. She explained that in lieu of a traditional Scottish feast, she was leaning into her American roots. Neil shouted, "Away with ye!" but everyone knew he was kidding so everyone laughed. Ruby had made, she said, smash burgers. They were a staple in her favorite New York diners. The beef came from Highland cattle, and the buns were made with a mixture of soft white flour and ground oats.

"The oats are because Scotland," she said, suddenly feeling shy again. The guests clapped, and Ruby did a little bow before bounding back into the kitchen where she got back to work, pouring thick cream into a bowl and sweetening it with a drizzle of honey. She whisked the mixture by hand, her muscles straining against the movement. She was dolloping it into a serving bowl in small clouds when the curtain parted again. This time, it was Brochan, his arms piled high with empty dinner plates.

"No bother," he said before she could protest, then set them into the sink. He retreated, walking backward through the curtain with a flourish of his hand. "I was never here." Ruby giggled to herself and finished arranging shortbread cookies on a platter with Donnie's chocolates and plump fresh blackberries. She had gone foraging earlier that week and found them growing in a patch near Moss Glen Falls. She served the dessert family style, a simple end to a decadent dinner.

Grace offered Ruby her seat next to Brochan, and this time wouldn't take no for an answer. While Grace brewed coffee and tea, Ruby nibbled on a cookie and listened to the chatter.

"I can't deny their presence is good for our businesses," Sofie said, then added in an aside for Ruby's benefit. "We're talking about Anne Dunbar's quest to turn Thistlecross into a tourist destination."

Oh. Cool. Super casual dinner party conversation.

Ruby set the cookie on her plate and looked quickly at Brochan before glancing Carson's way. Hadn't Dunbar mentioned that Carson wouldn't write the contract? How much did he know? He maintained a cool, neutral countenance that Ruby couldn't puzzle through.

Brochan raised his wineglass and looked around the table. "All I'm saying, Sof, is that if this little town is going to make it, it's got to be with what, and who, we've already got. Tourists come, but they don't stay. The people who belong here . . . that's who matters."

When Brochan said this, all the feelings that were accumulating in the cup of Ruby's heart tumbled over the lip. He looked at her with those last words, and he wasn't looking away. Beneath the tablecloth, he squeezed her thigh so far up her leg, any fool could tell that he hadn't innocently missed her knee. She swallowed hard to suppress a tiny moan.

Unaware of the shenanigans happening under the table, Mac spoke up for Sofie. "Well, that's a convenient stance for you, Brochan, seeing as the entirety of your business comes from Thistlecross residents. But Sof and me, we rely on out-of-towners to stay in the hotel. And who do you think buys all her soaps? I haven't seen an order placed from you. Nor any of you here." Mac looked accusingly around the table. "It's all folks from abroad, on her wee Etsy shop."

Ruby made a mental note to buy some patchouli soap from Sofie that week.

"So you're saying if someone wanted to drive Grace out of business, you'd be all right with that?" Brochan was continuing to trace his fingers over Ruby's thigh in tender swirls, making the contrast to his clipped tone all the more stark.

"That's absolutely bonkers; I didn't say that and now you're just drawing connections where there are none," Mac retorted. Brochan's fingers stopped traveling her leg just long enough to squeeze, his thumb almost meeting the edge of her underpants under her denim. He opened his mouth to further the argument, but he was stopped by Grace, who assertively cleared her throat.

"Enough," she said, placing her hands calmly on the table. "We've had quite our fill of politics talk for a family dinner, haven't we? Besides: no problem was ever solved on a Sunday evening. Mondays are for figures and puzzles. Now relax. Eat another biscuit."

Ruby took a bite of her shortbread and let the cookie soften in her mouth. That's right; no problem *was* ever solved on a Sunday. Thankful for the permission, she pushed all her worries straight out of her mind, replacing them with the sensation of Brochan's hand. She touched his knuckles briefly before letting her own fingers flutter down to his leg.

"Oh!" she said out loud with a start, realizing that she'd landed in the valley between his thigh and groin—an area that was straining with the canvas of his pants, pulled taut from his hardness. Everyone in the room looked her way, and Brochan held perfect stillness in his expression as he covered her hand with his own and pulsed once, hard. "Oh . . . I'm just so glad you all came tonight," Ruby said, fumbling, with her free hand, with the rumpled napkin on the table. "It's nice to be a part of this."

Everyone nodded, then busied themselves with their berries and cream. Ruby blushed and Brochan chuckled before letting go. She quickly retrieved her hand to safety and sat on it.

Once everyone had eaten their fill, Sofie, Mac, Brochan, and Neil stayed to help clean up. Differences of opinion and sharp words forgotten, they reminisced about the gaudy color the postal office had once been painted (apparently it was a dreadful sort of chartreuse before it found its way to its current sensible pale blue), and laughed about some national political figure's recent gaffe. (Ruby had no clue who they were talking about, but she enjoyed the story all the same.) As she wiped plates dry with a flour sack towel, she wondered if Brochan might walk her down the over-grown path, and if so, what might happen when they reached her door. She was mid-daydream when Sofie grabbed her forearm and said she'd been dying to see the cottage since Ruby moved in.

"Nice to have a bit of a feminine touch about it finally," she said and started for the exit, dragging Ruby behind her. "Come, show me your queendom. Mac, don't wait up. We're going to have a dram at the cottage. Just us girls."

Ruby almost protested—she watched Brochan's mouth work itself from a disappointed frown to a gentle smile—but Sofie's youthful enthusiasm and eagerness reminded her too much of

Lee to resist. And she missed Lee. And it would probably be good to have *two* friends in Scotland.

The women spent another hour together, sharing one of the Traveler's wines poured into teacups and sitting cross-legged on the velvet quilt. Sofie admired Ruby's additions and decorations, and praised Brochan's handiwork. She chattered happily about her dreams to quit hospitality work and make soap her full-time gig. She bemoaned Mac's inability to load the dishwasher properly. ("Plates go on the bottom!") She asked Ruby questions about New York City. And after she'd finally left, Ruby realized, curled up in bed with a dreamy smile plastered to her lips, that not once for the entire time had she thought about Anne's secret, her cookbook proposal, or any other generally existential life quandaries.

Yay, friends.

Chapter Twenty

Monday morning. Someone was knocking at the cottage door. Very loudly. Very rudely. (Or was that just the red wine?) Dancing around the edges of a dream, Ruby turned onto her stomach and covered her ears. The knocking persisted, and she peeked out from under her sleep mask. It felt like morning, but the cottage was still dark. "Yeah?" Ruby mumble-shouted and sat up, pushing the mask away and pressing the heels of her hands into her eye sockets. A stray bit of hair had come out of her braid; it tickled her ear. *What time was it?*

The door swung open and Brochan stepped in, apparently no longer shy after last night's overtures. "Heads up!" he said, tossing a waterproof anorak to Ruby. It hit the side of her head and fell to the floor, on top of her dictionary and a historical novel she'd been reading late into the night after Sofie left.

"Huh?" She was still half-asleep. "New project idea for the cottage," she said, flopping back down onto the mattress and pulling the quilt around her like a cocoon. "A *lock*."

"Let's go, then, Roo," he said, coming around to where she lay, and squatting to pick up the rain jacket. It was then Ruby realized that his eyes were shining and there was excitement in his voice. Maybe even a little mischief. A split second later, she realized that Brochan was two inches from her bed and she looked like the walking dead. *Eek*.

"Go where?" she said, sitting up and pulling her sweater over her pajama top. She yanked on the hair elastic and worked her braid loose. "It's the middle of the night."

"To the Isle of Skye. We're having a proper adventure day. You've been in Scotland far too long without seeing the Hebrides. And you deserve it, after treating us all to a feast last night. And I'll correct you: It's almost sunrise. Come on, then!" He was boyish and youthful in his enthusiasm. "I have tea in the truck. And scones."

Ruby was fully awake now. The Isle of Skye was one of those awe-inspiring islands off the western coast, and home to some of the most beautiful vistas the country offered. It was, she supposed, the kind of place Anne wished Thistlecross was. Ruby swung her legs over the side of the bed.

"Are we—are you—are you taking me to the Fairy Pools?" She had wanted to visit the picturesque pools and small waterfalls on Skye since she first started researching her new home. But she couldn't believe that Mr. Tourism Sucks was about to bring her to one of the most populated and photographed destinations in all Scotland.

Brochan did a poorly executed tap dance move and shrugged, then made for the door. "Get ready and meet me in front of the Cosy Hearth in half an hour. We've got a drive ahead of us. Oh, and bring your wellies."

Buckled into Brochan's forest-green pickup truck with a travel mug of milky black tea in her hands, Ruby's curiosity was about to eat her alive. "I have so many questions," she said, biting into of one of Grace's day-old pastries.

"No doubt you do," said Brochan, handling the gear shift and balancing his tea between his knees. He was wearing khaki-colored canvas pants and a flannel button-down in shades of gray and green, rolled up past the elbows, as always. "But I'm keeping this a secret."

A secret.

Her loyalties between Anne and Brochan wavered every time she actually saw her crush. Sure, she'd promised her new friend. But was Anne bringing her on an adventure to the Isle of Skye? Had Anne tried to feel her up underneath a dinner table? No. And definitely not. This was her moment. She had him all to herself, and they both had hours ahead. If she was going to warn Brochan about Winkler, she had to do it now. Now or never.

Wait.

She had done a pinkie swear.

Shit.

Never, it is.

Ruby ran her hand over the worn leather of the seat. The vehicle was old and well loved, but its interior was immaculately clean. "What kind of truck is this?" she asked.

Brochan raised an eyebrow. "Do you really care? I'll happily

143

talk about adventures in converting a truck from petrol to diesel if you want, but I'd rather not bore you."

Ruby laughed. "Nope. I do not care. Caught in a lie." She took a warming sip of tea. "But here's a question I actually do want to know the answer to: Your bumper sticker; is that about Scottish independence? I didn't take you for a hashtag kind of guy." There was a rectangular sticker on the back of the truck that read *#indyref2 #yes*—Ruby had noticed it as Brochan helped her step up into the cab.

"Oh, I'm not. Never understood the whole InstaFaceSpaceChat thing. But I support a second independence referendum all the same." Ruby asked him to tell her more about it, and he did. "In the first one, Scotland remained in the UK by mere margins." Brochan swerved to avoid a big bump in the road. "A lot of Scots— this one included—feel that it's time for another vote, properly executed this time."

"But if Scotland votes itself out of the UK, what happens with Brexit?"

"Well, ideally, we'd break from the UK but remain in, or re- enter, the EU. Then there's border tariffs and that whole nightmare to sort. But getting another vote on the books is the first step. Then we'd have to actually convince our fellow Scots that we're strong enough to break from Britain and take our future into our own hands." Brochan raised his fist in a rally.

"I think you can do it!" Ruby said, trying to be encouraging.

"I know so. Tell all your friends. Indyref2. Make it happen. Vote yes."

"Will do. Okay. Next question: Seriously, where are you taking me?"

Brochan took mercy on her and explained that they weren't visiting the Fairy Pools but a lesser-known place called Brother's Point. Brochan promised her that the Fairy Pools paled in comparison to the sweeping views of Brother's Point (or Rubha nam Brathairean, he annotated effortlessly). Brother's Point, Brochan explained, was also far less popular with visitors. "If you're going to battle the midges, you might as well see something truly worth the effort."

Ruby reached in her tote bag to make sure she'd brought some netting to wrap around her face. The small, biting midges were no joke . . . and Ruby was an experienced veteran of blackfly-ridden summers in upstate New York.

As Brochan drove westward toward the bridge that would take them to Skye, Ruby watched the scenery grow wilder and more coastal. She could smell seaweed and peat, and she felt excited. But even so, even still, a cauldron of bad vibes bubbled in her belly.

Tha sinn air ruighinn," Brochan said, parking the truck on a patch of grassy gravel. "We've arrived." Noticing Ruby's incredulous stare, he chuckled as he pulled on his rubber boots and gathered a few items into his knapsack. "I speak the most marginal amount of Gaelic. For entertainment purposes only." The drive had taken almost three hours, and although the sun should've been in its full morning glory, they were surrounded by a wet fog that was doing its part to uphold Skye's reputation as the Misty Isle. Ruby put her boots on, too, and they walked down a rocky trail that petered out to a pebble-laden beach. Ruby clapped in delight when she saw sheep munching kelp near the water's edge, and Brochan smiled, then took her hand. She looked up at him, noting a contented serenity in his eyes she hadn't yet seen. He seemed deeply at peace here, on Brother's Point. They passed the sheep and began an ascent, up the ridgeline of the landmass. It was wet and marshy in places, and their boots made a satisfying squelch with each step. They walked the spine toward its tip, Ruby's fingers trailing Brochan's, their touch at times becoming light but never breaking. When they reached a meadowed plateau, Brochan slid his knapsack down and stretched his arms toward the sea. He breathed in deeply and his chest rose and fell, as purposefully and powerfully as the waves crashing beneath them.

Ruby shielded her eyes from the sun and looked east; she could see the isle of Rona off in the distance. Kilt Rock, she knew, lay to the north. There were so many places to see in this unbound country. Would she ever visit them all? Would she ever stop feeling like a tourist? Maybe, if she stopped stressing about it. Ruby recommitted herself to just being present and enjoying the day, whatever it brought. She turned her attention to Brochan, who had laid down a blanket and produced another thermos of tea. The two drank and took in the view.

"I love it here," he said. "I don't come often, but it always makes me think about my mum. This was apparently her favorite place in all Scotland."

Apparently? Ruby studied Brochan. He swallowed and his Adam's apple bobbed in his throat. He turned his eyes away from the water and toward Ruby. "I've never come here with anyone else, actually. Always been alone with my sad-man thoughts." He gave her an ironic little eye roll.

"So why me?"

Brochan offered her the thermos and looked back out toward Rona. "Because you're my favorite person in all Scotland."

"That is absolutely not true."

Brochan leaned back in the grass, propping himself up on his elbows. "There you go again. Can't accept a compliment."

Ruby tried to laugh it off, calling to mind Anne's warning about Brochan. "I bet you've used that line on loads of women."

Brochan looked upset. "Och! That's not true." He picked a blade of grass and split it in two, right down the center. "Be gentle. I haven't felt this way in a long time. Not since . . ."

"Since the cider mill?"

"Her name was Margaret. Is Margaret. She's not dead. Ha ha? Not funny. Sorry. Yeah."

"She really got you good, huh?" Ruby said. She knew exactly what that felt like; to be gotten, and good.

"She sure enough did."

"The other week you said it was no big deal. What really happened?" She leaned back, too, so they were on the same level. "If you want to share, that is."

"We almost got married," Brochan said, and Ruby's heart plummeted. How could you ever get over something like that? "But for the better part of the year that we were planning our future, she was planning on moving. To New York. For her schooling. She didn't tell me until a week before our wedding. Apparently I was just to come along for the ride."

"Is that why she has an apple emoji next to her name? Because, you know, the Big Apple?"

"I did that when she first moved away, to remind myself not to ring her."

"People in Thistlecross really have a New York fetish, huh?"

"Sorry?"

"Margaret moved there. Anne did, too. Are you sure you've never sublet a studio in Hell's Kitchen?"

"I don't know what that means."

"Never mind. It's not important. Wow, Broo. I'm so sorry."

"Eh. I could never leave Thistlecross. I guess in the end I cared about the town more than I wanted to be with her. But it laid me out for a long time." Brochan shredded a few more blades of grass. "It hurt, Roo, that someone I loved could keep such a colossal secret from me."

Ruby nodded righteously but inside she felt like a husk of a human being.

"How do you plan a fecking wedding without telling your future husband that you'd like to tear up your lives and move to another country?"

"I guess you just really have to like apple cider?"

"Trust issues."

"What?"

"You asked about what kind of relationship trauma I had. I suppose that's the answer."

Was now the perfect time or the worst time to tell Brochan about her conversation with Anne? He reached over and pinched the curve of her ear and ran his thumb all the way down. He pulled gently on her earlobe, and it felt so arrestingly erotic that Ruby promptly settled on *worst time ever*, and strengthened her resolve to keep her promise.

Chapter Twenty-One

They drank their tea and ate some crackers and nectarines that Brochan produced from his bag. They took pictures of each other with their cell phones and then, very quickly, quite sneakily, Brochan threw his arm around Ruby and took a selfie of the both of them together with the water crashing and frothing and spreading out below. When they reviewed the picture Brochan said, "I look like an eejit," and he took another one, but this time he turned to Ruby and pressed his lips against her cheek, so that in the picture her eyes looked surprised and half of her face was engulfed by a large Scottish beard.

After that, Brochan said, *Kilt Rock?* And Ruby said, *Oh yes*, so they retraced their steps and buckled themselves back into Brochan's truck. All but five minutes later, they stood at the cliff's edge, watching the water from Loch Mealt tumble over the edge of an almost hundred-meter—quick google: about three hundred and thirty feet—rock face.

"Why is it called Kilt Rock?" Ruby asked, and Brochan explained that some people (a thinly veiled "tourists" disguised as a cough) thought the striations in the rock looked like the pleating of a tartan kilt.

Once they'd had their fill of sweeping sea views, it was time for lunch. They stopped at a pub and ordered smoked salmon sandwiches with dill on thick pieces of pumpernickel bread. They both licked crowdie cheese from their fingers, after which Ruby begged their teenaged server to bring the recipe.

"Erm, it's pretty common in Scotland, ma'am," the kid said, clearly wondering why anyone would need a recipe for crowdie cheese, but shrugged his shoulders, permanently slouched from a young lifetime spent on TikTok and WhatsApp, and disappeared into the kitchen.

"Am I really a ma'am?" Ruby asked Brochan across the table. His accent had made the word sound like "mum," and that unnerved her. A little.

"I think to him, every woman over the age of sixteen is a ma'am."

He came back with a torn piece of paper and a few scribbled ingredients and said, "The chef laughed when I asked for this . . . but I hope it helps."

Ruby read the list and instructions out loud: "Whole milk, cream, salt . . . Oh! This is basically fresh farmer's cheese. How do we feel about putting some of the garden parsley into this?" Ruby was sitting across from Brochan, her back against the wall on the banquette. He was in a heavy wooden chair, smiling as he watched her scribble quickly in her slim notebook.

After lunch, Ruby tried to sneak her credit card to the waiter but Brochan already had sneaked his credit card to the waiter, so she just had to deal with it and let him pay. Which was hard. Because Ruby had not been on a proper date with a good man in a long time. She wasn't used to dating men who didn't ask, "How do you wanna split the bill? Venmo or . . . ?"

It made her feel awkward and special at the same time. Especially since he had been so vulnerable with her earlier.

Brochan looked out the window and supposed they should head back to Thistlecross.

No!

Not yet!

If they left now, they would be stuck in the car for three hours, and Ruby would be out of brain-occupying activities, and she might accidentally crack and tell him everything, and he might be angry with her, and that meant he'd no longer gaze at her with such naked desire that she felt like she was getting scorched by the sun.

Ruby raised her hand at the table, like she was back in primary school with an urgent question to ask.

Brochan laughed.

"Yes, Roo?"

Ruby cleared her throat and explained that although she understood the Fairy Pools were dreadful—Top Ten Worst Tourist Attractions in Scotland of All Time—she still very much wanted to see them. And since they were so close, and because they had the whole afternoon ahead of them . . .

Brochan's face fell.

"We don't *have* to, really." Ruby scrambled to course correct.

She could always come back, on her own. Maybe do a tour bus or something.

"Yes, we do," he said. "What a selfish bampot I've been all day, dragging you around this island without a thought or worry about what *you* wanted to do."

Ruby's own relationship trauma, the doubt and insecurity that had become a fortress around her heart, was eroding.

"Yes, you were, enormously selfish. So make it up to me; take me to the Fairy Pools."

And of course, Brochan did.

They walked the path toward the Black Cuillin mountain, along gravel and over wet stones that dotted small rivers. Brochan held Ruby's hand tightly this time, to keep her steady as she traversed the slippery spots. When the path became too narrow for them both, he let her go before him. An elderly woman with her husband watched Brochan walk behind Ruby, just one pace, with his arms outstretched, in case she fell. The woman nudged her old man and smiled. Brochan concentrated on Ruby's steps. Ruby remained oblivious to all this, breathing in the damp air and listening to the sound of the water, trickling in places and rushing in others. She was just so happy. She led them past the first and largest waterfall. She led them past the second one, wide and expansive; populated with bikini-clad twentysomethings applying Instagram filters and counting Likes. When they reached the end of the path, Ruby plopped herself down on the ground with her heart open toward the sky and said, "Hooray."

Brochan sat down next to her and watched her as she watched clouds.

They were in front of Bealach a'Mhaim, a three-sided hillock, or saddle if you're being technical about it. They were mostly alone; the tourists flocked to the main waterfalls and pools.

Eventually, she turned to her side and cradled her chin in her hand. She inhaled and closed her eyes. She held on to her breath for a moment and then let it go. When she opened her eyes, she decided to do a brave thing. "So. I know I keep saying I moved to Thistlecross to write a cookbook. But you know something; I think it's actually because I wanted it to become my home. Is that naive?"

"It's hopeful. I don't know if they're the same, but it's nice, either way. . . . New York wasn't home, then?"

"Nope. I guess I never got around to setting down roots there. I mean, I was able to get rid of all my possessions in a single weekend."

Brochan grinned at her. "Home is more than a dining table."

"Well, I know that. But I always felt like I was waiting for my life to start. Even as I had my dream job."

"So how is the trial run going? Have we passed the test?"

"It's the homiest home I've ever known. Does that mean it's my home? I don't know. I keep thinking, *What if I love it here, but it's not the right place for me?*"

"If you love it, then it's right. Doesn't have to be any more complicated than that."

Ruby sat up and threaded her fingers together in her lap, resting the backs of her hands against the worn black denim. She could feel his eyes fixed on her.

"I got so lonely in New York. Sometimes, I still do. But less often here. Way less often. I don't feel like I'm an island so much anymore. The Isle of Roo on the Isle of Skye." She let out a small, sad laugh, then looked up and continued spilling her guts.

"Earlier this year, when I turned thirty-five, I realized my entire sense of identity was built around my job. I was working late—on my birthday, with literally nothing better to do—and I thought, *Oh my God, I have no idea what I really want to do with my life.* Once I realized that, I knew that there was no reason for me to be in New York any longer."

She touched the tip of her nose with her index finger and thought. "But I thought Scotland might hold a clue. Ridiculous, I know. What if I completely, utterly fail at everything I came here to do?"

"Failing means you're playing. That's something."

"I guess so."

Brochan didn't say anything for a few minutes.

Ruby couldn't bear that sort of silence.

So she spoke again.

She said, "Well, what are you thinking?"

Brochan's voice was slow and measured. "I sure hope you stay."

He reached over and wrapped his arm around Ruby, pulling her closer toward his body. She snuggled in and placed her hand on his knee. His fingers squeezed her waist. Hers drummed his knee. They stayed quiet for a long time. The sun was still relatively high in the sky, but the quality of light had softened, turning the grass into gold. Eventually, the horizon would become pale lavender, then indigo. But for now, everything was brilliant. Brochan's lips grazed the top of Ruby's head. Ruby's heart jumped. Brochan was quiet. Ruby was quiet.

And then, Ruby spoke.

"Brochan?"

She could feel him hesitate, waiting.

"Who are you?"

Brochan pulled his torso away from Ruby so he could look into her eyes, but kept his arm around her. "I'll be needing more context to that question," he said.

"You get what I mean. At least, I think you do," she said. "I know lots of little details about you: Brochan. Best handyman in town. Likes carbs and dairy (so: can be trusted). Drives a pickup truck. Once engaged. Not a fan of apples. Romance novel enthusiast. Patriotic Scot. Best damn smile in town." She paused, and Brochan gave her a winning one. "I like you. I like all those details. But I don't know who you are. I don't know your last name, which is insane. I don't even know why the Cosy Hearth matters so much to you."

"Intrepid reporter that you are," Brochan said, kissing Ruby's curls for a second time. "All right. But fair is fair; we'll be swapping stories, then." He stood and offered his hand to her. "And I'll be needing a whisky to loosen my tongue."

They retraced their steps as a light rain started to fall, staying close to each other on the walk. Brochan held his anorak around Ruby to shield her from the elements. And from the tourists.

He drove them to a small inn near the pools. Like the Cosy Hearth, its walls were cobbled and old. It looked dark and moody and just about perfect for cozying up with a glass of brown liquor.

After he parked his truck, Brochan ducked inside the small office attached to the bar and told Ruby to order two of whatever she wanted. Paralyzed with indecision—how do you choose a scotch for a Scot, in Scotland?—she was still agonizing over the bottles lined up behind the bar when Brochan returned with two keys swinging on metal rings. "What's this?" she asked him, taking one.

"I'm not brash enough to think I can drive three hours back to town after the amount of whisky it'll take for me to tell you all my deepest secrets," Brochan said and sat down next to Ruby, motioning for the barkeep.

"Is this going to be a very long night?" she asked, feeling color creep into her cheeks.

"This is going to be a very long night," he confirmed.

Chapter Twenty-Two

Brochan prompted Ruby to tell the bartender what type of flavors she preferred in a glass of whisky. "Hmm." She thought about it for a moment. "Well, I like intensity." Ruby blushed for what felt like the umpteenth time since arriving in Scotland. "I mean, in terms of flavor. I guess you could say I consider the word *smooth* to be a detractor. So." Ruby paused again. "Wild. Fiery. Aggressive. Does that make any sense? This is probably not what you're asking. . . ." Her voice trailed off.

Both the bartender and Brochan smiled. "You've got a good one there," the bartender said to Brochan with a conspiratorial aside, and pulled a bottle of Laphroaig 10 from the shelf. "A proper Islay lass, I'll say."

"Naw, mate, the Quarter Cask," Brochan countered. The bartender raised an eyebrow and swapped the bottles. "Your lad thinks something of you, then," he said. He poured a generous amount into a glass and handed it to Ruby. She brought it up to her nose and her toes curled in delight. A riot of scents shouted at her, and she spoke them out loud as each one introduced itself.

"Campfire smoke. Licorice. I don't know . . . iodine?" She looked up. "I love it."

Brochan explained that the aroma she was experiencing was characteristic of whisky made in Islay, another one of the Western Isles, and that the flavors that followed would deliver on the big promises in the nose. "Seaweed, vanilla cream, black pepper, and maybe cardamom?" Ruby recited after her first sip. "Like somebody mixed brackish ocean water into a chai latte and added booze. It's so good. How did you know?"

Brochan shared a quick wink with the bartender. "Americans love Laphroaig."

Ruby's jaw dropped and she smacked his thigh. "Ew! Way to stereotype me."

"Was I wrong?"

"That I like Laphroaig? Or that I'm American?"

Brochan cocked his head and smiled devilishly. After asking for a Balvenie Sherry Cask, he performed the same ritual. "Grace's Christmas fruitcake. Sweet cream. Apricot jam." He offered Ruby a sip, and told her about Speyside whisky, known for its floral, honeyed nose and rich, dried fruit flavors. "Of course, living where I do, I'm partial to Speyside," He handed his credit card to the bartender. "Keep it open, and bring some chips, yeah?"

"I've learned so much about scotch, and I somehow still feel like a complete beginner. Like there's volumes I don't know," Ruby said.

"You are. And there is!" said Brochan. "But I'm happy to serve as your instructor. First of all, if you're in Scotland—and you are—it's whisky. Not scotch. Now, the whiskies of the Highlands present an interesting categorical challenge because—"

Ruby shook her head and raised her right eyebrow. "Oh, no you don't." She pressed both her palms into his chest and he caught them with his own hands. "You. Talk about you. Tell me everything."

"That's such an open-ended demand. I don't even know where to start."

"Just tell me about something that's important to you."

Brochan reached for his glass and took a sensual, slow sip. A sly grin curled the edges of his lips upward. And then he began. "It was a dark and stormy night. . . ."

Brochan Wood never knew his mother. Elisabeth Wood died in childbirth. *We did all we could*, the doctor explained to her husband, Grant, as he sat under a humming fluorescent light, his back heaving with sobs. *The baby fought valiantly and is doing fine. Would you like to see him?* As Grant held his son's fragile body for the first time, his heart cracked open, right down the center and almost all the way to the bottommost seam. It was broken, from love and pain both. Grant's heart would have torn completely were it not for his son; and so in a way, the baby had taken a life and saved another. The child fixed his gaze on Grant and didn't let go.

He is wise beyond his years, Grant thought. *He has already seen too much.*

"Brochan," Grant whispered, christening the boy with his name. "Brochan, how are we ever to go on?"

For the first few years of Brochan's life, Grant went through the motions. He operated his pub, which sat on the eastern side of Thistlecross; he distilled and aged whisky for his customers and he cooked haggis the way he had learned from his father. He changed his son's diapers and bathed him in the kitchen sink in his flat above the pub/local watering hole/meeting place/post office/civic center. The pub's name was the Grottie Hermitage, and it had never felt more like a recluse's home than it did in those years. Even though it had originally been named ironically.

He mopped the floors and he listened as his friends and neighbors told stories and drank, their laughs growing louder and their hearts becoming lighter as the night went on. Grant drank, too, and he kept drinking after everyone had left. With each sip, his grief grew heavier and thicker. With each night spent in dull quiet, alone, Grant sunk lower into despair. The things that once brought him joy became rote, and then they became burdens. And then he stopped doing them. Grant removed many of the leaded glass panes in the windows of the pub, because they had been Elisabeth's favorite feature in the building. In their place, he installed dusty old panes from a box in the root cellar, so burdened with age that it was difficult to peer inside, and near impossible to look out.

Slowly, slowly, Grant retreated into himself. He was living in darkness, because he had never planned on living without Elisabeth. There were days in which his twin sister, Grace, feared his heart would shatter; that the man would drop, lifeless, to the ground. Grace lived in the next town, earning a modest living as a seamstress. She called her brother and when he didn't answer, she worried. Grant began shuttering the pub one, two, then three nights a week. On those evenings, he would sit alone while his friends and neighbors worried. First, they knocked and called out to him, and then they peered through the windows. Then they called his name. Finally, they stopped coming. Grant remained alone. He did not cry anymore, but he did drink. And when he drank enough, he would shout, and he would yell. When his memories grew too dark to bear, he would stumble to the stone cottage at the end of the path and sleep a heavy, stuporous sleep. But there was no relief from his nightmares, so he could not rest. He would forget to feed his son, and he would press his son into his sister's arms and say, "Take him; I cannot."

Grace Wood moved into the flat Grant had once shared with his wife. She slept on the sofa and she took care of the boy. And she bathed him in the kitchen sink, and she rocked him as he cried and sang to him as he slept. She unlocked the door to the pub, and she invited their friends and neighbors back inside. Although she did not distill whisky as her father and brother had done, there were plenty of barrels left to bottle and share. She mopped the floors and cooked haggis and poured beer and poured whisky and served coffee and baked pastries. As the boy grew, she sat him in a high chair in the kitchen and she fed him scones with soft yellow butter, and she fried toast with a hole cut out of the center and an egg cracked into that hole. And sometimes, she would think, *Maybe everything is going to be all right, even though it is hard.*

Although Grant was no longer making whisky, he kept drinking it. He stopped coming to the pub at all, Grace running it in his stead. They went on this way for four years and never spoke of it. Because Grace was afraid and Grant was impenetrable. Grace kept doing what had to be done. Everything hurt, but life continued after it had left Elisabeth.

In the fifth year after Elisabeth's death, a stranger came to town and visited the pub. The stranger's name was Louis Winkler. He wore a shiny blue suit and a wide tie. He carried a briefcase and he was from the United States. He asked who the owner of the Grottie Hermitage was. Grace said, "That's Grant. You can find him at the bottom of a bottle of whisky." When she said this, she tilted her head to the end of the bar, where Grant was sitting sullenly with, indeed, a large glass of brown liquor. The stranger loved that, because it was just what he imagined Scots were like— drunks who couldn't hold their tongues—and he was pleased to have been proven right.

The two men talked. The stranger had a proposition. He was opening a gastropub in Boston. It was going to be the first of many; it was going to be a huge success. It was going to be Scottish themed, and it was going to be called the Wee Tartan Bagpipe. Winkler needed an authentic Scot to manage it and be the face.

What did *be the face* mean?

Just draw folks in; make it seem real. Talk with an accent, you know, that sort of thing.

Winkler's brother had traveled through Scotland a few years prior and had eaten at the Grottie Hermitage; he'd loved it. The memory had never left him. When he came back to Massachusetts, he had told Winkler about the pub and the haggis and the whisky and Grant. *He served me the best hospitality I've ever experienced*, he said.

And now Winkler wanted to offer Grant a job. In Boston. For a lot of money. *How much money?* More than you've ever dreamed of; more than you'll know what to do with. Enough to keep your family well.

Grant was quiet. He was quiet for a long time.

Eventually Winkler said, *I can tell you've been through some hard times.*

He said, *That just means you'll be more successful than any man, because you know what it means to be down and you know how to fight.*

After a year, two years, maybe I'll make you a partner.

Brother, this is the best offer you're ever going to get.

He said, *Everybody deserves a fresh start.*

Grant finished his whisky and he poured another and he poured one for the stranger named Louis Winkler. And then Grant said yes.

Ruby's glass was empty and her eyes were welling with tears. No man had ever shared this much of himself with her. She knew that everyone felt broken in their own unique way, but until this moment, she hadn't been with anyone who was willing to bare it all to her. It felt as though Brochan was telling her a secret she'd been longing to hear. Beneath her tears was a hot flush of guilt, guilt that she was still holding Anne's secret inside her. And beneath the guilt was a bright flash of excitement. Ruby realized that with the sale of the Cosy Hearth, Brochan's father might be coming back. Coming home.

Brochan's glass was still half-full, but he wasn't drinking it. He was looking at the floor. His shoulders were strong but his face was sad. Ruby reached for Brochan's cheek with her fingertips. He held them to his face but did not look at her.

"What happened next?" was all Ruby could ask. The puzzle pieces were falling into place.

Brochan released Ruby's hand and replaced it with his whisky. He drained it and winced, then motioned for another round.

"That's the most exciting part," he said with a sad smile. "My father left Thistlecross when I was five, and I haven't seen him since." Ruby's face registered horror. "He sold the bar to the town; such a bloody chancer. He owned the building; it was handed down to him from his father . . . could have just handed it right over to Grace. Apparently Winkler needed capital for his 'restaurant.'" Brochan rolled his eyes toward the wooden beams on the ceiling. "So Grace started renting it from Thistlecross and reopened it under the new name: the Cosy Hearth. And, aye, Grant left me in Grace's permanent charge, sent her money every month to cover food and things for me. She's basically my mum. But not actually.

"I got a Christmas card from him once or twice, but we haven't heard from him in years. Supposing my ugly mug is too much of a reminder for him." Brochan rubbed the back of his neck.

If there was one thing Ruby had learned from being a journalist, it was to shut up when someone else is talking about real stuff, big stuff, so she dipped a fried potato in mayonnaise and waited for him to continue.

Brochan sipped his Balvenie and snorted. "The irony is, he's apparently massively successful now. The Wee Tartan Bagpipe has a staggering amount of franchises. He travels all over America, opening new locations and raking it in. Spreading his own special bastardization of Scottish culture across the land."

"I may not know a lot about Scottish culture, but I know enough to know that the Wee Tartan Bagpipe is a very stupid name for a pub," Ruby said.

"It's just a bunch of random words! It doesn't even make any sense. I'm half waiting to hear he's legally changed his name to Hamish McHaggis."

In spite of herself, Ruby laughed. "Can I ask about the Grottie Hermitage, though? That's not exactly an inviting name, either."

Brochan looked offended. "It is the best name for a pub, ever."

"Doesn't *grottie* mean—I don't know—gross? Dirty? And a hermitage—that's a secret home for a weird recluse."

Brochan sighed dreamily and scrubbed at his beard. "Aye. It was perfect."

Leave it to a man to name a dining establishment after a dingy murder shack in the woods. Grace had certainly spruced up the place since taking over. Ruby rested her chin in the heel of her hand, which was covered with the thick cable-knit sweater.

Summer evenings in the Highlands weren't so much hot and sticky as they were cool and dreamy. Or perhaps it was something else, sending a string of chills down her spine.

The perfect moment to tell him about her conversation with Mayor Dunbar had officially been incinerated. If she revealed it now, she'd look like a sociopath. Who could listen to a story like that, then admit, "Oh, haha, by the way . . ."?

They finished their whiskies and Brochan paid the bill. They passed through the lobby and up narrow stairs that smelled like old books and cedar chests. They walked down a hallway laid with a threadbare Oriental rug. They arrived at their rooms, twin versions of the same thing but with different numbers painted in script on the doors: One, and two.

"Me and you," said Ruby. "I guess this is it. Thank you." She breathed slowly to steady herself. "Thank you for the tour, and the scotch—I mean, whisky—and for sharing a little bit more of yourself with me."

They were both quiet and still. Brochan had said so much earlier. Now he didn't have to speak to let Ruby know what he was thinking. Ruby knew. She was thinking the same thing. But it was late, and they were both tipsy, far from home. They had waited for such a long time. They could wait a little longer. Ruby tried to think about all the words she'd looked up in her dictionary over the last few months, but nothing came close to describing how it felt to be standing this close to Brochan. There was no word for how hard her heart was beating, or how much her entire body called out to him.

Brochan smiled in the direction of the doors. "One and two. Me and Roo."

And although he did not take her to bed, he did take her into his arms. He held on for dear life, and then moved his hands upward. He gripped her chin between his thumb and the knuckle of his index finger. And there, at a small inn on the Isle of Skye, he kissed her for the first time. He kissed her for a very long time.

Chapter Twenty-Three

Ruby woke the next morning with her lips tingling. It had been lifetimes since she'd been kissed. (Well, unless you counted Finance Guy Aaron, Tattoo Artist Jason, Hot Yoga Lucas, and *Womp-womp* Seth. Which Ruby didn't. Count them.)

And nobody kissed like Brochan kissed. Ruby had felt shy at first but his urgency was irresistible. It encouraged her to relax into his touch. He'd held her face gently with his right hand; with his left, he found her waist underneath her sweater and gripped like he was afraid to let her go. He coaxed her lips open with his own and she began to soften—Kilt Rock slowly crumbling into the sea. She let her body become dwarfed by and assured in him. Brochan's hands had moved to Ruby's arms; he pressed her against the door marked *Two*. Ruby felt her shoulder blades grind against the wood as his palms ran down her biceps. She bit his bottom lip and pulled a bit at his beard, up near his earlobe. Just hard enough to make it feel good. And to let him know that he wasn't completely in control. That she had agency and wanted him as desperately as he seemed to want her. He responded by parting her thighs with his knee and kissing her deeper. His mouth tasted like honey and whisky and salt.

"You taste like mayonnaise," he murmured into hers.

She blushed and murmured back, "I always kiss with condiments. It's important to practice safe sex." He tried hard not to laugh, but laughed hard anyway, and lifted her up so that her legs were wrapped around his hips and her head was almost flush with the doorway. Her inner thighs felt warm and wet, and she wondered if he could tell. She hoped he could tell.

She squeezed him tighter as they continued to feast on each other. Finally, he set her down and hooked the collar of her sweater with his index finger, pulling it away from her skin. He kissed her there, then told her, "Good night." He told her that he'd be thinking about her, and asked that she do the same.

And oh, she had. For a good hour before she finally fell into a heap in the middle of the four-poster, she thought of him. She craved more.

But she was also frightened. Because when it's real, it's more delicate. It's more dangerous. That's why she had committed to a life of spinsterhood (*haha*; she rolled her eyes at herself). Because romance never lasts, and if she was searching for something, she sure wasn't going to find it in some Scottish man's bed.

Although . . . this time felt different.

But hadn't she thought that before?

But damn, could *this* man kiss.

Ruby desperately wanted a coffee, but the siren song of her cell phone was too strong to ignore. She connected to the Wi-Fi, opened

Instagram, took a deep breath, felt gross, hated herself a little, and then searched for Margaret.

Since Brochan wasn't on social media, she couldn't easily spot Margaret from his friends list. But she found Kyle. She got a little distracted on his profile, scrolling through pictures he'd uploaded to his feed of his rides with Brochan. She used her thumb and index finger to zoom in on one of the two of them holding post-bike beers, still wearing their helmets. The caption read *Bonkers good trails!!! Cheers mate #NoInstaB*. Cute. Once she'd exhausted every photo that contained Brochan, she searched Kyle's friends list for Brochan's ex-fiancée.

Ruby felt a little nauseous as the page loaded. There was only one Margaret, but the profile was set to private, and there was no last name. The picture was a meme; a cat typing on a computer, so it was hard to tell if this was *the* Margaret. As Ruby tabbed back to Kyle's page, her thumb accidentally hit the screen and sent a follow request to Margaret. She exited the app like her fingertips had just gotten scorched and threw the phone to the bottom of the bed. She flipped over onto her stomach and considered suffocating herself with the pillow. Then she retrieved her phone and undid the request.

What if she's gorgeous with amazing boobs and is the author of seven cookbooks? the evil side of her brain poked at her.

So what? the good side of her brain volleyed back.

You know what.

No, what?

How could you possibly compete with that?!

I'm not competing with anyone!

You're not? What did that text from Margaret say? Something about no strings?

MAYBE SHE'S A PROFESSIONAL PUPPETEER.

Or maybe he's been secretly having super hot sex with her all this time.

"Fuck off," Ruby said out loud and stepped out of bed. "Last night, he kissed *me*."

After a hot shower that washed away the prior day's salty sea air, she met Brochan downstairs for breakfast, bracing herself for the distance and cool demeanor men tend to slink back into once no longer fueled by strong whisky and dark hallways. Brochan was already seated at a table nearest the bay window, fiddling with the handle of his mug. Ruby approached, and he immediately scooped her into his arms and kissed her again (admittedly, a bit more chastely) before pulling away and twisting one of her curls into a corkscrew around his finger. He instructed her to sit down, and he retrieved a mug for her, menus for both of them.

They ate egg sandwiches on buttery biscuits with fat, round sausage patties, and drank buckets of coffee. They kept sneaking glances at each other but didn't mention anything that had been said, or done, the night prior. Ruby commented on the crumb of the biscuit, and Brochan entertained Ruby by making up a story about the very old man sitting alone at the other end of the room. He paid for their breakfast, and then they made their way back to Thistlecross. Back home.

When Brochan's hand wasn't busy with the gear shift, it was resting on Ruby's knee. There was something so confident, so assured in his touch, that Ruby was dying to double-check it was real. How could a man who claimed to have trust issues give himself so freely all of a sudden?

"Brochan?" she asked, looking over at him. He'd pulled his hair into a small knot at the nape of his neck, which accentuated the strength and width of his jaw. "Can I say something?"

He nodded and squeezed her knee. She turned her body toward him and nuzzled her cheek against her headrest. "I'm terrified."

Brochan checked his speed and relented a bit.

"No, your driving is fine. I'm wearing a seat belt." The left side of his mouth turned upward. "I'm scared because I'm having a hard time believing anyone could be so good."

"What do you mean?" he asked.

"All this. The surprise trip, the thermos of tea and snacks, paying for my meals . . . taking me to see the Fairy Pools . . . the *kissing*." Ruby inspected her cuticles and her voice dropped to a whisper. "Do you really mean it? Why did you even come to the cottage to help me with the greenhouse in the first place?"

Brochan's hand left her but only for a second as he merged onto the motorway. "Which question do you want me to answer first?"

"Um, the last one. About why you came around."

"Grace texted me about five minutes after you arrived and told me that her tenant turned out to be the most bonnie lass she'd ever met, and that if I didn't get my arse over there, she'd forcibly drag me."

ROCHELLE BILOW

"You're kidding."

"I'm not kidding."

"Grace is insane."

"Grace is the most sane one of all of us."

"But you didn't come right away; you waited."

"That's true." He waited a beat now. "But she really did ask me to fix up the cottage for you. I think she was a little embarrassed about it, once she realized that she liked you." Hearing that made Ruby feel a wave of fondness toward Grace.

"Next question: So why are you even single? Available?"

"Why are you?"

"Okay, answer my next-next question. About all the nice stuff you do."

"Ruby, most of those things are common courtesy," he said. "Anyone who kidnaps a woman and cajoles her into a road trip to a sea-battered isle sure as hell better have brought tea for the ride."

"It's just that no man I've been with . . . lately . . . would do those things. They've all been pretty much crap."

Ruby's brain flashed an image of Aaron, a week into their "relationship," ignoring her in bed while he scrolled through Facebook on his phone. He had never even taken her on a proper date. After that first night (which she had initiated and paid half of) all they did was hang out in his loft, stream Netflix, and eat dinners that she cooked. It was so different from how Brochan made her feel: special and rare. The realization registered on her face.

"Well. You deserve to be thoughtfully kidnapped with tea and kissed until your knees give out. And any man who thought otherwise was a right arse."

He drove in silence for a few minutes and Ruby let his words penetrate her heart. He continued.

"I'm falling for you, Roo. I want you. I want you so much I would set the world on fire just so you could warm your hands."

"That's a little dramatic, don't you think?" Ruby squeaked, but she was pleased he had said it, all the same.

"Fine, I'd set the world on fire so you could toast marsh-mallows."

She rolled her eyes at him.

"Canada. I'd burn Canada." He thought for a moment. "Maybe Alaska, too."

That satisfied Ruby. At least for now. She still harbored a fair bit of reservation and skepticism, but, she figured, a basalt cliff doesn't crumble in a day.

"Any other burning topics of conversation?" asked Brochan.

About that. "Um . . ." Ruby nibbled on her bottom lip and thought hard and fast. The deeper they got, the more intricate a deception she wove.

I promised Anne. The laws of sisterhood hold fast across international borders, right?

Brochan will find out soon, but it doesn't have to be from me. It shouldn't be from me.

Brochan was utterly intoxicating, but she'd never been the type of woman to put a man in front of her relationship with other women. And she wasn't about to start now. It wouldn't matter in a few weeks, anyway. She comforted herself with this idea and decided, once and for all, that she would never tell him the Cosy Hearth was about to be sold, and he would never find out that she'd known in the first place, and she could move to Scotland forever, and together they could save the town of Thistlecross from financial disaster *and* shitty chain restaurants.

This was a good plan. A perfect plan. What could go wrong?

"Roo?"

"No further notes," Ruby said. "Absolutely, positively not."

Ruby and Brochan arrived back in Thistlecross shortly before noon, and found Grace literally wringing her hands in the kitchen. Brochan had intended to drop off the picnic supplies and Ruby wanted to check in on a batch of no-knead bread dough she had in the pantry, slowly fermenting. The butcher block table was covered in flour, and from the smell of it, a batch of scones was quietly incinerating in the oven.

"Grace, were you worried? Didn't you get my message?" Brochan asked, touching his aunt on her upper arm. "I promised I'd keep Ruby safe and here she is."

Ruby's eyes jumped from Brochan to Grace. She'd known they were together, of course.

Grace shook her head. "No, no. It's . . ." She thumped her elbows onto the block and threw her head in her hands. Brochan looked to Ruby. Ruby approached Grace. She touched her back and waited for her to speak.

"When you're ready. We're listening."

"Might as well just spit it out. Anne Dunbar was here," Grace said. "She came to tell me that the town has received an offer to buy the Cosy Hearth." Grace swallowed the lump in her throat and clarified: "Buy it, kick us out, tear this place to its studs, and build a new restaurant in its place."

"Did she say who the buyer was?" Ruby asked.

"You remember the box of uniforms? It's him." Both women looked at Brochan after Grace spoke. His muscles flexed as his hands became fists. He bore down hard on his jaw. Ruby pretended to be shocked. She bugged her eyes and blinked them. Hopefully, it was convincing.

"Maybe you can appeal to Anne's better nature?" Ruby said.

"She has none," said Brochan. "I bloody knew it."

Grace shook her head. "It's hers to do with what she wants. The town owns this building, and the cottage, too. The . . . previous owner sold it when he left."

"It's all right, Grace," Brochan said gently. "She knows about my da."

Grace looked up from her palms, which had been catching tears. "So you understand, then, why this hurts all the more." Ruby nodded quietly. She was trying to empathize with Grace and Brochan, and she was scared to lose the only place that had felt like *home* deep down in her soul.

"It's one thing to sell scones to the Traveler. I didn't mind fading away, so long as I can do it in my own time. But now . . ." Grace's voice trailed off. "I'll have nowhere to live. Nowhere to go."

"She won't just turn you out on the street," Ruby said, but Brochan's face betrayed the fact that he didn't feel the same. He looked tired. Dejected. He looked every second of his years and then some.

"That bitch. That bloody, selfish bitch." Ruby could feel Brochan's anger reverberating from his body in waves, and she startled at the hot and dark word.

Brochan threw the thermos against the wall. The lid cracked and fell into the sink; the carafe rolled onto the floor. Ruby gasped. He stormed out of the pub, slamming the door so hard that the glass panes trembled. Grace continued to cry. Ruby wanted to say something—anything—that would help, but in that moment, she had never felt more like a tourist. She had never felt more like an outsider. She didn't feel confident that anything would make Grace feel better. But she had learned from years of watching her mother that the best way to show someone you care is to clean for them. So Ruby got to work.

Ruby scrubbed down the kitchen. She took the carbonized scones from the oven and wiped the butcher block table. She swept the floor and rinsed out the sink. Then she made Grace a pot of chamomile tea. "Sit," she ordered her friend, directing her to the big leather chair by the hearth. Grace seemed in a daze, but she did as she was told. Ruby hovered near her for a moment, biting both her cheeks at the same time. Finally, she figured there was no pussyfooting around things. Grace knew Ruby had spent the night away from Thistlecross, and she knew who she had spent it with. "Grace? I should probably . . . check on Brochan. He seemed upset. Like, really upset. Do you have any idea where he might be?"

"He's so much like his father, that one." It was an intriguing way of answering the question. Grace was looking into the hearth. "I've never told him that; I think it would only cause him even deeper hurt." She turned to face Ruby. "When Brochan cares, he cares more than anyone. Grant was like that until the day Elisabeth died. Always fighting to improve their lot; finding ways to make the Grottie Hermitage busier and the whisky better."

Ruby pulled out one of the chairs and sat down near her friend.

"*His place and his person*; that's what Grant always used to say. As long as he had his pub and his Elisabeth, he was invincible. I thought that when she passed, he'd throw himself into the business, and that worried me some. But then he surprised me and did the opposite; all the fight left him. And of course that was worse. I suppose Brochan told you all this." Grace took a sip of tea. "This is nice. There's honey in it?"

"He told me some things. Others, I'm still learning. Honey, yes. I added a little. Chamomile is too grassy on its own." She smiled. "At least, I think so."

Grace sipped again and continued thinking out loud. "So when Grant gave up on the Grottie Hermitage, it took me a while to work out what was happening. Finally, I understood: His place was never as important as his person. Without her, he couldn't see the point. Of anything. That's when it all fell apart. When he sold it and left."

Grace set the teacup down on its saucer. "What I am trying to tell you, Ruby, is that a Wood man can survive without his place. But once he's found his person? He'll never be the same without her."

Ruby set the soles of her shoes on the edge of the chair and hugged her knees. She was in the same jeans she'd worn to Skye. They had stretched out a little from two days of wear. "Do you," she started. "Do you," she tried again. "Do you . . ." (*almost there*) "think he's found . . ." (*so close*) "his person?"

Despite the tears still drying on her cheeks, Grace smiled. And that was her answer. "Brochan'll have gone to the barn. In the last year or so, it has become his respite." And then Grace stood, pulled Ruby to her feet, and gathered her up in a hug. Ruby wanted to cry then, for everything Grace had lost and for everything Ruby had gained and was afraid to lose.

She pulled away just enough to ask, "I know it turns your stomach to think about Winkler's restaurant here. But what if Brochan's father comes back, when the Wee Tartan Bagpipe opens?"

Grace snorted at the restaurant's name, but then looked serious. "I asked Anne. She said we'd all learn more in the weeks to come."

"If he did. Would that be good . . . or bad?"

"It would be complicated and it would be hard. But that doesn't mean it can't be good, also." She pulled Ruby in for another squeeze, then said, "Go to your person. Be strong because he's only pretending to be." Then she released Ruby and set her on the path to Brochan.

Chapter Twenty-Four

The barn was red and barny, just like Brochan had promised. It sat far back in a field lined with old-growth pines, a stone's throw away from the trees and—Ruby's ears perked—a stream. In the paddocks, shaggy rust-colored Highlander cattle munched on grass. *Wait. Brochan had cows?*

"Knock knock," Ruby said for good measure as she tapped on Brochan's barn. The door was whitewashed and had the same iron hardware as her cottage. It opened to reveal a very sheepish-looking Brochan, rubbing the back of his neck with his palm. *The way he does when he's thinking.*

Brochan leaned against the frame. "I threw a thermos."

"That you did."

"I was upset."

"With good reason."

"There's no good reason to break a thermos."

"I can think of seven, maybe eight good reasons to break a thermos."

Brochan didn't laugh.

"And one or two excellent reasons."

Still nothing. His face was awfully broody.

"Can I come in?"

He stepped aside glumly and she entered the barn.

She kicked off her shoes and stepped onto a large rag rug, made from scraps of blue fabric tied together in knots of varying sizes. She let her chest rise and fall twice before she crossed her arms and said, "So. You have cows?"

Brochan's resolve melted into a low chuckle. He closed the door behind Ruby and wrapped her up tightly in his arms. It felt wonderful. He took his time kissing her. "I do not have cows. But I do rent some of my land to a farmer. Who does have cows."

Ruby snuggled in closer and felt his chin settle on the top of her head. "They seem like very nice cows."

"They are. Nicest herd of cattle in the whole of Scotland. There was a survey."

Ruby looked up at him, still held captive in his arms. Her eyelashes fluttered. "God, Scotland is so weird."

Brochan pulled away a bit so that he could hold her gaze. "I'm lying. There was no survey. But Scotland is still weird."

"Maybe that's why I like it so much."

Brochan smiled knowingly and rubbed Ruby's jawline with his thumb. "Roo, you have the most beautiful eyes. They're the color of burnt caramel."

"How burnt is this caramel? Are we talking a light sugaring or dark?"

"Shite, you've got me there. I've never made caramel—surprise—but isn't it supposed to be good burnt?"

"Caramel is very good burnt."

She pulled his T-shirt back so she could press her lips to his chest. His skin was hot and she counted a few freckles hidden underneath the mat of hair. She grazed her tongue along his collarbone.

Brochan shuddered in pleasure. "Maybe a moderate amount of burnt, then."

She kissed him a bit more and let her hands wander around his waist.

Brochan slid his palms into her back pockets and pulled her closer to his body. "Will you be wanting a tour of the barn, then?"

Ruby felt him against her thigh and drew in her breath. She didn't want to wait for him to initiate any longer. Her lower belly roiled in need and one of her deep breaths caught in her throat. Whether this was for real or not, she needed him.

"No," Ruby said, "I do not want a tour of the barn. Not at all." She paused and listened to his heartbeat, so loud she could count it. "I hope that's not rude. It seems like a very excellent barn. Maybe you can give me a tour later? After I take care of some very important business?"

"What sort of business are we discussing then, lass?"

"Oh, you know . . . things." Ruby danced her fingers over his belt buckle, then down into his front pocket. She felt the crinkle of a condom's foil packet and gave a vixenish grin.

Brochan gripped at her face, holding her jaw and teasing the delicate hair around the nape of her neck. "You are my business."

"Brochan, that doesn't make any sense," Ruby said, her fingers working at his zipper.

He slid his hands up around the sides of her head and mussed her hair. Only this time, it was in the boyfriendy way, not the big-brotherly way. He put his mouth on her, right below her ear, and whispered into her skin, "This makes more sense to me than anything in the whole damn world."

And so it did.

And so they did.

An hour later (or was it two?) Ruby was lying on Brochan's bed, her cheek pressed into his chest and his arm draped around her. She was tracing circles on his sternum; he was absentmindedly tickling her hip. They were both quite naked. The most naked a person can be, really.

Ruby was thinking, *Wow wow wow wow wow wow wow*, but out loud she just said, "Brochan."

"Roo," he replied, an entire conversation in three letters, and flipped her over so that he was on top of her. He pressed her body to the mattress with his hips and thighs, and he reached for her delicate wrists. Once he had them in his grip, he brought them up over her head so that her knuckles grazed the wood wall behind her.

She arched her back and tipped her head to see what she was touching, and let out a soft "Oh!" Brochan had liberated the barn of its rotting planks and replaced them with a handmade work of art. Slats of wood in every shade—gray, pale brown, taupe, red, different red, new red, other red—fit together like pieces in a Tetris game. It was stunning, in a rugged sort of way.

Brochan took advantage of her position to pepper her chest

with firm kisses. Then he licked her; ran his tongue all the way up her neck. He was still holding her arms above her head, and she tried to wriggle free so she could grab at his back and pull him in closer to her. Even though he was already quite close. The closest a person can be, really.

"No," Brochan said. "Your hands stay there." He kissed his way down her chest and bit the patch of skin between her breast and her armpit. His voice rolled deeper into a low, gentle cadence. "Dinna distract me."

His skin was slick with sweat against hers, and his body, with all its masculine heft, felt comfortingly heavy. Even though Ruby had wanted this from the first moment she saw him, she was glad they had taken their time. It was worth the wait, worth every second.

"I missed you," she said, which didn't exactly relay how she felt, but she hoped he would understand all the same.

"I never knew how much I could want someone until I had you in my bed," he said, bringing her hands to his mouth and kissing her fingertips tenderly. "Your nails are short," he said. "And there's about a bushel's worth of compost wedged in them."

She laughed. "Meaning?"

"They're not talons. They make you seem more real to me, less like a fantasy." He rubbed her thumbnail between his fingers. "I like them." He released her hands and trailed his mouth to her stomach. "I need you."

Ruby writhed a bit, twisting up the sheet in her fists. "How *much* do you need me?"

"Absolutely the largest amount of needing."

Ruby was happy with that answer.

Brochan continued his journey down the terrain of Ruby's body, and when he got where he had intended to go, he kissed her. Oh, how he kissed her. Brochan did things with his tongue that no golf-playing finance guy would ever do. Unspeakable things.

Ruby was as warm and soft and sweet as she had ever been.

He moved his mouth to her inner thigh then and looked up at her. "Are you ready for me?" he asked.

"Oh yes. Very ready. Awfully ready. The most amount of ready!" She crooked her finger in the air and coaxed him closer.

Brochan's hair fell down around his face as he lowered himself on top of Ruby. His right hand found her left again, and with his other, he cupped her head and gripped her curls. He yanked back authoritatively. Ruby gasped in delight.

She liked that she didn't have to ask him for the things that drove her wild, and that everything he did was everything she desired. When he entered her, it was like he had always lived there, inside. It felt like he was finally coming home.

They went slowly, lazily, at first, like a dance and a conversation. Brochan would draw himself almost entirely out of Ruby, causing her to squirm around and grab at him with her short, mild-mannered nails. *Come back!* she'd beg, and only then, only a second *after* she'd asked, would he bury himself inside her. Each time he pulled away, he was acknowledging Ruby's hesitation and fears. And every time he met the deepest part of her, he was reassuring them both that *yes*, this was real and good and he was here, right here, and that she could trust him.

Ruby was about to lose her mind. "Brochan—" she said.

"Let's go together." She reached her mouth up to his. He kissed her roughly, sucking on her lip and pressing his forehead into the bridge of her nose. He didn't speak, but he moved faster. Ruby tightened herself around him, willing him to stay. Their bodies moved in rhythm and their faces remained close, touching. When they finally released, Ruby shouted and slammed at the wood wall behind her. Outside, a cow mooed. Brochan collapsed onto her, his ear over her heart, which was drumming joyously. They stayed together, just like that. They stayed there for a long time.

Chapter Twenty-Five

"So. Tour," Brochan said, standing stark naked at the sink and pouring a glass of water for them to share.

"Finally," Ruby said, wrapping his gray sheet around her like a cloak. It was nighttime now; the sky had darkened.

Brochan delivered the water and she drank heartily. He took the glass from her hand and replaced it with a tumbler of whisky. "Sip. Tell me all about what you taste."

Ruby let the sheet relax and it fell down around her shoulders. She brought the liquor up to her lips and considered it thoughtfully. "Caramel," she noted immediately.

"Is it burnt?" Brochan asked. Ruby playfully bopped him on the nose.

"No, like caramel sauce, with butter and cream in it." She sipped and held the liquid in her mouth for a moment. It sang out; it was so vibrantly alive that Ruby couldn't believe she had ever put ice cubes in her whisky. (Maybe someday she would confess this to Brochan; maybe she wouldn't.) "I feel like I've tasted it before, but I can't place from where." She wrinkled her nose, trying to correctly place the memory. "There are so many happy things in this glass."

Brochan took a sip and handed it back to her. He tucked one of her curls back into place. "There are so many happy things in this barn."

Ruby warmed. "This is heavier than the Balvenie you had last night. It's almost meaty. But then I taste it, and it's all— 'Baked oatmeal! With toasted coconut! And a brown sugar sprinkle!'" She handed the whisky back to Brochan, and he sipped, and observed all these things, too.

"Come here. First stop on the tour."

Ruby dropped the sheet and grabbed his T-shirt, which had, in the heat of things, landed in a bowl of apples on the counter. She pulled it over her head; it smelled like sweat and campfire mixed with eucalyptus mixed with peppermint. A curious scent, but a scent all Brochan. Ruby crossed the smooth wood floor, laid with chunky, knotted wide planks, to an open doorway that must have once been a stall for horses. In it now was a copper whisky still, the shape of a drum.

"Can I . . . ?" Ruby extended her arm out toward the still. "Can I touch it?"

Brochan laughed, big and booming. "Yes," he said. "It's not in operation."

Clearly not. But it was magnificent. The fat little still was obviously old. It looked weathered and wore a rustic patina. It was covered with a bulbous top, and the seam between the basin and lid seemed to have been sealed with a sort of paste and broken countless times; next to the still sat a coiled tube in a tin wash-basin. The tubing was made of copper, too.

"This was what my great-great grandfather used to distill whisky," Brochan said proudly. Although the still seemed laughably rustic today, he said, it was standard for the era. The coiled tube—commonly known as the worm—would have been kept in a tub of cool water to affect the condensation levels. And that seal? It would've been made with flour and water. As the years and technology advanced, this still was kept at the Grottie Hermitage as a reminder of the past. By the time Grant (at his father's name, Brochan swallowed like he was trying to take a bitter medicine without tasting it) was distilling whisky, he had a modern still. Which he had sold for cash before skipping town. Of course. The bastard.

Brochan didn't just like drinking whisky, Ruby realized. It ran in his blood.

"Wait, Brochan. Do you make whisky?" she asked. "Did you make *this*?"

"What's in your glass? No, that's Grant's work again. Hate the man, love his whisky. What you're drinking is over thirty years old. It's special." Ruby nodded. She could taste that.

"And, no, I don't make it. I've been bottling the last of Grant's barrels over the years. And I've learned enough that I could, but it probably wouldn't be very tasty. And"—he slapped the copper kettle affectionately—"I don't have a working still."

Ruby started to argue, but Brochan wasn't being modest. Making whisky was hard. She understood that much about it.

"Really, it's as much art and craft as it is science. It takes a long time to become a master. And a long time to age it. Patience is a requirement." He waited a moment. "I damn well would like the chance to try, but there haven't been too many opportunities here in Thistlecross."

"So this is how they made Speyside whisky back in the day?"

"Well, there was no 'Speyside' in the 1850s," Brochan explained. "The regional variations we use now are interesting to think about . . . but can I be honest?" Ruby gulped. *Honest. Right.* "I think most of it is just marketing lingo. Every distiller's product is different, but you can play with the variables to create whatever 'type' of whisky you want. You can make a smoky, peaty monster in the Highlands. Just like you'll find some refined beauties in Islay."

Ruby came closer and touched her knees to his shins. Brochan held the glass to her lips and tipped the amber liquid onto her tongue. A trickle escaped the corner of her mouth and she licked it up. Brochan set the whisky on a windowsill and stooped down to kiss the place where the liquor had landed. She made a small noise of satisfaction. Starlight hinted at a low, long bookshelf along one wall; a makeshift kitchen against the other. The barn was homey without being fussy. It was the sort of place you could imagine making a life in, especially if you imagined doing so with a bearded Scot.

"Refined beauties, eh?" Ruby asked.

He looked at her with adoration. "You are a bizarre and wonderful woman," he said.

"I'm a sleepy one," she said, enjoying the warming sensation of whisky in her body.

"Well then you, wild little Islay lady, ought to be put to bed," he said, picking her up and tossing her over his shoulder. As he strode across the floor, Ruby pounded his back with her fists but she was joking. Because she was quite happy. The happiest a person can be, really.

Chapter Twenty-Six

For the next handful of weeks, Ruby and Brochan held space for joy and dread alike, for fear and bliss both. Now that Anne had ripped the bandage off and finally broken the news to Grace, word was spreading like heather seeds on the wind. A town meeting was scheduled for the fifteenth of August, at which "all questions and concerns would be entertained and thoughtfully addressed," if you believed the message posted on the Thistlecross Facebook page. Brochan was readying himself for war. He had questions. The man had *concerns*. Although everyone around the Cosy Hearth was largely ignoring the feeling of impending doom, Brochan had made a few comments in passing to Ruby. From those comments, three things were clear:

1. *Brochan held Anne solely responsible for the sale of the pub/deterioration of the town's morals.*
2. *He did not want Grant to come back.*
3. *He was prepared to fight tooth and nail—or at least, word and fist—to stop the Wee Tartan Bagpipe from opening its doors.*

What could Ruby say about all this? Nothing; she could say nothing at all.

Grace and Neil were aligned with Brochan, of course, but beyond that, the ranks of his soldiers looked a little sparse. It seemed that although everyone else in Thistlecross was sad about the loss of the Cosy Hearth (and thus the memory of the Grottie Hermitage), they generally agreed about three things:

1. *A shiny new restaurant would bring in a new wave of tourists and their money—which the residents of Thistlecross needed.*
2. *It was quite a shame, and they didn't want to say it out loud, but when you got right down to brass tacks, the fact was that no one ever went to the Cosy Hearth anymore. Except for Neil, and honestly, how much longer was he going to be kicking around? Awful; they felt just awful for saying it. But there it was.*
3. *Mayor Dunbar was kind of a wench and was probably not going to change her mind, so why bother arguing?*

Sofie and Mac stopped coming to the Sunday suppers, which was sad because after their red wine chat, Ruby had started to think of Sofie as a pal. Not a replacement for Lee, but a sweet, unexpected joy in her new life. And after a few weeks, everyone else but Neil stopped coming, too. So Ruby and Grace put a pin in things and went back to their casual dinners around the bar with Neil and Brochan. At times, Carson would wave and smile apologetically as he passed a window.

Now that the cat was out of the bagpipe (*Wait*—), Ruby felt a shameful sense of relief. She was no longer keeping a secret from Brochan, she rationalized, so she could just focus on supporting him through this stressful mess. And she did want to support him. Really, she did! She just wasn't entirely sure how: what to do or say.

Obviously losing the pub to a gross plaid-themed chain restaurant would be tragic. But his father might be coming *home*. There was hurt, but didn't he want the chance to start over? To know the man who had created him? Ruby couldn't be sure, never having been abandoned by her father.

She thought about all this one morning as she harvested spicy arugula leaves from her garden. Ultimately, it wasn't up to her to dictate how Brochan felt about all this. She could hardly count herself a warrior in this battle. She wasn't even a resident of Thistlecross. Well—she amended, letting fantasy run far afield—not yet, anyway. She would attend the town meeting by Brochan's side, squeezing his hand when he got heated, and being there for him afterward. That's how to be in a relationship, right? Ruby had all but forgotten.

As for how to show up for her new friend, the mayor of Thistlecross? That was a little trickier. Ruby hadn't quite worked it out yet. Because Ruby was rather otherwise occupied.

Because there were happy times that month, too. Romance novel times. Falling in love in your midthirties or your almost forties is a unique sort of beauty. It's every bit as exciting as you remember, but you're older and wiser than the last eight hundred times. So you tend to vacillate between proverbial cliff jumping and retreating into the safe space of solo nights with elastic-waist pants, takeaway food, and streaming movies.

Except Ruby didn't have internet in the cottage. And there weren't that many options for takeaway. And she was really quite smitten. So when she and Brochan weren't hiking through the pine forest near Moss Glen Falls, taking day trips to taste whisky at Glenlivet, or screwing for hours with Ruby's back against the door of the cottage, the floor of the barn, or literally any semi-flat surface, she was writing to him. On nights they spent apart, Ruby leaned into the boldness that she felt when armored with the written word. What seemed too forward, silly, or trivial to ask in voice flowed rather easily through the pen. She would write a question or two in her wild, looping script, and decorate the paper with a small painting, usually an animal or flower she'd seen near the pines. She would then seal the message in an envelope and make the short walk to Brochan's barn, where she leaned the letter up against his window—the pane that was decorated in leaded glass. The pane that matched hers. And then she would bolt away, because they had promised to take the night off from seeing each other. Promised to give each other room to breathe.

But Brochan always replied promptly, like he'd been waiting for her all along. By the time Ruby woke the next morning, there would be a folded piece of paper waiting on *her* leaded glass window.

Dear Brochan,

What is your favorite part about being Scottish? What is your least?

xx,

Roo

Hullo. Roo–

My favorite part is literally everything.

My least favorite is literally everything.

It's a unique sort of self-loathing, being Scottish.

You have a fine arse.

Brochan

Broo,

What do you like best about my arse?

Roo

Roo. What don't I like about your arse.

But perhaps best is when you're on top of me, having your way, and I reach for it and hold on tightly, guiding you as we move together.

Second best is how it looks in those black pants of yours.

Third best is how you do that little squirmy thing and pretend not to enjoy it when I smack you there.

But I know you do enjoy it.

Dear Brochan,

A hard but important question:

What is your dream job? It's okay to say, "I already have it."

I used to think mine was working for a food magazine, then writing a cookbook, but I don't think either of those things anymore. I don't know what comes next.

Help!

Roo,

Fixing other people's leaky pipes is not my idea of career satisfaction.

(Probably not a big surprise there.)

In my perfect world, I'd be distilling whisky. No question about it.

That's the dream.

I think that you should just keep doing what feels good, and see if anything interesting happens from there.

I don't know if that helps. I hope it helps a little.

You,

If you were here or I were there, where and how would you be kissing me? Use lots of details and describe everything.

—Me

I would be there. Because I could never ask you to leave your cosy wee flophouse in the middle of the night. So I would come to you. You'd be in bed and although you'd try to get up when I arrived, I would tell you to stay exactly where you are.

The first spot I'd place my lips would be at the edge of

your eye, where the creases and crinkles of your past smiles live. (Is that obnoxiously fancy? Yes, and I don't care.) My touch would be light, it would be gentle, because you are delicate and small and wild and I don't want to startle you.

So I would take my time, touching my lips all the way up your neck. And then I would kiss your right cheek. Your left. Your forehead, with tenderness. Your chin, with a smile. And then I would bring my mouth to yours, and I would kiss you patiently and carefully.

Missing you—
Broo

Do you believe in astrology? I do and I don't.

Same. But maybe a little more on the "don't." And a lot less on the "do."

Okay, Ruby, it is absolute drivel. You have to know that???
But the fact that you believe in it somehow endears you to me even more.

Damn it.

Dear Brochan,
What is your biggest fear?
From, Ruby

Dear Ruby,
That is not the sort of question one can casually answer through an overnight post.

But my second-biggest fear is the Headless Horseman of Glen More. On the Isle of Mull. Spooky stuff. I'll take you there sometime. If you promise to hold my hand.

Of course, Brochan wrote letters with questions for Ruby, too.

Who's your favorite musician? You can't say "It's so hard to choose!" You must choose.
  P.S.: I know it's not Stevie Wonder . . .

Broo,
  Oooh, but it IS so hard to choose. Ugh. Okay. Gun to my head? Stevie NICKS. Absolute goddess. Just so damn good. Fleetwood Mac!!!
  Roo

Roo.
  I must admit, I'm pleased by your answer.
  I sure would like to lay you down in the tall grass, anyway.
  What do you like best about living in Scotland? What do you like least?
  Broo

Who's the journalist now? Those are excellent questions, Mr. Brochan.
  My favorite part about living in Scotland is, I suppose, the Sunday suppers. It makes me feel so sad that they've stopped. They gave me purpose. Here is a secret: I liked

them even better than I liked writing that stupid cookbook.
Although I could technically be doing them in New York,
they're more fun here, at the Cosy Hearth. It's like they
need to be here to survive.

My least favorite part about living in Scotland is
knowing that it was kind of, sort of, supposed to be
temporary. But don't I make the rules? And what is
"temporary," anyhow?

Must I always write a dissertation in response to your
simple questions?

Ruby,
Yes, you must. Because you are a writer.
Brochan

Ruby,
Why don't you move here for good?
Brochan

Was this all happening very fast? *Yes.*
Did Ruby have fears? *A zillion and one.*
Did she trust Brochan? *Weirdly, mostly.*

If this was a romance novel, Ruby thought, she would be
nodding her head seriously and saying, "He's the one. I guess it's
true: When you know, you know."

But this wasn't a romance novel, was it? This was Ruby's life,
full of doubt and ennui and cookbook rejections and wiry gray
hairs. She may have been falling for Brochan, but she was still

waiting for the other boot to drop. Everything was so excellent and so awful at the same time. Was she on the verge of setting her world on fire for an orgasm-fueled romp for the next six months? For the chance to toast some marshmallows?

She just couldn't shake the knowledge that something bad *always* happens when things start to get good.

Chapter Twenty-Seven

A week before the scheduled meeting, Ruby decided to do a sneaky thing. Well, another sneaky thing. Even sneakier than the first sneaky thing she had done.

It was Wednesday morning, and after Brochan had properly kissed Ruby goodbye, he set off for work. He had to pick up some bathroom tiles in Glasgow; apparently they were top-of-the-line stuff and worth the drive. Ruby half listened as he chatted about the renovation, making *aha*, and *mm-hmm* sounds at the appropriate places. But her mind was elsewhere.

As soon as she lost sight of his truck's dust trail on the road, she set her mug in the sink and yanked on a pair of pants and her favorite sweater. She ran her fingers through her curls and wiggled her feet into her shoes, pulling up on the heel to snug them on. She walked down Brochan's driveway and up the road and into the Cosy Hearth, where she found Grace cleaning up after the morning's bake.

"I'll deliver these to the Traveler," Ruby said, already starting to pack the scones—bacon and cheddar—into a cardboard box. "You stay here and relax. Have a second cup of coffee."

Grace agreed, happy to tick a chore off her to-do list, and untied her apron. Ruby waved, then set off toward town. She left the scones with the front desk clerk, who brought them into the kitchen. And then Ruby exited the hotel, took a left, and walked toward the town hall.

Anne was in her office with the door closed. Her receptionist, a young woman who had graduated highers the year prior, made Ruby wait while she spoke into the telephone.

"There's someone here to see you."

There was a pause on the line.

"It's a woman."

Another pause, and the secretary gave Ruby a quick once-over.

"No, dunno." A beat. "No appointment."

Ruby sighed and shifted her weight.

The receptionist held her hand over the receiver and said to Ruby, "What's your business?"

"Um," Ruby said, trying for an official sort of phrasing. "State business?"

The girl gave her a blank look.

"I mean—I need to talk to Mayor Dunbar."

"Obviously."

"It's kind of personal."

It was the receptionist's turn to sigh, as she relayed this into the phone. A moment later, the door behind her opened, just a crack. A set of ballet-pink nails snaked out around the frame.

"What's the secret password?" came Anne's voice through the gap, followed by conspiratorial, gleeful laughter. The door opened all the way, and there was Anne, in a cream-colored stretch linen dress. "A joke, obviously. I was rather sure it was you. God, how embarrassing would that have been if it *wasn't*?"

Ruby laughed. She had been a little nervous, but now she just felt good and light.

"Ruby, this is Ellen. Ellen is my brain. She's a star. Ellen, this is Ruby; she's new in town, but a friend. So she gets special privileges— you can drop the interrogation for her."

"Pleased," Ellen said, tittering.

"Doubly pleased," said Ruby, trying to put her at ease. Mayor Dunbar was a big presence; she was probably downright intimidating to a young woman. Hell, half the time Ruby was intimidated by her.

"Come on in," Anne said, waving Ruby through the doorway. Ruby sank into a gray velour chair across from the desk, on which Anne had perched. "It's been a spell since I've seen you."

"It has," said Ruby. "How are you?"

"Oh, on top of the world. Staggering under the crushing weight of civic pressure. Everything's braw, everything's shite. The normal."

Ruby gave a small smile. "So . . . you talked to Grace."

"As promised." Anne frowned. "It was just about as rough as I thought it'd be. Och, I felt like such a monster."

"Yeah. I think she was in shock for a while. Brochan was upset, too. I mean, he still is."

Anne unscrewed the top of a glass water bottle and took a sip.

"I'm putting our reconciliation rate at a negative one hundred at this point."

"He told me everything. About his mother, and his father, and the Grottie Hermitage, and about Winkler."

Anne gave a slow nod. "He told you . . . everything?"

"Yep. So I understand a little better why he's so pissed off. Why didn't you talk to him, too?"

"He does not want to hear from me."

"No, but is it possible he doesn't know how much Thistlecross needs the money? Maybe if he heard your side of things . . . ?"

"Maybe, but probably not."

There was a pause, and neither woman spoke.

"The real reason"—Ruby broke the silence—"the real reason I came was to ask if it was too late. If the contract hadn't been signed yet, maybe someone else could buy the pub."

Anne's eyebrow arched upward toward her glossy red hair. "Someone else? Like who?"

"Well, me," said Ruby. And again, that word: "Maybe?"

Anne's eyebrow disappeared under her razor-cut bangs. "Do you have that kind of capital?"

"I have a retirement account. And a decade of 401k, with matching from my old company. It's got to be at least enough for a down payment."

Anne didn't say anything.

"Well, how much is Winkler paying?"

"Ruby, over four hundred thousand pounds."

"Hold on." Ruby pulled out her phone and did a quick google. "Fuck. That's almost half a million dollars."

Anne made a *more-or-less* gesture.

"Well. I'm an idiot."

"No! You're sweet. I wish I could sell the pub to you, Ruby. But even if you were brimming with fat stacks of cash, Winkler's signed the papers. It's set in motion."

"When is everything . . . happening?"

"There's time. We'll wait for the dust to settle a bit after the meeting next week."

Ruby nodded stoically, still trying to shove down the fiery embarrassment she felt over thinking she could actually afford to buy the pub. "Do you know if Brochan's dad is going to be involved in this?"

"I do not. The less I'm involved, the better. But I bet he'll at minimum be a presence, in the beginning of things."

"Yeah, that's what I was guessing. Am I a bad girlfriend if I secretly want Brochan's father to come back? For his sake? Even if he claims he doesn't want him here?"

Anne's posture softened a little. "Oh, you're properly together, then?"

The tips of Ruby's ears turned pink. "Well, I don't know. He's never called me his girlfriend. At least, not to my face. But I care about him, in a way that feels big and real and . . . scary."

Anne reached over and grabbed Ruby's hand. She squeezed once. "I'm pleased that he found his way to such a bright woman. He and I may have our differences, but I'll always want the world for my best childhood mate. And, for my new best mate. Who is you."

Ruby squeezed back, then released her hand. "Thank you. So . . . are you dating anyone?"

Barking out a quick, prickly laugh, Anne got up from the desk. "No. The mayor of Thistlecross doesn't get a happily ever after. Or even a happy for right now. At least, not if she's a thirty-something woman who was bullied by half the town in primary school. All of whom now hate her guts and think she's wildly incompetent because she doesn't have a tube sock between her thighs."

"It seems so hard to be in your position. I don't know how you do it."

"I don't know that any mayor of a small town finds life *easy*. But, aye, I feel bothered over the fact that my predecessors were happily settled with a wife, two and a half kids, and a golden retriever by the time they took up office." She let out a sigh and her bangs billowed upward. "Sometimes, I wonder if I've completely bludgeoned any chance I have at romance. But then I remember: I wanted this."

"Can I ask, then—why you did? What made you want to run for mayor in the first place?"

Anne, who was pacing, stopped. "Because I love Thistlecross, Ruby. I love this town, and its odd little quirks, and even though they frustrate me to no end, I love every person in it. I love it better than anywhere I've been or anything I've done. I left when I was young, and that was both foolish and clever." She frowned seriously. "I've been enough places and done enough things to be in a position to help the town move forward. It's my responsibility."

The computer dinged, warning of a meeting in ten minutes. Anne moved toward the door, and Ruby followed, extending her hand. She pushed it aside, and gathered Ruby in a hug. It felt familiar and warm, and it made her want to cry. The women embraced, and Ruby couldn't help but notice that Anne smelled very nice, like green tea with handpicked jasmine flowers floating in it. Or at least, jasmine flowers that were marketed to have been handpicked.

"If it makes you feel any better, I'm a little jealous," Ruby said as they parted. "I wish I felt that way about where I live."

"You do, though."

Ruby cocked her head, taking this in. It was kind of true; after all, hadn't she just attempted to save a historical town landmark with like, seventeen thousand dollars? Plus, she had *at least* two friends here.

And, she thought, as she walked into the late-summer sun, despite the fact that she had absolutely, positively not planned on it, Ruby Spencer was falling in love.

Chapter Twenty-Eight

On August 15, Ruby was a jangle of nerves. She spent the morning baking with Grace, but neither woman was focused. Or steady. Grace did injustice to her name, dropping countless tools and spilling ingredients, while Ruby kept fudging up the measurements. Their worry hung in the air so thick you could have spread it on a scone with a butter knife.

Finally, Ruby set down her spatula and said to Grace, "We're a mess. Wanna talk about it?"

Grace chuckled. "You get bolder each day you're here, lass—you realize that?"

Ruby smiled proudly.

Grace thought, then spoke. "I'm just an old woman. I'm not keen to try and stop a train that's already set in motion. If the pub is sold, we will survive. If Grant comes back, I will welcome him. But it's the not knowing that's working away at me."

"Oof. That makes sense. But sometimes . . ." Ruby got quiet and ran her middle finger along the almost-empty bowl, collecting a streak of cream and depositing it in her mouth. "Sometimes, I *want* Grant to come back. For Brochan's sake. I think he should give his dad a chance to make amends. They'll never get anywhere if they don't at least meet. But am I just being insensitive?"

"Grant has a big heart and a frail conviction. Brochan has a long memory and a short fuse." She shrugged. "If only these damn men would put their pride aside and let the women make some decisions. We'd all be the better for it."

"Ha. Indeed. So what does all this mean for tonight—for the meeting? What do we do in this specific instance?"

Grace tucked her chin and put on a thoughtful face. "We do what women have done for centuries. We listen. We observe. We wait. And then, when the men have made an irreparable mess out of everything, we quietly do what we must."

"Sounds good," Ruby said, even though it sounded tricky.

Brochan was working on installing radiant heat flooring for one of his clients, which was a shame; Ruby could think of one or two things that would have distracted them both from the meeting-related anxiety. Instead, she decided to spend the rest of the afternoon tending the last planting in her garden. She had put hardy herbs, sage and rosemary, in the ground earlier that month. She hoped that they'd take her through the rest of summer; with the thermal cover they would stay toasty even as the season flirted with fall temperatures. As she yanked weeds from the earth, she wondered how she could have become so entangled in Thistlecross in only a handful of months. Just like that, she had a community, the potential for a job she liked doing. If things settled down, she thought, surely the Family Table would pick right back up. Location . . . TBD. She also had a vested stake in how the future took shape. She may never truly belong here, but, she thought with a rush of pride, Anne was right. Ruby's presence was felt. She had never experienced such a sensation in New York, where she was just another nobody taking up space on the subway.

The meeting was scheduled for six o'clock that night, so Ruby, Brochan, Grace, and Neil ate dinner together at the Cosy Hearth beforehand. Ruby tried to crack a few jokes, which went over like a lead balloon. Then she tried to get everyone to talk about their feelings, which, *hello*, was never going to happen. Finally, she gave up and forked beet and goat cheese quiche into her mouth, and scraped at the worn wooden corner of the bar with her fingernail. After the dishes were washed, they each took a quick swig of Grant's whisky. Neil looked thoughtfully at the bottle and asked Grace how much was left. "After this? A few. We'll have to start rationing it, I suppose." She replaced the cap and set the whisky back on the shelf.

"Someone should fire up the still again," said Neil. "Don't much care who." He reached into his vest pocket and took a pull from his personal supply. "Though I'm sure I'll be decomposing in a peat bog by the time anything new is ready to drink."

Ruby jabbed at Brochan's rib cage with her elbow and mouthed the words *dream job*.

Brochan grabbed the sleeve of her cream sweater and pulled her close. "It's just a pipe dream," he whispered in her ear. "I've got my place and my person. What more do I need?"

Grace's ears perked up, and she shooed Neil out the door as

she snuffed most of the candles, leaving the two on the bar burning. "We'll see you there, then."

Brochan rummaged around in his pants pocket for a moment with a mischievous look on his face. Ruby looked toward the door where Grace and Neil had just left. This was a setup!

"What on earth are you doing in that pocket?"

His smirk morphed into a genuine grin. "Never you mind." He unearthed whatever it was he'd been searching for, then pulled Ruby onto his lap. She perched nervously, waiting for whatever came next.

"I'm out of practice in telling beautiful women how special they are," he began, worrying his thumb over the trinket in his hand. "So forgive me; I'm likely to be awkward and dumb. But I'll try my best." Ruby's heart caught in her throat. *Oh my God.*

He continued, "I'd long since resigned myself to being on my own, which was fine. I wasn't willing to settle for a woman who didn't make me want to be a better man. A woman who I could be honest with, and who gave me that in return." Ruby swallowed hard. Brochan continued with a wink, "Even if that woman steals all the blankets in the middle of the night."

Ruby nodded. This was all so sweet, even though he was obviously the one who stole all the blankets. Brochan coughed nervously and her mind leaped forward. *Is this really happening? It's so fast. It's too fast? Do I want this? I think I want this. Think think think think think.*

He squeezed her waist with his free hand and looked soulfully into her eyes. "And you do. Make me want to be better. Just by virtue of being you. Curious, clever, sweet you."

"You think I'm clever?"

"Aye. I am continually impressed by your resilience and ability to try new things. By your bravery. By how you show up for your life."

They were so very different from each other, Ruby and Brochan, but then, the poles of his personality that were furthest from her own were the things she found most attractive in him. Was it really so hard to believe he could want her for exactly who she was? It was a tad easier to believe while sitting on his lap and getting showered with praise. And receiving whatever present he was about to give her.

Brochan opened his palm to reveal a smooth oval of wood strung on a simple gold strand. The wood was the size of a silver dollar and lacquered smooth with a pale stain. A necklace.

Instinctively, Ruby gathered her hair and lifted it as Brochan clasped the chain around her neck. The wood lay right at the diamond where her collarbones dipped into her chest. Where he liked to kiss her.

Not too fast. Just right. Just . . . perfect.

"It's rowan wood," Brochan said, and his round cheeks turned red as he added, "Rooan Wood?"

Just right. Just perfect.

Ruby loved the necklace. She loved Thistlecross, Scotland. She loved the Cosy Hearth. And she really loved Brochan Wood. She almost said that last part out loud, but she grew frightened that the gift of those words would be either too small or too large, and she didn't want to give him anything less than just perfect. So instead, she teased his mouth open with hers and whispered, "I love it. I adore you."

She wiggled around a bit, grinding herself onto his lap which was now firm with his excitement. She slow-walked her fingers all the way down from his throat to his zipper, and hummed as he grabbed her hand and kissed it feverishly.

"Lass, you are going to be the death of me. Or at least, make us late for this very important meeting."

Ruby nodded. "Girl Scout's honor; I won't distract you." Her face grew serious then, and she wrapped her arms around his neck.

"I know this isn't my fight, but I'm here for you."

"I hope so, Roo. Because, well—there's something I want to ask you. Later."

Ruby's eyes sparkled like fairy pools in twilight on the Isle of Skye. *Too fast? Too soon?* Her mouth started to form one of the zillion questions *she* desperately wanted to ask. Brochan quieted them all with a hearty kiss, then took her hand and led her to the town hall. She would not ask. She would not! She would find contentment in the uncertainty and she would wait.

But oh my, would it be hard.

Chapter Twenty-Nine

For the most part, these meetings came and went with little notice. Mayor Dunbar was always present, along with the council members, and maybe one or two folks who had a vested interest in decreasing the speed limit by two and a half miles per hour or something like that. All things considered, these meetings were sleepy, boring affairs that nobody cared about.

Until the fifteenth of August.

Everyone, by now, knew that the Cosy Hearth was going to be sold. But the details beyond that ranged from sparse—"The new owner is from out of town"—to the wildly embellished—"The building is going to be razed to the ground to make room for a goat yoga retreat center." So most everyone had shown up to the meeting to get some real answers.

Brochan let out a low whistle when he and Ruby opened the doors. It was standing room only, and that was being generous. His eyes scanned the space for a place to park their bodies, and was grateful when he saw Grace waving to them from across the floor. He made a pathway through the crowd, bringing Ruby along with him, and they squeezed into a row of folding chairs.

The ceiling was low, and Ruby felt a touch claustrophobic. It reminded her of rush hour on the 6 train in Manhattan. At least here, she was surrounded by friends and it didn't smell like pee. She closed her eyes and tried to recall what it felt like to ride the subway, but was surprised to discover that the memories had gone fuzzy and out of focus, as if they belonged to someone else. As if they'd never really been hers at all. Ruby wasn't sure what that meant, or if it was good or bad.

A gavel gave a few irritated bangs on a wooden block, and Ruby's eyes flew open, squeezing Brochan's hand once. He squeezed back twice.

One, two. Me and you.

Anne was sitting at a plastic table—the kind with legs that can be kicked in and folded underneath for easy storage—with three other official-looking people, two in cardigans and another in tweed pants. Oh, Scotland. How Ruby loved it. Even the town meetings were plaid-ier.

The room's chatter slowed to a gentle hush when Anne cleared her throat into a microphone set on the table. As she called the meeting to order, Brochan set his jaw. Ruby bit at her cheeks and played with her braid. Grace stared stoically ahead. Neil, the charming old devil, took another nip from a flask.

The room was carpeted with a thick, hazy feeling of unrest as the agenda items were ticked off. Anne had saved the best for last; the woman knew how to give good political theater.

"And finally, the moment I *assume* you've been waiting for unless you were all genuinely interested in the fold orientation on the updated town map." The room was quiet. "Oh, come now.

That was a joke!" Ruby laughed for her new friend, and Brochan gave her a fiery look.

Anne ticked off a summary of the deal. The town of Thistlecross owned the building containing the Cosy Hearth. It was currently being rented by Grace Wood as a pub; it was operating at a loss. A significant loss. An out-of-town buyer had expressed interest in taking over the property. Said buyer would keep the original structure, but perform significant repairs and upgrades. Said buyer would open a new restaurant in its place, one sure to bring an influx of tourism to Thistlecross. Their town would never rival Inverness, but if they had a waterfall, a snazzy hotel, *and* an American-friendly restaurant? Well, now . . . Said new restaurant had a proven record of success, and was well established in the States. The building's sale price was large. Shockingly large, which was excellent news for the town purse. Which was good for everybody.

There was a steady thrum of conversation as most folks in the crowd murmured in appreciation. They weren't here because they wanted to contest the sale. On the contrary, they were just about bursting with curiosity as to who was behind it.

"Are there any comments, questions, or concerns from the room?" Anne asked, her gaze steady but her voice wavering. Just a little.

"I have one, *Mayor*." Brochan raised his hand in mock respect for his old friend's authority. "Where do you suggest my aunt ought to live after you kick her out of her home?" Anne opened her mouth, but Brochan had more. "And her tenant?" He nodded in Ruby's direction and her chest reddened.

Don't look at me! she thought.

But Brochan was looking at her, along with everyone else in the room. He continued: "As far as I understand, Ruby Spencer signed a yearlong lease for one of the buildings on the property. And she has been using the kitchen at the Cosy Hearth for her work and business. If you won't honor the livelihood and home of Grace, a lifelong Thistlecross resident, perhaps your heart will be swayed by one of our guests?"

Ruby felt sick as her eyes bored a hole in the wood floor.

Oh, Brochan.

Please shut up.

A murmur went up through the crowd. Anne raised an eyebrow, and Ruby could tell that she was doing quick calculations about their previous conversations, and what had been said to Brochan, and what hadn't.

"Ms. Spencer?" Anne's voice was seasoned with a new touch of anxiety.

Ruby struggled for words and wove her fingers into a puzzle in front of her waist. "I . . . that's true. I've been living there. And using the kitchen. And I do love it. It's the sweetest place in all Thistlecross; at least I think so, anyway." Brochan nudged her with his hip. Ruby's discomfort and anger jockeyed for position in the driver's seat. "It would be a shame to lose it. A shame for the whole town, I think."

She looked at Grace, who was watching her closely. "But maybe, just maybe, there's some way to move forward with a little bit of the old and new together?" She was going off script. This wasn't what Brochan wanted her to say, but it was how she felt. "A new restaurant in an old town would be complicated. But what if it was good, too?"

The collective murmur became a din, and although it only lasted a second, she accepted Anne's look of gratitude.

Ruby could feel Brochan's disappointment at her response, but what did he expect? He had pinned her up against the wall, and *not* in the way that she liked. She hadn't expected to have to do public speaking tonight—or choose a side.

Grace looked worried; clearly Ruby hadn't "waited and observed" for quite as long as she ought to have. Everyone except Anne was unhappy with her performance. Screw it, she deserved to say what she thought. Her opinion was valid. And if she really was considering moving to Thistlecross for forever, it was important to do it on her own terms. Boyfriends were great and all, but—Ruby squeezed her eyes shut and chased away fear—what if things didn't work out?

"I have a question," called Sofie.

Ruby's heart swelled with appreciation for her new friend, although at that moment she would have fallen in love with just about anyone willing to take the spotlight from her. Sweet, sweet Sofie.

"Who's the potential buyer? Although I'm sad for Grace, I think the lot of us are looking forward to a new addition to our business district." She turned toward Grace and mouthed the word *Sorry!* "What sort of restaurant is it meant to be?"

"A fair question, Sofie, thanks for that," Anne replied, shuffling a few papers. "It's actually a restaurant with Scottish roots." Brochan snorted so loudly that he constricted his nasal passage and began to cough violently. Anne waited patiently. "The older among us will surely remember Grant Wood?"

The older among them nodded with serious expressions. The younger among them, who did not remember Grant Wood but knew his story and knew his son, whipped around to look at Brochan. A few jaws just about hit the floor.

"For the last few decades, he's been managing a growing group of restaurants in the States called the Wee Tartan Bagpipe." Anne raised her voice to barrel over a few groans. "And I'm happy to announce it's that very pub that'll be coming back to Thistle-cross. Maybe we'll even get lucky enough to welcome Grant back to town for a spell." Was it Ruby's imagination, or was Anne trying to meet Brochan's eye with that last sentence? Either way, he wasn't engaging.

Necks craned. The room quieted just long enough for Mac to wonder out loud, "Grant sold his pub to the town and he's . . . buying it back?"

"Well, technically no. That'd be the owner of the Wee Tartan Bagpipe."

"Fucking Wanker." Brochan's voice was low but Ruby heard it, and so did the man behind him.

"It's Winkler, actually." They whirled around. There he was. Louis Winkler. The lower half of his face had been worked into a grin, but his eyes were calculating. He wore a matte blue suit and a skinny tie. And he carried the evil-looking briefcase.

He set his case on the floor and the crowd rippled away from him. Winkler's eyes darted around the room as if scoping out the place, surveying it, and assessing what sort of damage he could do in the shortest possible time. At least, that's how it seemed to Ruby.

"Louis Winkler," he repeated, as if they all hadn't been hanging on to every word uttered in the last five minutes. "And, yes, I'm from the States, though I'm sure you've guessed that from my accent." He raised his hands in a *forgive me* gesture.

Ruby glanced up at the folding table, and saw that Anne looked irritated. Maybe *he* was going off script. Maybe this was just harder than she had anticipated. Maybe his overly dramatic entrance had thrown her. Regardless, Winkler had upended the meeting into chaos.

Next to Ruby, Brochan was seething. She sneaked a glance at him and saw that the veins in his neck were throbbing. Grace looked like she was about to cry. Again.

Winkler continued. "I hope you'll forgive my roots. I'm a fan of Scottish culture. And I do love whiskey."

Neil, who was awfully drunk by that point, cupped his hands around his mouth and hollered, "We can hear the *e* in your voice, ye American bastard!" A few people laughed; most everyone was equal parts horrified and delighted. "Here in Scotland, we drink whisky, not whiskey."

Winkler looked quizzically at the elderly man in the large vest with the gray comb-over, then he rolled his eyes.

"That's what I said. Whiskey."

Neil swatted a *never mind* at the air and slumped down into a chair.

"Anyway," Winkler continued. "It's a privilege to bring new life to your town. And although I myself won't be here for the majority of the construction of the restaurant, my business partner will oversee every detail." Winkler's eyes twinkled, but there was something untrustworthy beneath the shine.

"We'll be looking to hire for the full range of positions at the Wee Tartan Bagpipe. And we want to do it all locally; there's nothing better for a small-town economy than a successful restaurant. That's the level of commitment I plan to bring with my manager, Grant. I'll begin interviews tomorrow, at the Traveler Hotel. We're in particular need of waitresses, so if you think you fit the bill . . . come prepared to impress at eleven."

Louis Winkler cracked his right knuckle and he cracked his left knuckle. Then he twisted his lips into a very slow, very awful smile. "As I said, I do enjoy the Scottish culture. I think you'll agree that my restaurant will fit right in." And here, Winkler contorted his voice in an attempt to sound Scottish as he finished: "It's a bloody fun wee place."

Chapter Thirty

Winkler took a breath and then kept talking, but neither Ruby nor Brochan heard him. Brochan, who was seconds away from combusting, banged out the door without so much as a glance backward.

Ruby briefly wondered at whether she even wanted to go after him. There was the issue of him putting her on the spot, and forcing her into being his mouthpiece. And the issue of him being a hardheaded dum-dum who refused to consider anyone else's opinion. But then there was the issue of her being pretty sure she was falling madly, wildly, irreversibly in love with him.

Damn it, Brochan.

Ruby tossed a *see ya* look to Grace, and trotted out the door after him. She stood on the steps of the building, debating her next move, then made her way to his barn. *Swiftly.* When she arrived, she noted his truck still parked out by the old horse stalls, but there were no lights on in the barn. If he was sitting at home in the dark, he wasn't responding to her knocking. She reversed her steps down the drive, and somewhere in the dark, near her feet, a creature scampered. Ruby jumped and hurried to the Cosy

Hearth, but Brochan wasn't there, either. She stood in the doorway, biting at her cuticle and trying to figure where he would have gone.

If I were Brochan, what would I be feeling? she thought.

That's too complicated a question.

If I were Brochan, where would I go when I was upset?

I would go to the Isle of Skye.

But not the shitty touristy part.

The secret part.

But that's so far, too far for tonight.

And his truck is still here.

What does Brochan like about the Western Isles?

Feeling close to his history.

The wind, the rocks, the spray of the water.

The power.

Ruby set off for Moss Glen Falls, and although you'd never call her gait a run, you might consider it a sort of jog. If you were being generous.

I hoped I'd find you here," Ruby said when she found him there. Brochan looked up from the rock he was sitting on and gave her a sad smile.

"I wondered if you'd find me here," he said.

Ruby frowned, not sure of what to say.

"Am I that predictable?" he asked.

Ruby gave a sad smile back. "In lieu of Brother's Point . . ."

"Ah." Brochan didn't seem to have anything further to add at the moment. He stood and wiped off his pants before walking back to the path.

She fell into step with him. "So. Come here often?" Ruby said, then immediately regretted it.

"Ha. I do. Sort of. Normally, I like to be at the top of the falls."

"How so?"

"There's this split second before the water goes careening off the ledge. It's just an instant, but if you're there, you can watch potential energy become kinetic." *God, the man was so accidentally poetic.*

She nodded. "So why did you choose the bottom today, then?"

He shrugged, and touched his finger to her hip, then let go. "Supposing I just wanted to feel small. Because I do. Feel small, and powerless."

They were walking faster now, with no direction; just moving away from the waterfall and deeper into the pine forest. The farther they went, the quieter the night became and the better they could hear each other.

"Why did you say all that, back there?" Brochan asked, his voice at a low whisper.

"About the pub?"

"Yeah."

Ruby was afraid to look at him, so she watched the path as she spoke. "Because it's the way I feel, Broo."

His silence created space for her to keep on. "I don't know what it's like to be abandoned by a parent. Or to lose one. But I do wonder if your hurt over it is keeping you from considering the bigger picture."

Still, he didn't speak.

"For the record, I think that the Wee Tartan Bagpipe sounds truly heinous. And it wouldn't be the restaurant I chose to replace the Cosy Hearth. But I don't get to choose. And neither do you. So maybe we can find a way to unearth some good in all this. I refuse to believe this is a death sentence for you, for Grace, or for Thistlecross. Or for me."

"I think you're being idealistic. It's twee, Ruby, but you're seeing things as you wish they were, not as they are."

Ugh! Ruby pressed the heels of her hands into her forehead. He could be so dense. She didn't know what else to say, what would get through to him. Maybe this wasn't even her responsibility. She had been with him for, what? A month? Just under? "Maybe we're expecting too much from each other. Asking too much, too soon. I barely know you," she said, even though as the words left her mouth, she knew they were not true.

"Barely know me? I helped create your home here. Was there for you when you found out about your recipe book. Supported you with the Family Table. Ruby, I've been inside you. More than once. Not infrequently." He sighed, and moved close enough that they knocked into each other as they walked. "How much more do you need to know? What else do I have to do to prove that I want you? For real. For good.

"What do you want me to say? That every other woman I've been with has paled in comparison to you? That after I got my heart snapped in half by Margaret, I stopped trying? That I'd given up until you came to Thistlecross? That meeting you feels like fate, even though I don't believe in that sort of thing? That you're the person I've been waiting for? You're my equal; you're my better? I need you? Is that what you want, what you need? Do you just need me to say it out loud? Because it's true. It's all true, Roo."

No matter how much Ruby had wanted to move to Scotland to write a bestselling cookbook and find solace in living alone and become the Isle of Roo, none of that had happened. Other things had happened, instead. Complicated things. She had made friends, and fallen for a man, and found purpose in the act of feeding people. All that had happened when she wasn't looking. She had been so busy observing her experience, standing outside her body and watching someone else throw darts at a map of Scotland, that she had completely, utterly forgotten to live it.

Ruby wanted to stand up for her man, *and* she wanted to support her new friend. She wanted to assimilate into this new town, *and* she wanted to find a unique place for herself in it. She wanted everything equally, though none of it seemed to work together.

She had forgotten how messy life gets when you really show up to it.

The whole time they were walking, Ruby had been hurrying to keep up with Brochan's quick stride, but she grabbed his forearm now and swirled him around. They were standing in a small clearing with a few ferns scattered around the edges. Underneath their feet, a spongy bed of sphagnum moss spread out toward a small army of pines.

Ruby squeezed his arm tightly.

"I am sorry."

Brochan started to respond in kind, but she shook her head and dug her nails in harder. Brochan winced, just a little.

"I am sorry. Even though I tried to leave a whole suitcase of emotional baggage at Heathrow Airport, it followed me here." Brochan's face changed; the deep V between his eyebrows lessened and the crinkles around his eyes grew larger. Ruby grabbed his other arm and kept talking. "And you pushed me back there. So I got scared. Because I wasn't ready. But I'm ready now. I'll help you fight. I'll do whatever you need. Even if I don't always agree with you. Even though I'm still scared." She took a breath and released it, her exhale twice the length of the inhale. "Because sometimes I need to be pushed. Because Thistlecross is my place, too, now. And because I'm yours. Damn it, Brochan. Let's do this together."

He lifted his hands to grip her shoulders. She let her arms fall to her sides. And then he kissed her, harder than he ever had. The weight and urgency of his mouth on hers felt dizzying and disorienting. Their teeth knocked together until she relented and gave herself over to him. She softened her mouth as he molded his body around hers. And as he did, he walked her backward, pressing her up against one of the largest trees. She made a noise of curious pleasure, but Brochan just kissed her deeper. He moved from her lips to the underside of her jaw, and down to her chest. He took a bit of her skin in his teeth and dug in, making her jump.

His hands found their way underneath her sweater, and he wrapped his palms around her rib cage, his fingers reaching for one another across the span of her back. He continued kissing her neck with such fierce intensity that Ruby felt light-headed. She ran her hands through his hair to steady herself, raking the pads of her fingers down to his small bun held together with one of her elastics.

"I love you, Ruby Spencer," he said heavily as his thumbs worked their way underneath the band of her bra and pressed into her nipples. He grinned, finding them already firm and taut. Her breasts were very small and his hands were very large; she just barely filled the bowls of his palms. He lifted his face to hers. "I love every damn thing about you."

She moaned and almost said it back. "I . . ." but her mouth found his bottom lip instead of the words. He pinched her nipples so hard that she squealed. It had been so long since Ruby'd said those words. She had not said them to any of the random men she knew in New York. And it was entirely possible that she had never actually *felt* them, not once, not at all. Not even for Benjamin. But she wanted to say them now, very badly, in fact. What would it feel like to stop making lists and start letting life choose for her once in a while? What would it feel like to swan dive off the top of the falls? To become kinetic?

She snaked her arm up Brochan's back and she pressed her thumb into the side of his neck as he let out a primal groan. Ruby looked at the sky through the branches; a star winked at her. She allowed her body to melt as the words tumbled out.

"I love you back, Brochan Wood." Ruby's heart scurried around in her chest and she squirmed in anticipation. "I love you so much it scares me."

Hearing this, Brochan pulled his hands from her body and gently held her face. The curled lock of hair that was constantly refusing to stay in her braid leaped forward now. "I'm terrified, too," he said. "But if we promise to always be honest, and love each other fiercely, I think we'll be all right. Do you trust me?"

Tears pricked at the outside corners of Ruby's eyes. Her lips quivered. She nodded in silent affirmation. *I do trust you.* For the briefest of moments, she worried that perhaps *he* shouldn't trust *her*, but she firmed her chin and chased the thought from her mind. If she'd known how special Brochan was to become to her, she'd never have kept Dunbar's secret from him. And it didn't matter; everything was out in the open now. All they had to do was move forward.

That's all they had to do. Everything was theirs.

Ruby marveled that this man, hurting so much from the pain of the evening, could put all that aside just to make her feel safe. And yet, here he was. Here they were. He was so very good. She was so very his.

Scotland was not a mistake!

She wanted to say something that would allow him to touch the depth of her gratitude and love, but knew that words could never hold all of that weight.

Ruby lowered herself to kneel on the moss bed, allowing Brochan's hands to slide up to the top of her head. Hers found their way down to his waist. The tips of her sandals grazed the tree roots behind her as she worked his belt buckle free, and then his zipper. Brochan shuddered as she took him out of his pants. She took her time, letting her emotions tumble around between them.

"I love you; I love you, Brochan. I love you."

Now that the words had escaped her, they felt wonderful. She said them hungrily and loudly, letting them swell and fill her mouth until she couldn't take any more inside her, and he couldn't bear being held so sweetly. Brochan steadied himself with his hands on Ruby's crown and she pressed her legs into the earth to ground them both. The moon, almost full, shone through wispy clouds and bathed them both in light. A tawny owl called, announcing his place in the trees. The breeze rolled past their bodies, stirring up the scent of their sweat. And there, on the floor of a small forest in a tiny town in the Highlands of Scotland, she accepted everything he had to give her.

Chapter Thirty-One

The next morning, Ruby and Brochan walked hand in hand from the stone cottage to the Cosy Hearth. She swung their arms back and forth and smiled up at him. He grinned back. Everything sucked, but they had each other.

"Hey! Wait," Ruby said, stopping short and tickling his chest with her fingers.

"Hey yourself," he said gruffly. He tugged at both her earlobes with his knuckles. "Already? Again? I'm not complaining, but I might need a minute or two to recover."

She pulled back his shirt and bit the skin of his left pec. She really sank her teeth in, and he jumped and grabbed her belt loop, then kissed the top of her head.

"No, that's not what I want—I mean, yes. Obviously. All the time. Well, maybe after breakfast. But what I was going to say was: What were you going to ask me last night? Before the meeting? Before . . . everything?"

Ruby could see levers and pulleys rearranging themselves in Brochan's man brain. "Mm, situation dependent," he said cryptically. "I'm going to shut it for now."

"You are infuriating, and I love you, and you are infuriating," said Ruby, moving his shirt aside a little farther so that she could kiss the place she'd marked. "Did I mention I love you?"

"Funnily enough, I love you back. Despite the fact that you are a feisty wee thing this morning who ought to be filled up . . . with breakfast."

She laughed and took his hand again.

They both sniffed the air as they approached the old pub. Thistlecross was going to hell in a handbasket, but at least Grace would have made scones.

This morning, the pastries were mottled with creamy streaks of blackberries; Grace and Ruby had picked them earlier that week. Grace set the scones out on a serving platter along with a just-plunged carafe of coffee. At the bar, Neil sat holding his head in his hands as if it were a delicate glass marble, apt to shatter with too forceful a breath. Ruby wondered which was shouting loudest at him, the stress of yesterday's events or the troughs of whisky he had consumed. "Surprised you didn't wind up at the flophouse, mate," Brochan gently teased Neil while knocking his shoulder. "I was half expecting you to pound on the door round midni . . ." His words trailed off as he understood he'd just revealed that he, himself, had been an overnight guest at the cottage. Apparently deciding it was common knowledge, he finished with a sheepish shrug. "Midnight."

The curtain parted to accommodate Grace and the mugs she was carrying. She sucked her lips in under her teeth and nodded.

Ruby felt her joy fade. Just a little. She poured the coffee and handed a full mug back to Grace. "So. What happened after we left?"

Neil released his head from his hands and let it bang back onto the bar with a *clunk*.

"Help."

Ruby inched a coffee cup closer to him.

"Surprisingly little," Grace said. "Or unsurprisingly? Anne said that per the contract, 'building renovations' would start on the fifteenth of September. Curious that the owner of the business—hallooooo—wasn't part of these plans."

Brochan noted the bizarre timing with a snort. "Oh, sure. Right before winter sets in. A fine time to start a construction project in the Highlands."

Grace shook her head and Neil's fingertips crept toward the handle of his mug.

"Winkler said that they'll hire a construction crew that can make some changes to the facade before the weather really hits. A construction crew from out of town, no doubt. The bastard. Then they'll spend the winter working on interiors. All supervised by . . . well, by Grant, I reckon. It looks like he's really coming back. The residents of Thistlecross can, and I'm quoting here again, 'expect an exciting new beginning in spring of next year.'"

Ruby almost choked on her first sip of coffee. It burned her throat going down. A month. They wanted to start construction in a month? That was hardly enough time to change anything, let alone figure out how they all felt about it. The other week, Anne had made it seem like there was loads of time. And, she loathed to bring this up now, but there was the very small matter of her imminent trip home to visit her parents. She had mentioned it to Grace and Brochan earlier that summer, so they could plan to take a Sunday supper off, but that was before it all had come grinding to a halt. She was doubtful her vacation was on anyone's mind now.

As she had fallen asleep a few nights prior, her backside curled into Brochan's lap and thighs, she had wondered if he might want to come with her. To upstate New York. But what was the right time to introduce your sexy Scottish boyfriend to your parents? Before or after you announced to them that you were maybe, probably moving to Scotland for good? She slept fitfully, and in the light of day, decided it was more sensible to go it alone this time. Plus, she'd never traveled with a romantic partner. What if Brochan turned out to be the type who took his shoes off on airplanes? Or asked for a dozen bags of mini pretzels, then shoved them all in his pockets? Or—*oh god*—actually bought things from the *SkyMall* magazine? She couldn't be sure she would still love him if that was the case, and decided it was prudent to remain in ignorant bliss . . . for a little while longer, at least.

But back to pressing matters: "How can they expect you to pack up years' worth of cooking in this kitchen, let alone your home upstairs, in just a handful of weeks?" Ruby asked. Neil lifted his head high enough to slurp up a bit of coffee. Grace gave him a look she had perfected over years of tending bar and caretaking at the Cosy Hearth. She shrugged, signifying defeat.

Ruby reached underneath the bar, where she knew Grace

kept extra pens and a notepad. "What we need to do is make a list." She wrote at the top of the paper in capital letters:

IDEAS FOR HOW TO SAVE
THE COSY HEARTH (AND DEAL WITH GRANT)

Brochan raised an eyebrow. "Succinct."

"I'm serious. This is a maze. Let's try and find our way out." She immediately scrawled a few items, starting with one inspired by her fool's errand to town hall earlier that week.

1. *Raise the money to buy the property from Winkler (how??)*

2. *Ask Anne to place a hold on the construction, until the spring (to give us time to raise the money to buy it ourselves; see point no. 1).*

3. *Find a way to connect with Grant, despite all the shitty things he may have done to his sister and son (in case point no. 1 and 2 do not work out, but also maybe even still then???).*

"Curious about that last one, Roo," said Brochan. "How're you figuring on my da factoring into the solution at all?"

Ruby quickly clicked the pen open and shut a few times. "Well, if he's Winkler's partner, maybe he can help him see how special this place is. Maybe Winkler would be willing to open his dumb restaurant somewhere else."

"It's not a good idea to involve him." Brochan took a slug of his coffee.

"We'll never raise enough money to buy this place outright. Have you seen how much it was listed for?" Grace said sullenly.

"Uh, no," Ruby answered, doodling onto the notepad. "How much?"

"A lot."

Everyone was quiet for a minute or two, except for Neil, who was still slurping coffee and groaning.

Ruby caught Grace and Brochan exchanging looks. Her anger flared up briefly. "Listen. I'm sorry to be the one to say this, but if the restaurant does change hands, Grant is going to be a part of it. He's going to be a part of Thistlecross. Well, a part of it again." She paused, and let her voice turn gentle. "He's going to be a part of your lives again. Have you considered that maybe this is his way of trying to reconcile?"

Grace fiddled with the ribbon in her hair. "I thought about that."

Brochan slammed his fist on the bar and everyone's coffee trembled. Neil gave a look like he was a dog who'd been kicked.

"Grace, you know that's not it. Roo, I'm sorry, but you're wrong. If he had meant to reconcile, why wouldn't he have come to us first? Given us a wee warning? Extended an olive branch? Something. Anything. No; he's still the self-satisfied, money-chasing coward he always was."

Grace opened her mouth then decided against whatever she'd been on the edge of saying. She shrugged.

Ruby drew more squiggles around the border of the paper. "I

guess you're right. You know him better than I do. I wish there was something I could do from New York next week. I feel like a traitor for going away right now."

Recognition sparked in Brochan's eyes. *Ah, right. Her trip.* He took the pen from her and made an addition to the list.

4. *Find a way to fix this with what we already have.*

"I have no idea what that means in practical terms," he admitted, pulling Ruby close and kissing her forehead, his anger at his father and the situation directing itself away from the people gathered around him at the Cosy Hearth. "But I'm not going to put this burden on your shoulders, Roo. Yesterday, I was wrong to drag you into the center of things. If we're going to do anything, it's my responsibility to figure it out. Winkler is a bawbag, but Grant is my father. In theory, anyway. This is my burden."

Bawbag? That was a new one. Although, Ruby intuited, it was probably not listed in the Oxford Dictionary. She audibly sighed. Sure, she had been hesitant about taking up this fight. But hadn't she later told him she was ready to join in? She decided to hold her tongue for now.

"Depending on how long his hangover lasts"—she gestured to Neil, who was officially snoring into the cradle of his arms—"we can always chain him to the bar and call it a peaceful protest."

Chapter Thirty-Two

The last thing Ruby wanted to do was leave Thistlecross, but a promise was a promise. And airline tickets were nonrefundable. Every August, her parents rented a house on Cayuga Lake in upstate New York. And every year, they gathered there to reconnect, take hikes, grill steaks and burgers, and most of all, drink lots and lots of beer by the campfire. Even though plenty of other upstate families took lake vacations at the same time, there was a peacefulness to the place that made the Spencers believe like they had the whole waterfront to themselves. The trip always felt like a balm to Ruby's city-battered soul. Nothing could compare to a week's worth of mornings spent on the dock with a book, and evenings spent cooking with her parents. Not even Scotland. Even if Scotland contained Brochan.

She had, after all, floated the idea of him coming along, and he enthusiastically said he'd love nothing more. But after an anxiety-ridden twenty-four hours while he searched for flights, she rescinded her invitation and told him that perhaps it was too soon to have such an important meeting. Maybe he could just do a Zoom call with her and her parents one night?

Brochan had gathered Ruby in his arms like a bouquet of late-season heather and laughed. "Sure, Roo," he'd said. "At your pace, and when you're comfortable. I'm not in a rush." That patient generosity scrambled Ruby's brain even further, and she tried to re-invite him, but he shut her up with a smack on her bottom. "If you don't go, you won't miss me, and then I'll never get any slavishly devotional love poems from you," he said, closing the matter. Ruby rolled her eyes to the heavens and tackled him to the ground with a kiss so forceful it surprised even her.

The morning before her flight, Ruby woke in Brochan's barn to the sensation of his mouth on her inner thighs. He had been extra-sweet, extra-generous in bed and everywhere else for the last few days. Their *I love you*s had unearthed a tender trust in each other as if they'd cracked through the hard crust of a crème brûlée and were now greedily spooning up the custard underneath.

"Ooh!" she murmured and burrowed deeper into the pillows. "Your beard tickles."

"And you like it, and you want more," he said, his breath wild and warm on her skin.

"What else do I like?" Ruby asked, taking his kisses.

"You like it when it hurts."

Ruby blushed something fierce. "A little, yes."

"You like it more than a little." Brochan kissed her most secret place, then replaced his lips with his first two fingers. "You like it when there's a lot of pressure; when I stop being gentle and start ravaging you."

"A lot, yes." Ruby's eyes were closed as she succumbed to the

241

sensation of Brochan's fingers moving in rhythm. "Faster," she whispered.

"Speak up, Roo."

Her voice raised a fraction of a decibel. "Faster?"

Brochan kept at the same pace, and his eyes smoldered over her.

"*Go faster*," Ruby finally said, holding firm and loud.

He went faster.

"Go harder."

He went harder.

Brochan propped himself up on his forearm and watched Ruby's face twist and contort in pleasure. She was close to orgasm, and they both knew it.

"Should I keep on? Are you going to let yourself go? You're so fine when you do." He coaxed his fingers even farther into her center.

She struggled back toward the wall, away from his touch just moments before she came.

"Put yourself inside me," Ruby gasped, and Brochan was happy to oblige. Already naked underneath the sheet, he was ready for her. More than ready. The most ready a man can be. He grabbed at her waist and flipped her over, so that her face was crammed into the pillow.

"Lift your arse," he said, and she did, arching her back and braiding her fingers together. *Steady, Roo*, she thought, tingling in anticipation.

Brochan caressed her skin, running his hand over Ruby's back and down her leg. And then he took it away. Ruby waited without looking, and let out an eager purr. She wanted to be surprised when he entered her. But he didn't enter her just yet; instead, he brought his palm down hard on her flesh. Ruby yelped and Brochan smiled. They both knew there would be an imprint of his hand on her upper thigh.

"Now; I need you now!" Ruby was half demanding and half pleading, which she knew was Brochan's favorite way for her to be in bed. She kept a secret grin all for herself. As he rolled on a condom, she thought how lucky she was to have found a man who could take control in bed, but would never ask—or desire— obedience in real life. How lucky she was to have found Brochan. He steadied himself with one hand on the wall and eased himself inside. He blew out a low and heady breath. She drew hers in sharply.

Almost immediately, Ruby lifted her torso from the mattress so that her back was against his chest. She wanted to be close to him. As close as they could possibly get. And then a little closer than that. Brochan held her tightly, his arm across her breasts. He kissed her neck and she grew warmer, and more malleable in his hands.

As Brochan neared finish, he slowed down just long enough to whisper that he was ready. Was she ready? He didn't want to finish without her. Too exhilarated for words, she nodded, her curls smothering his lips. They both climaxed at the same time, their pleasure heightening each other's.

Immediately afterward, they dissolved into laughter. As they lay naked and sprawled on the bed, Brochan fingered the wooden medallion around Ruby's neck, and she rubbed at his calves with her toes. There they were, whisky and food nerds in their midthirties and almost forties without a clue who they were or what they were doing with their lives. But they had each other, and that made them feel like they had unearthed some sort of luscious secret.

Chapter Thirty-Three

Eons ago, Ruby had planned on hitching a ride to Inverness, where she'd take the train to Glasgow. From there she'd take a flight path that led her to New York, where she'd finally reunite with her parents. But that was before she'd met a generous Scottish man with a forest green pickup truck of unidentified make and model. Brochan insisted on bringing her all the way to Glasgow, and she gratefully accepted, happy to spend at least a portion of her journey with him. Home seemed to be an impossible distance away, although that intangible goalpost was suddenly looking a lot more covered in sphagnum moss.

He hoisted her duffel, stuffed so full it was bulging at the seams, into the cab and jokingly asked if she'd crammed a few rocks inside.

She poked his cheek with her index finger as they buckled in. "Make fun all you want, but losing your luggage is no laughing matter. I'm never traveling with anything more than a carry-on."

He grabbed hold of her finger and squeezed tightly. "I suppose that'd make your permanent move here a fair jot easier, anyway."

She blushed. He pressed her hand to his lips, then released her.

They rode in silence for half an hour, Ruby drinking in the view and Brochan effortlessly weaving through cars. She rested her forehead against the window and before long, the steady drone of the engine had lulled her into a hazy sort of consciousness. She was just about to dip into the deeper layers of sleep when she was jolted awake by a Pavlovian response to the sound of a phone ringing She blinked and sat up, searching for her cell. But it wasn't hers; Brochan pulled his phone out of his pocket, looked at it, sighed, and put it back in his pants.

"Spammer?"

"Naw."

"Tax collector?"

He gave her a pained smile.

"Undertaker?"

"Jesus, Roo."

"Tell me if I'm close, at least," she said, the words dissolving into self-satisfied giggles.

"It was Margaret. My—"

Ruby immediately sobered.

"I remember who she is."

They sat in a humid silence, the air thick with tension. Ruby didn't want to play the role of insecure girlfriend, but she felt an anxious swelling in her chest when she thought about Brochan's ex. Why was she calling him so early on a weekend morning? Wait. Didn't Brochan say she had moved to New York?

"It's the *middle of the night* in New York." Ruby's voice was a bare whisper.

"Aye," Brochan said.

"Yeah," Ruby echoed, waiting for more.

Brochan didn't give in.

"So . . . yeah?" Ruby's tone made the phrase into a noncommittal question.

Brochan kept his eyes on the road ahead and shrugged. "Haven't got a clue what she wants."

Ruby crossed her arms over her stomach. "Then why didn't you answer?"

"Because I don't care."

"Oh?"

"Yeah."

"It seems like you kind of care."

"I do not care."

"You do care!"

"Why are you trying to stir this into something?"

Ruby's chest flushed. She hugged herself tighter. "I guess I'm nervous. About leaving you. I know it's just a stupid week, but I've never been away from someone I love. And everything seems so uncertain. A phone call from an ex feels like a bad omen. You know?"

"Is that what they teach you in astrology?"

"Don't make fun of me when I'm being vulnerable!"

"I'm seriously asking: Is Mercury radioactive right now or something?"

"You're not being serious; you're being evasive. And it's Mercury in *retrograde*. But, no. It's not."

Brochan's posture softened. He reached across the car and placed one of his big palms over her thigh. "Roo, I'm sorry. I'm not going anywhere. Literally or otherwise. I'll be right here where you left me. Probably a stone lighter without your cooking to gorge myself on."

Ruby nodded and tried, and failed, to look cheerful.

"It was probably a bum-dial, anyway."

"Oh, maybe . . ." Ruby's voice dropped off.

Neither of them spoke again, and Ruby tried to ignore the overwhelmingly bad vibes Brochan's cell phone was suddenly serving up. Evil briefcase–level vibes. She shut her eyes and kept them closed. When she eventually dipped into sleep, it was with Brochan's flannel scrunched up between her cheek and the window, the fabric soothing her with his scent. Reminded of his steadfast goodness, she stayed that way until they reached Glasgow.

At the airport, she kissed him goodbye and promised to sneak back a small bottle of New York–made whiskey. "Don't bother," Brochan said, patting her rear with his hand and responding to her kiss with one of his own. "Unless you're planning on cooking with it?"

"Rude brute of a Scot," Ruby said and rolled her eyes.

"*Your* rude brute," Brochan corrected, and she had to admit it was true, and that she liked it.

"Promise me you won't do anything drastic," Ruby said, hoping that her request held weight for deadbeat dads and obnoxious ex-girlfriends alike.

"What's drastic?" Brochan wanted to know.

"I don't know. Anything you'd regret in the sober light of day?"

He pulled her in and up. She wrapped her legs around his hips, clinging on to his neck.

"And promise you'll tell me if there's anything I can do to help you and Grace," she murmured into his skin as he squeezed her tightly. "Remember, I said I'd help you fight. I meant it then, and I mean it always. So don't leave me out."

He released her to the ground. "I promise. If you promise to relax, and be with your family. We'll all be here when you return. Waiting for you." She danced her fingers over his nose, counting freckles. "Waiting for Roo."

As Ruby waved from the train, she felt her thoughts swirl.

What if my place was always meant to be here, in Thistlecross, with Brochan?

How does my part in this story change if Thistlecross changes?

How involved am I supposed to be in this battle? A little? A lot?

How is Anne doing, with all this?

What the fucking fuck did Brochan's ex-girlfriend want?

I forgot to pack snacks!

Chapter Thirty-Four

Many mind-bogglingly exhausting hours later, Ruby was drinking a cup of Earl Grey tea with her mom as her dad cooked bacon on the grill. The two women sat on Adirondack chairs, looking out over the calm expanse of Cayuga Lake. It was breakfast time. Or maybe it was brunch. Breakfast for dinner? Ruby was too tired to figure it out, but she didn't need to. She was just happy to be there. The gentle lapping of the water provided background music as Ruby told her mother all about Thistlecross. Well, almost all about Thistlecross. On their video calls, Ruby had been diligent about providing updates about Scotland life and the Family Table suppers. She'd hinted a bit about Brochan, but hadn't shared more than the bare minimum. But now her mom wanted the kind of details mothers always want when their daughters start dating handsome strangers. "Is he good to his family? Is he good to you? What do you like to do together? Have you talked about the future? Does he want childre—"

Ruby cut her off there with a laugh. "He is good to me, and to Grace, and to Thistlecross, which he considers to be his family at large. We love sharing food, talking about whisky, drinking whisky—don't look at me like that, I know you and Dad spent the entirety of the seventies sloshed—and, um, no. We haven't talked about what comes next. Not really. But I like him. I love him? I love him. That's enough for now, isn't it?"

"It's enough for me. But there's something else on your mind, Ruby Shoes. Tell me."

Ruby warmed at her childhood nickname. She clicked her bare heels together three times. "Oh, you know me. Just having a minor identity crisis." Her mom drank her tea and didn't speak, waiting for Ruby to fill the silence. *Damn, she knows all my interviewing tricks.*

Ruby gulped down fresh air and finally said what she'd been keeping secret from them. From herself, really. It was time to face the facts. "My cookbook got rejected." It seemed like so long ago that she'd gotten that email. "And I feel lost. I moved to Scotland for the express purpose of writing a cookbook. So I guess now I'm confused about what I'm actually there for. It seems like it could be Brochan, but I don't want to make big life decisions just for a man. That's so . . . clichéd."

Her mother reached over and stroked Ruby's forearm. "You may have forgotten, but I know who you are, and what you're doing. You're Ruby Spencer, from New York. You're a brilliant writer and a wonderful cook. You're in the process of transitioning to a new career. Are those answers not good enough?"

"Sure, for now. But what happens in April, when it's time to come back to New York? What's stopping me from staying in Thistlecross? What's stopping me from going back there in a week? I have a perfectly fine life here. But it feels deeply *blah*. I have the possibility of an extraordinary life there. But it's rigged with what-ifs and failures. I feel like every decision I make could be the wrong one . . . or the right one. How do you choose a place to live if you don't have a career? How do you know if a place is trying to choose you?"

"Big questions for such a small girl," her mom said with a kind smile.

"I mean, I am almost forty."

"You've got miles to go before forty. But even so, you'll always be my baby."

Ruby offered a weak smile.

"I'd be sad if you created a life so far away. But it's in a mother's job description to be sad when her children move on. It's also a sign of a job accomplished."

"Would you be mad if I told you that Thistlecross feels more like home than Ithaca ever did?"

"No—only if you told me that, then ignored it."

"I guess I don't have to have all the answers today. Which is good. Because I have zero answers. But no matter where I live, I do have to figure out how to earn money with my cookbook slowly fading into a bad dream."

Ruby's father brought over a platter piled high with bacon, pancakes, and scrambled eggs. "What's this about your cookbook?"

Ruby crunched into a slice of bacon. "Rejected, Dad. Your daughter is a failed author."

He shook his head resolutely. "Robert Pirsig got rejected more than a hundred times before *Zen and the Art of Motorcycle Main-*

tenance was published." Mark loved motorcycles. And he loved that book. Ever since Ruby was little, he'd been finding ways to sneak it into parenting lessons. Apparently he wasn't out of them yet.

"Please do not compare me to your favorite author; he was a literary genius and I'm just an ex–food writer."

"Right now, the only difference between the two of you is that you seem to be on the verge of giving up."

Ruby's mom nodded in agreement. Her dad didn't say anything further; he didn't have to. They ate breakfast in silence, watching a small sailboat make its way across the water. Her parents had planned on a day perusing the antique shops in town, an activity that did not, altogether, seem scintillating to Ruby. But that was just fine, because Lee had taken the day off from work, and was coming out to the lake for an afternoon of girl time.

When Lee's Jeep pulled into the gravel drive, Ruby dropped the book she'd been holding and ran at breakneck speed to meet her friend. The two women embraced tightly; and when they finally pulled away, Ruby had tears in her eyes. Lee's icy blond hair was held back by a pair of aviator sunglasses, and her expression twinkled with its familiar air of wild adventure.

"I missed you a lot, a lot," Ruby said, wiping her eyes with the sleeve of her flannel. Well, Brochan's flannel. She had liberated it from the truck when she left. It smelled like her man, and she fully intended on wearing it until the scent had faded.

"Missed you, too, baberooni," said Lee, twirling her friend

around to inspect her. "Hmm, well, you don't *look* any more Scottish than you did before you left."

Ruby pulled her in for another hug, then flung her arm around her shoulder as they walked back toward the lake house. They had a lot of catching up to do.

B y midafternoon, Ruby and Lee were sprawled out on a blanket on the dock, dipping carrot sticks and pretzels into a tub of hummus and sipping on rosé. Ruby was giving Lee the kind of details thirtysomething women always want when their best friends start dating handsome strangers. She was describing the handprint-shaped mark Brochan had gifted her when her phone pinged.

"Toss it to me?" Ruby held out her hand.

Lee wiggled her eyebrows dangerously, then swiped up to read the message. "Honestly, Roo, you need to put a password on this shit. Now, let's see. Ten bucks says it's a well-endowed Scot." Ruby was about to argue, but Lee raised her hand. "Obviously he's hung, don't lie to me." She cleared her throat and read out loud in a Scottish accent that somehow managed to sound more like a mashup between the American Deep South and Australia.

Hey, Roo. Some tidy news from the land of barley: Cosy Hearth construction project has been pushed back another month. Something about "pressing matters at the Wee Tartan Bagpipe stateside headquarters." We'll figure it out when you get back. Still thinking about your arse.

"Arse!" squealed Lee, flopping onto her back and pretending to make a snow angel on the blanket. She was a touch wine drunk by this point. She tossed the phone to Ruby. "Maybe I should move to Scotland."

Ruby hiccuped. She, too, was wine drunk. A touch and a half.

"If you do, just promise you won't become a conniving restaurateur."

Lee held up her arms in a *stop-the-presses* gesture. "Wait. What's the name of his dad's weird pub again?"

Ruby rolled her eyes. "The Wee Tartan Bagpipe."

"Okay, actually kind of cute. I don't hate it. But your snobbery is beside the point: Roo, did you know there's one of those in Albany? It opened up, I don't know, three months ago?"

Ruby's eyes narrowed. "Why . . . ? What? How . . . How do you know this?"

"Work, duh." *Ah, yes.* Lee was constantly traveling back and forth to Albany to report on stories for the paper. "I may or may not have eaten there with the politics team at the paper."

"Excuse you!"

"Okay, and I may or may not have also gone on a date there."

Ruby's eyes narrowed.

Lee grimaced. "Two dates?"

Ruby grabbed the wine and held it behind her back.

Lee lunged for the bottle. "Okay, fine, three."

"What the hell, Lee!"

"They have good boneless wings . . . ?"

"Which is not a Scottish food. And not actually made of chicken wings."

"But there's Guinness hot sauce!"

"Guinness is *Irish*."

"We're getting sidetracked here," Lee said, gesticulating with a carrot stick. "The point is, if you're going to stop this restaurant from opening in Thistlecross, you need to do some recon. Know what it's all about. Infiltrate enemy lines. Etcetera and whatnot."

Ruby clutched her wine. "I'm not even sure if stopping it is the best idea. But I know it's not my job. What are you saying, Lee?

"What I'm saying"—Lee peered over her aviators and clinked her glass against Ruby's—"is buckle up, baby. Because we're taking a road trip to fucking Albany."

Chapter Thirty-Five

The next day, as the sun rose over I-81, Ruby was indeed buckled into her best friend's Jeep. After spending the evening grilling with Ruby's parents (and admiring the vintage champagne glasses her mother had scored), the two friends fell asleep, sharing a double bed. It was just like their childhood sleepovers, minus the *Tiger Beat* magazines and plus two bottles of wine. Lee had a full day of interviews at the State Capitol, which meant that Ruby would be free to explore the Wee Tartan Bagpipe on her own. Whether or not she wanted to. Whether or not it was a terrible idea. Lee had booked a hotel with her work credit card, and told Ruby that they'd go out for a real dinner—no boneless wings allowed—to dish on everything afterward. Ruby felt a smidge weird about the whole thing for two reasons.

1. *She was abandoning her parents, whom she'd traveled from Scotland to see. But they'd assured her they didn't mind, that a road trip with her best friend was important, too, and that they'd have plenty of time later that week for family time.*

2. *She kind of, sort of, just a little bit, had not told Brochan she was going to the Wee Tartan Bagpipe. She had sent him a tipsy good night text, and the next morning he wrote back with a picture of Kyle and him on a ride. His text said,* **Missing your cooking, but had a banger of a bonus day full of muddy trails to make up for it. Can't wait to eat you, I mean, your food, again soon.** *Ruby knew that Brochan would have complicated feelings about her visiting the Wee Tartan Bagpipe, even if it was just on an ammunition-gathering mission. It didn't seem fair to tell him about it over a text, and besides, with construction being pushed back, they had more time. They could sit down together next week and talk about it all.*

3. *She had gone from food writer to failed cookbook author to pop-up restaurant chef to bizarro spy, and she wasn't sure that any good would come of that last one. Why had she even agreed to it in the first place? Damn it, Lee. Damn it, all-day rosé.*

That was three reasons. Whoops.

Once they reached the Capitol building, Lee grabbed her briefcase and tossed the car keys to Ruby. "You can check into the hotel after three. I'll meet you at the restaurant; our rezzies are for seven thirty." She looked her friend up and down, appraisingly taking in her braid, gray shoes, skinny jeans, and a faded black tank. "And make a little effort for me, will you? I'm your date." She winked and trotted up the steps, leaving Ruby to wonder what was so bad about Keds.

It was still early, so Ruby drove around until she found a coffee shop. She ordered a scone and a cortado, and sat down at a table next to an enormous monstera plant. The coffee was a revelation of dense steamed milk and expertly pulled espresso; just the right combination of sweet and bitter. But the scone may as well have been a doorstop. It was rock-hard and tasteless, and whatever fat used to make it was not butter.

Sitting there in that little café made Ruby's heart hurt. Because she missed Scotland. Which meant that she missed Brochan and his giant Scottish . . . beard. (She chuckled a little, and a woman reading at the next table gave her an irritated glare.) She missed her cottage and she even missed her mouse roommate who had, alas, returned. She missed the way the breeze betrayed whatever plants were flowering in that moment. She missed working in her little garden, and she missed the rhythm and flow of cooking with Grace. As Ruby drained her mug, she realized that what she was feeling was homesickness. It was a funny sensation. Until now, until Thistlecross, Ruby's pangs of sadness for home had been about her lack of one.

After a walk around the city park, Ruby checked her watch. 11:05; the Wee Tartan Bagpipe was finally open for lunch. GPS directed her to the strip mall where it lived; and as she pulled the Jeep into the parking lot, she heaved a great sigh. She already knew exactly what was inside: pockets of dim lighting, American whiskey parading as the real deal, and maybe a framed kilt or two in the vestibule. She'd sit at the bar, order a soft drink, do a quick lap on a visit to the restroom, then be on her way. Just to tell Lee she had. Maybe then she'd rent one of the city-sponsored bikes and explore Albany a bit before dinner. This would be dumb, but it would be over soon.

Ruby audibly gasped as she entered. The Wee Tartan Bagpipe was not so much a celebration of Scottish culture as it was a man cave that had been dipped in plaid paint. There was no shortage of televisions flashing *Sports! Sports! Sports!* content, and early-2000s-era alternative music blared over the sound system. Whoa; the last time she'd heard a Stone Temple Pilots song was . . . freshman year? Of high school?

Ruby stopped by the hostess's stand to read the menu, which read like a greatest hits album of dude-friendly bar snacks. Her eyes skimmed down: Bang-Pow Shrimp (*no thanks*), Spinach and Artichoke Dip (*cool idea, 2002*), Tater Tot Nachos (*tot-chos?*), American Haggis (*whatever THAT was*), Giant Skillet Brownie (*a.k.a. mass-produced brownie covered in forgettable vanilla ice cream*). . . . Aside from the "haggis," the menu could have been ripped out of the nearest Hooters and pasted onto the books here.

"Waiting for someone?" a woman chirped and jolted Ruby from her snarky read. Ruby's eyes followed the voice, which was attached to a very round, very large set of breasts draped in a purple plaid fabric. *How—literally how—were her nipples not escaping?* Ruby was mesmerized by the hostess's garment, a replica of the one Brochan had unboxed at the Cosy Hearth some months ago. Admittedly, it looked much better on this woman than it had held up against Brochan's broad chest.

"Um . . ." Ruby struggled to bring her attention to the

woman's face, which was sweet and pretty. "No, just me. I think I'll sit at the bar."

The hostess gave her a curious look but shrugged and motioned behind her. There were only a handful of other people in the restaurant. Ruby took her time on the walk, drinking in the fake-wood paneled walls, the dark green carpet, and the high-top tables scattered around the room. It was . . . well, it was really something.

She hung her messenger bag on the hook under the bar and eased onto a stool. In front of her was a dizzying number of taps, all advertising domestic beer. The bartender, who had raven hair and was wearing the same getup as the hostess, but in green, approached with a cardboard coaster. "Hey, babe," she said, and Ruby blinked. "What're ya thinking?"

Ruby took a small breath and smiled. She didn't want to be judgmental—after all, she didn't know this woman or her story—so she pushed away her gut reaction to the big breasts and penciled-on eyebrows and gave her best *we're in this together* smile.

"Do you do lemonade?" Ruby asked. "I'll start with that."

The bartender winked and clicked her tongue, then poured a tall glass filled with crushed ice. She set a plastic straw down next to the coaster and Ruby handed over ten dollars. "Keep the change," she said, hoping the generous tip would absolve her of the guilt she felt for being a bad feminist.

Ruby sat and sipped her lemonade slowly, letting questions swirl and gather in a small pool in her brain. *If Winkler started this place thirty years ago, what did it look like then? Did he know this was bullshit? He had to know, right? Grant totally knew this was bullshit. How could he possibly choose this over his family and his home? Over real Scotland? Wait, does Brochan know the Wee Tartan Bagpipe is like . . . this? Does Grace? Does Anne? Has anyone in Thistlecross actually been to a Wee Tartan Bagpipe?*

After forty-five minutes, Ruby figured she had absorbed enough fry oil through her pores to last the next decade. And honestly, she had grown pretty confident about things. Because even though sitting at this bar was the most depressing thing she had done in years, she felt something crystallizing into a conviction: she finally knew how she felt about the Wee Tartan Bagpipe, and its encroachment on her sweet little adopted town. She did not feel good about it!

Setting aside the complication of Brochan's dad, Ruby just couldn't get behind the idea of something like this in place of the Cosy Hearth. There was no way her new neighbors would stand for this crackpot representation of their culture, either. Even Anne would change her mind. Right? They had to. She had to. There must be some municipal magic that would get them out of the contract. Some loophole.

Renewed by a sense of clarity and purpose, Ruby took a quick trip to the restroom. She redid her braid and was just about to make her way back to the bar then bolt when she heard arguing.

There was an office next to the restrooms, and the door was slightly ajar. Ruby paused in the hallway, holding her breath. She was certain she recognized one of the raised voices.

"I don't see why you won't just let me pay her off, so we can be done with it," said the familiar voice.

"Because it's wrong, and you know it," hissed the unfamiliar one.

"You're telling me you actually *believe* her?"

"I am telling you that. And I'm telling you I don't want to be a part of this anymore. I can't. I'm too bloody old for it." The further the unfamiliar voice got into the last sentence, the more pronounced his accent became. He was no doubt a Scot.

"I'm sorry—what did you think 'partner' meant? That you wouldn't have to deal with the actual logistics of running a business?"

The familiar voice was followed by the sound of a fist slamming into a desk. Ruby jumped a little and pressed her body flat against the wall. *Oh my god.* She really was in a spy movie. "I didn't think that getting hit with sexual harassment lawsuits was a *normal part of running a business.*"

"Welcome to America."

"To hell with your America."

"Well, precisely, you Scottish bastard. That's why I'm sending you back home. You should be thanking me, frankly."

Shit, shit, shit. Ruby bit down on her cheeks and pedaled her knees back and forth. She felt like she was going to explode. Louis Winkler was here.

And more than that, Ruby was 99 percent sure she was about to run into her boyfriend's estranged father on a secret spy mission that had a fifty-fifty shot at saving Thistlecross and destroying her relationship.

Chapter Thirty-Six

I can't do this." Probably-Grant's voice was impossibly sad.

"What you can't do is back out of our contract," said Winkler, and there was a satisfied sneer in his voice. "Five more years. Five years, and then I can retire and you can do whatever you want. I hate to admit it, but the Wee Tartan Bagpipe just doesn't *work* without you. When we open a new franchise, you show up and do the Scottish thing and it creates a narrative. A story. It creates customer loyalty. You're what everyone wants. So yes. You will finish out the run here in Albany, and you will go to Richmond, and you will go to Pittsburgh, and then you will go to Scotland. I can't handle any more bad press. Northeast business is down and you know it."

Ruby heard the sound of footsteps making for the door, and she scurried from the hallway to the bar. She sank back down on her stool and before she knew it, she was calling the bartender over and asking about whisky. "Anything from Scotland? Anything at all?"

"Yeah, babe," she said. "Famous Grouse or Johnnie Walker."

Ruby considered her options. Honestly, she just wanted a drink. "I guess. . . ."

"Dinna do it." Ruby looked to her left; the Scottish voice from the office was lowering himself down onto the stool next to her. "If you care about whisky, dinna drink any of those."

Ruby stammered and tore a napkin to shreds on her lap. "Um, so, what do you recommend?"

"Krista," Grant said to the bartender, "would you please pour this woman a Balvenie Sherry Cask? And a double for me."

Balvenie. Yep. Definitely Brochan's dad.

Definitely.

Shit.

Shit, shit, shit, shit, shit.

Krista clicked her tongue again and reached under the bar for the secret bottle. She poured two glasses, neat, and set them down in front of Ruby and Grant. "Thanks," he said, then brought it up to his nose and inhaled. "I swear, this smells like my sister's holiday cake." Ruby shook her head in disbelief. It was almost exactly what Brochan had said, that night on Skye. Grant touched his glass to Ruby's, and she watched as he took a first slow sip. He looked *just* like Brochan. Same round cheeks (Grace had them, too). Same beard shape, except that Grant's was varying shades of gray and white, as was his hair. Familiar deep, dark eyes, for sure. They had the same build, although Grant was an inch or two shorter; and where Brochan's expansive torso was flat and trim, Grant's had gone soft. Everything about him just screamed *Brochan*. Everything inside Ruby screamed that she wanted Brochan to know this.

"This is wonderful; thank you," said Ruby as she took a small sip. Her mind was racing, every one of her synapses firing, as she tried to come up with a strategy. She knew she had to say something about Thistlecross to Grant; if she didn't, she'd only make things awkward and awful when he came to Scotland for the restaurant opening. But what should she tell him? And how much should she say? And how was she going to say any of it without admitting she was here for the sole reason of checking up on his restaurant?

Coming to the Wee Tartan Bagpipe was an awful idea.

Ruby was a terrible spy.

This was the craziest and dumbest thing she had ever done.

"I know who you are!" Ruby's face and chest immediately reddened. In lieu of having the right words, she decided to say the stupidest thing of all. *Super smooth, Roo. Just brilliant.*

Grant set his whisky on the bar. His face registered worry, and Ruby realized that whatever explanation was running through his mind had to do with the sexual harassment lawsuit he had been shouting about minutes earlier. *Even smoother.*

When Grant spoke, his words were measured and clipped, stripped of the congenial warmth they had carried moments before. "Do you? I'm sorry to admit I can't recall who you are. Have we met . . . ?"

"I'm sorry; that was a stunningly weird way to start a conversation," Ruby said. "Can I try again?"

Grant nodded; he was kind and patient when he listened, just like Brochan.

"My name is Ruby Spencer . . . I'm from Thistlecross."

Grant set his jaw. Ruby noticed that when he wasn't smiling, his face betrayed a deep, bone-aching tiredness. Two dusty-rose-colored smudges had settled into the delicate skin under his eyes. It was clear that Grant had not slept much lately. Ruby wondered if he'd looked like that since he left Scotland, or if this was all lawsuit related.

She hurried to clarify. "Well, not really. I'm from New York. But I've been living in Thistlecross for the last few months. Since spring. I . . . I know Brochan." Ruby placed both her hands on the bar to steady herself and bolster her courage. She looked at Grant with as much tenderness as she could muster. "I know what your whole family has been through."

"Oh . . ." Grant said. "Well, then." He took a hearty drink, then extended his hand to Ruby. "Hello."

Ruby shook his hand, not sure if the ball was back in her court. "Hi." She wanted him to start talking, but that didn't seem likely.

"Hallo," Grant said again, his Scottish accent becoming a shade thicker.

"I can imagine what you're thinking," she said, picking apart a few strands of hair at the bottom of her braid. "What is a New Yorker doing in Thistlecross, Scotland? What is a Thistlecross, Scotlander doing in Albany? Is she here to spy on us?"

Grant laughed then, big and loud. "It never crossed my mind that you might be a spy. But now you've got to come clean if you are."

Ruby smiled. Maybe this was going to be okay. He seemed nice. From everything Brochan had told her, she'd been imagining a monster. She decided not to hesitate: to come clean and tell him everything.

She explained that she'd been renting the stone cottage; he chuckled and asked if she'd meant "the flophouse." She laughed and said she supposed so. Then she told him about the Family Table suppers and how much she had fallen in love with the Cosy Hearth a.k.a. the Grottie Hermitage. She said she'd become friends with Grace and Brochan. Her cheeks betrayed her when she said Brochan's name, and knew that unless Grant was a fool he'd surely see the truth in their relationship. She dropped her voice to a whisper and said that she was at the town hall meeting when Winkler showed up, and she told Grant that building the new restaurant would mean displacing Grace, kicking her out of her home, and angering Brochan. Who was, all things considered, already quite angry. She admitted that he had probably thought about all this already.

"I'm sorry to be so forward, but I have to ask: Is this really something you want? Can't you see how it would hurt Thistlecross? And the people who live there?"

Grant sighed and rubbed the back of his neck with his palm. At that moment, Winkler strode past them with briefcase in hand. Ruby dove under the lip of the bar, pretending to rummage in her bag until he exited the building. When she resurfaced, there was a bit of paper straw wrapper stuck in the bottom of her braid. "Sorry. I don't know if he'd remember my face." She plucked off the wrapper and crumpled it into a ball. Grant glanced at Krista, who was busy chatting with a server at the other end of the bar.

"I can see there's no use in weaving a tale for you, is there?" Grant said. "You seem to know every card in my hand." He swallowed his whisky and reached for the bottle, which Krista had left on the bar. "To answer your question, Ruby, the New Yorker turned Scot and international woman of mystery: no. And, aye. I don't want this. I see how it would hurt my family. But my hands are tied."

"I just don't see how that's true," Ruby said. "You're Winkler's partner, aren't you? Doesn't a partner have an equal say?"

"If the partner is not a dunderhead who doesn't know how to read a contract, yes." Ruby's face fell. *Oh. This was bad.* "To be clear, I am the dunderhead. When Winkler proposed making me partner, I didn't exactly look at the fine print. I didn't know there was fine print. At the Grottie Hermitage, it was all just . . . in the family. There's an old piece of legal paper floating around somewhere, but Thistlecross moved a little slower. Less officially.

"Here, I'm a partner in name only; more like a glorified manager. Have been for more than thirty years. The Wee Tartan Bagpipe has changed a lot over the decades, but it's always been a disappointment to me. I thought it provided a way out. As it happens, it was all a trap."

A plaid, appropriated trap, thought Ruby.

"But you can leave, right? Why haven't you?"

Grant ran his thumb down the side of his glass. "I'm still paying back the money he gave me for Brochan and Grace."

"Wait, what? Brochan told me you sent money to cover his school expenses, but that was . . . money you earned, right? From selling the pub to the town? And, you know, *doing your job*?"

"Some of it, aye. But Grace told me how much damage I'd done to the reputation of the pub after Elisabeth died. You know about Elisabeth, I suppose?" Ruby nodded and took another small sip. "I ran that place to the ground; a well shan job of it. Nobody wanted to eat there anymore. And I left Grace with the mess. It was my fault, but my sister tried to fix it. There was never enough money for her to keep the lights on and pay the town for her rent."

"Sorry, I still don't understand. You were the one who sold the building to the town in the first place. Where did that money go?"

Grant gestured to the room around him. "Expanding the business. Opening up the first few franchises. Louis convinced me to put everything into this. He said I'd see it returned double." He hung his head and avoided Ruby's eyes. "I was drinking pretty heavily at that point. Does everyone just tell you their entire life story when they meet you, by the way? I don't mean to be saying all this." *But you are*, Ruby thought. *Keep going.*

"Anyhow, I invested all I had. Even sold my still. I really thought it was the right way to help Brochan, but when Grace let me know how rough things were in Thistlecross, I realized I'd been wrong. So I asked Louis for a loan, to help them. Back and forth we go."

"I hesitate to ask about the terms of the loan."

"I'm essentially a crofter for a corrupt landlord." Ruby knew that Grant was referencing the Clearances, the era in the late 1700s when Scottish Highlanders were evicted en masse from their land, or else forced to work an unsustainably small plot of land in exchange for astronomically high rent.

Grant gave a sad little smile. "Arguably the greatest tragedy in Scottish history, playing out here along the United States's eastern seaboard. The irony is not lost on me."

"So what happens now? You're just going to come to Thistle-cross and be his henchman?" Ruby realized she was pushing, maybe even being a little rude. But she had to get to the bottom of this. Nothing good ever came from being timid, that was for sure.

"I thought if I came back, I could make things better in Thistle-cross. If I was there. Find work for Grace in the kitchen, help Brochan out with a job, too."

"Brochan is doing just fine," Ruby spat out, suddenly defensive. "He's a general contractor, with his own home," she said. "But maybe you didn't know that."

Grant's eyes saddened and his shoulders slumped. "I mucked it up."

"You really did." A thought flashed in Ruby's mind. "And now a sexual harassment lawsuit? Grant, this will never fly in Thistlecross. We're a community there." Ruby realized that she was starting to sound a lot like Brochan. She was starting to think a lot like him, too. She really cared about her found town and everyone in it.

"Oh, no! It's not! I'm not!" Grant started and stumbled over his words. "The lawsuit is not about *me*." He pulled at his beard. "Saying this out loud makes me realize what a nightmare this has all become. But it's Louis. Winkler. An accountant at the Wee Tartan Bagpipe's headquarters said that he made a pass at her. She didn't take kindly to that, and he threatened to terminate her employment unless she—well, you can likely use your imagination. That's put a hold on progress in Thistlecross. Louis is a wee . . . distracted there."

Ruby studied him. "Do you believe her?"

Grant looked up from his lap and met her eyes. "I believe her."

Ruby breathed a little easier.

"Grant, do you actually understand why I'm here?"

"I . . . no."

Until that moment, Ruby hadn't, either. But suddenly, it was all clear.

"I'm here because Brochan and Grace—and I—want to stop the sale. We want to save the pub. I didn't plan on running into you, but at this point, I'd say you can either keep ignoring the reality of the situation and fight against us, or you can do the hard work and rally with us. I think that's what you want to do, but I can't be the one to make that choice for you, Grant."

They were both quiet. They were quiet for a long time.

Ruby was impressed with herself. She'd initially felt weird about coming here behind Brochan's back, but now she wished he were here to see her take charge.

"My grief has grown so large, I don't know what to call it," Grant finally said, staring into the empty glass.

Ruby did her zillionth brave thing of the year then, and placed her palm gently over Grant's hand. She looked at him even though he would not look back. "Call it home," she said.

Chapter Thirty-Seven

That night, wearing the dress Grace gave her, Ruby met Lee at a wine bar with soft, upholstered stools. Lee was a few minutes late, and she laughed when she saw her friend. "I told you to dress up, not play dress-up," she said, adjusting her jet-black bandage dress and flipping her bleached locks over a deep side part.

Ruby gestured to her tartan-print skirt and studied the red-and-green plaid for a moment before scowling playfully. "What's wrong with what I'm wearing?"

Lee motioned for the bartender and pointed at a bottle of gin. "Nothing . . . Lady Clodagh."

"Okay, again, with the Irish thing. Honestly, Lee, you are borderline offensive."

Lee laughed. "I'm taking that as a compliment. So. Start from the beginning."

"I know, and don't leave anything out."

Ruby spilled everything.

Lee's eyes were as round as martini glasses the whole time. "What're you gonna do?"

Ruby explained that she and Grant had spent an hour discussing the mess. Every possible solution seemed improbable until Grant floated the idea that maybe he should just start by showing up. In Thistlecross. At the beginning of September. As himself, not as Grant the manager-cum-henchman. Before leaving, he'd present the idea to Winkler as an opportunity to lay groundwork and scout staff while Winkler dealt with the mess he'd made at headquarters. But Grant's real mission would be mending the ties he'd spent the last thirty years severing. It was a no-plan plan, but it was the best they had. Ruby suspected it was the only real place to start.

Lee whistled. "Shit, girl. You think your man is going to go for that?"

Ruby dog-eared the corner of the wine list, then smoothed it back down. The selection wasn't as good as the menu at the Traveler. "I think he deserves a real apology from Grant. And who knows what will happen from there."

Lee popped an olive in her mouth. "That's not what I asked."

"Sure. There's a massive part of me that's convinced I'm making an even bigger mess. I basically invited him back to his hometown like *I* was the mayor. And now it feels too late to smooth it over without causing drama. I'm going to tell Brochan the second I get back to Thistlecross. He'll understand, and we'll work it out together."

Lee shook her head, and her momentary silence spoke volumes. She lifted the menu and studied the tapas section before knocking Ruby's shoulder with her own. "Hey, remember when you were going to move to Scotland for one year to become a recluse, drink scotch, and write a cookbook?"

"Ha. Yes, my whisky year. It all seemed so innocent. Well, best-laid plans, right?"

"Exactly. Turns out, you went to Scotland to get laid."

"Lee . . . that's . . . you're . . . no." Finally, Ruby gave up trying to reason with her best friend and just laughed. She held Lee's face in her hands and pressed their foreheads together. She didn't want to spend any time worrying. They only had a few more hours together before Ruby went back to the lake, and then back to Thistlecross. Back home.

Sometime after midnight, as Lee snored gently in the next bed over, Ruby's phone lit up. Brochan's name appeared on the screen, with a request to video chat. Ruby glanced at her best friend, then plunged her feet into her slippers and ducked into the bathroom.

"Hi," she said breathlessly, holding the phone at face level as she searched around for a place to sit. Finding nowhere appropriate, she sighed and put the toilet lid down, then settled in. Lee had booked a budget-priced hotel with the decor and ambiance to boot. All things considered, it was not the most glamorous place Ruby had ever taken a phone call.

"Erm, hello?" Brochan said, his bushy brows lifting to reveal mirthful eyes. "Shall I call back when you're done in the loo?"

"I'm in a hotel bathroom," Ruby said, and reached over to flick on a different switch, hoping the lighting was better. It was not.

"I can see that."

"Lee and I took a trip to Albany," Ruby said, meting out her words carefully. "We needed an adventure. She's in the room, sleeping. So." Ruby gestured and her hand hit the handle of a toilet brush. She winced as Benjamin's memory rudely interrupted their conversation. "I'm in here."

"I'm in bed," Brochan said, extending his arm and moving the phone farther away, so Ruby could see his body sprawled under a velveteen green quilt.

"Did you steal that blanket from my cottage?" Ruby whisper-squealed, happy that he had.

"Indeed I did. An equal exchange for my best flannel."

"Oh, well, you're never getting that back," Ruby said.

"And you've got to come home to me if you ever want to see your quilt again." Brochan pushed the fabric down a bit to reveal his bare torso.

"You're not wearing a shirt," Ruby observed.

"Right, because you stole it."

"Are you wearing pants?"

"In bed? Don't be ridiculous."

"Are you wearing underpants?"

"Are you?"

Ruby shifted on the toilet lid. "Yes."

"Take them off."

Ruby opened and closed her mouth. She'd never had phone sex, let alone FaceTime sex. (*Was that even a thing?*) The conditions were not ideal. The fluorescent light was hardly flattering. And yet. Through the screen, Brochan burrowed his arm under the quilt, and Ruby could make out the form of his hand wrapping around himself.

"You're *not* wearing underpants, then."

Brochan moved his hand slowly, slower than Ruby would have if it'd been her touching him, and repeated, "Take yours off."

Ruby stood and angled the phone down, toward her belly and then lower still.

"The palm trees!" Brochan broke character for a moment and laughed. "My favorite."

Ruby grinned into the camera. "I know."

"Off," he said, resuming his serious, bossy-Brochan voice.

"I feel a little nervous, Broo," Ruby said, edging her thumb into her waistband. "I'm scared to be on camera."

Brochan held the phone closer to his face so Ruby could see his expression soften. "You don't have to show me anything you don't want to," he said. "Keep the camera on your eyes so I can watch them light up when you touch yourself."

Ruby nodded, feeling comfortable and safe in his presence. Even if his presence was just on a screen. She stepped out of her panties. She turned around and flashed him a quick peek of her backside in the mirror, then hopped up onto the vanity ledge. "Is this okay?" The camera only caught her face and the upper part of her chest.

"It's perfect," Brochan said. "Now I can watch my favorite person as I imagine her hands on me."

Ruby trailed her own fingers down to her center and fluttered them over her skin. "Should I—should I touch myself, too?"

Brochan nodded and showed Ruby that he was doing the same.

"How?"

"However you like best," Brochan instructed, his voice catching as he got himself closer.

She started slowly, trying to match Brochan's speed. Neither of them spoke, but Ruby let a few faint gasps escape her lips, and Brochan heaved with anticipatory pleasure. It wasn't long at all before Ruby found a rhythm and quickened her pace, leaving Brochan behind. She had started by nervously watching him, but as she grew more confident she closed her eyes and focused on finishing herself off. "Oh, oh, *oh*!" she murmured.

She peeked out under her lashes and saw Brochan's huge smile emerge from behind his beard. "That's my lass," he said proudly. "How did it feel?"

Ruby nodded, unable to put the sensation into words. At least, not on such short notice, in a hotel bathroom at two o'clock in the morning. "I was trying to re-create the swirly thing you do." She paused. "But it's better with your tongue."

"Everything's better with you, as well," he said. "I was imagining your thighs around my legs."

"Did you—just now? Was I—?"

"Otherwise occupied? Yes. I did. With you."

"I missed it!"

"Your attention was exactly where it ought to have been."

"You're the best, honestly, Broo." Ruby sighed, and slid off the counter.

"We're the best. It's me and you. But until you return, it's me and Carson's bathroom renovation. I should get going; had a bit of a lie-in, obviously." It was almost seven in the Highlands, and the morning sun was throwing itself onto the bed in wide beams, making Brochan look like a piece of outlandishly handsome artwork.

"Hey. I love you," Ruby said as she waved into the camera.

"I love you, Roo."

Ruby ended the call. As she wiped the counter with a wad of tissues, a fierce and fiery blush spread across her neck, transforming into lighthearted laughter that bubbled up and out of her with abandon. She could not wait to get to Thistlecross.

Chapter Thirty-Eight

After an uneventful rest of the week and another marathon travel day, Ruby arrived at the Inverness train station. She was alone. And she was livid.

The day after their Albany adventure, Lee had driven Ruby back to the lake house and left for Ithaca, promising to visit Scotland soon. Well, just as soon as Ruby could procure an eligible bachelor for her to meet. Ruby snorted and smooshed Lee's cheeks in her hands and kissed her forehead, then sent her on her way. She had dinner with her parents, then snapped a photo of the sun sinking into the water and sent it to Brochan with the text, **Wish you were here, for real.**

That had been in the early evening, or after midnight in Scotland. But when two more sunsets came and went without a reply, Ruby started to worry. Why hadn't he responded? Why hadn't he responded to her follow-up text? Or her follow-up follow-up text? Was he mad? About what? Had she done something wrong? At first, she couldn't think of a thing, beyond the obvious. But that—her secret with Anne—that had happened ages ago. It didn't even matter. And there was no way he could have found out. She tried calling him, but got sent straight to voice mail. Rude!

That's when she started spinning out. Ruby had a sinking feeling that she was being deliberately ignored. Although that was of course better than the alternative answer she'd come up with (*Brochan's death by fire-breathing dragons?*), living through his silence seemed unbearable. Suddenly, Ruby couldn't get Margaret's phone call out of her mind. His ex had reached out (*AGAIN*), and he acted shady about it. Less than a week later, the man had dropped off the face of the planet. It was all just so suspicious. And so easy to torture herself over.

The week prior, they had made plans for her arrival back in Scotland; he was going to pick her up in Glasgow, right where he'd left her.

But when her plane landed, neither Brochan nor his truck was anywhere to be seen. She sent him an angry text (???????) and stomped off to buy a train ticket to Inverness. As the train chugged farther north, Ruby seethed. By the time she'd hailed a taxi at Inverness station, she was so angry that she slammed the duffel bag into the trunk, causing the zipper to break. A pair of palm tree–patterned underpants tumbled out, which Ruby snatched up and hurled into the rubbish bin on the curb. An act which she regretted immediately. They really had been her favorite pair.

She finally made it to Thistlecross, and marched straight into the Cosy Hearth. "Grace?" she called. "Grace, are you here?"

Grace doddered down the stairs and met Ruby in the bar, which was desolate and felt cavernous. "Welcome home," Grace said.

ROCHELLE BILOW

Ruby took three deep breaths. When she felt calm enough to continue, she responded. "Thank you. What is going on with Brochan? Please? He won't talk to me, so you have to."

Grace's sigh was weighted and heavy, but it didn't seem to lift any load from her spirits. "This is for the two of you to resolve."

"Resolve what?" Ruby's fingers rapidly undid and rewove her braid.

Grace shook her head and Ruby snapped her elastic back into place. "I guess I'll just take a quick bath and then go find out for myself." She was halfway out up the stairs when she remembered something important. She had to tell Grace about Grant. About the fact that he was coming to Thistlecross. In, um, two weeks. Grace would understand. And not judge her. And maybe, if Ruby was lucky, tell her what to do next.

Grace listened patiently as Ruby described her visit to the Wee Tartan Bagpipe and her conversation with Grant. Her face registered only base emotion as Ruby finished confessing. "So he's coming here. To Thistlecross. I think he means well. You have to give him a chance! He's your family, after all."

Grace's mouth opened slightly and she shook her head. "Oh . . . Ruby."

"Is that okay? Are you mad? It was his decision, really. I was just . . . the catalyst." Ruby twisted the toe of her shoe into the stair.

Grace lowered herself onto one of the bar stools and motioned for Ruby to come sit next to her. Ruby looked questioningly at Grace. Grace patted Ruby's hand. "It will be a gift to see my brother again. Life's surprises are just small miracles, in the end.

But I know someone who might need a little more convincing. And what you've just told me complicates matters a touch."

"Please," Ruby begged. "I need to know what's going on."

Grace looked around the room as if someone might've been hiding behind the armchair, then gave an almost imperceptible nod. A few nights ago, she told Ruby, Brochan and Kyle had gone to the Traveler Hotel for a drink. "I just can't justify keeping those sour beers in stock here," she told Ruby. "And the boys do like them."

Three goses deep, Anne Dunbar walked in—she'd planned on having a nightcap by herself. To everyone's surprise, the three old mates ordered a bevvy together. For old times' sake. Or for something new. After that, they ordered whisky. For atonement of friendship wrongs committed. By the end of the night, thoroughly drenched in alcohol, Brochan and Anne had forgotten why they'd held such trivial grudges against each other in the first place.

"That's great!" Ruby said, forgetting, just for a second, to be upset. It would be so cool if the three of them could hang out. Well, if Brochan hadn't already left her for his ex.

Grace gave Ruby a pitying look and continued.

And then, in a whisky spritzer haze, Anne told Brochan that she adored his girlfriend. It was an offhand comment, one meant as a compliment and made in attempt to bring them all closer together.

"But you don't know Ruby," Brochan had said. The two women had only just met at the town hall meeting. And that didn't count.

"Sorry, mate, she's amazing and essentially my girl now," Anne had said, and laughed, as she recounted their first meeting. She was so caught up in the alcohol, and the good feeling of being reunited with her old friends, that it wasn't until the very end of the story that she noticed Brochan's face. Recalling the memory of her pinkie swear with Ruby, Anne sat up very straight and squeezed her eyes shut. She whispered "shite" and waited.

Brochan grew quiet, then uttered two words before standing up, depositing a wad of cash onto the bar—leaving a full glass of Balvenie behind—and walking out the sliding glass doors.

Anne's face was ashen as she confirmed to Kyle what Brochan had murmured on his way out: "Ruby knew."

Despite being terribly jet-lagged, Ruby *flew* to Brochan's barn.

As she streaked by the cattle and down his drive, she understood, for the first time, the ramifications of her decision to keep Anne's secret. It wasn't just withholding important information, which was bad enough. Ruby had betrayed his trust. Brochan had told her that he was scared to be with a partner who kept secrets. And that was exactly what Ruby had done.

She slowed to a walk and tried to get her thoughts to follow suit.

So maybe I didn't deserve to be stranded at an airport, but I understand why he's angry.

I never meant to hurt him.

I thought I was trying my best.

My best apparently sucks.

How can I explain this to him?

I guess I could just be finally, fully honest.

She wasn't sure how to have this conversation, but that seemed like a good place to start. She'd tell him she understood how badly he was hurting. And even though he might try to push her away, she would apologize. They could get through this. They had to. They were Broo and Roo!

With a quick knock, she called for him. "Brochan? It's me."

There was no answer, but she could hear two voices coming from inside. She almost banged harder, but fear gripped at her and instead she hovered her ear next to the door. She could make out Brochan's clipped tone.

"I don't know if she'll forgive me, Margaret."

MARGARET? Ruby smashed her face up next to the wood.

"B, she will. Oright, yes; keeping our relationship a secret from her was bad. But you two are so good together. You're, like, neeps and tatties."

B??? Ruby couldn't listen a second longer. She pushed open the door and tumbled into the barn.

Her heart cracked as her eyes landed on Brochan, leaning against the reclaimed wood wall, on the floor next to the bed. His legs were wide and knees were bent; bare feet on the floor. His work shirt was unbuttoned to reveal his chest; in his hand was a glass of whisky. By his side, and just as shoeless, with a glass of her own, was Anne.

Chapter Thirty-Nine

Oh," said Ruby. "I . . . it's me." It took everything she had, but she kept her eyes on Brochan as her hand found its way to the wooden medallion at her throat. She touched it lightly and then let her arm fall limply to her side.

"Ruby, this is not how it looks," Anne said, jumping up and taking a step toward the door, then a step backward. She looked from Brochan's chest to her bare feet to the bed. "Admitting it looks bad."

"Putting it mildly," Ruby fired back. It looked like they had just had very sexy sex. Or were about to. Or both. She paused a beat before adding, "*Margaret.*"

"Margaret Anne," she said with a shake of her head. "Nobody calls me Margaret. Well—almost nobody." *Oh, so Brochan had a secret nickname for her? That made things so much better.* The mayor's hair cascaded over her shoulders like a waterfall, and she ran her hand down its length, cupping it in her palm toward the ends. "I should have told you we dated. But it was so, so long ago. And I thought it was his responsibility. I can't believe he didn't."

Brochan set his whisky on the floor and strode across the

barn to meet Ruby. He put his hands on her shoulders, but she shook them off. "Your childhood best friend is the ex-girlfriend you're still obsessed with? How could you keep this from me?"

"He's not obsessed with me," said Anne at the same time Brochan said, "I'm not obsessed with her."

The three of them were standing in an uncomfortable little circle. Ruby pointed at Anne's chest. "You keep texting him! And calling him!"

"I can explain that," Brochan interjected.

"I don't think you can. Clearly you aren't finished with each other. And, oh my *god*, here I am, keeping secrets and playing the loyal fool for both of you." Ruby's remorse and shame was all red-hot rage now.

Anne touched the crook of Ruby's elbow with her pale pink nails. Ruby glanced down at them and noticed, for the first time, how sharp they looked. Like ten perfectly manicured, high-gloss arrowheads.

"Ruby, I'm sorry. I want to talk about all this, but you two should, first. I'll go," she said. She pulsed gently on Ruby's arm, then stepped into her pumps by the door. "Tell each other the truth," she said. "And listen."

Fuck off, Ruby thought as the door shut, feeling ashamed of her strong reaction, but unable to settle on anything lesser. A heavy silence hung between Brochan and Ruby.

"So," Ruby said, starting to pace. "Let's sort this out. You found out I had kept a secret from you—to protect your heart— and you decided to punish me by leaving me in the lurch at a foreign airport miles from my home?" Brochan started to speak, but Ruby barreled over him. "Despite the fact that you were keeping a much worse secret from me this whole time. You had about seven thousand opportunities to tell me that the mayor of Thistlecross was your ex-girlfriend. It could have come up in conversation very naturally. Unless you've been sleeping with her all along! Which clearly, you have been. And to think, the only reason I kept *her* secret was because I thought she was my friend. I'm such a feckin' eejit." Ruby clapped her hand over her mouth. *Wait, was that my first Scottish-ism?*

She stopped pacing and faced him.

"Say something," she commanded.

"I never meant to hurt you."

The words rattled around Ruby's skull; they were the exact ones she had come here to tell him. But her hurt suddenly seemed more important than his. More painful! More pressing!

She wanted to beg him to tell her he hadn't touched Anne, hadn't kissed her, hadn't slept with her, but she was too scared to ask. If he had, everything would be over. There was no way out of that. Not for Ruby. Not after Benjamin, not again. They both let the silence grow.

"And also, it would have been very easy for you to tell me you knew about the sale of the Cosy Hearth. We both kept secrets from each other," said Brochan steadily. "But Margaret and I have been over for a long time." He took her hands and brought them to his chest. "I'd never cheat on you."

Ruby wavered. Even if that was true—if they hadn't been intimate—hadn't he wanted to? Hadn't Anne? Or, whatever, Margaret? Ruby mind tripped back to that first text she saw. *No strings.*

This had all gotten so messy. There were layers upon layers of lies.

And, ugh, Ruby knew that things were about to get even worse.

"Ah, fuck," she said. "Brochan, I went to the Wee Tartan Bagpipe in Albany and I met your dad."

Brochan released her hands and took a step backward.

"I didn't mean to—to meet him. It was a freak accident. I didn't even know he was going to be there." Now he began to pace. "Damn it, Brochan, Yes. I'm sorry. I'm sorry I kept a . . . couple of secrets from you. But I never meant to betray your trust. You have to realize that when Anne told me, I had no idea . . ." She stopped, then decided to push through the familiar calcification that was rapidly spreading over her heart. "And I was only trying to help." She pulled her hand through her curls, trying to emulate the smooth motion of Anne's hand, but her fingers got stuck halfway down. "After the town hall, I honestly didn't think it was that big of a deal. Because you knew everything that I knew. And apparently more."

He shot a pained look in her direction, out from beneath his moody brows.

"But we did meet, your father and me. And we talked about everything; about what happened, and Winkler, and just all of it. He regrets leaving Thistlecross, Brochan. He regrets leaving you."

Ruby picked up Anne's abandoned glass and took a big, messy gulp. She sank onto the bed.

"And he's coming here, in two weeks, to try and make amends."

She offered the whisky to Brochan, but he sat, unmoving, and continued to let the seconds tick by in agonizing slow motion.

Finally, she said the only thing she could think of.

"Do you need a thermos?"

"It's not a joke, Ruby."

"I know."

"He's not a good man, and I don't want him here."

"I know," she said again, unsure of what else she could possibly offer.

"And yet you invited him."

"I was trying to help. I thought I was doing the right thing."

"Aye, that's just it, isn't it? That's the problem."

Ruby didn't know what he meant, but she knew it wasn't good. It was annoying, the way he was getting angry with her when she was trying to be angry with him. She felt short of breath, like her lungs were being crushed under the weight of a thousand bagpipes. A thousand wee tartan bagpipes.

Finally, Brochan turned to look at her. "I don't know if we can trust each other again. When you first showed up, I thought you could be a fling. I never expected you to actually want to stay, and that seemed fine. Then you charmed me, straightaway, and I figured, *What the hell—if anyone is worth the risk, it's her.*" He spat out the next string of words: "But if this was meant to be real . . . why has it been so hard for us to just be honest with each other?"

Fling.

Fling, fling, fling, fling, fling.

FLING.

Any of the beautiful, special moments that hadn't been annihilated by the image of Anne next to his bed were dissolved by *fling*. What a tiny, disgusting word.

"So, what? I handle something differently than you would have, and suddenly I'm a stupid tourist who doesn't understand your arrogant Scottish man brain? Just because I haven't lost a parent doesn't mean I haven't been hurt. Just because I didn't grow up here doesn't mean I can't belong. Or maybe there are some things *Margaret* just does better."

Her anger had frothed his into a frenzy.

"Ruby, you're twisting my words. I didn't say any of that." he said, his voice now edging toward a shout. "But now that you've brought it up, aye; I am finding it hard to find faith in you right now. My da willingly abandoned me when I needed him most. So forgive me for not entirely trusting a woman who's so lost, she doesn't even know where her loyalties lie."

Ruby blinked twice. *One, two. Fuck, you, Broo.* She jumped up from the bed.

"Loyalties?" She polished off the whisky in a single swig; it hurt as it tumbled down her throat. "Loyalties? Yes! Let's talk loyalties! Let's talk about you revenge-screwing your secret ex-girlfriend in your dirty old barn because you got *mad at me*? You're a child."

Brochan stood and his hands flew up to grip his scalp, then balled back down in fists. "I didn't fuck her, Ruby!"

"And I'm supposed to believe that?"

"About as well as I'm to believe anything you say."

The alcohol that Ruby had knocked back so aggressively was not sitting well. Not at all. She could feel the fire coming back up her throat, and she knew what was next. She covered her mouth with both hands but couldn't contain the enormous belch that rocketed out.

Brochan's lower lip trembled, and he almost allowed laughter to escape.

Apparently that was all he needed to pull him back into his body, back into his heart, because the next thing he said was, "Oh, Roo. I love you so much."

He tried to reach for her hand, to pull her into his arms, but she snapped it back away from him and made for the door.

No. He does not get to touch me. He doesn't deserve that. Not anymore.

She stood up by herself and paused with her hand on the doorknob. What the hell: Why not be honest? She hadn't come to Scotland (twice now, technically) to trudge along blindly, feeling adrift and dissatisfied. Ruby Spencer was sick and tired of men playing the romantic lead until it was time to actually show up and do real things—hard things!—and Brochan Wood was going to hear all about it.

"Ruby, please," he said, and he looked so handsome and wounded that she wanted to cry. But only for a moment. She launched into it.

"You know, I can handle challenges in my life. I've been doing it perfectly well on my own for years now. But it's nothing compared to the predictable disappointment this turned out to be." She made a rapid swirling motion with her index finger at the word *this*, circling the space between them. Her eyebrows were stitched together in angry arches and her hair was falling into her face. She looked crazy. She sounded crazy. She probably was crazy, at least a little bit. She didn't care. She waited for him to interject, or argue for himself—for them—but he remained quiet, looking at her under heavy eyelids.

"Life gets weird and messy. And doing life with another person is even harder. I had given up on the idea I'd find a man who was ready to dive in with me. After the romantic weekend getaways. A man who could deal with imperfections and mistakes and awkward growing pains. You want honesty? Here's some: That man just doesn't exist. He sure as hell isn't you.

"Turns out, *B*"—she sneered out his ex's nickname for him—"you were just another notch in my bedpost."

She slammed the door behind her. As she walked back to the cottage, hugging herself tightly, tears streaked down her cheeks. The sky was cloudy and the road was quiet, and even the cows had run out of things to say.

Chapter Forty

Ruby hated Brochan Wood. She hated him and the way he wore his ugly flannel shirts rolled up past the elbows. She hated his red-brown beard and his dorky cheeks. She hated the way butter got stuck in his mustache and smelled weird if it had been there for a few hours, and she hated that when they fell asleep together, he starfished all over the bed, encroaching on her side and suffocating her with his hairy man body. She didn't care about him and his whisky pipe dreams and his beautiful ex-girlfriend. She didn't care at all! Ruby hated that 49 percent of her wanted to run right back into his arms. But 51 percent hated that he hadn't run out of the barn into hers. Stupid, stupid Brochan.

She slowed her pace and dried a few tears with the back of her hand. What was she thinking? No—scratch that. What was she feeling? Ruby was hurt and scared, and at the same time, she wanted to be brave. On the one hand, hadn't she intended to make a life here with or without him? Hadn't she specifically committed to that on the night of the town hall meeting?

But on the other hand, which was a very big hand, later that night she had told him she loved him and given him a blow job.

So . . . complications. Ruby couldn't imagine forging forward with her dream to make a fresh start here if Brochan was around but not hers. What would that even look like seeing him on the street? Showing up at the same bar on Friday night? One does not simply live in Thistlecross and be without Brochan. Brochan *was* Thistlecross. He was all of Scotland—the whole damn country, from Edinburgh to St. Kilda island. She hated herself for letting her connection to this beautiful, wild place become tangled up with a man.

And then there was the issue of Anne, a.k.a Margaret. Could she live in a place where the mayor was her ex-friend and also her ex-boyfriend's ex-girlfriend? All the excellent things about living in Thistlecross were getting scrubbed clean. Could it be her place if she didn't have any people here?

Ruby's head hurt and her heart was heavy.

And she needed a scone.

Back in the soft, warm respite of the Cosy Hearth, Ruby felt a little calmer. She told Grace about her argument, and Grace held her so tightly against her chest she thought she might pop.

"I don't fault you for what you did. It was brave of you to take matters into your own hands, and it was a wise thing to invite Grant here. In many ways, you've been more courageous than I have in the last thirty years. A Wood man plays at being strong, but the truth is, his person is his pillar."

Ruby tried at a smile, but it came out as a grimace. "If only that were enough." She picked at her pastry, dunking bits of it in a mug until they were saturated with strong black tea. "Grace? Is Anne . . . ? Do you think they . . . ?" She couldn't bring herself to finish either of those sentences.

"Oh, now. My boy was smitten with her something awful when they were young. But I've never seen him light up the way he does with you pottering around my kitchen." Grace offered a comforting nod. "After they went their separate ways, he swore he'd never get tangled up with her again, and I'll admit I was glad for it. She's a lovely lass, but she's not for him. Nor he for her."

A piece of Ruby's scone broke off and floated in the tea, like a crumbling island. "Was my lie as bad as his lie?"

Grace crossed her arms. "I don't think that matters."

"How, now?"

"He loves you. And you're his person."

Ruby looked out the window to where two rowan trees mingled, their branches touching.

Grace followed Ruby's gaze. "It's beautiful, isn't it?"

"What's that?"

"The way the trees look as though they are reaching for each other."

Ruby agreed that it certainly seemed that way.

"But of course they aren't. They're only growing, on their own terms, next to each other. When they find each other, it's by accident. That is what makes it beautiful."

Grace pressed the pads of her thumbs into Ruby's cheeks and wiped away two tears that had been racing down either side of her nose. It felt so good to be touched like that: gently and kindly. Ruby's heart surged for Grace as her friend smiled with her eyes.

"And Brochan will come around. In his own time."

Ruby wasn't so sure about that; they had both said words they could never take back. It was one thing to lob insults at each other. Honestly, a once-in-a-while fiery fight could be kind of hot. But this was deeper than makeup sex. They had revealed a lack of trust, a crack in the very foundation of their relationship. And Ruby didn't have to be the town handyman to know that a house built on shaky ground was not a house that would stand for long.

"But the fact of the matter is"—Grace knuckled under Ruby's chin and guided her gaze up, steering her attention back to the present—"my brother is coming to town, and if the Wee Tartan Bagpipe is half as bad as you described, he'll be needing a proper Scottish supper."

Ruby slowly nodded. Right. Life goes on, even when men suck. Especially when men suck. She had set this chain of events in motion, and now she had to see them through. Her mind started whirring and spinning with options. *Did they dare be brave enough to reinstate the Family Table dinners for Grant's arrival? If they did, who could they invite? Who would come? And, obviously most pressing: What would they cook?*

"Invitation only," said Grace, reading Ruby's mind. "We'll pick who comes, so it's a gentle reentry for Grant. He's been through a lot, and he needs to be handled with care."

Ruby wondered if Grace had forgiven Grant long ago, but had simply given him the space and distance she thought he needed. How was that even possible? Ruby was a thread puller; she'd pick at a loose strand until her sweater was a pile of yarn on the floor. Even now, she wanted to run back to the barn and outline a clear ending with Brochan. To create boundaries and rules. But Grace wasn't like that. Steady, stable Grace. Grace, who was already rummaging through the cupboards, pulling out spices and jars of dried goods.

Ruby followed suit, reaching for a notepad. She divided the paper into two with a horizontal line. In the top half, she wrote:

GUEST LIST FOR GRANT'S SUNDAY SUPPER

1. *Grace*
2. *Ruby*
3. *Grant*
4. *Neil*
5. *Carson*
6. *Sofie*
7. *Mac*
8. *Brochan (Is this weird?)*

Ruby tried to stuff her anxieties about Brochan back in her emotional duffel. Despite the fact that they seemed to be at an end, it was *his* father coming to town. She wanted to give him the chance to make his own decision about how to handle that. And besides, it would be a good trial run: Could she do Thistlecross with Brochan present but not at her side? It seemed like a long shot, but they were in the fourth quarter, with seconds left on the clock. At least, Ruby thought that's how sports metaphors worked. Or were there halves in a basketball game? *Focus, Roo.*

On the bottom portion of the page, she wrote:

WHAT THE HECK ARE WE GOING TO COOK
FOR THIS MEAL?

Grace nodded in approval at the first list, then tapped at the second heading with her index finger. "Ruby Spencer, we've got some work to do."

Chapter Forty-One

For the next few days, Ruby didn't have time to parse out how things had gone down with Brochan. And Anne/Margaret. Which was fine, because neither of them had reached out to her. Obviously they were very busy having excellent sex. Which was also fine, because Ruby did not care at all. Ruby was very, *very* busy cooking.

Together with Grace, she pored over old recipe cards, written in impeccable script by Grace and Grant's parents, and by their parents before them. The recipes that made up the Cosy Hearth's canon were old. They had soul. Ruby and Grace used those flavors as inspiration, brainstorming ways to breathe new life into the food Thistlecross had been eating for generations. They wanted to create a meal that walked the line between traditional and creative: a little home-grown comfort married with a touch of modern freshness. "So everyone at the table feels seen and heard," Grace had said.

Ruby's stand-in Scottish mum had another trick up her sleeve. Toward the end of the week, as Ruby worked her hands into a batch of savory pie dough, Grace motioned for Ruby to join her at the door of a broom closet. Ruby ran her hands under the tap and wiped them dry.

"Go on," Grace coaxed, inviting her to turn the knob.

What Ruby had assumed was a boring storage nook was actually an intimate room. This one was tiny, with low wood beams and cool stone walls. There were a few wood barrels stacked in a corner; Ruby tapped one with her knuckle to find it empty. The windowpane featured the same leaded glasswork as the one in her cottage. And in Brochan's barn. The focal point of the room was a beautiful fireplace, covered in a patina of ash and black soot. It felt old. It smelled like must and wood. It looked like Scotland. "This . . . It's . . . I mean," Ruby stammered, realizing that she'd been seeing the two chimneys on the building for months without questioning the source of the second one.

Grace grinned. "Welcome to the Cosy Hearth."

Ruby ran her hand over the mantel in disbelief. So this was the *real* Cosy Hearth. How many more secrets was this little town holding? Ruby smiled for the first time in days. Probably more than she'd ever unearth. That was one of the things she loved about Thistlecross: there was always something new to learn. It was quiet and unassuming, but it was wild, too. It wasn't boring. It challenged her.

Grace spread her arms out like the room was a gift. "This is where Grant—and his father, and his father—used to age their whisky. I've kept it shuttered since he left. Although I'll admit I always held out hope that Brochan would find himself here someday, bottling his own. It seems like the right place for our supper, doesn't it, then?"

Ruby didn't speak, just continued trailing her fingers over the dusty surfaces, drinking in the room.

Worried Ruby's silence indicated dissatisfaction, Grace continued to make a case. "It's not too small, see. We can move the bar tables in here, push them together to make a communal one. It's close to the kitchen, and we can clean out the hearth."

"It's beautiful," said Ruby, and this time, the tears that filled her eyes were gentle and sweet tasting. She couldn't help it; she thought of Brochan. She wondered if he had any memories or feelings connected to this room, then reminded herself that she shouldn't care.

Grace shook her head. "Of course, we'll serve the good whisky. Unless"—she looked momentarily concerned—"Neil's drunk it all." Ruby's mouth turned up into a smile that turned into a laugh; and it felt magnificent, even though tears were still pricking at the outside edges of her eyes. Especially because of that.

"Grace, can I tell you something a little crazy?"

Grace nodded but held up her finger. *Wait.* She reached into the cupboard and pulled out one of two bottles nestled in the back. The last of Grant's whisky. Aged in barrels for more than thirty years and every bit as clever and complex as it had been on bottling day. She broke the seal and took a sip, then handed the bottle to Ruby, who delighted in this breach of propriety. Ruby sipped, and wiped her mouth.

"Even though I have my parents back in New York, something about you . . . and this place . . . it just feels like home. You feel like family. Like *my* family. Learning from you and cooking with you has been one of the great joys of my life."

"I couldn'ta said it better myself," said Grace, slipping into the deepest version of her Scottish accent that tended to appear whenever she felt sentimental (or got tipsy). She held Ruby's face in her hands and smiled. "I do feel as though you're the daughter I never had."

Ruby's heart swelled as the whisky swirled in her veins.

I'm not alone. I'm not the Isle of Roo.

I have two families. And they love me!

No matter how many men come and go and thrill me or trick me.

The whisky year was a massive success.

Quitting my job and moving to the Scottish Highlands to write a cookbook was the smartest and best thing I've ever done.

Ruby's runaway train of thoughts screeched to a halt at a giant flashing sign.

I know what cookbook I'm meant to write.

"Grace," she said, reaching for the bottle of whisky. "I have an idea. . . ."

Chapter Forty-Two

For the rest of that week and into the next, Ruby was immensely grateful for the distraction of the impending dinner party and her new, infinitely improved cookbook project. It was good to keep occupied, because the second she stopped working, a dumpster of hot garbage emotions smoldered in her brain.

She had undeniably destroyed things with Brochan, but then he had undeniably destroyed things with her. Who was to blame? She waffled here, before reminding herself that it was him. Duh. It was clearly him. She deserved someone who would be a strong and equal partner for her. Someone who would not screw his ex-girlfriend and lie about it for months. Someone who wouldn't hold a double standard, requiring her to be perfect while sliding deeper into a hurtful lie himself. She wanted to believe that "nothing" had happened with Anne, but what she had witnessed was at least a little something. And a little something was more than Ruby could bear. Her faith was shaken. This was always the way things went for Ruby: there was always some glaring flaw that made it impossible to settle down with a man. Something she couldn't ignore. It was just frustrating that she'd been strung along for so long this time.

But (complications) in the most secret chamber of her heart, she still wanted her person to be Brochan. If Ruby thought a little harder about things, she caught glimpses of another possible explanation. That she was the one keeping herself single. That her standards and expectations were pushing men away. Maybe she needed to figure out where she fit in before she could find a man who fit her. Now that she knew where she belonged, she understood who she was. She hadn't really grasped those things when she and Brochan first fell into bed together. This newfound confidence made her wonder if, this time, with Brochan, *she* was the one who'd destroyed all that good stuff; stuff they'd built together . . . just because things got hard. In this scenario, Brochan had indeed lit the world on fire. And Ruby had burned the marshmallows.

She worked on her new cookbook proposal late into the night, her fingers flying over the laptop keyboard every evening. Finally exhaustion took hold, and a few days before Grant's arrival, she woke to the late-morning sun. She stretched and yawned, then padded outside to open the henhouse. "Ladies," Ruby said, gathering a few eggs from the nest basket. The chickens strutted down the walk and scratched at the dirt. As Ruby turned toward the Cosy Hearth to make breakfast, she passed by the leaded glass window of her cottage. There, leaning against the pane, was a neatly folded piece of paper with her name on it. Well. Her nickname.

Ruby dropped the eggs in surprise and they splattered next to her shoes, but she ignored the mess and strode to the window in three big leaps. She opened the paper and read, her lips quietly forming the words out loud.

Roo,

    Well. It's been over a week without you starfishing all over my bed as we sleep, and I must report that I don't like being without you. I don't like it at all. I've tried to give you space, but I miss you and I'm ready to talk. If you are.

    I didn't tell you about Margaret because I was afraid that if you knew how close she was—that she was here, in Thistlecross—you'd leave. But that was rubbish, and I'm an arse. As you know. I carried that hurt for years, and it clouded my vision. My anger at her got in the way of my love for you. But, Ruby, I never kissed her, never touched her, never wanted anyone but you.

    I understand why you invited my father. But I'm still angry at him, and I'm afraid I'm not able to forgive what he did. What if I'm dead inside? Ha. Sorry. That's not funny at all. I wish you were here tonight, so we could talk about these things and you could help me make sense of them.

    Grace told me about the Family Table, about Grant's

dinner. I want to be there to support you, but I don't want
to see my da. I don't think he deserves it. I don't know what
to do, and I don't know what you want. Meet with me?
There's still something I want to ask you.

Talk with me? Be with me?

Broo

Ruby sank onto the ground and let the paper flutter into her
lap. She pulled her cell from the pocket of her jeans and took a
picture of Brochan's words. She sent it in a text to Lee, who'd been
talking Ruby off the ledge all week. She responded immediately.

Lee: well? thoughts and feels??

Ruby: He lied about her for months and months.

Lee: about the same length of time you lied to him

Ruby: I lied by omission.

Lee: um, roo. so did he—literally the same sitch

Ruby: Can I forgive him?

Lee: IDK . . . can you?

Ruby: This is Benjamin all over again.

Lee: it is not

Lee: practically speaking this is not the worst thing a man has
ever done

Lee: practically speaking you're still in love with him

Lee: and he's hung

Lee: haha

Lee: sorry

Ruby: You are a filthy animal.

Ruby: Weird thing is, I was kind of getting used to Thistlecross
without him. It is lonelier. Less sexy obviously. But still good.
It still feels like home.

Lee: what if you gave him a chance to be a good guy?

Lee: are you going to write him back?

Ruby typed out three skull emojis and then deleted them.
She typed out one weepy-eyed emoji, then deleted it. Finally, she
just wrote, **I don't know**, pocketed her phone, and went to hose the
egg yolk from her shoelaces.

Chapter Forty-Three

Ruby had invited everyone on the list—except Brochan; Grace had taken care of that—to Sunday's dinner. Mac, Sofie, and Carson all gave enthusiastic yeses. Neil was obviously in, having spent the last week "helping" the two women by telling stories and entertaining them with jokes as they cooked.

But now, she was in the kitchen alone. She had just wrapped up a tray of peeled vegetables and was heating milk on the stove for the purpose of having a warm mug of something when she heard the door to the pub creak open. Ruby paused, her hand on the saucepan, waiting. It was late, and Ruby didn't have the energy for whoever this was.

"It's me. Don't shoot! I brought chocolate."

Ruby sighed as Anne pushed aside the curtain and entered the kitchen, depositing a box of chocolate-dipped shortbread on the butcher block table. "Curiously, this is from New York," she said. "It's the best I've found. Don't tell anyone I said that. Kidding, of course. No more secrets. Tell the world!" She offered a smile.

Ruby turned the package over in her hand and studied the ingredients: *flour, butter, sugar, salt, chocolate.* It seemed impossible to screw up something with so few ingredients, but good short-bread was hard to find. "Thanks. I'll try it later."

"So, this whole situation is absolutely fucked," Anne said, settling down onto a stool. "And as much as I'd like to blame my eejit ex-boyfriend, most of the responsibility is mine." She took a chance and sneaked a wink at Ruby. "Besides, he's no longer my eejit ex-boyfriend. He's your perfect current boyfriend."

"You both say nothing happened between you two, but . . . how can I believe that? You literally asked him for a one-night stand. I *saw* the text."

Anne cringed. "Uff. I did, that. I was desperate, and horny. Do you know how long it's been since I've had a pump with a man? He was wearing JNCO jeans and we shared an Irn-Bru." Ruby crossed her arms and bit her lip to keep from laughing. "Texting Brochan was desperate and dumb. We hadn't really spoken in *years*. And that was before I knew you two had taken up. And before I knew you, full stop. I wanted to get off, but not as badly as I want you to become my mate."

Ruby stirred the milk as it started to bubble around the edges.

"We were together ages ago. Bairns, really. We did get engaged; I can't deny that. And I loved him. I did. But it never felt right. Not like you're meant to feel, when you're *in* love. We were . . . comfortable. I think we mistook inside jokes and pet names for intimacy—like the way he insisted on calling me Margaret." She pinked a little around her cheekbones. "He never got me all hot and bothered. I never felt like I *needed* him. I was young. Immature. So instead of talking about all that, I moved to another country. Problem solved, however madly."

"I may or may not have tried that tactic," Ruby admitted.

"But he's still my childhood best mate, and I still care about his happiness. I was chuffed when I met you, and realized that you two were . . . falling in. It seemed right. I wanted it to work for you."

"So why did you go over to his barn? The night I came back? Why did you call him the week before? Nothing in this situation inspires confidence that you two are ready to move on."

"Och, Roobs. Can I call you that? Please don't say no. It's twee. Don't hit me with that pan, but I can't tell you. I know! Secrets. I was helping him with a project. I cannot say any more, but I promise that's all it was." Anne held out her pinkie and put her other hand on her hip. Ruby didn't take it. "It's a good secret, not a scary one." Anne wiggled her finger and gave one last attempt: "Hens before mens?" She shifted her weight, and Ruby took note of her shoes: an old pair of running trainers. No heels. That was different. It made her feel a little better.

She tentatively reached out and gave Anne's littlest finger a pulse. "I just can't shake the feeling that it's you two against me. Even if you're not romantically involved, you're conspiring together. And I hate that."

"I hate that you feel that way, too! If anything, I want the 'us' to be you and me. Not you and Brochan. Because I am a selfish wench. But I'll settle for being your clinger."

Ruby poured the milk into two mugs. She hadn't been anything but a "me" for a decade. Now she had to decide which Scot to form an alliance with? "I don't even know what to call you," she said, handing a mug to Anne.

"Anne, please. *Margaret* makes me think of my miserable childhood. Also, it was my grandmother's name and she was a wicked bitch." It was just impossible not to give in to this woman. Anne. She was wild and fun and she reminded Ruby so much of Lee, it made her heart hurt. Well, Ruby reasoned, if she was going to walk away from a partnership with Brochan, at least she could build a solid friendship.

"You don't want to come to dinner on Sunday, do you? For Grant? He's coming back early—I'm sure you've heard."

"Aye . . . but no. I want to. Grace may not want me there. And Brochan . . . it would be odd. I'm sorry; you've invited me twice and twice I've turned you down."

"Anne, when has this entire year not been odd? I don't even know if Brochan is coming."

Anne reached for the package of shortbread and untied the twistie. "I'll chew on it." She held a cookie out to Ruby. "But you should talk to him before then. I know he wants to talk to you. And ask you something. . . ."

"Blah," said Ruby, freeing a cookie from the plastic.

After they'd demolished the shortbread, Anne gave Ruby a tight hug. As she watched her friend wave from the path, Ruby felt a small glimmer of hope. Hope for Thistlecross, and for her future in it. Uncertainty and fear, but hope, too.

She tidied the kitchen and prepared to walk back to her cottage. Ruby thought about Anne's advice. *Talk to him. Listen to each other.* She grabbed the notepad from under the bar and scribbled onto a piece of paper, without bothering to address it or sign her name.

Can you promise you will never hurt me again?

Once night had fully cloaked itself over Thistlecross, Ruby tiptoed past the cows, hushing a few as they mooed their hellos. She deposited the piece of paper on Brochan's window, then went back the way she'd come.

She woke early and peered out the window. No note. But when she opened the door, she almost stepped on a bundle of blossoming heather, tied together with twine. Below the bouquet was the same paper with her question, and Brochan's response.

No. But I promise that I will try with everything I have.

It was honest. But was it enough? Ruby just couldn't get her head on board with her heart. She put the heather in an empty honey jar and filled it with water from the hose. She set the jar on top of the note on her windowsill, stole one last glance at the flowers, and went off in search of breakfast.

Chapter Forty-Four

Grace had plans to leave early to pick Grant up at Glasgow airport. But first, she brought Ruby to the whisky barrel room. "Brochan was here last night with Kyle. They delivered something for us. Well, for you, I reckon."

Gone were the tiny bar tables and rickety chairs. In the middle of the room: a large oak table, each of the four sides left rough and natural. It looked like it belonged in the woods, right next to Moss Glen Falls. It was a fairy-tale table. Grace had brought in two chairs from the dining room for the spots at the ends, but the long sides were accompanied by matching benches. Ruby ran her fingertips over the wood. It had been lightly lacquered. In the corner, almost too small to see, Brochan had etched his initials along with the words, *for roo*. Ruby swallowed a cry. What had he said, on Skye? *Home is more than a dining table.* She felt a surge of anguish as she waved Grace off.

No man had ever tried to buy her forgiveness with a custom-made table before.

But then, no man had ever manipulated her, lying about his

ex-fiancée for months, then gotten mad at *her* for lying. Then questioned her loyalty, and insulted her integrity.

Some red flags were just too bright to ignore.

Ruby and Neil were eating popcorn and battling each other in backgammon when Grace and Grant returned in the afternoon. The two Wood siblings burst through the door in a fit of laughter. Their joy was downright infectious; Ruby couldn't remember ever observing Grace this happy or animated. She loved to see it. Apparently the reunion had gone well.

Grant clapped Neil on the back as Grace looked on, and the old man's eyes shone with memory-tinged tears. He clapped back at Grant, and the two of them shared a look of deep knowing. Then Grant approached Ruby, removing his cap. "There she is," he said. "The American Scot." Ruby beamed, and Grant turned shy for a moment, extending his hand. "I'm grateful for your visit. You were right. I had to come back. No more faffing around." He frowned. "But Brochan . . ." His voice trailed off and he set his hat on the bar.

Grace interjected. "So. What happens now is we have a dram, a quick lie-down, then banter over a hearty dinner. No problem was ever solved on an empty stomach."

Grant hugged Grace tightly and kissed her cheek. "My wise older sister."

Grace crushed his head in her arms, then let it go and smacked his cheek. "Older by two minutes, you miserable fool."

After Grace had passed out glasses and poured a bit of whisky into each, Neil narrowed his eyes and said to Grant, "I'm pleased you're back, Grant, if for no other reason than our stores are about to run out. Why did you stay away for so long?" Grant started to speak, but Neil held up his hand. "I know why you left. I know why you thought you needed to. But thirty years? More than? It's not about Scotland or Thistlecross or that bastardization of a pub you run over there. It's about your family. Your son, for Christ's sake."

"Neil," Grace said, touching the old man's shoulder.

"No, it's all right, Grace. I should answer for myself," said Grant. "I got lost. And I let myself stay that way because I was hurting. I did so much wrong by my son. By all Thistlecross. I should have warned you about Winkler and his plans. I knew that and I know it. I'm sorry that I didn't do it, but I was . . . I was ashamed." Looking directly at Grace, his voice sounded like a tender plea. "I don't deserve any of your forgiveness. But I'll spend the rest of my life trying to earn it." He held a sip of whisky in his mouth, and his shoulders involuntarily released in pure pleasure. The whisky really was that good. It always had been; he'd just forgotten.

Satisfied, Neil nodded.

Grant drained his glass. "Great mercy, Grace, what whisky is this? Not the Balvenie? It's delicious."

Grace, Ruby, and Neil all exchanged looks before bursting into laughter.

"It's *yours!*"

Chapter Forty-Five

A few hours later, it was time for dinner. Ruby walked to the whisky barrel room to do a last check of things, and stopped short when she saw her reflection in the mirror by the loo. She'd swapped her braid for a low, loose ponytail. Grace had tied it back with one of her ribbons, a rusty orange. She was wearing her favorite black jeans; the ones that hugged her hips and sat high on her waist. The ones that made her arse look stupendous. Tucked in was a simple tan blouse that cut into a modestly low V and showed off her collarbones. Resting in between them was Brochan's necklace. She held the medallion in her palm, then wrapped her fingers around it and squeezed. When she released it, the wood felt pleasant against her skin.

She had swiped a bit of matte red stain over her lips that stood out in a stark sort of beauty against her naked face. She looked nice. She felt content, if not complete. But who *ever* felt complete? She was here. In her place. With her people. As she studied herself in the mirror, she realized that she felt different than she had in the spring. More confident. Ruby had come to realize that all the parts of her Brochan said he loved—her spunky fearlessness, her willingness to dive in and try new things—were inside her before he noticed them. She had loved them about herself first. All those little details made up who she was—not her city, not her job. Not her man. Her identity had been there all along.

Brochan had become part of her, but he wasn't her whole story. She was who she was. She was Roo.

At seven o'clock, a polite knock sounded at the door of the Cosy Hearth. Mac and Sofie arrived with two bottles of Bordeaux. Ruby brought the wine to the dining room and set it on the table. As she did, she caught a glimpse of her engraved name. What if Brochan came? What if he didn't? She shook her head to clear the cobwebs. No matter what, there would be dinner. And wine, and whisky. And laughter, and probably some tears, too.

Oh, Scotland.

By 7:15, Neil, Grace, and Grant had joined Sofie and Mac in the bar. The atmosphere was cautious and polite. Brochan was nowhere to be seen. Or, curiously, Carson. Ruby started to feel anxious and sneaked a nip of the Laphroaig she'd poured into a mason jar earlier. Her sip was overzealous, and it scorched going down. *Note to self: Ask Neil about getting a flask.*

By 7:30, Grace announced that they'd be eating "with or without the stragglers." There was a collective gasp of admiration as they shuffled in to the dining room. Ruby shone with pride that overshadowed her concern about the missing guests. In the middle of the table was a scattering of acorns and a collection of candles. She'd also strewn a few handfuls of colorful lentils and beans around the centerpiece in a haphazard sort of pattern. A smoldering, steady fire was going in the hearth, just enough to provide ambiance without sending anyone into the sweats. The lighting was soft and tender, and she'd put a few drops of cinnamon and pine essential oils in a brass basin that was being warmed from below with a nubby candle. The air smelled like fall, and the room looked like magic. It was stunning, really. Just the sort of place you'd picture if you were daydreaming about an intimate dinner party in a small town in the Highlands of Scotland.

As everyone settled around the table, Ruby arranged the first course onto two large serving platters. She shimmied her shoulders and wiggled her hips in a happy dance. This was going to be a great meal. And it was the perfect nod to her new cookbook.

She had made fresh crowdie cheese, dotted with chives from the garden. She'd done a beer batter dredge, coated the cheese curds with rolled barley and breadcrumbs, then gave it a proper fry in some bacon grease. On the side: a ramekin of beer sauce spiked with honey and mustard. She zested a bit of lemon over the cheese nuggets and hit it all with a shower of fresh parsley. Ruby would be lying if she said she hadn't been the teensiest bit inspired by the menu at the Wee Tartan Bagpipe. There really was something winning about salty snacks and beer. For balance, Ruby also served a salad, a tangle of arugula and mustard greens. The creamy vinaigrette was made with hazelnut oil, cider vinegar, and puréed whisky-soaked prunes, which provided just the right amount of sweetness. The prunes were her secret weapon. A quirky and rather uncool secret weapon, but then, that's Thistlecross for you.

Everyone who was present ate heartily, but Ruby couldn't help feeling disappointed that not *everyone* was there.

For the second course, Ruby made individual bowls of lamb stew, encased in a generous layer of flaky dough—half soup, half savory pastry. It had been Grace's idea: when the guests cracked into the crust with their spoons, a rush of steam and aroma would escape, revealing the peas, carrots, broth, and lamb. Of course, there was a side of neeps and tatties, and Ruby hadn't done a thing to them beyond cooking them to Grace's specifications. They were perfect as they were, and would never need to change. Grace helped Ruby carry everything to the table, along with a few loaves of bread and butter flavored with big hunks of roasted garlic.

After the initial exclamatory praises, a comfortable silence settled over the room. For a few minutes, all one could hear was the clinking of flatware against bowls, and the occasional *Oooh!* and *Mmpf!* Satisfied with the reception, Ruby tucked into the soup herself. It was rich and buttery, with a brightly acidic note from the wine in the broth. This was absolutely going in the cookbook. Which—well—now seemed as good a time as any to spill the beans.

Ruby clinked a fork against her water glass and everyone looked at her expectantly, thinking about dessert.

"You'll be wondering about sweets," Ruby said.

From the far end of the table, Neil gave a rousing "Huzzah!"

"But first, I want to say two things."

Grace nodded encouragingly.

"Wait."

Ruby turned, knowing who the deep, slow voice belonged to before she saw him. In the doorway was Brochan. Brochan, looking strong and calm, and smiling like the man she'd never stopped loving. Not for one minute. On either side of him stood Anne and Carson.

Chapter Forty-Six

The room went silent. Finally, Neil spoke. "If this was a proper romance novel, you'd have come on time for dinner." He rolled his eyes and scraped up the last bits of his stew, then shoveled the spoon into his mouth.

"We're late. And I'm sorry. But"—Brochan locked eyes with Ruby quickly before turning his gaze to his father—"we're here."

Across the table, stoic tears slid down Grant's beard. Grace watched her brother meet his son for the first time in more than thirty years, and her hand trembled as she held it over her mouth.

"Well sit down, then," Neil barked. "Your lass was about to say something."

Mac slid over to make room for Anne and Carson. Brochan took the seat next to Ruby, his thigh pressed firmly against hers. She didn't move. He reached for her hand but instead of taking it, put something in her palm. Her fingers curled around a small metal shape. She could feel its curves and knew before she looked: It was a duck-shaped cookie cutter.

Damn it, Brochan.

"Well?" Neil prompted.

Ruby laughed nervously. Brochan had shaken her. The flowers, the note, the table . . . those were all good. Fantastic. Dramatic and exciting. But not enough to crack through her armor. But now. But this cookie cutter. This tiny, dumb gift. It brought her right back to their first meeting. It brought her home.

She cleared her throat. "Right. No pressure or anything. First, I want to say thank you. I know that for a while, I was just 'that weird tourist staying in the flophouse.' And maybe you still feel that way. Sometimes I do." There was a low chuckle that rolled over both sides of the table. Ruby continued. "Over the last few months, I've realized something: fitting in isn't about how long you've been in a place or how far away you've gone or if you come back. It's something you feel. In your belly. It's a warm feeling, like when you drink too much of Grant's whisky." The chuckle came back around, making its way to Ruby. She took a sip from her mason jar, for courage. And warmth.

"After I spent years feeling like I didn't have one, Thistlecross has become my home. It may not be perfect, and I may not know exactly how I fit in, but I love it. And I hope it loves me back."

"Welcome home, dear," said Grace.

"Also, Grace and I have an announcement." Ruby took a dramatic pause. "We're writing a cookbook!" There were a few confused looks exchanged across the table. "I mean, I know that's what I originally came here to do. So maybe this doesn't seem like a big deal. But it is! For months, nothing I came up with felt right. That's because I was missing my partner in crime. Or rather, my partner in thyme."

Everyone groaned.

"I think that finding Grace was the reason I was meant to come to Thistlecross, after all." Brochan pressed his thigh against Ruby's again, and this time she leaned into the sensation.

"The name, what's the name of the book?" Mac asked.

Ruby nodded at Grace.

Grace cleared her throat and her cheeks colored prettily.

"*The Cosy Hearth Cookbook: Secrets from a Scottish Kitchen in the Heart of the Highlands.*"

"It's perfect," Brochan said, and the whole table agreed. "Thistlecross is damn lucky to have you. It does love you back. Very much."

And then, with that gentle proclamation, Ruby decided to give in. To let Brochan be a good guy. To stop finding fault with men and start working toward a life with the one she loved. There was so much for them to talk about, to explain and figure out. But there was time for that. She lived in Thistlecross, after all! Well, she would once her visa renewal was accepted. "Thanks, Broo," she said and crossed her arms. "So. Why were you late?"

Brochan looked around the room, stopping when he met Grant's eyes. Ruby could sense his body tense, and then release, as he shifted his gaze toward her. "We—Margaret, sorry, *Anne*, Carson, and me—were working on something. It was a secret. But I think we're done with those here. So it's time for me to start blethering."

Brochan looked into his whisky as he spoke the next words. "I also learned something this summer. I used to fight anything that wasn't Thistlecross through and through. You've seen me distrust people and lose faith in them." Brochan raised his gaze toward Grant, then he looked at Ruby.

"But if family can become strangers, then tourists can become family."

He placed his hand on Ruby's shoulder and she glowed from the inside out.

"Marg—shit, Anne! I'm trying—and I have come up with a plan—it was her idea, really." He squeezed Ruby's shoulder harder. "That's what we were working on when you came home from New York." Ruby looked at Anne, who nodded and smiled. *Their secret. And his question.* Curiosity bubbled up inside her. Brochan continued, "And Carson helped make it happen."

Carson's small, neat mustache was no match for his broad smile as he handed a folder to Brochan. Brochan's eyes twinkled with that familiar Wood family charisma. He took a deep breath, and then he exhaled, twice as long. And then he began.

Chapter Forty-Seven

The crux of it was, Brochan explained, that the sale of the Cosy Hearth was impossible to reverse. The contract was legally binding. Unless *the contract itself* was voidable.

"Anne realized that in the middle of the night a couple of Saturdays ago, and rang me in the morning." He looked pointedly at Ruby, and she understood the mysterious call on their way to the airport.

Anne jumped in to further clarify. "I phoned him because if this really worked—if we really could stop the Wee Tartan Bagpipe from opening—we needed a new plan for the building. One that could make a haul of money. And I knew Brochan could help. If he'd actually answered my calls, we could have sorted this sooner," she teased from across the table, and Brochan shrugged unapologetically.

Finally, chance brought the old friends together, the night at the Traveler Hotel bar. Anne had finally worked up enough (liquid) courage to launch into her pitch, when she drunkenly revealed the secret she and Ruby had been keeping from Brochan. "It put me even further off track from my plan," she said lightheartedly. "Luckily, Brochan loves his Thistlecross too much to ignore my calls forever."

"When Anne came to the barn that evening, she wanted to create a new plan for the Cosy Hearth," Brochan followed up. "I was angry at you, but Anne convinced me to listen. Also gave me a damn earful about not picking you up at the airport." Anne rolled her eyes at Ruby and Ruby rolled hers back.

Brochan continued: "The clever thing is that I'd had a similar idea for weeks now. I thought we could build off what you and Grace were doing, with the Family Table. I just didn't know how to make it real. I almost asked you, Ruby, in August. I'm glad I waited. Because now it *is* real. And we can make it happen together."

With business still at a slow crawl, Brochan explained, the pub truly did need a refresh. But instead of doing things the Winkler way, they reckoned they could tackle it the way they always had in Thistlecross: with conviction, scrappy know-how, and family.

"We'd like to renovate and reopen the pub ourselves," he said, suddenly a little shy. "And we'd like to call it the Family Table." Grace and Ruby locked eyes and shared a surprised look.

"Anne can handle the marketing, finally get us on the map and such. This pub has always been the heart of Thistlecross. Now we just need some good slogans and campaigns to make other folks see that."

"Och! It's more complicated than that!" Anne argued.

"I know," Brochan said. "Do half the banger of a job you did at the Traveler, and we'll be turning tourists away. We need them—the tourists." He coughed. "It's only a matter of attracting the right lot. The sort who like sweet old pubs, not shiny chain restaurants.

"And here's the big finish. We could go back to our roots. We could be more than just a pub. We could be a distillery. A proper one, with a bottling line and distributor—all that. I don't know how to make whisky properly, but . . ." He paused, filling the room with an audible exhale, directed into his lap. Three, four, five more seconds ticked by. Then Brochan raised his glass in his father's direction. "Supposing someone could teach me."

"Wow," Ruby said very quietly.

Grant's tears were flowing freely again, but his eyes danced with happiness. Grace's cheeks were fire-engine red.

Brochan turned to the contents of his folder, which were three packets of paper, held together by metal clips. "Carson helped us make preliminary contracts. It's why we were late; I wanted to have something to show for tonight. Contracts . . . that are fair to everyone."

Grant shook his head and raised his glass. "I'm an eejit!" he offered by way of good-natured confirmation.

"God love you," Grace murmured.

"There are three contracts here. One for each of us: Grace . . . me . . . and you, Roo."

"Me!?" Ruby almost spat out her whisky.

"Well, Grace can't be running the kitchen all by herself. Not with the amount of business we're about to step into."

Ruby placed her hand on the side of his face, feeling the familiar scratch of his beard against her palm. His glorious beard.

The beard she loved forever and ever. "Me, seriously? I know nothing about running a business."

He held her hand in his own, his calluses and rough spots melding into her softness. "Well, neither do I. But you're a damn fine cook, and you have that certain . . . je ne sais quoi." He grinned knowingly. "I've made many mistakes over the last few months, but there's no way I'm ready to let you go. As a partner. As my person. Thistlecross needs you." He held her face with his other hand, his fingertips touching lightly on her temples. Everyone was watching and it was a little awkward, but Ruby didn't care. Because she was just so happy. So very happy to be together again. Brochan shook his head and a bit of hair escaped from behind his ear.

"Ruby Spencer, *I* need you."

Ruby tucked the hair back into place then took his hands in hers. She said yes with her eyes, so it could be a private thing they shared first. Then she turned to the room and said, "Well, of course!" and everyone clapped and laughed.

"But wait!" Grace said. "What about the contract with Winkler?"

"Right," Brochan affirmed. "Take it away, Anne."

Anne swirled the whisky in her glass. "Like Brochan said, I knew that we had to find some fault with the contract. But I don't know anything about that. We needed a lawyer. And what better lawyer than the curmudgeon who had refused to help with the sale in the first go?" Carson gave a salute. "Car's always been on our side. The man is a proper hero; he pored over the document for days."

"Everything seemed to be tight and neat," Carson said. "It wasn't until my second pass that I found it."

"He's brilliant," said Anne.

"See, I was searching for something that would render the contract voidable—some proof Winkler had made a misstep, or failed to deliver on the terms. If I could find that, we could exit the contract without a breach." Ruby nodded, pretending she understood the terminology Carson was slinging around. She was catching the general gist of it, anyway.

"While everyone was moaning about the September renovation date, it turns out putting it in the terms and conditions was genius. Well—accidentally so," said Anne.

Carson smiled encouragingly. "Yes; when Winkler pushed back the construction start date, he did so without a formal amendment to the contract. So while the contract remains watertight in almost every way, we're able to declare it voidable." He paused, and added for clarity: "The contract is as good as toilet roll."

Ruby jumped up from the table, overcome with emotion and too amped to sit still. "Dessert!" she cried, running into the kitchen as her friends and neighbors chattered excitedly. "We need dessert!" She whirled around, gathering everything together, then reappeared a few minutes later with a serving tray full of puddings. They were a Scottish spin on crème brûlée, sweet cream with swirls of honey, and topped with a sugar sprinkle. Before caramelizing the tops with a small kitchen torch, Ruby added a few lavender buds. The heat of the sugar crust activated the floral scent, sending curls of it into the air.

She was halfway back in the barrel room, balancing the puds

on a massive tray, when she slipped on a spot of grease by the doorway. She went down with a terrific clatter, landing on her rear with the desserts all around her. Pudding was all over the floor. Pudding was all over Ruby's pants. She wasn't hurt, but she was embarrassed. And disappointed. For a moment, she couldn't move or speak.

She sat in horrified silence for another beat. Brochan jumped from the table and made it to her side in a single stride. "Are you all right then, Roo?" he asked. She looked from the pile of broken ramekins to the tableful of friends and to her man. As he helped her up, she finally released the breath she'd been holding. She started to titter. Soon the whole room was cackling; they laughed so hard their sides ached. Brochan led Ruby back to the table and wiped a smudge of cream from her wrist.

This was not sexy, cool, tourist Scotland. This was not *Outlander*, and it definitely wasn't *Braveheart*. It was Thistlecross, birthplace of the golden retriever and home of Moss Glen Falls and the best, scrappiest Scots in the whole damn country. Neil reached for the very last bottle of whisky and gave Grant a tentative look. Grant nodded—*If not now, when?* Everyone passed glasses down to Neil, who poured a bit more into each.

Brochan handed Ruby the dram and rubbed the end of her hair ribbon. "I like this. It's nice. It suits you."

She felt dizzy with pleasure, intoxicated with whisky and his sweaty-smoky-minty scent. She offered the tip of her nose for a kiss. He gave it to her, and then arranged his features into a serious expression. His cheeks grew a little slack, and his lips pouted slightly.

"I have a great deal more to say to you in private. Ninety-nine percent of it is an apology." He shook his head quickly, trying to erase the pain of the last couple of weeks. "I don't want to stifle you from being the woman you are. I should have trusted you. Roo, your free spirit, your adventurous self, your willingness to try things, even if you might fail at them. Those are the things I love best. I saw it all when I watched you with that electric drill; saw a million reasons to adore you in that moment. Every single one was perfect. Just like you. You're my heroine." He took a breath. "And you deserve to live inside the romance novel of your dreams."

"Shh . . ." Ruby pressed her finger to her lips and then to his. She giggled. "I have a list.

"One: We both said hurtful things that we didn't mean. So if you need to apologize, I need to apologize double.

"B: I was such a hypocrite! I was terrible! Holding you accountable for all the wrongdoings of mankind, while sneaking and keeping secrets; it wasn't fair. I showed up in Scotland so angry I hadn't found the perfect man that I almost gave up on the one who is perfect for me.

"Roman numeral three: I am awfully excited to open a restaurant with you. But wait! Will you be my boss, or will I be your boss?"

Brochan laughed, deep and throaty this time. "Lass, either you are drunk or I need to revoke your list-making privileges."

Ruby hiccuped loudly. "Oh, I am quite drunk," she said, "but the happy, lovely kind that can only come from whisky."

He lowered his voice so that just she could hear. He continued to fondle the ribbon in her hair and looked at her with reverence and desire. "If this were a romance novel, what would happen next?"

Ruby felt the familiar Brochan-shaped swelling in her heart that dropped into her belly and continued south. She lifted herself slightly off the bench so that she could reach his ear. The left side of her mouth slid into an easy grin, and her lips tickled his skin as she whispered, "Take me to the flophouse."

Epilogue

"Make love to me like Islay," Ruby said as her cheeks flushed. Brochan's lips worked his way down her neck and explored her collarbone. They were in the barn, on the old butcher block table from the pub. Brochan had made a new one for the Family Table, a bigger one that would allow Ruby and Grace to work together without bumping into each other. But nobody could bear getting rid of the old prep table; not when it had seen them all through so much. So they brought it to the barn, where Ruby and Brochan had been living together for the last six months.

Make love to me like Islay. It was an odd thing to say, but of course he knew just what she meant.

"No," he said, bringing his face close to hers. He kissed her mouth, deep and slow. "Like Speyside."

"Islay," Ruby repeated, pulling away. She leaned back on her elbows to expose her throat to him. "Wild and fierce and raw and hard." Brochan grabbed at her waist and pulled her closer to the edge of the table, so that his hips were nestled between her inner thighs. She shivered with anticipation. He released her from the constraints of the top button of her jeans.

"Speyside." He guided her back to an upright position, and lifted her hand with his own. "Speyside." He rubbed her palm with his thumb and wove his fingers into hers. "It's honey and flowers and oranges and Christmas cake and taking our time. Being thoughtful as I explore you. It's your beautiful hands holding a glass of sherry and me not being able to take my eyes from them. From you."

Ruby brought her fingers to his mouth and touched the corner of his lips. Outside, a rooster crowed. Which was weird. Because it was the middle of the night. But you can't control roosters. As everyone knows.

She smiled like she had a secret she was dying to tell. "Make love to me like Scotland."

Brochan scooped small, lovely Ruby up into his arms and made the short walk to their bed. He tossed her onto it and she landed softly. Her face was half-hidden by curls but there was no concealing her flushed cheeks.

He struck a match and lit a taper, then brought it over to the windowsill. "Scotland is a vast country, Ruby. After a year of living here you ought to know that."

She bit her lip and grinned wickedly. "I have all night."

The next morning, Ruby woke early, while Brochan was still sleeping. True to form, he had sprawled out so much that his big arms and muscular legs were covering three-quarters of the bed.

But Ruby loved him, so she was only a little grumpy. She was curled up at the edge; from her side of the mattress, she could see the stall where the whisky still had once lived. She smiled as she thought of its new place of honor, tucked into an alcove near the bar at the Family Table. It was just for show, but customers loved seeing it—especially now that Brochan and Grant had bought a new still with a bank loan, and were distilling their own whisky.

During Grant's visit, he and Brochan spent many quiet, private hours together. They went walking at Moss Glen Falls, and Brochan showed his father the work he'd done on the barn. Eventually, the men's conversation shifted from construction projects to the past. Ruby wasn't privy to what words had been exchanged, but she knew they were of the healing sort. At the end of Grant's trip, Brochan surprised everyone—including himself—by asking Grant if he would consider staying on at Thistlecross. If he would consider being a partner in the new business. Grant said yes.

Making whisky was a tangible task for father and son to use as they continued to cautiously form a relationship. Through Grant's lessons, Brochan learned the trade he'd always dreamed of, and Grant found himself feeling passionate about his career once more.

They had years to go before the first bottles would be ready, and years to go before either man would feel at peace with all that had passed, but it was work they were committed to. And excited about. (Just ask Brochan to explain the virtues of their recently purchased French oak barrels, and oh, were you in for an evening.) Although whisky was required by law to age for at least three years, in the meantime they had plenty of fun with lesser-aged spirits; they even tried their hand at gin, an experiment that had Lee seeing double on her trip to Thistlecross last month.

Lee. That visit had been so nice. She and Brochan got along like brother and sister, which meant they were arguing by day two, trash-talking each other in a game of horseshoes on day three, and crying big crocodile tears by day five, when Lee had to leave for New York. Ruby missed her already, but she'd be back in June. Apparently she and Kyle had hit it off? Had a thing? Whatever happened, it had involved a lot of gin and furtive giggles. They'd been texting like mad ever since.

Ruby's parents hadn't made it out yet, but Brochan had joined a few of their family Zoom calls, and Mark had even started emailing Brochan questions about whisky, which was very cute. Ruby hoped they would come soon; she knew they were eager to meet the mysterious Scot who had stolen their daughter away. Now, in bed, Ruby smiled even bigger from the warren of Brochan's warm body. She couldn't believe how much had happened since Grant had returned to Thistlecross.

With Carson's lawerly help, Grant had been able to gracefully exit his contract with Winkler. The man had a way with loopholes, that was for certain. As for Winkler: Well, who knew, really? And who cared? No one in Thistlecross. As soon as Carson pointed out the voidability of the contract, Winkler decided to cut his losses rather than drag it into court. He had enough legal troubles as it was. Besides, the Wee Tartan Bagpipe was busy optioning West Coast franchises (whether or not California was ready for Scottish Bang-Pow Shrimp). And as it turned out, he didn't need to worry about losing Grant as his GM. Krista, the raven-haired bartender, had been vying for a management role, and she was already running a tight ship for all the New York Wee Tartan Bagpipe locations. Ruby felt guilty for having judged her so harshly; Krista had even instituted a "Thursday Ladies Night" tradition, in which all the female servers were given the night off and replaced with men in *very* short kilts. It sounded wild. Ruby kind of wanted to go. You know, to support Krista and everything. She had made a commitment to stop judging other women and start considering them all as allies.

Margaret Anne Dunbar was enjoying the challenge of rebranding the pub and keeping Thistlecross humming along. She'd registered the Family Table as an official stop on a national "Historic Highlands" tour, which had piqued the interest of tourists and Scots alike. Although no closer to finding a date, she had gotten her wish: She and Ruby had become real, honest-to-goodness friends. Between their regular whisky spritzers at the Traveler and their online yoga classes, the two women had become inseparable. Ruby had initially been worried it'd be weird, becoming friends with her boyfriend's ex, but it was only a little weird, and only in the beginning.

The Cosy Hearth had closed for a few weeks in the winter, during which Brochan gave everything a thorough scrubbing, sanding, and new shine. Grant found a small house near the town hall to rent. He helped Brochan scour the Highlands for more leaded glass panes, and together the men installed them in random windows throughout the main dining room of the pub. The designs were all different, without a common artistic theme. The effect was a bit chaotic but very lovely. Just like the people who ran the pub. They reopened officially as the Family Table just in time for the Christmas holidays. The first night was packed, with Brochan's oak table at the center of the room. Everyone in Thistle-cross, it seemed, was present; even the tourists staying at the Traveler Hotel, which had promised to advertise Grace's authentic Scottish breakfast served daily at the pub.

Ruby had worked with Grace to give the menu a makeover, too. Some of the classics remained (no one would ever dream of nixing neeps and tatties!), but Ruby's American-Scottish burgers were a hit on Friday nights, and nobody could resist her fried crowdie cheese with honey-mustard ale sauce. When they weren't churning out dishes for the now-bustling pub, Ruby and Grace were working on their cookbook. Her agent had loved the idea ("Scotland is so hot right now," she had said). Happily, a few publishers felt the same way. Ruby accepted a book deal and split the advance halfway with Grace. *The Cosy Hearth Cookbook* was due out in two years, and in the meantime, they were busy writing and cooking together in a perfect unspoken rhythm, like they had been all along.

The pub was closed on Sundays; they all deserved a rest. Although sometimes Ruby missed the intimate nature of their old Sunday suppers, she liked her new routine even better: In the kitchen at the barn, Brochan prepared dinner for *her* while she curled up in the big leather chair with a novel and her dictionary. They'd taken the chair from the pub, too—there'd been no room for it, with all the new dining tables. As for the barn, it was starting to feel like home. And starting to look like it belonged to Brochan and Ruby both. A few of her watercolor paintings were tacked up above the bookcase, and they'd kept the velveteen quilt from the cottage. A small ceramic tray on her nightstand held the wood medallion necklace every night while she slept, and a few lotions and tinctures lined the shelves in the loo.

Ruby loved the fact that in less than a year, she'd gone from living in one of the biggest cities in the world to a glorified chicken coop to a barn. Every once in a while, she would feel a small pang of nostalgia for her tiny stone cottage, but she didn't miss walking to the pub every time she wanted a bath. Plus, she had to admit that the stone cottage made for a much better whisky storage closet. Brochan, Ruby, and Grant hadn't decided what to do with the beautiful secret room in the pub, now that the barrels lived at the cottage, but they had a few ideas kicking around. And they had time to figure it out.

Ruby poked Brochan in his ribs. "You're crowding the bed, Broo," she said.

"I'm allowed to crowd the bed on Sundays. New rule," he murmured sleepily, but turned to his side and gathered her into a hug so that he was a big spoon and she fit against him perfectly.

"Oh!" Ruby sat up with a start.

"Mmm?" Brochan massaged her shoulder with his eyes closed.

"The mail! We never got it from the box on Saturday!"

Brochan laughed into his pillow. Ruby had been anxiously watching the post for days; she'd sent in for a renewal of her work visa and was waiting for the updated card. This one would have a proper photo of her, taken in her new home country.

Ruby pulled on Brochan's flannel, which, arguably, was Ruby's flannel at this point. She ran out the door and down the drive in her bare feet and a brand-new pair of palm tree underpants. It was early April, almost one full year since she first arrived in Thistlecross. The grass was covered in dew, and it tickled her toes. The air was still cool and wet, but Ruby felt warm.

TRA-LA!

There it was, waiting patiently in their postal box. She tore back into the barn and jumped onto the bed, almost landing on Brochan's stomach. He had put the kettle on for coffee, and he hoisted himself up now, seated against the wood wall. "Come here," he said, and Ruby wiggled into his lap. He kissed the top of her head. "Let's see about Ms. Ruby Spencer, my Scottish lass."

She ripped open the envelope. When she dreamed of this moment, she pictured herself doing it purposefully and slowly, but Ruby was not the kind of woman with that kind of restraint. As she lifted her new identification card from the pile of papers, both Ruby and Brochan peered at it curiously. The picture had been taken mid-sneeze, and Ruby looked supremely unglamorous. Her curls had obstructed her face, and her right eye was squeezed shut. Her mouth was half-open; her nose scrunched. *No do-overs*, the clerk had said. *You get one go at it, and hope it's a good one.* Ruby had smiled then, because even if it was the rule for visas, she knew that life was generous with second chances.

The kettle yowled. She turned to Brochan and kissed him

with all her might. She kissed him so hard that she bit him, but just a little and only by accident.

"Wow," said Brochan. "I love it."

Ruby Spencer hugged the card to her chest, then held it out and admired it again. "It's a good one."

Acknowledgments

Heartfelt thanks to my agent, Sharon Pelletier, for spending years guiding me patiently toward the right project. For helping me turn a curious idea into a real-deal book. Sharon, you are damn good at your job, and I love being one of your authors.

Thank you to my editor at Berkley, Kerry Donovan, for embracing Ruby and Brochan with all the love and thoughtfulness in the world. It is a marvelous feeling to be understood; even more so if you are an anxious writer. You give me that gift.

Thank you to the entire team at Berkley and PRH: Fareeda Bullert, Megan Elmore, Yazmine Hassan, Christine Legon, Jessica Mangicaro, and Chelsea Pascoe. You helped this book shine in ways I never imagined possible.

Thank you to Rita Frangie and Mallory Heyer for bringing Ruby and Brochan to life on the (very beautiful!) cover.

Mary Baker: Where would I be without your efficiency, technology lessons, and Grape Nuts ice cream recommendations? You make ironing out the details feel like a breeze.

To Martha Schwartz for teaching me about semicolons and

for the thorough, excellent copyedits, and to Lynsey Griswold and Cheryl Murphy for the proofreading and cold reading.

To my early readers, especially Katrina and Jen: bless you for being game to read a half-finished manuscript and offer helpful feedback. I owe you a dram.

I can't imagine this book—or Brochan!—having come to life without the aid of my UK-based friends. Lachlan: Thank you for feeding me, for sneaking me the good whisky, for answering questions about rude slang words, and for teaching me about *real* Scotland. Julie, Jason, and Steven: thank you for stopping to help a crazy American stranded on the side of Loch Lomond, and for making me see the good in a flat tire. Charlie: thank you for driving me all over Islay for days. Thank you for buying me coffee and tea, and for making me laugh, and for sharing some of the island's best-kept secrets. Rachel: for making a rented room feel like home, and for guiding me to the places that anchor this book. Jody: for saying hello and sharing conversation. Never has a three-hundred-hour ferry ride been so enjoyable.

Padraig: I'm indebted to you for the help with the book's Scots Gaelic. Although Brochan claimed his knowledge was for "entertainment purposes only," I'm so very glad that it's spot-on.

Thank you to the crew of gentlemen at the Ardnahoe tasting room. I promised I'd include you in these acknowledgments, and even though we were rather tipsy at the time, I'm honored to do so. I doubt I'll ever meet another whisky drinker with tasting notes as creative as yours.

To all of the whisky writers, distillers, experts, and lovers who helped me understand scotch on a deeper level. Charles Maclean:

I'm grateful for your thoughtful insight into the history and evolution of distilling.

My mother, father, and sister: thank you for cheering me on from the very beginning—for your encouragement and unwavering love. We have a special thing, the four of us.

To the Cape Cod crew: Roger, Nancy, Dana, Paul, Abby, Dave, Lily, Matt, Sam, and Eliana. It makes me happy that our time together was a part of this book's evolution, even if it did mean proofreading "spicy" scenes at the dining table. Thank you for welcoming me into your family—the love I have for you is big, and grows each day.

Thank you, Jake. Thank you for your ever-patient encouragement. Thank you for helping me add ~legal flair~ to the story. Thank you for providing sympathy and advice both, so unselfishly. Being together is the very best thing.

Keep reading for a special preview of
Rochelle Bilow's next rom-com!

———————————

Home—sort of—again, Annie slipped in the back door. Her dad had never locked it when she was growing up. On an island with fifteen hundred people, "Why bother?" he'd said. She tiptoed up the stairs, skipping the creaky one at the top. *Don't wake up, don't wake up, please don't wake up*, she thought, slipping past the master bedroom into her own. It was a dance she'd done dozens of times as a teenager, sneaking in late. Not because she would've gotten in trouble—she didn't have a curfew, and Samuel had never once grounded her—but because waking him up meant suffering through an hour of chitchat and a mug of his overly bitter, very yellow turmeric tea. Samuel was a sweet man full of love, but he could be much too much. As her mother had decided so many years ago.

She collapsed onto the papasan chair and screwed up her face like she was going to cry. Deep inhale. Bigger exhale. She was almost there. She let out an effortful howl, like a feral kitten, but no tears came. Annie simply wasn't a crier. She hadn't cried when her mom had packed up and left Alder Isle; hadn't cried when, on graduation night, her best friend, Ernie, told her to forget he'd ever existed; hadn't cried during any of the hundreds of times her male coworkers and bosses had berated her during dinner service.

Annie hadn't cried when, three weeks ago, she had been fired from her job as the executive chef at Cowboy Bean, one of the hottest restaurants in San Francisco. In California. In the whole country.

Annie didn't cry because if she cried, she felt weak, and her entire life had been one long test of her strength. She wasn't weak. She sat up straighter, which, irritatingly, was difficult to do in a papasan chair. Over the last decade and a half, she had done many harder things than cook in a beautiful seaside restaurant for the summer. Even if that restaurant was located in her absurdly small, insufferably cheerful hometown. Even if she no longer had any friends here, just ghosts and shameful memories. But, hey: at least she'd get to work with the best produce, meat, and seafood Maine had to offer. The thought of fresh lobster, steaming and fire-engine red, made her mouth water. Maybe this wouldn't be so bad after all.

Maybe.

Her mind fast-forwarded a few weeks, and she pictured herself at the restaurant pass, inspecting each plate of risotto or striped bass or roasted chicken before it went out to customers in the dining room. Garnishing each one with torn basil leaves and snipped chives. Adding a crack of black pepper. Making it look perfect. Doing the thing she was good at. Redeeming herself for everything that had happened at Cowboy Bean. She pictured herself a few months from now, with enough money saved up to move somewhere new. She imagined herself brave enough to take on another executive chef role. It was the next job after sous chef; it was the title she'd wanted her whole life. Too bad her first shot at it had turned into such a disaster. She pictured herself far away from Alder Isle, with a second chance at her dream job. She pictured herself happy.

It would happen. She could make it. All she had to do until then was keep her head on straight, do her job for four months, and not get distracted. Nobody and nothing—especially not some tiny island—was going to keep Annie down.

However. That job didn't start until tomorrow, and right now what Annie needed was a swim. Restaurant workers had a reputation for living the hard and fast life—late nights; greasy, salty food at 3:00 a.m.; cocaine and hard liquor—but Annie was part of a smaller faction who fought valiantly against that stereotype. She may have been a rule breaker as a kid, but there was no room for that sort of thing in her line of work. Rule breakers couldn't keep up. They weren't disciplined enough to stick around the cut-throat, perfection-required environment of a restaurant. She'd learned that fast, and now she lived a rigid and regimented life . . . in and out of the kitchen. Annie thrived on rules. Rules for her cooks, rules for herself. Rules about relationships (don't get too close to anyone, ever) and rules about routines (stick to them).

She was a sprinter in high school, and still ran a fast mile. Most mornings, she'd rise at a decent hour, even if she had worked late the night before. She would clock a few miles before coming home and making a green juice with whole grain toast and a poached egg. Annie didn't eat junk food, didn't do drugs, didn't party with her coworkers.

Well. Mostly didn't.

Blergh.

Her joints felt too thick and rusty for a run today, though. And she *was* back in Maine. She brushed her teeth and splashed water on her face, then took the stairs two at a time, down to the yard to retrieve her trusty chariot, the red Schwinn that was glossier and sleeker than any decades-old bike had the right to be. She flung her towel around the back of her neck and swung one leg up and over the bike, then started pedaling away from town. She had decided to do what teenager Annie would've done after a hard night. She'd go for a swim.

On the eastern side of the island was a rocky public beach with parking spaces for a few cars. It was never busy—most people swam at the abandoned mining quarries closer to town—but if you walked a quarter mile north through the woods, you'd reach another, secluded little cove. Locals didn't bother with it; the water was too cold and the beach was too steep. Tourists didn't know about it. And it just so happened to be Annie's favorite place on Alder Isle. When she was twelve, she and her best friend, Ernie, had named it Dulse Cove, for the squishy seaweed that floated around its edges. Her breath caught in her throat as she took the curves dangerously fast.

Ernie.

Ernie was still on Alder Isle. She was sure of it. He wasn't the leaving type. Of course, she'd thought about that when she made the decision to come back. But he had essentially told her to drop dead in 2009, and they'd never spoken again. What was she supposed to do, send him a pin of her location with the message **u up?** They used to be inseparable, but now he was just a painful memory. One of the ghosts. She shuddered to think what she meant to him. If she meant anything at all.

They'd see each other when they saw each other. No amount of planning could make that meeting go smoothly. It would be weird, and he would get awkward, and she'd probably say something accidentally mean, and they might even laugh about stuff. If they were lucky. If they talked about it at all. But it didn't matter. Not really. He wasn't a part of her life anymore. And her life was no longer in Maine.

She jumped off her bike and ditched it behind a large rock, then jogged down the overgrown trail, pulling her tank top up over her head. At home, she'd changed into her swimsuit, a high-waisted bikini with marigold-colored bottoms and a sporty emerald green top. She could hear the waves gently lapping. It was low tide. The air felt heavy and wet, smelled like brine and oysters and cold mud.

Annie hated Maine, but she loved this.

As she approached the beach, she stopped short. There was a pair of beat-up sneakers and a gray T-shirt by the shore. She wasn't alone. Annoyance immediately tugged the corners of her mouth into a frown. This was *her* spot. *Hers.* Nobody else even knew about it. Nobody except . . .

Annie lifted her gaze from the pile of clothes to the shoreline.

There, emerging from the water with glistening skin and dripping hair, was Ernie.

Ernie. Ernie Callahan, of childhood-best-friend fame.

Annie blinked and shook her head. He hadn't yet noticed her, and she took the opportunity to study him in the early-morning sunlight. Unlike the rest of Alder Isle, he'd changed.

Okay, yes. His sandy blond hair was still styled like a 1990s dreamboat, middle part and all. Although she couldn't see from the distance, she knew his eyes were the same shade of pale gray-blue. Like a junco's wing, her father would have said. Did say, once. But that was where the familiarities stopped. Sometime in the last eighteen years, everything else about Ernie Callahan had grown up.

His chest and shoulders had graduated from skinny to muscular and lean, with strong-looking forearms. He had a swimmer's build, finally, to match his water-loving heart. In spite of herself, she smirked when she noticed the touch of pink around his collarbones. That boy always burned so easily. But his abs had never been that . . . *damn.* And his waist. Annie lifted her hair off her neck and quickly tied it into a low ponytail. She suddenly felt very hot, and her inner elbows were awfully sweaty. Ernie came closer. He'd noticed her— but did he recognize her? She kept staring, too shocked to look away. His waist was whittled down to a narrow V with the faintest trail of white-blond hair at the band of his swim trunks. She chanced a look at his face, afraid to catch his eye, and saw that his bone structure looked more mature, too. Gone were the cute, toothy grin and chubby cheeks. The man on the beach was all strong jaw and de-fined cheekbones. Even the explosion of freckles that covered his entire upper half, from forehead to hipbones, seemed sexier, like they'd been chosen as carefully as a fashionable outfit.

Holy raging shitballs, she corrected herself. This was *Ernie* she was ogling at. Absolutely not. She had already decided she was not going down that road. Almost fifteen years ago exactly. It was a choice that had cost her their friendship, but it had been the right one. The kindest one for both of them. They were older now, and maybe more mature. But even the Pop Rocks–and–Coke sensation dancing on her tongue wasn't enough to convince her that her instinct to tackle him to the ground and kiss him—hard—was a good idea.

Annie shook off the spell his slow walk out of the ocean had cast. Just in time, because now he was standing in front of her, close enough for her to confirm: Yep. Same slate blue eyes. Same extra-dense spray of freckles across the bridge of his nose.

"Oh. Hey, Annie."

"Hey, Ern."

"You're standing on my towel."

She took a half step to the left and he reached down to grab it. She felt his breath dance over her knees as he rose to stand, meeting her eyes again. He looked good. She was nervous. None of this made any sense. She suddenly wanted him close, closer than he'd just been. Closer than he'd ever gotten.

But she wasn't going to admit any of that. Not to herself, not to him, not today, not ever. Instead, she said, "That's it? After fifteen years . . . that's all I get? 'You're standing on my towel?'"

Ernie tousled his hair with the towel and shook it out. "I haven't exactly been practicing the perfect opener. You told me you were never coming back to Alder Isle, remember?" He let that sink in. "What are you doing here? You visiting Samuel?"

Annie's chest immediately splotched with red. She crossed her arms and hunched, drawing her shoulders in close to hide her embarrassment. "I'm back for the summer, actually. I was in California, but . . ." She paused, her lips still parted. She'd already foiled her plan. Everyone at the restaurant had to believe she'd come back for good; Jarrod wouldn't have hired her just for a season. But she'd just told Ernie the truth without even thinking. Well, a partial truth. They used to share everything—no secrets, no lies—but she barely recognized the Ernie standing in front of her. And his last words to her, before *You're standing on my towel*, had been *Have a nice life*. She finished in a rush: "I was in California, but I decided to spend a few months at home. Dad's not getting any younger, all that."

"I know what you mean." A rain cloud crossed over Ernie's face, and it was somehow worse than the chilly, distanced look in his eyes. "How long you been back?"

"A day. Not even."

"What'd you do?"

"Fucked around and got into trouble."

And there it was. The tiniest dimple at the corner of Ernie's lip. It always betrayed his biggest laughs. The ones that got Annie going, too. The dimple grew now as his eyes got lighter, and he did laugh. It sounded familiar, but older. Wiser and more confident. Still just as gentle. "Oh, Annie. Get over here."

He opened his arms wide with the towel held up behind him like wings. She stepped forward and snuggled in. Their height difference was still the same—her 5'5" to his 5'9"—and her cheek landed on his chest as if nothing had changed. Even though, of course, it had. It all had. She wrapped her arms around his waist and his found their way around her back, the towel covering them both. His skin was chilly from the sea and still a little wet. He smelled like Dr. Bronner's almond soap. Like a marzipan cookie.

"Don't be mad at me anymore," Annie whispered into his armpit as he kissed the top of her head. Her stomach surged in a new and unfamiliar way.

"I never was." He stepped away, just an inch, just enough so he could knuckle under her chin and bring their eyes to meet. Her heart hammered in her chest. She felt shaky, but his embrace was strong. "Annie, I . . ."

Absolutely not.

"Race you to the water!" Annie shouted as she broke away from him and tore down the beach, expertly skipping her way over the jagged rocks. When she got to the seaweed and sand, she stripped off her shorts and turned around to toss them over Ernie's head. He was right behind her, and she scored, the nylon fabric covering his face. "*Haha!*" She laughed loudly, then pulled her bright blond hair from its elastic and shook it out as she splashed into the ocean, her knees up high. The water was arrestingly cold; it took her breath away as it hit her stomach. She didn't stop because she knew it was too easy to lose your nerve. Too easy to give up and retreat if you didn't plow through like you had never been scared at all.

He was hot on her heels, chasing her through the first ten yards. Once the grade steepened and the water got deeper, she slipped underneath and swam for a few seconds before surfacing. When she bobbed up, Ernie was gone. She looked around, momentarily worried before feeling both his hands wrap around her ankle and pull her under. "*Ernie Callahan!*" she shrieked, the last two syllables of his name bubbling with seawater. They play fought under the surface, pulling each other close and pushing away, before rising once more, gasping for breath. They could both touch the ground, and Annie sunk down so she was almost entirely covered by the water. She didn't let herself rise up out of the chill because she knew how easy it was to quit if you admitted there was something more comfortable close by.

She licked her lips; she had swallowed a mouthful of ocean and tasted salt. "You got faster," she said, sinking even lower. She was now in almost up to her chin. His shoulders and chest, dotted with a night sky's worth of freckle constellations, were above the water.

"Did I? Or did you just get slower? What's that mile time now, track star?"

"Kindly fuck right off," she said, laughing. "It's seven minutes, seven ten if I've had a couple beers the night before. Don't judge. I got old."

"No judgment, Annie Pants," he said, and gave her a sideways glance to see if she'd notice the reappearance of her childhood nickname. How could she not?

"You still pole vaulting?"

"Oh yeah, every morning before work," he said, then quickly added, "JK."

Annie smiled at the abbreviation. They may have grown up,

but they'd forever be millennials. She danced her fingertips over the water. He cupped his palms together and squirted some at her face. There was the briefest of pauses when she wondered if she should bring it up—the big fight they'd had on graduation night so many years ago—but he spoke first. "Wanna get breakfast? The Gull's Perch is still open for another couple hours and I have a feeling that a biscuit sandwich oughta help your hangover."

"Hangover? Barely know her."

Ernie knocked her shoulder with his own. "You don't look as green as the morning after prom, but I know a hungover Annie when I see one."

"I honestly still cannot look at peach schnapps without feeling ill."

"I honestly never could."

She rolled her eyes, and without speaking, counted down on her fingers from five. When she reached one, they both dove underwater and swam for shore.

Rochelle Bilow is a food and romance writer who previously worked as the social media manager at *Bon Appétit* and *Cooking Light* magazines. A graduate of the French Culinary Institute, she has also worked as a line cook, a baker, and a wine spokesperson. Her first book, *The Call of the Farm*, a swoony farming memoir, was published in 2014. Raised in Syracuse, New York, Rochelle now lives in northern Vermont.

Ready to find
your next great read?

Let us help.

Visit prh.com/nextread